The shattering of glass made Sara scream. "Hello?" she called. "Is someone there?"

There was no reply. *The pitcher fell, that's all.* She took a deep breath, held it, exhaled, did it again, then stood, her legs rubbery as she flushed, then opened the stall door.

The white pitcher lay in shards on the floor. "Damn," she muttered, as she took a handful of paper towels from the dispenser and started cleaning up. "Damn it."

Somewhere behind her, in the shower room, she could hear faucets dripping, slowly and steadily. Then a shower turned on. Sara, brushing the last shards of glass into a towel, raised her head. *Who could be in here?* Another shower came on, and another. *Do nuns shower at two in the morning?* That was ridiculous, but someone was in the shower room, and she—or they—hadn't answered when she called out. The thrum of water against tile increased as more showers turned on.

Sara tiptoed across the floor toward the shower room. She flattened herself against the white tiled wall and edged along until she came to the open entryway. She peeked around the corner, at first seeing nothing but steam.

She jumped as a shower head near her suddenly came to life. Not believing her own eyes, she watched as the hot water handle turned by itself. "No," she whispered.

*"Sara . . . Sara . . . Sara . . ."*

The words echoed in her ears. They came from the middle of the shower room, but she still couldn't see anyone. Steamy mist, like fog, pulled apart and then wafted together again, over and over. *"Sara . . . Sara . . . Sara . . ."*

Something began slowly to glide toward her, a wavery oblong of steam that took form as it neared her . . .

Books by Tamara Thorne

HAUNTED

MOONFALL

ETERNITY

CANDLE BAY

BAD THINGS

THE FORGOTTEN

*The Sorority Trilogy*
EVE
MERILYNN
SAMANTHA

Published by Pinnacle Books

# MOONFALL

## TAMARA THORNE

PINNACLE BOOKS
Kensington Publishing Corp.
http://www.kensingtonbooks.com

*This one's for Douglas Clegg and Raul Silva*
*Two of the World's Greatest*

Thank yous go to the bewitching Jessica Hartwell for insight, Carol Scott, Pharm. D., and the pharmacy crew for information and enthusiasm, and Paul Najarian, M.D., for keeping me in stitches. Although the "death drug" mentioned in this book exists much as described, the information supplied by medical professionals has been freely adulterated by the author.

Kay McCauley, you're terrific; John Scognamiglio, you're sensational; Doug Clegg, you're the magus of mirth. Q, I'm glad you're U; and Gary and Duong, thanks for doing that voodoo that you do so well.

Finally, I'd like to thank the most important men in my life: Nigel, for being so familiar, yet never biting too hard, and my darling Damian—you've got me under your spell . . .

# PART ONE
## HALLOWEEN, 1972

# One

Beano Franklin poked John Lawson in the ribs. "Come on, pull my finger!"

"Cut it out," John muttered, his gaze never wavering from the dark apple orchard that lay beyond the orange and yellow lights strung around the picnic area of Parker's Cider Mill. Beano had been after him for five minutes now, even though John's parents were standing right behind them, along with just about everybody else in town and God knew how many tourists.

"Come on, Lawson!"

He sounded pretty desperate and John smiled to himself, thinking that his friend must be about ready to burst. If it had been anyone but Mom and Dad and Grandpa Gus in Beano's direct line of fire, he might've been tempted to comply. "Ask Winky," John murmured, ignoring the digit wagging under his nose.

"He took off with Paul and Doug, remember, Bonehead? To get our supplies for later?"

"Oh, yeah." John had managed to put their plans out of his head for the last couple hours, but Beano's words made his stomach squiggle with fear and excitement about what would come later tonight.

Standing on John's left was Greg, his ten-year-old brother. Dressed true to his character as a little red devil complete with pitchfork, he was tugging on John's sleeve. He turned. "What, Squirt?"

"What're you doing later?" he demanded loudly. "I wanna do it, too! And don't call me Squirt!"

Behind them, John felt his mother lean closer, listening, so instead of strangling Greg, he smiled at him. "We're camping out at Winky's, Squirt. Only high school freshmen. Sorry."

The boy's freckled face slipped into a frown, and just as he opened his mouth to complain, Beano saved the day, sticking his finger in Greg's face. "Quick! Pull it!"

The frown instantly inverted and Greg yanked for all he was worth. Nothing happened. Greg opened his mouth to protest.

"Silent but deadly," Beano reassured him.

An instant later, Mom said, "Oh, dear," Dad cleared his throat, and they, along with everyone else in the immediate vicinity, edged away. "Christ," John sputtered, trying not to inhale any more stink molecules than he had to, "what crawled up your ass and died?"

"Two chili dogs with double sauerkraut, dill pickles, and jalapeños. Look! Here comes Caspar!"

Old Caspar Parker, the man behind Moonfall's annual Halloween Haunt, stepped out in front of the crowd, dressed in denim overalls, a blue and white checked shirt, and a yellow Parker's Cider Mill baseball cap, all liberally spattered with fake blood. His wrinkled face was expertly made up in corpse colors—grayish-white with blue mottling around his eyes and cheeks and a trail of blood drizzling from one corner of his blue-black lips. The bloody gash painted on his neck was even wider than the grin on his face.

"Have you folks had a good time tonight?" he called in his booming voice. The cheers and applause threatened to rip his widening grin in two. "Anybody sighted any gargoyles in the sky?" Hoots and whistles and more cheers answered him, and John felt Greg move closer to him; the squirt still believed the gargoyles decorating St. Gertrude's School for Girls could fly and might get him some dark night. John hadn't been intrigued by the gargoyle stories for a long time, but Greg was a sort of nervous kid. He turned his attention back to Caspar and his shenanigans.

Every Halloween, Parker's Mill hosted a costume parade, pumpkin-carving contest, apple-bobbing, a dance, and a hayride, but the best part was the Haunted Barn, which Caspar enlarged and changed every year. This time, he'd outdone himself with the addition of a hologram ghost swaying from a noose in the rafters.

At the ripe old age of fourteen, John knew Caspar's haunted barn was a little lame, a trifle hokey, but he didn't care. His buddies—Beano Franklin, Winky Addams, Doug Buckman, and Paul Pricket—all liked to make fun of it, and John went right along with them, knowing full well that they secretly loved it as much as he did. Even John's dad, who was also the sheriff of Moonfall, admitted that Caspar's not-too-friendly ghosts could sometimes get a rise out of him.

"Quiet, please!" Caspar called out, setting the stage for the night's final event. He cupped his hand around his ear. "I believe I hear hoofbeats."

The hushed crowd looked to the orchard as the faint sound of a horse's hooves came from the loudspeakers, distant at first, then louder and louder, closer and closer, until the sound stampeded around them. A spotlight went on deep in the orchard just as a savage whinny ripped the air. Deep maniacal laughter followed. All around John, people caught their breath. Greg grabbed his hand and held tight.

There was shadowy movement in the orchard and John Lawson shivered in anticipation. An instant later, the Headless Horseman, on his midnight stallion, galloped out of the apple grove, an ominous black silhouette brandishing a fiery-eyed jack-o'-lantern. Steam blew from the animal's nostrils as it halted before the crowd and reared up on its hind legs.

The horse came down and the Horseman, his cape blowing in the wind, his white shirt covered with blood from neck stump to waist, held the pumpkin-head higher. "It's All Hallows' Eve and the night belongs to the spirits now! Go to your homes and lock your doors, or you," he pointed at a man at the far edge of the crowd, "or perhaps you," he pointed at a little girl ten feet away, "or *you*," he pointed at John, or maybe Greg, "will be doomed to die and join us in our ghostly revelries forever! Lunatic laughter rippled through the air, then the Horseman spurred the stallion. John watched horse and rider until they melded with the night.

"Wow!" Greg let go of John's hand, fearless once more. "He pointed at *us!* Isn't that great?"

John ruffled his brother's hair. "Great, Squirt!"

"Don't call me that!"

Beano nudged John. "Here come the guys. Let's go!"

"Mom? Dad?" John turned to his parents. "We're going to

Winky's now, okay?" He hoped he didn't sound as nervous as he felt.

"Are you boys still planning to sleep outside?" his mother asked. "It's awfully cold."

"No, ma'am," Winky said, as he and the others joined the group. "My dad said we can camp out in the family room." The other boys groaned, then Winky added, "He says we can watch the all-night horror movie marathon. The Black Widow's hosting."

"The Black Widow!" Doug Buckman breathed. "Boy, I'd like to get my hands on those—"

Beano elbowed him into silence.

Mom turned to John. "Did you remember your toothbrush, honey?"

*Oh, God, I'll never live this down.* "Yeah, I remembered."

"Be polite to Mr. and Mrs. Addams, John." With that, she kissed his cheek and he wanted to sink right into the ground as the guys snickered behind him.

"Ben," Dad drawled. He looked big and imposing in his sheriff's uniform.

"Yes, Sheriff Lawson?" Beano asked, his plump cheeks coloring.

"Your brother and his friends used to stir things up on Halloween night."

"Huh?" Beano was all innocence. "Brian's in college back east. And his friends, well, Raul's in college, too, and Martin's in Vietnam, and Cal, he's in Canada—"

"The thing is," Dad said, moonlight glinting off his badge, "I know *they* aren't here to t.p. Jeremiah Moonfall's statue this year."

"How'd you know—" Beano blurted.

Dad smiled tightly. "I'm the sheriff, that's how. I also know that these things sometimes become traditions, kind of like the Halloween Haunt. The point is," he continued, looking from boy to boy, "this is *not* to become one of Moonfall's traditions." He gave them a genuine smile. "So, boys, if you see anyone hanging around the town square on your way to the Addams place, make sure and let me know."

"Sure," Beano said, and the others echoed assent.

# Two

"Are we still gonna do the statue?" Paul Pricket whispered, as he stepped out the sliding glass door of Winky Addams's family room into the moonlit night. "I got us a dozen rolls of pink toilet paper! *Pink!*" He pushed his wire-rimmed glasses back up his ski-slope nose.

"Shit, man, I dunno." Beano looked at John. "Think your dad's watching the square tonight?"

John shrugged. "He's got the night off, but one of his deputies will be on duty."

"Which one?" Doug asked, digging in his ear. "Man, I think I got a piece of candy corn stuck in here."

"You're just saying that because you like to eat your own ear jam," Beano observed.

"Eat *me,* Franklin," Doug said, still digging. "So who's on, Lawson?"

"Cohtek, probably." John rubbed his chin thoughtfully. "Knowing him, he'll stay at the station and watch the Black Widow unless a call comes in, so we're safe."

"Cohtek's favorite place is between a chick's legs," Beano said, right on cue.

"Between her tits," Paul said, craning his neck for a last look at the horror hostess's amazing cleavage.

"God, you're dense, Pricket." Beano underscored his disgust with a belch that made his Adam's apple waggle.

"It's ten-thirty already." Doug Buckman tapped his watch. "If it gets much later, all the girls'll be in bed and we won't get to see anything."

"He's got a point," Winky agreed.

"We gotta go—"

"Shhh, Buckman, not so loud. You wanna wake up my parents?" Winky glared at him then looked to John, one eyelid beginning a nervous dance. "What do you think we should do first?"

"Let's go to St. Gruesome's. We can stash the toilet paper in the bushes by the statue and do it on our way back."

Silently they nodded agreement, then Winky led the way around the perimeter of his darkened house. Then, with soldierly stealth, they moved along the edge of the orchard until they reached the apple shed, where they'd stashed their bikes.

"This is gonna be so great," Doug gloated, as he pulled open the door and flicked on a dim flashlight. The sweet smell of apples filled the air and he smacked his lips loudly. "Naked girls everywhere, getting in bed, showering, washing their panties—hey!" he squawked suddenly. "What the hell are *you* doing here? Lawson!" he hissed, "get your ass in here!"

"Now what?" John muttered, as he pushed past Doug and saw Greg, still wearing his devil costume, perched on an apple crate, arms crossed, a shit-eating grin spreading across his freckled face. "Shit! What the hell do you think you're doing here?"

"I'm going with you guys," he said, nodding toward his red stingray bike. He gave his brother a coy look. "If you don't let me, I'll tell Mom you cussed."

"We're not going anywhere," John said, as calmly as he could.

"Yeah, right. That's why you all got flashlights and there's a pair of binoculars in Doug's bike basket."

"You're full of it, Squirt." John forced a smile. "We just came out for some apples."

"If you don't let me go with you, I'll tell Dad you guys are gonna t.p. the statue." He pointed at Paul's bulging backpack waiting near the door. Two pink rolls of tissue poked out of its open top.

Beano stalked toward Greg, hands out, reaching for the kid's neck. "I'm gonna teach you—"

"Knock it off!" John stepped in front of Greg and looked

Beano in the eye. "We either go back in and watch TV all night, or we take the squirt with us."

"Don't call me Squ—"

John whirled and angrily grabbed Greg's collar. "Be quiet!" He pulled his little brother forward, then bent so they were nose to nose. "Okay. You can go with us, but you'll be in deep shit if Mom and Dad ever find out anything. *Anything!* Now, swear."

"Cross my heart and hope to die." Greg swallowed hard. "Stick a needle in my eye."

"John, we can't take a chance," Winky said. "He's too young, he might make noise."

"No, I won't!" Greg practically squealed. "I swear it. I just want to do some of the t.p.ing!"

"We're going to St. Gruesome's first," John told him. "Where the gargoyles are. You still believe they can fly?"

The boy hesitated. "Huh-uh. No way." His eyes widened. "Why are you going *there?*"

"To see the naked chicks." Beano leered at him and licked his lips.

Greg backed up a step. "I thought nobody could get inside."

"My brother and his buddies got in," Beano bragged, as he walked over to a half-filled apple box and extracted a big red one. He bit into it and chewed loudly. "And now *we're* getting in." He turned and walked toward Greg. "But you know what those nuns do to you if they catch you?"

"What?" Greg asked, eyes widening.

"They take your pants down, so you're butt-naked in front of all those girls, and then they tie you up and whip you until you cry!"

"No way," Greg murmured, but it was obvious that he thought it might be true.

"He's telling the truth," John said solemnly. "Remember Raul? They caught him. He couldn't sit down for a week!"

"Maybe I could watch your bikes or something?" Greg suggested softly. "I just want to t.p. I'd puke," he added disparagingly, "if I had to look at naked girls, anyway."

"Yeah, like you ever seen one, you baby," Beano sneered.

"Are you sure we can trust him?" Winky asked John.

He nodded. "He'll be fine with the bikes."

"I promise, guys." Greg turned on his smile again.

"Okay." John tried to hide his nervousness. He wasn't as sure of Greg as he pretended—the kid was easy to spook. For that matter, he himself hadn't even been that hot to go to St. Gruesome's tonight, at least, not until his brother almost blew the whole thing. Now it seemed worth the risk.


Five minutes later, John was in the lead as the six pedaled hard up Apple Hill Road. He caught the good scents of burnt pumpkin and woodsmoke in the air. There was no traffic, and Moonfall, cloistered in mountains, shrouded in their shadows, was deathly quiet behind the wind in their bicycle spokes. Silently the boys circled into the town square and left Paul's backpack hidden near the statue of Jeremiah Moonfall, then continued on like ghosts in the night.

Originally, they were going to go on foot, following the stream that led the two miles cross-country from the Addamses' place to St. Gruesome's, rather than risk the road. But the Appleseed Orchard lay in between, and crossing it was risky because of Bert and Ernie, the Dobermans who roamed the orchard at night. And to make it worse, when—*if*—they finally reached the forest that edged St. Gruesome's property, they would have had to do some seriously treacherous climbing, and that would have been time consuming and dangerous in the dark. It had taken some doing, but in the end, John, backed by Paul and Winky, had finally convinced Doug and Beano, who still liked to play soldier, that the road was the only way to go.

John turned off Apple Hill Road, raising dust with the wheels of his aging mountain bike. He breathed a sigh of relief as they cruised across Apple Heaven's parking lot. The store, owned by St. Gruesome's, was primarily a bakery where the nuns sold fresh apple everything—pies, cakes, breads, butters, jellies, jams, and sauces—the same things that all the rest of the Moonfall stores sold. They also sold "Heavenly Mincemeat

Pies," which Beano, the gourmet of the group, swore were so good they must have been blessed by God Himself. John couldn't bring himself even to taste mincemeat. As far as he was concerned, dark brown glop belonged on the sole of your shoe, not in a warm pie crust.

They rode behind the store and dismounted, then walked their bikes up a small rise, then down, carefully skirting the chain that blocked the private dirt road to the school. John glanced back toward the main road and was happy to see it was out of sight. That meant they were, too.

All around them were St. Gruesome's orchards, and beyond those loomed the pitch-black forest. The old orphanage, once a monastery, was invisible, hidden behind woods at least a mile farther down the winding road.

As John stared into the forbidding darkness, fear began nibbling away at his resolve. The night was utterly still; no birds sang, no leaves rustled. The only sound was his breathing and that of his friends. Everything around them seemed to be waiting, and he began to wonder if the stories about spirits roaming the land on Halloween night might hold some truth. Overhead, a night hawk cried and he fought down a shiver. *Think about the girls, numbnuts!* Sternly, he told himself that his hands were trembling because of the chill mountain air. When he was half-convinced, he looked at the others. "Hey."

Winky's flashlight bobbed around. "What?"

"No lights."

"Nobody's gonna notice," Beano hissed, turning his on, too.

"We can't chance it."

"But it's too dark to ride without them," Winky protested.

"We walk the bikes."

"John's right," whispered Paul, always the voice of reason.

"Then we might as well just leave 'em here," Beano grunted.

"You're not gonna leave *me* here!" Greg's eyes shone wide in the moonlight.

"No," John said. "We'll take them with us. We can ride back—it'll be safe to use the lights coming out."

Winky nodded sagely. "Especially if we need to make a fast getaway."

Beano forced a belch. "Okay, let's move. I wanna see some pussy tonight!"

# Three

Tonight the torch would be passed. Freshmen or not, once word got around, they'd be the kings of Moonfall High, the rightful heirs to the windows and peepholes of St. Gruesome's. That's what Beano Franklin kept saying as they stumbled blindly along the dirt road to St. Gertrude's Home for Girls. John was sure Beano's bravado was born of sheer terror. He was also wondering, not for the first time, if Beano's older brother and his buddies had ever actually come out here. He was beginning to think Brian Franklin's stories about frustrated virgins who soaped each other's backs in the showers and massaged one another in bed were pure and utter bullshit. Right now, trying not to shiver, he couldn't believe he'd ever bought such crap.

They had entered the forest about fifteen minutes before, and that was when a claustrophobic black glove shutting out any trace of moonlight had enfolded them. The air, syrup-thick, barely seeped into John's lungs and his exhalations were equally difficult. He was light-headed and his legs were rubbery. Something screeched among the trees and he imagined he heard leathery wingbeats. If he'd been alone, he'd have turned back long ago, but in front of his friends and his little brother, he refused to show a trace of anxiety.

"Look!" whispered Paul. "There's a light!"

Sure enough, when he craned his neck, John spotted a small glowing rectangle of yellow high between the pine branches. "We're almost there. We gotta move real quiet now."

Not speaking, watching the single light splinter into a dozen or so more, they neared the old monastery. The pines thinned, allowing a stray moonbeam to illuminate the high stone walls surrounding the buildings. A wrought-iron gate loomed not twenty feet away, gargoyles crouching on either side. Even in the dim moonlight the eyes seemed to be watching them, and John hoped Greg would be okay.

"You hear something?" Paul whispered softly.

"Singing?" Winky asked, as the boys moved their bikes off the road and parked them in the shadows of a pine grove.

The sounds were soft, feminine, faraway. "Yeah," John whispered. "Chanting, maybe."

"It kind of sounds like a mass," murmured Paul, the only Catholic among them.

"A mess?" snickered Beano.

"A *mass*. Like a death mass, or something."

"Monk music," John whispered. "Do nuns do it, too?"

"Yeah, sure. I mean, I guess." Paul paused and they listened to the rise and fall of the voices that seemed to be coming from somewhere behind St. Gruesome's. "It sounds weird, though."

Maybe it was Paul's words, or maybe it was the eerie rise and fall of the voices, or maybe both, but something made John's flesh prickle up in goosebumps. "Is Halloween a holy day, Paul?"

"All Saints' Day is . . . the day after Halloween." Paul pushed his glasses up. "But it's not a big deal or anything." His face gleamed white in the thin moonlight as he gazed around at the others. "Maybe we shouldn't go in if they're having a religious service."

"What're you, Pricket?" Doug whispered. "Chicken?"

Beano cleared his throat. "Hey, Pricket, what's black and white and red and black and white and red?"

Paul rolled his eyes, nervousness forgotten. "Sunburned nuns."

"Huh-uh." Beano leered. "Nuns in a blender. Now, quit being a pussy and let's go inside."

Doug, Beano, Winky, and even Paul looked ready to go in, so John put his hand on his little brother's shoulder and guided him over to the bicycles. He felt sorry for the kid, who looked ready to pee in his pants. John wasn't feeling much braver, but he gave Greg a confident smile. "Your job's really important, Squirt. You have—"

"Don't call me Squirt."

"Shhh. Don't talk . . . whisper. Look, you have to stay with the bikes. If anybody comes along, hide behind the trees and stay still. Be quiet. After they're gone, alert us by doing a whippoorwill twice, then count to a hundred slow and do it again. And don't worry about those stupid gargoyles. They're just statues. They can't do anything."

The boy nodded, eyes wide. "But what if you don't come out?"

"We'll be back, Squirt, don't worry." John pulled his flashlight from his back pocket, then took off his watch and briefly shined the light on its face. Then he handed both to Greg. "But just in case, it's quarter to twelve now. If we're not back by two, you should go home."

"He'll tell on us," Doug hissed.

"No, he won't," John muttered. He turned back to Greg. "Can you find your way by yourself? Just follow this road back to Apple Hill, then cross—make sure you look both ways—and go home. Did you leave your window open when you snuck out?"

"Sure, but you're coming back, aren't you?" He cast another nervous glance at the gate.

"Of course we are. We're just making plans in case the nuns catch us or something, so you won't get in trouble, too."

"Okay."

Greg's voice sounded small and alone to John as he rejoined his friends. When he told Greg to leave if they didn't come back, it was mostly selfish—if Mom and Dad found out they'd brought the kid out here, he'd be in about a million times as much trouble as he would if he got caught by himself. But now, leaving the little booger there by himself, he felt really guilty. Greg had to be scared spitless.

Beano tugged his jacket sleeve and glared at him, then at the iron gate made of ornately spiked black rods. The gargoyles leered down at them, grinning winged dogs, or monkeys, or something. Their stone eyes seemed to glitter. "It's not locked. You go first, Lawson."

"Why me? Why not you, for once? Or Doug?" It was a stupid question. He didn't know why—maybe because his dad was sheriff or something—he always went first. It was kind of funny that they thought of him as the big, brave leader, when he secretly knew that even Paul Pricket was braver than him. All he ever did was go along with whatever scheme Doug and Beano came up with. Just like Winky and Paul, he didn't want to look like a wuss.

"Okay," he heard himself say, as he put his hand on the latch. He could feel the gargoyles watching him as the gate creaked on its rusty hinges and began slowly to open. He shivered as a nightbird screamed over the singing. "Let's go."

# Four

The sun shot hot needles of light through John's closed eyelids. Groaning, he turned his face away, felt something moist and cold against his hot cheek. He lay still, eyes closed, head pounding, unable to think, unable to move, not knowing or caring where he was.

Slowly, his senses began to awaken. First, there was the smell of the moss pillowing his cheek, the rich odor of damp earth, the tang of the pine forest. Woodsmoke wafting on a gentle breeze, and on that same breeze, a fine spray of cool mist washed over his face. All-encompassing thunder filled his ears; the roar of water.

*Witch Falls?* He groaned softly, clearing his throat, tasting bile and dust. His stomach rose into his throat, then subsided. *What am I doing here?* The thought came sluggishly, as if his brain had been turned off and rusty gears were struggling to turn again. It felt a little like the time he'd taken one of the Valiums that Beano had pinched from his father's pharmacy, but much, much worse.

*Beano!* Memories surfaced of riding along Apple Hill Road, he and the guys. Leaving toilet paper at the statue, then riding in the dark and wondering if spirits might really walk on Halloween night.

"Beano?" he croaked, slitting his eyes against the bright morning light.

His eyes registered Witch Falls twenty yards away, but his brain took forever to process the information. *What am I doing here?*

Birds sang in the trees.

*The whippoorwill call!*

"Greg!" Suddenly remembering his brother, he pushed himself up on his elbows. "Greg!" he cried again, now seeing other boys sleeping nearby. Beano's husky body was curled into a ball; Paul lay on his stomach, his glasses gone. Farther away, he recognized Winky by his red windbreaker and Doug by his army jacket and his godawful snore, audible even above the crash of the Falls.

"Greg!" Head pounding, John pushed himself to his feet, his legs as shaky as a newborn fawn's. After a moment, he walked—staggered, really—over to Beano. "Franklin! Wake up." He poked him in the ribs with the toe of his sneaker and Beano groaned.

John walked unsteadily around the clearing, checking the others, poking them, calling for Greg at the same time. The meadow was small and serene, with wildflowers and grasses growing around old pine stumps, trees cut down for some cabin that was probably long gone by now. John and the others came here often in summer, just as their parents had before them. His dad called the area "the Mezzanine" because it edged the Falls, which rose another twenty feet above them and dropped nearly as far down into a deep, clear pool that eventually fed Apple and Moonfall Creeks. The Mezzanine was a natural diving board, a place John loved.

He walked away from the Falls now, though, calling Greg's name, his mind clearing as the headache began to let up. Last night, they'd . . . they'd what? Planned to t.p. the statue, and . . . *what else? To come here?* That seemed right. *But why?*

Approaching the path that led out of the clearing, he saw a flash of red among the trees. "Greg?" He trotted into the shadows. "Greg?" The bikes were parked under one of the trees, just like they'd left them last night.

*Greg stayed with the bikes.* ''Come on, Greg, this isn't funny!''

''God, my head's killing me.''

John jumped at the sound of Beano's voice behind him. ''It'll clear,'' he said, turning to his friend. ''Listen, have you seen Greg?''

''Shit, no. What happened?''

''Yeah. What happened?'' Doug Buckman joined them, rubbing his temples. ''Christ, my mouth tastes like I was sucking on dog turds.''

''I can't find Greg. He was supposed to stay here with the bikes, remember?''

He saw momentary confusion in both boys' eyes. Then Beano nodded hesitantly. ''Maybe the little booger ran off.''

''No, his bike's here.'' John squinted into the forest, then turned to his friends. ''Do you remember coming here last night?''

''Yeah.'' Beano scratched his lank hair, dislodging a yellow oak leaf. ''I mean, I guess so.''

''The bikes are where we left 'em,'' Doug said.

''We came to camp out, remember?'' Beano said slowly.

''So what'd you do, Franklin?'' Doug asked. ''Drug the food? I can't remember shit.''

''Fuck you.''

''Guys,'' said John, putting his hands up. ''Knock it off. We gotta find Greg.''

''Probably, he went home,'' Doug said. ''Remember, you told him to go home if we didn't come back?''

''Come back?'' Beano asked. ''We were camping out. Why would we tell him that?''

''He was supposed to guard the bikes,'' John said slowly. He could barely see into the fog blotting his memory. ''I guess we didn't want him to bug us, so we left him here for a while. Maybe we fell asleep and he left. I remember . . . I remember I asked him if he'd left his window open so he could sneak back in the house, and he said yes.''

Doug's brown eyes lit up. ''St. Gruesome's! Shit, guys, we

were going to go to St. Gruesome's and see the girls. Like your brother used to, Beano.''

"Nah," Beano said. "He made all that stuff up."

"He *what?*" Winky Addams asked, as he stumbled into the group.

Beano actually blushed. "He wrote me from college and said it was all a fake. He said we shouldn't go out there, that there was nothing to see."

Doug grabbed Beano's sleeve and yanked him closer. "You lied?"

"Hell, no. Brian did. He said so in his letter."

"You didn't tell us!" Doug growled. "You let us go out there and—and . . ." Looking lost, he let go of Beano.

"I think maybe we *talked* about going to St. G's," John said slowly. "But we decided to camp out instead."

"Yeah," Winky agreed. "Man, I feel like shit."

Behind Beano, Winky, and Doug, Paul Pricket got to his feet and paused, feeling for his missing glasses. Seeing John, Paul raised his hand in a just-a-minute gesture, then walked cautiously toward the cliffside—Paul couldn't even read the big E on the eye chart without his specs. John watched curiously, then realized by Paul's arm movements that he was unzipping his fly. He turned his attention back to the other three, who were still arguing.

"Guys," he began, "we gotta find Greg—" As he spoke, he glanced up at Paul again, and even from this distance, he could see the boy's back stiffen. Elbows moved slightly— putting the weasel away—and then Pricket just stood there, unmoving.

"Paul!" John yelled.

The other three turned to look.

Paul didn't answer, didn't move.

"Paul!" John was running, running, and the little meadow seemed to go on forever before he reached him. "Paul?"

Paul turned then, his face pale and strange. He stared at John with fathomless eyes.

"What's wrong?" John asked, as the other three arrived, and

suddenly he knew. As the pit of his stomach filled with cold sludge, he stepped closer to the edge of the cliff.

"No." Paul grabbed his arm, tried to pull him back. "No, John, don't look."

He barely heard him. Shaking Paul off, he took the final step and looked over the edge. Below, Greg floated, face down, just below the surface of the pool, his red windbreaker puffing out of the water. "No," John whispered, as he felt the others gathering around him, staring down.

*"No!"* he screamed. Without thinking, he bent and dived. The fall went on forever, then he broke the water. Ice cold, impossibly cold, it seized his body, crushed his chest.

He pushed to the surface, saw Greg floating three feet away.

"Greg!" he gasped, and with one powerful kick, moved close enough to grab his brother. *"Greg!"* He turned the boy in his arms, saw the open eyes, dull with death, the raw flesh and mashed cheek and jaw bones, and wanted to die himself.

"I'm sorry," he whispered.

"Is he okay?" Doug called from above.

John looked up at the four pale faces lining the cliff. His voice deserted him, but he was dimly aware of the heat of the tears coursing down his cheeks. He looked at his brother again. *The water's so cold, sometimes people come back to life after being in cold water . . .*

"Is he alive?" Beano called.

John didn't answer, just held onto Greg and swam for the water's edge, to where a steep trail led to the top of the ridge. The air felt warm as he climbed out of the chill water. Turning, he grabbed his brother under the arms and pulled him out.

Greg was stiff and John knew then he wouldn't be coming back; all the CPR in the world wouldn't do it. Dimly he felt tears coursing down his cheeks, but his emotions were dead as he grimly pulled the little body—so much heavier in death than in life—up the path.

"Here, John." He looked around, saw Paul squatting on a rock just above him. Beyond, the others were strung out up the trail, waiting to help. "Here," Paul said quietly. "Hand him to me."

"No, it's okay. I can do it."

"It's too steep," Paul insisted. "You can't do it by yourself. Hand him up."

"He's dead." John's emotions, so ordinary a moment ago, nearly choked him now.

"I know. Let us help you."

With that, Paul reached down, and somehow, with those skinny little arms, pulled Greg up to the rock, then turned toward Doug, who reached down from his perch and took the body. John watched it all, until, waiting on the cliff's edge, Beano Franklin pulled the body up and out of sight.

"John?" Paul Pricket, his eyes dark, agonized, watched him. "Take my hand, John."

Dumbly he stared at Paul's fingers. Greg was dead, and it was all his fault.

"John!"

Unthinking, he grabbed Paul's hand and hoisted himself up, then waited while Paul climbed the rest of the way. He stood on the rock, unwilling or unable to move, and after a moment, he looked toward the waterfall.

Far above, on the bridge over the top of the Falls, he saw the old witch, Minerva Payne, looking down at him, her gaze inscrutable. He looked away and began climbing. When he reached the ridge, she was gone.

# PART TWO

## AUGUST 1996

# Five

"Who found her?"

Sheriff John Lawson swallowed hard and forced himself to look over the edge of the cliff. "Anonymous caller. Female. Scotty didn't recognize the voice. So, do you think it's a suicide?"

"Can't say yet." Frank Cutter, Moonfall's physician and coroner, scratched his round jowls thoughtfully. "But I wouldn't be surprised. Wouldn't be surprised if it's foul play, either. You okay?"

John could feel the doctor's eyes on him. "Yeah." Standing on the cliff at the rim of the Mezzanine at Witch Falls, staring down at the pond, at his deputy taking photos of the woman's body floating just below the water's surface, was almost more than he could bear. It reminded him too much of that terrible day over twenty years ago, when Greg ... *God I hate this place!*

Until now, he'd returned only three times since the accident: once on the one-year anniversary of Greg's death, again after Doug Buckman committed suicide here at age sixteen, and finally, six years ago, as a deputy investigating the death of a John Doe. Each time, it was more difficult and he wondered what he had ever seen in this place. "I'm fine," he said at last, not looking at Cutter, noticing instead the early morning dew, already drying under the rising August sun.

"Go ahead."

At the sound of his deputy's voice, John glanced down. Scotty Carroll was putting the lenscap on his camera as two EMTs began wading into the red-tinged pool and began maneuvering the body into a stretcher basket they would use to haul up the corpse. As he watched, Scotty began climbing back up the same trail John had traveled so long ago. A moment later he arrived topside, wet to the waist and shivering despite the fact that it was already warm out. The water was always chill.

"Her wrists are slit." Scotty's face was pale. This was his first dead body.

John nodded. "Go on back and get changed, then take care of the film."

The young man nodded gratefully and walked off, keeping to the edges of the clearing to try to avoid damaging any evidence that might still be waiting.

"Suicide, then," John said to Cutter.

"I'll tell you after the autopsy." He eyed the sheriff. "It's not like you to make snap judgments, John."

Morning sunlight streamed through the pines, highlighted the flowers, and glinted off the waterfall. The air smelled fresh and warm, fragrant with the forest and the cold scent of water. The Mezzanine was a beautiful meadow, but he hated it with all his heart. He feared it. "I'm not judging, Frank. I'm hoping."

"John, you've got to let it go someday."

His eyes burned. He couldn't look at Cutter. "I know." He shielded his eyes against the sun and stared up at the top of Witch Falls, half-expecting to see Minerva Payne, the old witch, watching him.

# Six

The Moonfall sheriff's office had changed very little since John Lawson's father had been in command. Located in the town's historic business district just off Apple Hill Road, the small, square building, clad in wood siding and a western false front riser, was really concrete and stucco beneath. The "historic" facades of downtown Moonfall had been added in the early sixties, when the town council decided that a good crop of tourists was at least as profitable as a harvest of apples.

Other than St. Gertrude's, a onetime monastery dating back to Revolutionary War days, a few cabins, and the Baptist church from the Civil War era, every building in town had been built after the turn of the century. The western look amused John

Lawson: monks and then farmers had settled Moonfall, with nary a cowboy in sight.

Despite this, he liked the look of the town, with its old-fashioned soda fountains and tourist traps masquerading as general stores and smithy shops. Moonfall Market only sold meat from behind an antique glass butcher case manned by One-Thumb Isaacson, but Franklin's Pharmacy was Moonfall's jewel, with windows displaying rainbows of antique apothecary bottles and jars that cast prisms of delicate color across the sidewalk every afternoon.

Even the lobby of the sheriff's office bowed to the western ambiance. An old-fashioned brass desk bell decorated the tall cherrywood counter which hid the dispatcher's desk. The walls were adorned with reproductions of photographs from the Lawson family albums: Tobias Lawson, the Baptist minister who'd built the old church, had arrived shortly after Jeremiah Moonfall, and the Lawsons figured as importantly in Moonfall's history as the Moonfalls, though they showed up less—probably due to their mundane surname and a lack of success with apple-growing.

The Moonfalls had died out after selling their land to the Parker clan, who later became the most prosperous apple growers on the mountain. The Lawsons had stuck to preaching until Henry, John's father, turned to law enforcement. And although Henry had died in the line of duty in 1973, barely six months after Greg's death, John's desire to follow in his father's footsteps never wavered. If anything, his death had only strengthened his resolve. It must have, he reflected, for him to return to Moonfall after college and hire on as a deputy in a town he thought he never wanted to see again.

Maybe, he thought as he pushed aside his half-finished report on the Jane Doe, just maybe, Greg's death had had something to do with it, too. He still held on to the hope that it hadn't been an accident, if only to assuage his own guilt, but the only indication he'd ever had of that was his and his friends' foggy memories. He swiveled his desk chair, then stood and crossed his disorderly little office; hidden from public view behind a closed door, it was piled high with notebooks and papers,

Wanted posters and mail, mostly junk. The scarred green desk blotter was the only relatively clear thing in the room. It held only a framed photo of his thirteen-year-old son, Mark, and two mugs, one filled with pens and chewed pencils, the other containing cold coffee.

Three tall oak file cabinets against one wall dated from the thirties. The fourth, a beige metal one, had been added by his father around 1970. It was three-quarters filled, mostly with traffic violations and accident reports.

He opened the top drawer and flipped to 1972, then pulled out a manila folder labeled "Lawson, Gregory," in faded blue ink. His fingers trembled as they closed around the tabs. He'd looked inside before, always wondering what he'd forgotten about that Halloween night so many years ago. *Death by misadventure.* That was the finding of his own father. *But . . . what if?* He shut off the thought, knowing he was only trying to get around his own guilt.

"Sheriff Lawson?"

At the sound of his dispatcher's voice, his fingers opened, dropping the file back in place, a kid caught with his hand in the cookie jar. "Yes, Dorothy?" he called, shutting the drawer.

She opened the door, her round face cheerful and motherly—grandmotherly, he corrected: Dorothy had worked for his father as well.

"There's someone to see you," she confided. Anything Dorothy said sounded as if it were a state secret.

"Isn't the intercom working?" he asked, as he did whenever she opted for knocking—which was all the time. She was great on the radio, so her dislike for the comm line seemed absurd.

She gave him a long-suffering look, but didn't bother to dignify his question with a reply. "Shall I show her in?"

"Show *who* in—"

A bony hand appeared on the edge of the door and pulled it farther open. Dorothy looked surprised as a nun, in full-habit, came into view.

"This is important," said the nun, as she whisked past Dorothy, "and I'm in a hurry." Shutting the door in the dispatcher's face, she stared at John with squinty dark eyes. "May we speak?"

She looked jarringly familiar, and the musty cinnamon scent she gave off was something he had smelled before, something that made him feel slightly queasy. Occasionally, he saw the nuns in town, and he realized that's where he must have run into her. He returned to his desk chair, then gestured at the seat across the desk. Her long, angular face, faintly traced with wrinkles at the eyes and between the pointy nose and thin, pursed lips, made him think of the Wicked Witch of the West. If nothing else, this horse-faced nun had to be a creature from a Catholic schoolboy's worst nightmare; all she was missing was a ruler for knuckle-rapping. For an instant, his voice deserted him. He cleared his throat. "Please sit down, Sister."

"Mother," she corrected him, as she settled into the chair. "Mother Superior Lucy Bartholomew. Head mistress of St. Gertrude's Home for Girls." She extended her hand. It was all stretched skin on bone, dry and hard and cool. The word "reptilian" came to mind.

When her eyes bored into his, he had to fight an uncharacteristic urge to cringe. "What can I do for you?"

"I wish to report a missing person." She folded her hands on his desk.

"A student?" he asked, thinking that if he were a girl under this woman's care, he'd certainly run away. "Or one of your nuns?" he added.

"A lay teacher named Lenore Tynan."

The sight of the imposing nun had momentarily made him forget about the Jane Doe found at Witch Falls this morning, but his professionalism came back in full force now. "How long has she been missing?"

"We saw her at dinner last night. When she didn't show up for breakfast, I sent Sister Regina to her room to check on her. Miss Tynan wasn't there, but there was blood on the bed and splashed on the floor and walls."

"Can you give me a description of Miss Tynan?"

"Five foot six, one hundred and ten pounds, light red hair,

twenty-five years old." The nun ticked off the data in the tone of a teacher repeating a lesson to a class of idiots.

As John studied the woman's stern face, his stomach began to churn at the thought of visiting St. Gruesome's. He'd never gone near the place after Greg's death. There had been a call or two during his time on the force, but he'd never had to go himself. "Mother Lucy," he began, "we found the body of a woman matching your description this morning."

"Where?" she asked, her composure firmly intact.

"Witch Falls," he said, his insides puckering.

Her expression hardened. "That accursed place." There was no sadness in her voice, no remorse. "What was she doing there?"

"Maybe you can tell us. I'd like to take you over to the coroner's office to identify the body."

"Certainly, but I'm in a hurry." She rose and waited until he came around the desk and opened the door for her.

# Seven

"That's Lenore Tynan," Mother Superior Lucy Bartholomew said the instant Frank Cutter folded the sheet back from the young woman's bruised, lifeless face. The three stood in Cutter's tiny morgue, gathered around the body on the metal table. The room was cold and white, and the tang of antiseptic mingled with the vague odor of decay and the mildewed cinnamon scent that wafted from the nun. John wasn't sure which of these was the most nauseating.

"You're certain?" John asked, as Cutter hesitated, the top of the sheet in his hovering fingers. "You don't need another look?"

"I'm positive." Lucy clipped the words off. "Cover her up."

"I'll need to ask you some questions," John began.

"I realize that, Sheriff." The nun stepped to the door, put her hand on the knob, and turned back to face the men. "I'll receive you at the school later today. Stop at Apple Heaven and ask the sisters to unlock the entry gate for you.''

With that, she opened the door and stepped briskly out.

''Mother Lucy?'' John called, and she halted, turning to glare at him.

''Yes?''

''Don't let anyone into Miss Tynan's room before I get there.''

''Naturally,'' she practically barked, then pulled the door closed behind her. An edge of black hem caught in it and John grinned at Cutter as they heard a muted oath of some sort. The door reopened minutely and the black cloth flashed out before the door slammed closed again.

The doctor crossed his arms, whistling low. ''That nun was worthy of Sister Mary Margaret, the meanest sixth-grade teacher at St. Martin's Elementary.''

''I didn't know you were Catholic,'' John said, averting his eyes from the sheet-draped body on the metal table beside them.

''I'm not. I kept getting into trouble in public school, so my parents sent me to a Catholic boys' school.'' He chuckled. ''I'm afraid it didn't take.''

''You? A troublemaker? What did you do?''

''Played doctor, what else?'' When Cutter smiled, as he did now, he bore an uncanny resemblance to Mel Tormé. ''And I must admit, I did lose all interest in that game at St. Martin's.'' His smile faded and he glanced at the draped body of Lenore Tynan. ''Mysteriouser and mysteriouser,'' he said softly.

John followed his gaze. ''Have anything for me yet?''

''You arrived during my first breather of the morning. You know that church potluck yesterday? Seems like about half the Baptists in town got hold of some bad potato salad.'' He shook his head. ''Talk about having a run of customers!''

John smiled in spite of himself. ''Sure it's just the Baptists? That nun had my stomach clenching the whole time she was here.''

''Some nuns have that effect. Don't worry, if you weren't

at the picnic, you're safe . . . unless Gus brought you a plate. Did he?"

"No. He's all right, isn't he?"

"He'd better be. I ordered your grandfather to stay away from cholesterol—mayo, eggs, et cetera, so he wouldn't have touched the stuff."

"No, that means he won't tell you if he did." John shook his head. Augustus Lawson, retired Baptist minister, was as old and spry as Caspar Parker, and he delighted in disobeying doctor's orders. John figured the old man would outlive them all, cholesterol be damned.

"I'll call him later." Cutter's expression became serious as he looked down at the sheeted corpse. "You ready?"

John took a deep breath and looked, too. "As ready as I'll ever be."

Cutter folded the sheet back, revealing the nude body of the young woman. "See this, John?" He took one of the corpse's arms and carefully turned it to expose the wrist. The hand was bagged, and just above that, a deep horizontal gash revealed a white glint of bone beneath pale, bloodless tissue. "The other arm's the same. She meant business."

"Then you *do* think it's a suicide?"

The doctor laid the arm back down. "The angles are right for it. And notice—except for a few scrapes she probably suffered in the fall, there are no obvious signs of trauma. Of course, I haven't done a pelvic yet, so we can't rule out rape, but on the surface, it appears to be suicide."

John nodded, wishing Cutter would cover up the pitiful, pale body. "That's a relief. This town doesn't need a murder, especially with tourist season coming up." The truth was, *he* didn't need a murder, especially one that would have him poking around St. Gruesome's. Fleetingly, he wished the place would burn to the ground before he could arrive there today.

Cutter raised an eyebrow. "Your boys haven't found the knife yet, have they? Or the anonymous caller?"

"Not so far as I know." Two of his three day deputies, Scotty Carroll and Wyn Griffin, were scouring the Witch Falls area as they spoke. "If she's a suicide, Frank, what was she doing at the Falls?" Despite his wish to be done with this case, he couldn't overlook the contradictions, couldn't deny his instincts. "There's blood in her room, but she made it all the way to the Falls. And there didn't appear to be more than a few drops on the Mezzanine."

"We don't know how much blood is in her room," Cutter observed. "Maybe she started to cut, then finished it at the Falls. Maybe you'll find the blade in the water."

"Blade," John said. "Razor or knife?"

"I'd say razor, by the looks of the cuts," the doctor replied, as he picked up one dead white hand and examined the fingers through the plastic encasing it. He shook his head and came around to the other side of the table and repeated the process. "A single-sided blade, or maybe a small, very thin-bladed knife."

"Why start in her room, then change her mind and go to the Falls to finish?" John probed. "Privacy?"

"Maybe so." Cutter covered the body and crossed to the sink. "The cuts were made crosswise," he called over his shoulder as he washed his hands. "That's the slow way— Hollywood style—maybe she realized someone could walk in on her."

"Do you know if the teachers' rooms have private baths?"

"I have no idea," Cutter said, drying his hands. "I've never made a housecall at St. Gertrude's."

"You're kidding."

"Nope. As I understand it, they've got their own doctor on the premises. Always have had. When are you heading out there? I'd like to go along."

"I'd like you to," John said, and meant it. "Half an hour?" he asked, knowing that was the doctor's lunchtime.

Cutter consulted his watch. "I'll be ready."

John took his leave, wondering if he had time to stop by the Gingerbread House and question Minerva Payne, who lived near the Falls. He had never told anyone about seeing the old woman—"the old witch," in those days—at the Falls the day his little brother drowned, but he would never forget. Scotty had said the caller who reported the body sounded like a young woman, and Minerva Payne, though unbent by the years, was at least as old as God, so she probably wasn't the caller. He consulted his watch again and decided against visiting her just yet. The decision lifted a weight from his shoulders. Although the day he'd locked eyes with her he'd seen sympathy in them, he'd been frightened, and to this day he'd never done more than nod a greeting.

Old childhood myths never really died; instead, they gained power with each new generation. Moonfall's current generation of kids still loved to tell stories about the "old witch." In his day, Minerva could make you sick just by looking at you, but the most popular story today—that she could turn you into a gargoyle decorating St. Gruesome's—was a minor one twenty-five years ago. He knew they were all ridiculous—he even knew it when he was a kid—but whenever he thought of her, a little thrill still wormed through his belly. It was a fun sort of fright, though; nothing like the lead that filled his gut at the thought of returning to St. Gruesome's.

# Eight

Minerva Payne set a sheet of fresh molasses cookies on the counter to cool, then walked out into the sales room of the Gingerbread House and began sweeping the spotless floor. Anything to keep busy, to keep her mind off the vision of the young woman floating in the pool below Witch Falls this morning. Nothing worked; not the morning baking, not the sweeping. No matter what she tried, the image remained.

Minerva lived in an old log cabin deep in the woods bordering St. Gertrude's land, and each morning she walked the half mile through the woods to her bakery and candy store on Apple Hill Road. Today, as usual, she had taken the short detour to the bridge spanning the Falls, where she paused to take in the fragrance of pines and fresh water, to feel the rushing power of nature. And there, in the pool, she'd seen the girl, forlorn, dead, her hair fanning around her in the dark water. *It's almost time. It's almost time again already.*

The last time she'd seen a body in the pool was in 1972, when the little Lawson boy had died. She'd seen the other boys that morning, the horror on their faces, but they hadn't seen her, except for one, John Lawson, who'd grown up to be sheriff. Because he saw her, she had expected to be questioned, at the very least, but Henry Lawson never came around. John hadn't told. She liked him for that, even though they had never spoken in the ensuing years. He would think of her now, however, with this new death, and she had a feeling that soon the silence would finally be broken.

*It's almost time. October will be here soon.*

Sheriff John Lawson had only one son, a bright boy with mischievous eyes and a kind smile. He came into her shop often and wasn't afraid of her, like most of the kids. He would die this October unless she could stop the cycle.

*And what makes you think you can stop it, old woman?* She'd never succeeded before, and she was old now, so very old. It was becoming difficult to maintain her appearance, to perform tasks that had been easy only a few years ago. This morning, when she had placed the phone call, even making her voice sound young and full of life had been a drain.

Minerva returned the broom to its place, hidden out of sight behind the doorway to the kitchen. Her heart beat hard against her chest. She couldn't give up now. Not now. This would be her last chance.

Unable to stand still, she crossed to the front door of the Gingerbread House, hearing the familiar sound of the little bells over the door as she opened it. She stepped out into the noontime August heat. The shop stood alone on its small lot, surrounded by Moonfall Forest, though no one called it that: it had been Witch Forest—and Witch Falls—for as long as she could remember. Across the road was the Snowflake Orchard and a clutch of antique and gift shops. Just west of Minerva's shop were Moonfall Park and the Falls, then the orchards of St. Gertrude's and the nuns' store, Apple Heaven. Directly across from the Apple Heaven was another tourist center with shops, a museum, and a petting zoo. From there, the road curved out of sight and down through town, then there were yet more orchards.

Long ago, when the first monks had built their monastery, there had been only forests. The monks planted crops and orchards—peach, pear, and cherry—to feed themselves and those they took in, but it wasn't until Jeremiah Moonfall arrived around the time of the Civil War that apple orchards were planted. By then, the monastery, deserted for more than twenty years, had been taken over by the elements, though, within a year, it took on new life as St. Gertrude's Convent. As more settlers arrived, more apple trees were planted. Today, Moonfall was still small by any standard, but to Minerva, it seemed vastly populated.

As she was about to go back inside her shop, she heard a car approaching from somewhere below. She waited. A moment passed, then a black and white sheriff's cruiser came around the bend. For an instant, she thought it was coming to her place, but its right blinker flashed and the car slowed and turned into the Apple Heaven lot. She recognized John Lawson's tall, lanky form as he got out of the cruiser and entered the store. Shortly, he returned and pulled out of sight behind the store. *Going to St. Gertrude's.* So that's where the young woman had come from.

Minerva wasn't surprised at that, but she was at her own mild disappointment that her long overdue meeting with John Lawson was not yet to be.

# Nine

They drove past the orchards and into the forest surrounding St. Gertrude's Home for Girls, and as the pines and firs, the sycamores and aspens, thickened and spread their branches across the narrow dirt road, John felt as if walls were closing in on him. Between his sudden claustrophobia and the queasiness that had been growing since they'd turned off at Apple Heaven, he wasn't happy.

"It's beautiful out here," Frank Cutter said. "If you must be an orphan, what a place to be one."

How could the man sound so serene? "You have the soul of a poet," John said, then paused. "You ever come out here as a kid, Frank?"

"Me? No." A low branch brushed its leaves across the top of the cruiser. "I was never invited. I wore thick glasses then, and got straight A's. Classic nerd." Cutter hesitated. "I always meant to as an adult, just to take a look, but, you know, the years go by. What about you?"

"No." John suppressed a cringe. After finding Greg's body, the gang had decided not to tell anyone they'd been on their way to St. Gruesome's that night—especially since they weren't sure themselves. They said they were merely having a clandestine camp-out and Greg had invited himself along. When the doctor and his dad had questioned them, they'd all stood by their story.

He felt a sudden urge to confess, but stopped himself. *Confess what?* How could he explain a feeling, a hunch? A few bad dreams meant nothing. The only fact that supported any of their fuzzy memories about that night was that they'd found Paul's toilet paper–loaded backpack in the town square. And of course they'd kept that bit of information to themselves.

The fact was, they'd wound up at the Falls, and none of them knew how or why, or, more accurately, why they thought they'd been on their way to St. Gruesome's. Over the next few days, Beano and Winky had grown more and more certain that all they'd ever planned was a camp-out, and as the weeks passed, they remembered more and more details of the night, as did he and Paul Pricket, though perhaps they were persuaded by a need to belong. Only Doug Buckman stoutly maintained that they had gone to St. G's that night, but he could remember no details.

After that, the boys began to drift apart, uneasy with each other and the confusion they shared. Doug Buckman died in 1973 and Paul moved to Redlands the same year. Like John,

Winky Addams and Beano Franklin still lived in town, Winky running the family orchard and Beano, his father's pharmacy, but the three of them, by tacit agreement, were little more than nodding acquaintances.

"There were always stories about the old abbey," Cutter was saying, "And there were always boys who claimed to have come out here and spied on the girls. Maybe the tales of ghosts and gargoyles were started to keep the youngsters away."

John glanced at him sharply and was relieved to see that the doctor was oblivious to his discomfort.

"Of course, all those females—nuns and young girls, all those *virgins*—supplied the boys of Moonfall with all sorts of fantasies, but that was all. Except maybe once when I think some kids might've actually come out here."

"When?" John asked, as a tire bounced over a small pothole. What was Cutter getting at? He felt like a kid himself right now and didn't have the nerve to be direct with the doctor.

The physician glanced over inquisitively. "Remember Brian Franklin and his buddies? Maybe they were a little before your time."

"I remember. They bragged about coming out here every Halloween. I thought it was all bull."

"Maybe it was, but one November first in '70 or '71, Mrs. Franklin brought Brian in with a mild concussion and a gash on his back that took about twenty stitches, inside and out."

"Why do you think he was out here?" John asked, relieved.

"It was the day after Halloween and he'd been gone all night. He claimed he and his friends had been climbing the chainlink fence at the schoolyard and he'd fallen off, cutting his back and bumping his head. His friends backed him up, but I had a hunch they weren't telling the truth. There should have been multiple cuts and scratches if it was chainlink, but this wound was single and wide and he was damned lucky— it missed his spine by a fraction of an inch. The boys were all a little confused about what they were doing at the school. You know . . ."

Cutter's words trailed off and John was sure he was going to compare Brian's confusion to his own in '72. But then the doctor cleared his throat and added, "Your dad and I talked, and he became very curious about the whole thing, too. He even went to the school and checked the fencing for ripped material, blood, that sort of thing."

"Did he find anything?"

"No. But shortly after that, we met at Winesap's Tavern for a drink and got to talking. He'd noticed the spiked gate. Nasty thing, he said. He thought Brian's injury was more consistent with the spikes around the abbey than the schoolyard. But the boys stuck to their story. Your dad did speak to the nuns, though."

John slowed as the trees thickened above them. His stomach was doing flips for no good reason. "When was that?"

"A few days after Brian's accident. They said they'd had no trouble, so he let it drop. Any reason you're so interested in ancient history all of a sudden?"

"No reason," he lied. "Dad never mentioned coming here. All I really remember was that he was positive that Brian Franklin was the leader of the t.p. pack. He warned us not to follow in Brian's footsteps . . ." In his mind's eye, he could see the light reflecting off his father's badge that Halloween night. *If you see anyone hanging around the town square on your way to the Addams place, make sure and let me know . . .*

"Something wrong? You're looking pasty."

"I'm fine." The trees thinned slightly and he saw bits of gray stone buildings looming between the most distant branches. The last few yards went quickly. "My God." John braked as the outer walls and gates of St. Gertrude's came into view. For a horrible instant, he thought he was going to be sick, then it passed. The dirt road continued on around the stone and wrought-iron enclosure. Behind the outer walls, the Gothic turrets and steep roofs were clearly visible. "No wonder they call it St. Gruesome's." John pulled the car slightly off the road and killed the engine, then stared at the old monastery. These buildings bore no resemblance to Father Junipero Serra's famous California missions, with their graceful arches and tile roofs. These medieval structures looked more like San Quentin dressed up with bizarre touches of Notre Dame.

But it was the narrow, spiked front gate with its gargoyles—
ugly, grinning monkey-faced creatures crouching on either gate-
post—that took John's breath away as he stepped from the
cruiser. Queasy again, he forced himself to ignore the feeling
as he took a camera and a briefcase containing a fingerprint
kit, tools, and evidence bags from the back seat. He shut the
car door, then turned and looked at the gate, his stomach in
knots.

"Speaking of spikes . . ." Cutter said, joining him, his own
bag in hand.

*I thought the gargoyles were watching me when I opened
that gate . . .*

In his mind he could hear the rusty creaking of a gate. Sudden
images flooded him in photographic black and white as he
remembered taking hold of the bars and pushing the gate slowly
open under the leering gaze of the creatures. The memory, if
that's what it was, lasted only an instant, then fled, a nasty little
fantasy, a piece of a nightmare. He felt Cutter looking at him
and said, "Ugly, aren't they?"

The doctor nodded, studying the gargoyles. "I've seen pictures of them, of course, but these are more remarkable than
I'd ever imagined." There was a tightness in his voice that
belied the calm words. "The work is magnificent."

"Maybe so, but those things are as ugly as sin. *I'd* hate to
be an orphan here." *You've been here. You* were *here.*

One corner of Cutter's mouth crooked up. "Ugly, yet beautiful. I'm surprised the nuns don't give tours. Judging by these
fellows," he gestured at the small gargoyles, "they could have
a healthy business if they showed off the place."

"When we were little kids we thought they could fly," John
said. *Don't worry about those stupid gargoyles, Greg. They're
just stone.*

"So did we," the doctor said. "When we camped out, we'd
listen for them. We thought they screamed like banshees, but
any night bird's call satisfied us."

"They'd fly out to steal babies for the old witch in the
woods," John added, as they moved to the gate. He hadn't
thought about those ridiculous old stories in years. *Greg was*

*afraid of them.* "Let's go." He made himself put his hand on the gate latch, trying to ignore his racing heartbeat.

The gate swung open smoothly, without creaking, and the two men stepped onto the flagstone path that led across the lawn to the buildings. Despite the grayness of the structures, once the barred gate was behind them, St. Gertrude's didn't seem as forbidding. White wooden benches encircled the thick trunks of some of the sycamores that dotted the vast manicured lawn. Here and there were pristine chairs and benches of gracefully ornate wrought iron that looked as if they wouldn't dare rust. At the west end of the lawn were a few picnic benches in the shade of a cluster of oak trees.

And straight ahead were the buildings, all with steep-pitched roofs that seemed to grow taller with each step. John could make out gargoyle waterspouts crouching at the edges of the gables and Gothic gingerbread vining along the eaves of all the buildings. To the left was a chapel overgrown with ornamentation with a tall scrolled cross above the door. A low privet hedge began at the rear of the building and John could see that it encompassed a small cemetery behind, the graves presided over by a weeping angel.

To John's far right was the narrow end of a three-story rectangular building, and directly before him was the long main building, three stories of heavy rough-cut gray stone, relatively simple despite the gargoyles and gewgaws. A large cross-gabled entry at the top of a dozen wide stone steps broke the flat rectangle. The building looked cold and ominous, reminding him a little of the old schoolhouse in *Prom Night*.

He could see the roofs of a few smaller structures peeking out from behind and between the chapel and main buildings, and from somewhere out of sight came the sound of a lawnmower. The smell of freshly cut grass wafted on the air, but otherwise the place seemed deserted.

They walked up the steps and John tried one of the massive oak doors. It swung silently open and they stepped into the cool interior. His stomach protested; he continued to ignore it. The entryway was lit from high above by sunlight streaming in through a stained-glass skylight which cast dancing colors across the polished wide-plank oak floor. On each side was a closed door, one with a brass plate reading "Administrator," the other blank. Twenty feet farther, the main corridor crossed, then the entry hall deadended at another stained-glass window, this one an arched starburst of dark colors barely touched by the sun. A madonna-style statue stood before the window. A single ray of muted crimson light fell across the alabaster face like a bloody gash. Fascinated, slightly repelled, John took a step toward it.

"May I help you?"

John turned and saw the administrator's door had opened and a tall elderly woman in a long black habit was staring at them from the doorway. Cutter stepped forward and extended his hand, introducing himself. She nodded curtly and looked to John, who swallowed bile and introduced himself.

"Mother Lucy said you would come," she said, without bothering to give her name. "Follow me."

With that, she turned to the wide entryway, approached it, then looked back at them, raising an eyebrow. Cutter stepped forward and held one of the doors for her. She exited like royalty and the men had to move quickly to keep up with her.

She led them across a walkway toward the dorm building. As they passed the windows of the main building, John caught glimpses of students and nuns in classrooms—no summer vacation for the orphans. Farther along, he heard a sonorous voice droning in what he assumed was Latin, and as they reached the corner and turned, girls' voices raised in song. It was Monk Music, as he used to call it, and it raised the hackles on the back of his neck. A moment later they reached the dorm, and again the nameless nun waited while Cutter opened the door for her.

The dormitory was long and dimly lit, the paint old and yellowed, the walls dotted with paintings between closed doors, ugly pictures of suffering saints. John barely noticed them as the nun approached a stairwell and led them up. The second-floor landing was the same, murky light coming through small colored glass windows and twenty-five-watt bulbs. The place reminded him of a run-down WPA apartment building on a grand scale, but at least his nausea had abated.

One more flight—the last—and the nun turned right, her black robes fluttering behind her. Toward the end of the corridor she halted and peered into an open room. Yellowish light poured through the doorway and a voice issued from the room. "Hello, Sister Agatha." A second voice echoed the greeting.

Irritated—he'd told them to stay out of the room—John stepped briskly into the doorway and silently groaned as he took in the buckets, rags, and mops. *Christ, why me?* He surveyed the rest of the room: the walls were pinkish and red-streaked with watery blood, the small bed stripped, not only of its linen, but its mattress as well. Only a circular rag rug that extended beneath the bed and spread across most of the floor remained intact, and despite its multicolored braiding of autumn reds, oranges, and browns, John could make out a number of blood spatters, an especially heavy one near one edge of the bed. That was, at least, some testimony to the site of the incident.

He started to open his mouth, but Sister Agatha cut him off. "This is Sister Bibiana," she said, as a short, round nun pulled rubber gloves from her hands and came forward, her face dimpling in a cheerful smile.

"Just Bibi," she said. "I'm sorry the room's so messy, Sheriff, but we're working hard." Color flooded her cheeks as she spoke. John wondered if she was embarrassed that two men were standing in a woman's bedroom.

Again he opened his mouth, again he was cut off by the administrative nun. "And this is Sister Mary Oswald."

"Sheriff," she said, not bothering to put down her mop or come forward. She was blond, he assumed, since the black cowl covered her head. Of average height and weight, her skin almost white against the habit, she had pale everything—lips, eyes, and eyebrows, the last so pale that he wasn't sure if she actually had any.

"Ladies. Sisters," he amended, "I asked your Mother Superior not to allow any one in this room until Dr. Cutter and I arrived."

"Oh, well." Sister Bibi started to giggle nervously, then

stopped, putting one hand to her mouth. "We were already working when Mother returned, so she said to go ahead."

John glanced at Cutter, who looked as annoyed as he felt. "Please stop now and leave us to our work. We need to take photos and samples." He turned to Sister Agatha and ignored her sour expression. "Please tell your Mother Superior that I'll need to speak with her and the rest of you when we're done here. Also, make sure that your resident physician will be available."

The two younger nuns bustled by, Sister Mary Oswald giving John a shy smile as she passed. Sister Agatha only nodded before following them.

# Ten

"I guess that's the best we can do, under the circumstances." John Lawson put the lenscap on his camera and turned to Frank Cutter, who was sealing an envelope containing fibers he'd scraped from the rug. "Did you find anything in the lavatory?"

"It's spotless. Not a drop of water or a dirty towel anywhere. We'll have to check the laundry facility on the way out, but I don't think we'll find anything." Cutter put the envelope in his bag. "What's next?"

"You wished to speak with me?"

John looked up to see a tall, elegant man in a charcoal suit standing in the doorway. He raised his eyebrows. "Who are you?"

"Richard Dashwood, M.D.," the man said, stepping into the room.

As John introduced himself and Cutter, he couldn't stop studying Dashwood's face. The man was between thirty-five and forty and almost too handsome, with thick, dark hair, high cheekbones, a strong jaw, and a hawk nose. But it was his eyes, long, hooded, and dark, that captured John . . . and made him uneasy. Uncomfortably familiar, Dashwood's gaze seemed to pierce through to his soul. He took an instant dislike to the man, and that was something that rarely happened. It intrigued him.

"Dashwood," Cutter said, as he removed his latex gloves. "The name's familiar." He walked up to the other doctor, peered at him. "You're too young to be . . ."

"My father was St. Gertrude's physician before me." Dashwood's manner, the serenity in his appearance and voice, combined with a slight British accent, reminded John of Basil Rathbone as Sherlock Holmes relaxing with his violin. "Dr. Cutter," Dashwood continued, "I've heard of you as well, and I'm sorry to make your acquaintance over such an unfortunate incident." He turned his attention to John. "Haven't we met before, Sheriff?" A Mona Lisa smile crept across his lips.

"It's possible," John said. "I've lived here all my life." The eyes drew him in. Something about them flickered through his memory but was gone before he could identify it. "You don't sound like a native, though, Doctor."

"I was schooled in England." One eyebrow arched slightly. "Poor Miss Tynan," he murmured. "She never should have come here, didn't have the temperament for it."

John walked over and pushed the door shut, then moved to a round dinette table and indicated one of the chairs. "Have a seat, Dr. Dashwood." He waited for the physician to seat himself, then sat opposite him while Cutter leaned against the cold radiator on the wall between them.

"Tell me about her," John began. "What didn't she have the temperament for? Teaching?"

"She didn't have the kind of personality that could thrive in a school, especially a girls' school. She was very sensitive, very soft-hearted." Dashwood leaned forward slightly. "Some of the sisters are, well, rather harsh. There's only one other lay teacher, our gym instructor, Esther Roth, and she isn't the easiest person for a young woman like Miss Tynan to get along with, either. Then there are the girls, and, well, you know how they are."

"No," John said, "I don't. Please tell me."

"Miss Tynan was very good with the younger girls, but she taught at the high school level, and adolescents—especially young women—can be very difficult to handle. Miss Tynan wasn't suited to the job."

"Did she talk to you about her problems?"

"Yes, a little. She came to me for something to soothe her nerves. She requested Valium, or at least Xanax."

"Did you give her something?" Cutter asked.

"After examining her, I suggested herbal tea. Chamomile, actually. And I gave her advice on some simple relaxation techniques. We talked, and I realized that she was young, inexperienced, and really just needed to, ah, tough it out, as they say. I told her these things—in much kinder words, of course—and tried to build up her self esteem." Dashwood looked down at his hands, then back at Lawson, his expressive eyes filled with regret. "I'm afraid I underestimated her mental instability. If I'd realized, I would have referred her to a psychiatrist. Perhaps she would still be with us."

"You believe it was a suicide, then?" Lawson asked.

"Depression?" Cutter asked simultaneously.

"Yes to your question, Sheriff, and no to yours, Doctor. Or, more precisely, perhaps depression was part of why she took her life, but I've been thinking about something she mentioned a few times. She said it lightly and I didn't take her seriously. After all, she was a grown woman."

"Go on," John prompted. There was absolutely nothing to dislike about this man, but his aversion was growing by the second. Maybe he was simply responding to Dashwood the same way he'd seen his ex-wife react when she encountered a woman she perceived as more beautiful or intelligent than she. *That's not important; concentrate.* "What did she say?"

"She said she thought she saw one of our alleged ghosts. That it spoke to her."

"And what did it say?" John tried to cover his skepticism.

"It told her she was going to die. Her phrasing was cautious; she said she had probably imagined it, and she tried to laugh about it."

"I would take it seriously," Cutter said, "if a patient told me that. Joking or not, it's important."

"I would have, Doctor, except for the fact that she asked

me to prescribe sleeping pills, or at least, the Valium or Xanax she'd requested earlier. I knew from her history that she had used these drugs for extended periods, and as I'm sure you're aware, they can be quite habit-forming. I believed that she probably concocted the ghost story in order to get the drugs I had previously denied. I thought it likely she had a substance abuse problem."

"So you gave her nothing?" Cutter asked, in a much calmer tone.

"In addition to the tea, I eventually gave her some over-the-counter antihistamines. Completely safe, and they make most people sleepy."

"How long ago did this ghost business begin?" John asked.

"She began to complain about her nerves about six months ago—only a few weeks after her arrival. The ghost stories began about two months ago."

"I see," John said, thinking that drug abuse really was a definite possibility. "I'd like to see her medical files."

"Dr. Dashwood," Cutter began. "Just out of curiosity, was it the ghost of a headless monk?"

John wondered about that, too—the headless monk tale supposedly dated from the earliest days of the monastery.

"No, our monk has only been reported in the chapel and in the cemetery behind it." Dashwood cleared his throat. "This ghost is one of our 'ladies in white.'" To show he was a nonbeliever, Dashwood forged a wry smile. "This building— the living quarters—has only one, but it's said she wanders every floor. Sometimes sobbing is heard in conjunction with her visitations. There have even been a few reports of doors opening or closing by themselves; as with all good ghosts, she's often invisible. The main building, which contains the school, has two; one that haunts the janitor's storeroom, and another, commonly known as 'The Screamer.'"

"Sounds delightful," Cutter said dryly.

Dashwood sat back and folded his long-fingered hands. "I thought that Lenore Tynan was at most trying to obtain drugs, and at the least, merely a little anxious. The ghost stories have that effect on some of our students and even an occasional teacher, and as I said, she spoke of it jokingly. In retrospect, I realize that she must have been genuinely delusional, and that she was experiencing a nervous breakdown. I wish I'd realized it sooner, but she was a quiet girl who kept to herself. Her conversations with me were very stilted. Cautious, you might say."

"I see," John said, after a brief but heavy silence. The queasiness was returning and the longer he looked into Dashwood's weird, dark eyes, the worse it became. He wanted to end the interview. Now. "I appreciate your cooperation, Doctor. Rest assured I'll return your records as soon as possible."

"Of course." Dashwood glanced up as someone rapped sharply on the door. "That will be the Mother Superior," he said, rising as the knob turned. "If there's nothing else, I'll fetch Miss Tynan's files for you."

"Thanks, I'll be in touch." Lawson and Cutter stood and followed Dashwood to the door, which opened to reveal Mother Superior Lucy Bartholomew, whose expression implied she was wearing the tightest panties in town. She entered the room and the odor of mildewed cinnamon clinging to her made nausea worm more deeply through John's gut.

Dashwood stepped forward and took Lucy's hand in both of his. Instantly the woman melted, her face relaxing into something resembling beauty. Color bloomed in her cheeks as she beamed at the man. "Doctor, thank you for cooperating with the sheriff's investigation," she purred without a glance at John.

"I'll see you later, Mother Lucy." Dashwood let go of her hand and glanced back. "Gentlemen."

John nodded and Dashwood left them to Mother Lucy, whose expression hardened to cement as soon as the physician was gone. "Sheriff, Dr. Cutter, follow me, please. The sisters are waiting."

"John," said Cutter, looking at his watch. "I have to get back. Baptist bellyaches," he added for Lucy's amusement, but she only scowled.

"I'll run you back right now," John said quickly. "I'll be back soon, Mother Lucy. Actually," he added, relief flooding him, "I'll send two of my deputies, and they can complete the questioning in half the time."

"Very well." Lucy clipped off the words. She pulled the door closed behind them, then escorted them briskly out of the dorm and off the property. When the gargoyled gate slammed shut behind them, John actually began to feel good for the first time that day.

# Eleven

"I have a customer," Minerva Payne told Mark Lawson as the bells over the door of the Gingerbread House jingled. "Let's go see who it is."

Mark nodded, his mouth full with a chunk of freshly cut fudge, then followed the old lady out of the kitchen, only to stop dead in his tracks when he saw his father, in full uniform, approaching the counter.

"Mrs. Payne," he began, then spotted his son. "Mark, what are you doing here?"

"Nothing," he mumbled around the fudge.

"Mark was just helping me in the kitchen, so I gave him a piece of candy," Minerva said, smiling at the sheriff. "I hope that's all right—it's not too near dinnertime, is it?"

John Lawson looked taken aback, then shook his head and gave her a strained smile. "No, ah, that's fine. I just didn't expect to find him here." He looked at his son. "You told me you and Corey Addams were going over to the Parkers' today."

Mark looked a little sheepish. "We did. I just stopped here on my way home."

"Where's Corey?"

"He didn't stop. He's afraid of Minerva."

"Mark!" Lawson said. "Mind your manners."

Minerva chuckled and rested her hands on the boy's shoulders. "That's all right, Sheriff. Mark is refreshingly honest, and he really is one of the few Moonfall children who aren't afraid of me." She smiled and ruffled Mark's hair. "Some of the adults are afraid of me, too. Afraid I'll turn them into frogs, or some such nonsense." She paused. "You'd best run along now, Mark. Your father needs to speak with me."

"Really?" Mark asked. "What about, Dad?"

"Business. Look, go over to Gus's and help him do some chores."

"Ah, Dad—"

"He's cooking us dinner tonight, so give him a hand. I'll be there in an hour. Now, scoot."

Minerva watched the father watch the son as he scuffed his way out of the store, noted the affection in John Lawson's eyes. It was a painful thing to see. "Sheriff? I thought you might pay me a visit today," she said briskly.

"What made you think that?" Anxiety laced his voice, and she knew he was trying hard to hide it.

"Why, that poor young woman in the pond, of course."

"Were you the one who phoned about her?"

"No, Sheriff, but it's all over town. You can't keep something like that secret for long."

"Who told you?"

"I don't want to talk out of turn."

"You won't. This shouldn't be common knowledge yet. I need to know."

"Very well. Deputy Griffin told me."

"He already questioned you?"

"No, of course not. Why would he ask an old woman like me about something like that? I gave him a potion that loosened his tongue."

The sheriff's mouth worked, but nothing came out. Old ideas died hard.

"The potion was coffee and a Danish, Sheriff Lawson." There were two wicker chairs near the window, and Minerva walked over and sat in one, beckoning him to do the same. "Old bones. They pain me when I stand too long." She waited while John Lawson settled in the chair. He'd been a good-looking boy, and he'd grown into a fine figure of a man with a strong face and thick hair, just like his father, and old Gus before him. As Mark would be one day. The Lawsons were of fine stock. *And why shouldn't they be?* She smiled to herself, then studied John. "Would you like some coffee, and perhaps a tart? I just took them out of the oven—and they're not apple."

He actually smiled at that and she saw some of his unease drain away. Moonfall humor dictated that no resident would be caught dead eating apples if other fruit was available. "No, but thanks for the offer."

"Hot lemon," she told him.

"I'm on duty."

"Let me assure you, they contain no alcohol." She laughed her low, throaty chuckle again. "Now, you have some questions?"

"Yes, Mrs. Payne, I do."

" 'Minerva' will do better."

He nodded, then asked several questions about her whereabouts the previous night and this morning, if she'd seen or heard anything unusual; exactly the sort of thing she expected.

"You can ask me anything, Sheriff," she prompted, when he fell silent. "Isn't there something else?" She wanted him to bring up his brother.

He gazed at her, his mask dropping for an instant to reveal the frightened boy she'd seen so long ago. Then his expression turned all-business again. "I have just one last question: why did you expect me to come by to talk with you, yet find it humorous that Deputy Griffin might do the same?"

Bones creaking, she rose slowly from her chair, then looked down at John Lawson. "It's very simple." She bent slightly, staring into his eyes. "You and I have unfinished business. And why not? You never told anyone about seeing me at the Falls twenty-four years ago."

Slowly he nodded, then stood. Unlike many men, he was taller than her, but only by an inch or so, and he tried in vain to avoid her eyes. "I don't know what you mean."

"Yes, you do. And we must talk about it soon. Before Halloween, John, *long* before." At those last words, he flinched visibly. "Why didn't you tell, John?" she persisted.

For an instant, she saw the glint of a tear in his eye, but he had great self-discipline and it disappeared quickly. "I don't know," he said hoarsely, then turned and walked out the door, shutting it so hard that the glass panes vibrated.

"Remember, John. You must remember," Minerva whispered. "You couldn't save your brother, but you *can* save your son."

# Twelve

"What the hell is the matter with me?" John ranted, as he paced his grandfather's old-fashioned veranda. He turned around and looked at Gus, who sat on the porch swing, calmly lighting one of his foul-smelling cigars. The butt glowed red in the twilight. "I'm the goddamned sheriff, for Chrissake, and I practically tossed my cookies the minute I walked through the gates of St. Gruesome's."

"No need to swear, Johnny. No need to berate yourself, either. We've all got our demons." Gus leaned forward. "And yours are out there at the abbey."

John walked toward his grandfather, then leaned against the white wooden porch railing, facing him. "My demons are at Witch Falls. St. Gertrude's has nothing to do with them."

"Sure it does, boy. Sure it does." He pointed the cigar at John. "You were going there on Halloween to have some fun, but something happened and you ended up at the Falls."

"What makes you think that?"

"Overheard you boys making plans." Gus blew a smoke ring.

"What?"

"You and your friends thought you were pretty clever, hunkering down behind the wisteria vine near my bedroom window, didn't you?"

"You *eavesdropped* on us?" John asked, shocked. Of all his family, it was Gus he'd always felt closest to, Gus he had trusted the most.

"Not on purpose, but I couldn't very well help it for a while. Remember why I moved in with your folks?"

"Sure. You broke your leg." That was an understatement. Mom and Dad had been after Gus to sell his huge old Victorian house—he'd been widowed for a decade and was still puttering around there by himself. One night, a drunk slammed into his car on the winding road below town. He was lucky to survive, but his leg had been shattered in several places. When he got out of the hospital, he went to stay in the Lawsons' single-story California bungalow, and he never left, though he talked about it—at least, until Dad died. Then there was no question of his leaving. Mom died when John was still in high school, and he and Gus grew even closer. Yet he'd never brought up Halloween of 1972 until now.

"Broke it good, too," Gus was saying, around puffs of smoke. "Almost missed the Haunt that year, but there you boys were under my open window, and I couldn't help listening."

"You knew we were going, but you didn't rat on us?"

"Heck no, boy. What'd you take me for?" He chuckled to himself, then began puffing out a series of smoke rings, bull's-eyeing each one through the last.

John watched fascinated, afraid of what his grandfather might say next. "Maybe we'd better get home," John said finally. "It's getting late, and Mark's probably cross-eyed from watching that oversized TV of yours." He pushed himself away from the porch rail, then Gus fixed him with The Look.

"Did you go to St. Gruesome's that night, Johnny?"

For a moment he couldn't answer, then he realized that was something else he, Doug, Winky, Beano, and Paul had talked about under the wisteria, and irritation replaced anxiety. "You overheard us, Gus. Why don't *you* tell *me?*"

"You went, all right." The old man sat forward, his thinning white hair blowing across his forehead in the evening breeze. "You might think you didn't, but you did. I don't know what happened out there, John, but St. Gertrude's is at the core of your problems."

"We didn't go. We were going to, yeah, but then Beano said that his brother made up all his stories about going and had written to him telling us we shouldn't go. So we went camping instead."

"Why is it that five boys didn't know whether they went to St. Gertrude's or not? You boys argued back and forth for weeks, then Doug Buckman died and you all stopped seeing each other." He grunted. "The way I heard it, you convinced one another you didn't go. Don't you remember?"

*Walking our bikes up the long dark road. The gate, the gargoyles watching us.* "There's nothing to remember. We were just making up stories." *Minerva Payne said we have to talk. How come you never told them you saw me, John?* "Serves you right for eavesdropping." John said this lightly, then crossed the porch and opened the screen door, raised his voice. "Time to go home, Mark. Get a move on!"

Gus stood, flicking ash from his dwindling cigar. "You ever want to talk about it, Johnny, you know where to find me."

"Thanks, Gus, but Greg's death is not something I want to talk about. Ever."

Mark flew out the door as Gus nodded. "Just keep it in mind. See you two next week?"

"Sure. Come on, Mark. 'Night, Gus."

" 'Bye, Gus," Mark tossed in, running down the steps.

John followed his son to the car, not looking back at the house until he was inside with the engine running. Gus was still on the porch, invisible except for the glowing cigar butt. *Damn that old man. Damn Minerva Payne, and damn Lenore Tynan for starting it all up again.*

# Thirteen

Sobbing. In the dark.

Kelly Reed came awake slowly, thinking the sounds were borne of some fleeting nightmare, but as she lay there in the dark, the soft, heartbreaking cries continued.

"No." Kelly whispered the word, willing the weeping to stop. As always, the sounds were close, so close that she was afraid that if she reached out, she would touch whoever made them.

She didn't know who was crying; she'd never known in the entire six months she'd been a resident—*resident, hell, I'm an inmate!*—at St. Gertrude's. Her roommate, a snotty senior named Marcia Crowley, claimed she had never heard it, and alternately told Kelly she was crazy, on drugs, or hearing the ghost of Jenny Blaine, the girl rumored to have killed herself in their room over a decade ago. Then Marcia told her friends, and they all made fun of Kelly. Whenever the nuns weren't around they called her "Ghost Girl." The worst was in the showers, where they liked to hide her clothes.

The sobbing, closer now, continued, and Kelly ducked her head under the covers, sure that if she didn't, she'd feel someone else's breath on her cheek. *What if it's Marcia, playing a trick? Her friends are probably all hiding in a corner, laughing at me.* They'd done that once a couple weeks ago, and she'd hidden, as she did now. Since then, on top of everything else, they'd started squawking like chickens at her when no one else was around.

The sobbing went on, louder now, louder than she'd ever heard it. "Marcia, cut it out," she hissed beneath the blankets.

Someone sat on the end of her bed. She felt the mattress depress and pulled her feet up and away, waiting for the sound of the bedsprings. But she heard nothing except the crying. *It's Marcia and Buffy and those other twits, trying to yank your chain. Don't let them do it again!*

Sudden anger killed her fear. Steeling herself, she swallowed hard and yanked the covers off. "I said, cut it out!" she cried, fumbling for the light switch. "Cut it out *now!*" Her hand closed on the bedside lamp and she quickly found the switch and pressed it.

Light blossomed in the room and there was no one there except Marcia Crowley, sitting up in bed, blinking and pushing her long blond hair out of her eyes. "What the fuck's wrong with you?" she demanded, her voice thickened from sleep. "You see another ghost?"

"You didn't hear it?" Too angry to be intimidated, Kelly swung out of bed. Her knee-length white nightgown had crept up over her thighs and she pulled it back down without even being embarrassed. She stalked the room, looked in the closet, behind the curtains, under the beds.

"Poor little Ghost Girl," Marcia taunted, wide awake now, and grinning her cheerleader grin. She curled a golden lock around her finger. "Did that mean old lady in white come visit you? Maybe she pulled up your nightgown!" She giggled.

Kelly opened the door and peered out into the corridor. Nothing. Turning toward Marcia, she put her hands on her hips. "You used a tape recorder, didn't you?"

The other girl shrugged. "I don't know what the hell you're talking about. Hey!"

She jumped out of bed as Kelly started opening bureau drawers, looking for a tape recorder. "Get out of my stuff!" She grabbed Kelly by the shoulders and tried to yank her away, but Kelly shook her off and started tossing her socks and underwear on the floor.

"My locket," she whispered, as the small gold chain with a heart almost slipped through her fingers. She fumbled it open, relieved to see the tiny picture of her mother still inside. It was her only possession, the only connection she had with her past, and she'd worn it forever, through all the foster homes she'd lived in since her mother had died. She'd worn it until she'd ended up here, at St. Gertrude's, where the nuns forbade the girls to wear jewelry. It had disappeared from her dresser three months ago, and it hadn't even occurred to her that someone had stolen it. *How stupid can you be?*

The ghost forgotten, she turned to face Marcia. "You—" Marcia leapt at her, driving her to the ground, pulling her hair, digging her nails into her arms. Kelly fought back, got a grip on Marcia's hair, and yanked her down. Simultaneously, she forced her knee up into the other girl's stomach, knocking the wind from her, the same way it had stopped one nasty foster brother from picking on her. Marcia raked her nails down Kelly's cheek and Kelly heard herself scream, but she didn't let go, then Marcia started screaming, too.

Vaguely, she was aware of the door opening and nuns in dark nightgowns pulling them apart. One of them started prying her fingers from Marcia's hair with so much force that she finally let go, afraid the nun would break them.

They were apart. Someone was holding her from behind by the arms, and Sister Mary Oswald held Marcia the same way. The blonde's nostrils were flaring and there was spittle running from her mouth. Kelly twisted her neck, saw that she'd been captured by Sister Agatha, mean and old and surprisingly strong. On the floor between them lay the locket, the chain broken.

Mother Lucy stood in the doorway, arms crossed, face grim, supervising it all, and behind her, Kelly saw Buffy and Jan and the others, all watching with glee.

"What's going on here?" Mother Lucy asked abruptly.

At that, Marcia went into her act, crying loudly and turning to embrace Sister Mary Oswald. She lifted her tearstained face and said to Lucy, "Kelly tried to steal my locket. I woke up and tried to stop her, and—and—and—"

"It's all right, Marcia," Mother Lucy said, and Sister Mary Oswald held the girl to her breast and stroked her hair. Lucy turned. "All of you, back to your rooms this instant!" The faces disappeared.

Lucy, a woman carved in stone, pulled her black robe tighter around her and approached Kelly, pausing only to scoop up the locket. Sister Agatha's grip tightened.

"Is this true, Kelly?" the Mother Superior asked harshly.

"No!" She felt her lower lip trembling and felt blood trickling down her cheek, but she refused to give in to tears. "She's lying, Mother. That's my locket. Remember, when I came here, you said to keep it in my bureau, that I couldn't wear it? I did, and I told you it disappeared, remember? It has a picture of my mother in it. Look and see!"

"She's lying!" Marcia sobbed. "That's my locket. That's my mother in the heart, see? She has blond hair, just like mine."

Lucy opened the heart, looked briefly, then shut and pocketed it. "Kelly, you've been a troublemaker ever since you've been here. You've sinned repeatedly, lying, making up stories to scare the other girls, and now stealing." She looked over Kelly's head, at the nun holding her. "Sister Agatha, clean her up, then put her in the solitary room for the night."

"But it's *my locket!*" Kelly cried.

Lucy's hand flashed out and slapped her bloodied cheek. Shocked, Kelly said nothing. "Don't cause yourself more trouble, young lady. In the morning, you're going to see Dr. Dashwood, and then I'll decide on your punishment." Lucy turned her back on Kelly. "Marcia, I'm sorry this happened, and if this girl gives you any more trouble, I will remove her from this room. She'll stay in solitary every night."

Kelly let herself be led away, thinking that whatever solitary was, it had to be preferable to being tortured by Marcia Crowley.

# Fourteen

*Monk music sung in feminine voices, minor-keyed and beautiful, enveloped him. He was on his back, tied down; dark figures, the singers, moved around him, and above, the moon watched it all. A shadow began to eclipse the moon, and then he saw the bare outlines of a face hidden under a cowl. He could see only the eyes, preternaturally bright, brilliant whites, irises the color of night, boring into his own, digging into his soul. "Tell me your name!"*

"No!" John Lawson came bolt upright in his bed, his cry still on his lips. The full moon shone through the window, casting abstract shadows across his bedroom, and the sheets, tangled around his legs, were damp with sweat. He reached up and turned on the light, saw his body sheened with droplets of perspiration. "Christ," he muttered. The nightmares were always at their worst when the moon was full. "Christ Almighty."

"Dad?" Mark stood in the doorway, clad in boxer shorts and an ancient Rude Dog t-shirt. "You okay?"

"Fine, son, just had a whopper of a nightmare." Thinking that he was getting tired of being asked about his well-being, first by Frank Cutter, then Gus, now by his own son, he climbed out of bed and began straightening the sheets.

"Maybe you should get some sleeping pills, huh?" Mark's

question was innocent enough, but it only reminded him of Dashwood telling him about Lenore Tynan's alleged drug problem. "I think I'll get some warm milk instead." He glanced at his watch, saw it was past two in the morning. "You want some?"

"Nah, not unless you're going to put chocolate in it."

"Sounds good." He knew he shouldn't let Mark stay up just because he wanted company, but what could it hurt? After all, he didn't have to be up for school in the morning.

In the kitchen, which was white and sterile because Barbara, his ex-wife, had wanted it that way and he'd never had the time to strip the paint and restain the cabinets light oak and replace the chrome handles with copper, Mark got out the Hershey's chocolate and sugar while John took a pan from a cabinet and the milk from the brushed chrome refrigerator. *Ugly and cold.* The whole room was as ugly and chill as the insides of the too-large refrigerator. He had to do something about it. *Someday.*

Mark was oblivious as he started jabbering about basketball scores, moved on to Parker clan gossip gleaned from his friend Pete, and then to plant collecting, the latest hobby in a lifelong fascination with collections. At one time or another the boy had collected everything from snails to rocks to feathers to the screw-on caps on soda bottles. Now it was plants. Herbs, to be precise. The kid was talking about wild mugwort, and as John brought two cups of chocolate to the kitchen table, which was chrome and glass and all Barbara, he looked at his son. "Mugwort? What in the world is mugwort?"

"It's an herb. It's kinda fuzzy and it grows all over Witch Forest. It keeps ghosts away."

John burned his tongue on the chocolate and set it down again. "Ghosts? I thought you didn't believe in ghosts!"

Mark snorted, then blew on his chocolate too hard, spattering the glass with tiny brown drops. It improved the looks of the table, as far as John was concerned. Made it homier. " 'Course, I don't believe in ghosts, Dad. It's just lore."

John smiled. "Lore?"

"Minerva—" He cut his sentence short, watching for a bad

response, but John kept his smile pasted in place. What else could he do? Tell him the old lady was a witch, that she sent gargoyles out to fetch babies? Even he'd never believed that.

"Go on."

"She says herbs were the first medicines, they weren't just used for casting spells 'n' junk like it says in witch books. Like foxglove, it was heart medicine—"

"Digitalis," John said.

His son beamed at him. "*You* knew that?" he asked in amazement.

"Sure. And garlic kills worms," he added, exhausting his knowledge of medicinal herbs.

"Wow. Did Minerva teach you?"

"No." He couldn't help smiling. "That's pretty common knowledge. "You know, like when Gus puts in his garden, he always plants a couple rows of beets around it to distract gophers?"

Mark nodded. "Minerva says he should put marigolds in, too, because they keep bugs away."

"You sound like you know Minerva pretty well," John ventured. "How'd you meet her?"

Mark looked at his chocolate. "At the Falls."

Alarmed, John tried to sound calm. "The Falls?"

"Yeah, well, me, Pete, and Corey were messing around, you know, hanging out on the Mezzanine—"

"I warned you about swimming there. You didn't—"

"Well, no, but everybody does it." He rolled his eyes in anticipation of his father's next remark and beat him to it. "And if everybody jumped out of an airplane without a parachute, would you?" he asked, mimicking John.

He couldn't help being amused, but it also bothered him— he could never comfortably use the standard "would you jump off a cliff" metaphor. "So you were at the Falls *thinking* about diving in." He spoke lightly.

"Well, yeah, I guess. But Minerva came along. She was spooky, just sorta standing up there on the bridge, looking down at us. Scared the pee out of Corey and Pete." He sat up straighter to brag, "But not me. They ran off, and I stayed and talked to her." Mark lowered his voice and looked at his cup again. "She told me how your little brother died and all and, well, don't worry, Dad, I'll never swim there again."

John felt a flash of anger at Minerva Payne for talking about Greg. *But why? Is his death all yours? Did she invade your territory?* Here she'd stopped Mark from doing the one thing he really didn't want him doing. *I ought to thank her.*

"Dad?"

"What?" he asked after a long pause. "What, Mark?"

"How come you never told me what happened to your brother?"

"Well . . . I guess because it's really hard for me to talk about. It hurts."

"Like when Mom ran off with that lawyer from Claremont and never came back?"

That had been a relief for John, but he knew it was horrible for his son. Barbara had never communicated beyond the divorce papers. She'd thrown her own son away. "Yeah, Mark," he finally said, "Kind of like it was for you when Mom took off."

The boy was silent for a long moment, then asked, "But worse, huh?"

John looked at him, saw a reflection of himself in the hazel eyes, straight mouth, brown hair, even in the bone structure and the faint summer freckles across Mark's nose. He'd inherited little from his mother, a drop-dead beautiful lawyer who'd left when she couldn't talk John into going back to law school and bettering himself by wearing a suit and arguing in court and attending the right dinner parties with the right people and the right wine. No uniformed cop for her; not even head cop would do. *Still bitter after all these years.* He had wanted her to leave, had told her to leave after he'd found out about the affair with the infamous Claremont lawyer, an ambulance-chaser who'd hit it big.

"Dad?"

"Mark, losing Greg was really hard for me. I was his big brother and I was supposed to be looking out for him. I was responsible." He said the words with as little emotion as he could, but still there was a catch in his voice.

"You feel guilty," Mark observed in his childish, blunt way.

"I sure do. That's why I don't want you playing around there." *If anything happened to you, I couldn't go on.*

"I know. Minerva says it's not your fault, though."

"What?" John sat up. "What did she tell you?" *Does she know something? Did she see something?*

Mark shrugged. "Just that aside from it being dangerous, I shouldn't swim there because you felt like it was your fault your brother died, so it would really upset you if I played there."

The irritation at the old woman's interference was still there, but lessening. "Mark, this is important. Did she say *why* it wasn't my fault?"

Mark finished his chocolate, then looked his father in the eye. "No, huh-uh. She just said it wasn't and it was too bad you didn't get that."

"Get that?"

"Y'know, like understand, or something. Dad?"

"Yeah?"

"You get lots of nightmares," Mark said abruptly.

"I do? What makes you think that?"

"You make noises, creepy noises, in your sleep. Sometimes you yell, but not usually as loud as tonight."

*Christ.* "Really?"

"Yeah; it's spooky."

"I'm sorry. Some people talk in their sleep."

"You just make scared sounds. Dad?" he repeated.

"What?"

"Do you dream about your little brother?"

John studied his son. "I can't ever remember the dreams when I wake up, but yes, I think I probably do."

"Minerva told me how to remember dreams."

"Wait a minute. Did you tell her about my nightmares?"

"Huh-uh, swear to God. She told *me*, though."

"What? That's impossible."

"Huh-uh. She knows stuff like that because she's an herb woman. That's like a really old-time doctor. She says most of the herb women were killed off in the witch hunts because they knew more about medicine than the men doctors from Europe and they didn't like that. So they burned them and hanged them and drowned them, and all sorts of gross stuff. But she's one, and she knows. She says you should write down your dreams and you'll start remembering them.''

John had had just about all the strange conversation he could take for one night. Exhaustion and irritation were setting in for real now, so he just stood up and took the cups to the sink. Left them there, nice and dirty, for tomorrow. Barbara would never have let him do that. ''Mark,'' he said, finally, ''why in the world would I want to remember dreams that scare me so much?''

The boy shrugged once more and walked to the kitchen threshold. ''Gee, I dunno, Dad. Maybe if you remember your dreams, you won't feel so bad about your little brother. 'Night.''

''Night.'' John watched his son slouch down the hall. *Out of the mouths of babes.* He waited another minute or two, then opened the cupboard and got out an old half-full bottle of Scotch, poured a couple fingers in a juice glass, and downed it. Liquid fire burned his throat. It felt good. Very good. He screwed the lid back on the bottle and put it away, knowing that if he allowed it, he, like Lenore—*the lost Lenore,* came a whisky-mellowed thought—could become dependent on a drug or two to get him through the night.

# PART THREE

## SEPTEMBER, 1996

# Fifteen

*I must have been nuts to come back to this place.*

Sara Hawthorne, a flight bag over her shoulder and a suitcase in her hand, shivered as she walked along the poorly lit stone corridor of the St. Gruesome's dormitory. It was colder here than she remembered, damp and chill, with cobwebs in the ceiling corners and chipped paint on the doors. When she was a girl, perhaps she'd paid less attention to such things, or maybe here on the third floor, where most of the teachers lived— *where I'm going to live*—the upkeep and heating weren't priorities. After all, most of the other teachers were nuns, and didn't they believe in austerity, in self-sacrifice and denial?

The corridor, lit only by dim, fly-specked bulbs and trembling prismatic rainbows cast by the afternoon sun through small stained-glass windows in the left-hand wall, seemed to telescope before her. The windows did not depict religious scenes, but were simple diamond patterns, the dark colors made darker by a layer of grime, completely hiding the view of the garages and outbuildings, and the big stone kitchen, where the nuns made cider and prepared apples and mincemeat for Apple Heaven.

Sara's eyes followed a reddish reflection across the stone floor and up the wall, and almost against her will, she paused to study one of the portraits that studded the corridor. The paintings, all of saints, were hung throughout the halls, and Sara remembered that a nun, Sister Elizabeth—*Sister Lizard, that's what we called her back then*—was the artist. This was one of the tamer pictures. Labeled "Saint Wolfgang," it depicted a lean, bloodied man, quite naked, shielding his head from a horde of descending demons that reminded Sara of the flying monkeys in *The Wizard of Oz. Sister Elizabeth wasn't so talented, after all.* She wondered if the nun was still in residence, still creating her gruesome pictures. Recalling the sister's intense, oddly asymmetrical features, the pursed full lips and grim set of her piggy mouth, she hoped not.

"Somethin' wrong?"

Startled by the high-pitched male voice, Sara turned to see a grizzled old man approaching, her garment bag and other suitcase in hand. Scrawny from the top of his bald head to the toes of his surprisingly white Reeboks, he grinned at her with big, tobacco-stained teeth.

"Nothing's wrong," she stammered, thinking he looked vaguely familiar. "I was just . . . the doors aren't numbered, and I don't know which room is mine."

"Two doors down," he said, joining her before the painting. He glanced at it and whistled through his teeth. "Sister Liz, she likes to keep her saints naked." Shaking his head, he gazed at Sara with his dark little rodent eyes. "Too bad she don't do more of the women." He cocked his head like a chicken. "You look kinda familiar."

"I lived here about ten years ago," she told him as they began walking.

He nodded. "Most girls leave here, they never come back." He stopped in front of a yellowed door. "Here 'tis."

Sara hesitated, realizing that the nun who'd greeted her downstairs hadn't given her a key.

Evidently, the old man could read minds. "No locks on these old doors," he told her, gripping the knob. He turned it and the door creaked open. "Ladies first."

"I think I remember you, too," she said as they entered the room.

"Basil-Bob Boullan," he told her. "Been the caretaker here for almost forty years." He flipped the light switch.

Setting her luggage down, Sara stared around the room, relief flooding her. Though windowless, the room was reasonably sized, light and airy, and freshly painted, the oak floor gleaming around a large braided rug, old and worn, but clean. At one end was a twin bed, neatly made with a light blue quilted bedspread. A simple pine nightstand with a hurricane lamp sat beside it. There was also a very old vanity, dark wood, ornate, but scarred, that cradled a dented copper basin. Sara glanced around, half expecting to see a chamberpot, but the only other furnishings were a small pine table and two matching chairs, a chest of drawers, a faded easy chair with a side table and lamp, and a half-filled bookcase. A narrow door hid a dinky closet.

"There's a fridge in the corner, there." Basil-Bob pointed at a squat white refrigerator behind the table. "And you've got a hot plate and a few dishes there, in the bureau." He glanced behind him. "And that's a real nice bed. Got a new mattress and everything. Old one got spoilt."

She nodded uncomfortably as Boullan crossed to the bed and placed her luggage beside it. "There's no bathroom?" she asked, glancing around in hopes of seeing a door she'd missed.

Boullan cackled. "That'll be last door at the end of the hall."

*If I were smart, I'd leave right now.* Even though she knew the students had communal baths, she'd assumed that the teachers' rooms had private facilities. Wondering if she could afford a room in town, she smiled at the caretaker. "Thank you, Mr. Boullan."

"Basil-Bob'll do." His eyes crawled over her body. "You got yerself any more questions?"

*Only about a million of them, but I won't be asking you.* "I'm supposed to meet with the Mother Superior in half an hour. I'm sure she'll tell me everything I need to know." She tried to smile, but her discomfort at having this man in her room was growing by the second.

"You want me to show you to her office?"

"Um, no thanks. Unless it's moved, I know the way."

He showed no signs of leaving, so she went to the door and held it open for him. "Thanks for your help. I need to freshen up now."

He shambled over to her and stood in the doorway. He looked like he ought to be dirty and malodorous, but his dark green work clothes were as immaculate as his joltingly white running shoes. "You need anything, you come and see me."

"Thanks."

He started out the door, then paused, turning to face her again. "Don't let the funny noises at night bother you none."

"Funny noises?"

"At night. It's just the ghost."

"The ghost? I never heard any ghost stories concerning the dormitory." Despite her immediate skepticism, the hairs on the back of her neck prickled up.

Boullan nodded. "Got us another lady in white. She wanders all over the place and likes to walk along this here hallway sometimes. Why, the last teacher who had this room, Miss Tynan, she was so afraid to go out to the bathroom at night, she got herself a piss infection, laid her up for a couple weeks."

"Did she leave because of the ghost?" Sara asked, trying not to smile.

Boullan's expression turned somber. "Maybe she did. Maybe she just did, now." His beady eyes bored into hers, raising real goosebumps this time. "Killed herself, she did. That means you get to go straight to Hell, do not pass Go, do not collect two hundred dollars." He leaned in conspiratorially. "Slit her wrists, you know. Did it right here in this room—that's why I had to paint the place and getcha the new mattress. That's where she done it, on the bed. Squirted the walls, yes, ma'am. And the floors and the bed."

He went on, spouting details, but Sara barely heard him. She was thinking about Jenny Blaine, her best friend and roommate when she'd lived here in the mid-eighties. She'd died the same way, and Sara was the one who had found her. "Basil-Bob," she began.

He stopped talking and stared at her. "Yup?"

"I really can't talk any longer right now." She tried to keep her voice steady. "We'll speak later, if you like."

"Sure thing." He turned on his heel and strode silently down the shadowed corridor. She watched him until he reached the stairs, where his Reeboks squeaked as he turned.

Back in her room, Sara pulled the door closed behind her. She decided that after her meeting, she'd go into town and at least buy some sort of lock for her room.

The bed where her predecessor had sat to slit her wrists was as pristine as the white, white walls. She wondered how many coats of paint it had taken to cover the bloodstains. When Jenny had died, she'd scrubbed and painted over the stains herself, five coats, but when the light was just right, she'd thought she could still see them, dim red shadows across the walls.

Jenny Blaine was the reason Sara Hawthorne had returned to St. Gertrude's Home for Girls. Jenny didn't kill herself; she was murdered, of that Sara was sure. Her death, along with other foggy memories of other girls' disappearances—runaways, the nuns said—still haunted her. At sixteen, three months after Jenny's death, she'd run away herself, unable to sleep another night in the room where Jenny had died. She'd hitchhiked to San Francisco and had herself legally emancipated, so that she could work and attend school. Her new freedom should have been wonderful, despite the hard work, but she'd taken the horror with her.

Sara's insides felt hot and liquid as she quickly brushed her dark brown hair and reapplied lipstick. Despite the therapists, despite her attempts to write down her memories, they all eluded her, except for the vision of that bloody room, of Jenny. She was haunted, not by ghosts, but by the past, and now it was time to see justice done for Jenny Blaine and to exorcise her own demons, the ones that caused the nightmares and the nervousness with which she met each day.

After she received her teaching degree, she worked in Marin County, California, for a middle-grade school, thinking that now that she had her career, she would finally forget. But it didn't happen. Finally, she sent a résumé to St. Gertrude's, hoping that giving herself a chance to solve the mystery of Jenny's death would soothe her nerves. She never really expected to hear back from the home, but a few months later, Mother Superior Lucy Bartholomew—the selfsame nun she'd so feared when she was a student—wrote to her. Shortly after, they interviewed by phone and Sara was offered the position. *And here I am, only slightly in shock. What the hell am I doing here?* It had all happened so fast she'd barely had time to think about her actions.

Shaking her head, she took her briefcase from her flight bag, glanced in the small, round mirror over the chest of drawers, then squared her shoulders and walked out the door to make her appointment. Coming back here was the hardest thing she'd ever done, but now that she was here, she decided, nothing—*nothing*—would stop her from finding out what had really happened to Jenny Blaine.

# Sixteen

Mother Superior Lucy Bartholomew's office was the same dark and depressing chamber it had been when Sara was a girl. Both the office and Mother Lucy appeared to be untouched by time.

The office and outer room, where Mother Lucy had kept her waiting for forty-five minutes before admitting her to the inner sanctum, were also the same. Sara suspected that the nun, whom she remembered as being compulsive about punctuality, had kept her there for the sole purpose of producing feelings of awe and anxiety before the meeting. But all it did was make Sara remember how much she had hated the woman.

Six wooden straight-backed chairs designed to become unbearably uncomfortable within five minutes of use were the only furnishings in the waiting room. There were no tables, no magazines; it was a claustrophobic room meant for frightening young girls who were sent to see the Mother Superior. Some of Sister Elizabeth's most vile saintly effigies adorned the dark-paneled walls as further insurance against any future misbehavior.

Each portrait bore a small bronze plaque identifying its saint. During the long wait, drowsy from boredom, Sara had examined all four paintings several times. One depicted a naked St. Pelegia falling from a roof. Another portrayed St. Genevieve, also nude, trying in vain to shield a burning candle as the devil's fingers reached out to extinguish the flame. The other two were of St. Denis, a headless man unclad except for a cross, carrying his own mitered head on top of a book, and St. Margaret of Cortona, contemplating a rotting corpse that lay at her feet while a dog nipped her thigh. The paintings were of poor to mediocre quality and reminded Sara of the ones from Rod Serling's old *Night Gallery* series.

Now, in the inner office, sitting on another hard, straight chair facing Mother Lucy at her massive scrolled desk, Sara tried to keep her eyes off the two paintings that framed the Mother Superior. They were the worst of all. The largest, in a gilded frame, was of Lucy's namesake, St. Lucille, and with each furtive glance, Sara became more convinced that the Mother Superior had actually posed for the nude portrait, which showed the martyred St. Lucille, gashed throat and dark eye sockets as prominent as her breasts, proffering a platter. On the platter were her own eyes, which seemed to follow you around the room. To Lucy's left was a smaller painting in a matching frame. It depicted St. Gertrude, the school's namesake. Unlike Saints in the other paintings, St. Gertrude was dressed; she wore the robes of an abbess. Her face was somber and gaunt, and in her outstretched hand she held a flaming heart. At her feet were a dozen gray rodents that were supposed to be mice, but looked to Sara more like rats, with their long pink tails and protuberant teeth.

After opening the door and waiting silently for Sara to enter, Mother Lucy returned immediately to her large crimson leather desk chair. Ignoring Sara's outstretched hand, she told her to be seated, then wasted no time on pleasantries. "Why did you apply for work here, Miss Hawthorne, when you were so eager to leave us before?"

Sara stared at the woman, at a loss for words. Even though she had a story prepared, Lucy's bluntness stunned her.

"Well?" Lucy demanded.

"I've spent many many hours in church, praying about this decision," Sara began. This was an out-and-out lie—she had never been a believer, and any leanings she might have had been destroyed by the acrimonious nuns of St. Gertrude's, with their grim stories of devils and demons and the endless hours of indecipherable Latin recitations. There had been no warmth here, only chill judgment and disapproval; St. Gertrude's was truly a little piece of Hell on Earth.

"Miss Hawthorne? Continue, please."

Lucy was buying it, and that gave Sara more confidence. "I've felt guilt and great remorse since the time I ran away. I knew I was a coward, and no matter what I achieved, the feelings wouldn't go away. I thought they would disappear after I began my career, but they didn't; instead, the feelings grew stronger. I had to come back." She paused, keeping her gaze on Mother Lucy's beady little eyes, half believing her own tale, she'd rehearsed it so often. She took a deep breath. "I was called here, Mother, to serve you and St. Gertrude's and to help the soul of Jenny Blaine."

"Blaine . . . your roommate who committed the ultimate sin."

"Suicide," Sara murmured. "I didn't do my duty to her as I should have, and I feel that if I had, she might not be . . . gone now."

"Explain."

"She was depressed, and she needed me to listen to her. I didn't take her seriously."

"She told you she was going to kill herself?"

Of course she hadn't—Jenny had been the only bright spot in Sara's life. She was the one who had listened to and consoled Sara, reassuring her that they'd both be free soon. They'd made plans. Jenny, due to graduate that year, would go to San Francisco, find a job, and go to college, and Sara would join her the following year. Jenny had even said she might be able to pretend to be a long-lost aunt and free her right away. Instead she'd died, horribly and alone, and Sara had gone north by herself. "Yes," she finally told the Mother Superior. "Jenny told me she was thinking about it, and I didn't believe her. I even teased her, and I doubt that God will ever forgive me. That's why I must spend my life in service. That's why I came back. To face my demons." Literally, she thought, looking at Lucy's long, tight face.

"You've changed," the Mother Superior said, after a long pause.

"I hope so."

"You were a very quiet girl, good at your studies, but very

nervous, as I recall. It was a shock to us when you disappeared. I hope you know how worried we were about your welfare.''

*About as worried as I was about yours.* "I'm very sorry I worried you," she said humbly. "I was a selfish child."

"I'm glad you've realized that." Lucy fitted a pair of reading glasses over her narrow nose, looked at the papers on her desk—Sara's résumé and cover letter—then removed the little half-glasses. "I'm impressed by what you've accomplished on your own."

"Thank you."

"We're glad to have you here with us at St. Gertrude's Home for Girls. We have a handbook," the nun said, opening a drawer and pulling out a blue booklet. "It outlines the basic rules and regulations for our students and teachers, our expectations for the behavior of both, and our policies on disciplinary actions." She passed the book across to Sara. "Please read it before you begin work Monday morning."

"Thank you. I will. May I ask a question?"

Mother Lucy attempted a smile. "Of course."

"Your caretaker, Mr. Boullan, told me that the teacher I'm replacing committed suicide."

"That's true."

"In the room I've been assigned?"

"Yes. What of it? Does it frighten you?"

It did, but Sara shook her head. "No. I was just curious."

"We don't have any other rooms available."

"It's fine. Really. I was wondering, though, why there's no lock on the door."

Mother Lucy cocked her head like a chicken, one way, then the other, her squinty eyes narrowing until they were barely visible. "There are no locks on *any* doors at St. Gertrude's."

*I'll bet there's one on yours.* "Why not?"

"Policy. It's in the handbook. Do you have any other questions?"

"Today's only Thursday. Why don't you want me to begin work tomorrow instead of Monday?"

"Tomorrow, you have to complete some tests. The weekend is yours, although after that, you'll be working half-days on

Saturdays with the girls in some of their extracurricular activities. I'll have a schedule for you next week."

"Tests? What kind of tests?"

"The usual. Psychological evaluations, and a physical." Lucy paused, then added, with another fake smile, "It's nothing to concern yourself with. Our Dr. Dashwood, as you may recall, has his offices in the basement of this building, and he will conduct the entire procedure. Be at his office at one o'clock sharp. You'll be done by suppertime. That's six P.M., in the cafeteria at the far end of this building. Or, if you like, as long as you're not on cafeteria duty, you may eat in your room. You must supply your own food, though."

Sara nodded impatiently. "Why do you have tests? I've been certified by the state, and I had a complete physical a few months ago. It's in my records."

"Policy—"

"It's in the handbook," Sara finished, barely containing her anger. "Is there anything else?" she asked, rising.

"Always be respectful, Miss Hawthorne. Our teachers are role models for our students."

"I'll remember that. May I leave?"

"Of course. Please close the door on your way out."

Sara took the handbook and moved to the door. "I will. Thank you for your time."

A bell rang as she let herself out of Lucy's inner sanctum. She crossed the lobby and opened that door—which had a locking knob—and walked out into a sea of girls clad in blue and white. Classes were out for the day.

There were all ages here, though most of the girls were at least twelve or thirteen. One group, junior or senior, she thought, stopped in their tracks and scrutinized her from her sensible, low-heeled shoes to the top of her head. The girls had a look she knew well, a certain perfection of hair and shortness of skirt that identified them as the reigning clique. At public schools, they were often cheerleaders who spent time flirting with boys and gossiping. She forced herself to smile at them. "Hello, girls."

They stared at her.

"I'm Ms. Hawthorne. I'll be teaching history beginning Monday."

"Oh," said the one who seemed to be the leader of the pack. She had long, wavy blond hair and cornflower blue eyes. "What grades?"

"High school."

The blonde finally smiled. "Then we're all in your classes. Since Miss Tynan offed, I mean died, Sister Elizabeth has been substituting. She's kind of a pain."

Several of the other girls nodded.

"I might be a pain, too," Sara told them.

Another blonde, a tiny girl with short, curly hair haloing her face, giggled. "At least you're not a nun."

"No, I'm not." The girls were loosening up. *Maybe this won't be so bad, after all.* "What are your names?"

"I'm Marcia Crowley," said the one with the long, wavy locks.

"Cindy Speck," said a pink-faced girl with straight, shoulder-length black hair. "And this is Marybeth Tingler." She punched the girl next to her, a fragile redhead with limpid green eyes, gently in the arm. "She's shy."

Sara smiled. "Hi, Marybeth." She looked at the remaining three. "And who are you?" she asked the little curly-haired blonde.

"Buffy Bullock."

"Jan Sutcliff," volunteered the girl next to her. She had wire-rimmed glasses, light brown hair, and an overdeveloped figure.

"I'm Blaire Fugate," said the last girl, who looked like she was twenty-one, at least. She had thick chestnut hair that curled under perfectly at her shoulders, large blue eyes, and lashes so thick and sooty that they made her appear to be wearing make-up. She was as tall as Marcia Crowley, but with a more developed figure. She smiled, showing perfect white teeth behind full lips, and although she had been the last to speak, Sara thought that she was probably second in command of the clique.

"I'm glad to meet all of you," Sara told them, then glanced

at her watch. "I have some things to do right now, but I'll see you this weekend, I'm sure."

"Okay," Marcia and Blaire said simultaneously. Sara saw them glance at each other and knew there was a rivalry between them. *So what else is new?* The girls said goodbye and started out the lobby doors. Sara followed slowly, and as she opened the door for herself, she saw a slightly younger girl, awkward and gangly, with wavy carroty hair, walk widely around them as she came up the steps to enter the building.

"Hey, Ghost Girl," called Marcia Crowley, "you'd better be careful or I'll get you put in solitary forever!"

The girl wrapped her arms tightly around her books and, head down, passed them. As she approached Sara, Marcia and Blaire turned around, mouths open. Seeing Sara, they shut them, turned, and hurried down the steps, the whole pack giggling.

Sara put her hand on the girl's shoulder. Startled, she flinched, then looked up, her eyes wide, like a frightened doe's.

"Are you all right?" Sara asked gently.

The girl nodded, not making eye contact.

"I'm Sara Hawthorne, the new history teacher. If you want to talk, come see me, okay?"

"Kelly Reed," came Mother Lucy's voice from behind. "You're supposed to be on your way to study hall." The nun approached, glaring at the girl.

"It's my fault," Sara began. "I stopped her. There was a little trouble, some girls teasing her—"

"The only trouble is Miss Reed," interrupted Mother Lucy. "Don't let her shyness fool you. Run along now, Kelly." She clapped her hands twice and the girl took off, nearly running.

"She's a known thief, and her attitude is terrible," Lucy said. "I advise you to be very wary of her."

"I'll remember. I want to go to town to buy a few things before it gets much later. I'd better get going."

The Mother Superior nodded and Sara took off, walking rapidly around the school building and past the chapel, to the garage area, an old stable, at the rear of the grounds. Disgusted, upset, she unlocked her little white Sentra and slipped inside, dropping her briefcase on the seat next to her.

She ground the ignition and took off too fast, making the car buck. She slowed and drove the dirt path around the school and out. A mile of forest and she'd be among normal people. She was amazed; she hadn't though St. Gertrude's could be as awful as she remembered. She'd been wrong.

# Seventeen

Kelly Reed glanced behind her to make sure no one was looking, then quickly slipped out the door at the east end of the school building. There, she again checked for people, quickly ducking under the stair rail and jumping down behind the hedges as a small white car tore out of the garage. She caught sight of the driver—the new teacher who'd wanted to talk to her—just before the car disappeared behind the cemetery, heading toward the road to town. Maybe she was leaving already. Kelly didn't blame her.

She tucked her schoolbooks out of sight under the neatly trimmed hedge, then peered around. Everything was quiet. She unfolded her long legs and stood, stepped out, and walked slowly across the lawn toward the ugly stone chapel. If someone saw her, they probably would think that she was just taking a walk.

She walked up to the chapel's steps, feeling the gargoyles watching her from above. She hated the things and sometimes imagined she could actually see their stone breasts move as they breathed. But that was stupid. She walked along the back of the chapel and into the cemetery, crossing the small yard quickly, glancing up only as she passed the weeping angel. The statue was so beautiful that it seemed out of place; trapped here, just like Kelly.

A moment later, after making sure the road was clear, she slipped through the cemetery hedge, then darted across the road and into the pine forest beyond. *Safe at last!* Or she would be, once she was off St. Gruesome's property and into Witch Forest.

It took only ten minutes to get to the north fork of Moonfall

Creek, but it always seemed much longer. The forest on this side of the stream looked no different from Witch Forest on the other side, but it *felt* very different, as if the trees, the pines and sycamores and oaks, were bending down, watching her, just waiting for the right moment to trip her with a root, then wrap her up in woody tendrils and pull her under the earth to feed upon at their leisure. She shivered and glanced around. "Grow up," she muttered, as she sat down on a large boulder where she took off her shoes, stuffed her socks into the toes, then tied the laces together. Rising, she approached the edge of the creek, which was only about ten feet wide and fairly shallow this time of year. Still, she had to be careful because the water ran rapidly and the streambed was filled with slippery rocks.

Lifting her shoes by the laces, she twirled them above her head and let them fly across the stream. Her clothes would dry if she fell, but she couldn't take a chance on the shoes. That old bitch Lucy would stick her back in solitary, like last month, after Marcia had told her she'd stolen the locket. *My locket.*

Holding her skirt up around her thighs, Kelly began picking her way across the freezing cold stream. When she'd first been sent to solitary, she'd thought it was great to be locked, all alone, in the tiny room in the basement. She didn't feel imprisoned, but safe behind the windowless walls. There was a hard cot, a scarred up old desk and chair, and a lamp. And her schoolbooks, of course. Even in solitary, she was expected to do her work. The first few hours were fine, but there was no place to pee, except over a drain in the floor, and no water to drink. They left her there for a long time—later, she found out it was almost two days, and they hadn't given her anything to eat or drink. It was hell, and old Mother Lucy was right: she didn't want to go back.

She stepped out of the water on the east side of Moonfall Creek, retrieved her shoes, then sighed happily and lay back on the forest floor to let her feet and legs dry before putting the shoes back on.

It was amazing, the difference in atmosphere on this side of the creek. Maybe it was all in her head, but the trees seemed taller and more sunshine came through to dapple the ground, with its thick cover of pine needles, acorns, pinecones, and the first few red and yellow autumn leaves. She sat up and put on her shoes, turning so that she didn't have to see St. Gruesome's forest, which looked dark and grim. The trees reminded her of the Ents in *The Hobbit*.

She stood and made her way through the forest, moving with more leisure now, enjoying the singing of the sparrows, the harsh complaints of the obnoxious scrub jays. A gray squirrel saw her and sat very still for an instant, then scrabbled up an oak tree, where it watched her from a branch, its fluffy tail twitching. Kelly laughed. "Silly thing. I won't hurt you."

It occurred to her that she'd never seen a squirrel on the other side of the creek, and she began walking more rapidly. Soon, she heard the thunder of Witch Falls, and she considered going there, then remembered that's where they'd found Miss Tynan, who'd been so nice to her. She shivered and kept going until she came to the east fork of the creek and the narrow, well-worn footpath that followed it. Glancing up through the trees, she tried to gauge the time. *Probably past three.* That meant Minerva would likely be at her cottage by now, home from the Gingerbread House. She turned south and followed the path toward the cabin.

Ten minutes of travel brought her to Minerva Payne's house. She slowed as she approached, enjoying the sight, wishing she could move in and live with her.

The cottage, in the middle of a large clearing, was built of logs, like a cabin, but it had two stories, and there was a slight curvature to the walls that gave it a fairy-tale appearance, especially with its steeply pitched thick-shingled roof and a riverstone chimney rising gracefully into the sky. Around the cottage were stone–edged flowerbeds full of marigolds, petunias, and periwinkles, and instead of a lawn, the walkway was surrounded by vegetable gardens full of huge red tomatoes, cucumbers, peppers, onions, zucchini, and melons. Once, Kelly had asked Minerva how she grew so many vegetables when they had sun for only a few hours each day, and the old lady had chuckled and told her that everyone knew she was a witch.

Kelly didn't know what to say, then Minerva laughed and talked about composting, vitamins, and things like that.

Off to the side was a pumpkin patch that blazed orange, and behind the cabin were blackberry bushes and an herb garden filled with cooking herbs like chives and garlic, oregano and rosemary. There were other herbs, too, and shortly before Miss Tynan had died, Minerva had finally told her why there were all the stories about her being a witch: she was a healer, like a medicine woman, and that, she explained, was what real witches were, until the Christians came along and declared them evil servants of the devil—a devil the healers didn't even believe in.

Kelly loved to think about that and the fact that Minerva made no effort to hide her contempt for the nuns. She understood her fears about the ghost, and she even warned Kelly to be careful around the nuns and never to talk about her visits to the cottage. *Yeah, like I'd ever tell them anything.*

There was no smoke coming from the chimney, but the day was warm, and if Minerva was home, she wouldn't have built a fire yet. Kelly approached the door, which was made of heavy planks and had a black iron knocker at eye level. She rapped on it, but the sound seemed to be absorbed by the wood. The multipaned kitchen window was open, so she leaned toward it and called Minerva's name.

"Here I am."

Startled, Kelly turned to see Minerva coming up the path. "Hi, Min—"

There was a boy walking with her, carrying a basket covered with a gingham napkin. He was maybe thirteen, a year or so younger than her, and he was staring at her. She started to blush.

Minerva smiled. "This is Mark. Mark, this is Kelly. You have some common interests and I thought you'd like to meet."

"How did you know I'd be here?" Kelly asked.

"Minerva knows everything," said the boy.

"Let's go inside, shall we? We'll have tea and these tarts Mark helped me make."

"Ah, geeze . . ." Now the boy was blushing. "I just watched," he told Kelly.

Tentatively, she returned his smile. He was six inches shorter than she, but she liked him anyway and suddenly wished she'd combed her hair.

# Eighteen

John Lawson sat back in his chair and put his feet up on the desk, glad to be out of the patrol car and back in the office. Scotty Carroll was out of town, on vacation until Monday, and Wyn Griffin had called in sick, so John had ended up working his ass off. Fortunately, Jeff Thurman, the pride of the night shift, had shown up early, bless him, and now, as the afternoon shadows lengthened, John stretched his neck to one side then the other, relieving his stiff muscles. He laced his fingers behind his head and relaxed for the first time today. His boots could use a shine, he noted, but that was a job he secretly enjoyed. Though it couldn't compete with fly fishing, it was therapeutic in its own way.

Moonfall had been quiet since the death of Lenore Tynan a month ago. The reports had come back a few days after her body was recovered and there had been no real indications that she had met with foul play. They had found bloody towels—makeshift bandages—at they bottom of the pond, plus a small amount of blood and the weapon—a single-edged razor blade—at the edge of the Mezzanine, dropped among the rocks. Tynan's fingerprints were on it. After that, John had closed the case, and although he was relieved to be done with it, doubts continued to eat at him.

First, there were the nuns, who had disobeyed his request and frantically cleaned the room. He and Cutter had talked it over several times, and he had eventually agreed with the doctor, whose Catholic schooling gave him a whiff of expertise, that they were, after all, dealing with nuns, who wouldn't be inclined to answer to any authority that wasn't from on high. Between that and the fact that the ever-unpleasant Mother Lucy claimed that Sisters Bibiana and Mary Oswald began cleaning up Tynan's blood-spattered room on their own while she was at the sheriff's office, it all pretty much made sense. Too, there had been her attempts to get tranquilizers and sleeping pills.

Richard Dashwood was a thorn in his side. There was no logical basis for his misgivings; the man had more than cooperated with him and had shown him every courtesy, but dealing with him had been an unaccountably unnerving experience. Dashwood had given him the most logical reason for Tynan's trip to the Falls—she had been intent on committing suicide and hadn't been able to secure any sleeping pills to do the job, hence the razor blade and then the jump. John forced himself to discount his unease, because he suspected it was born of personal dislike, not a cop's instinct.

The other person who had set off his suspicions was St. Gertrude's caretaker, Basil-Bob Boullan, an old letch who was somehow simultaneously seedy and obsessively clean. Despite the fact that he leered at the girls and the nuns alike, no one had a bad word to say about the man and John had to let that drop, too.

The only other thing that still gave him pause was a slight chemical imbalance found in Tynan's blood. It was a very minor thing and Cutter had concluded that it was an unimportant allergic reaction to a food or an over-the-counter drug.

Apart, these things meant nothing, and together, not much more. Maybe it had been Gus's talk later that night—*We've all got our demons, and yours are out there at St. Gertrude's*—that had upped his anxiety. And that, combined with Mark's revelation that old Minerva Payne seemed magically to know he was plagued by nightmares, had made him overly suspicious, when all he really wanted to do was close the case and forget about it and the memories it stirred.

Right after the discussion with his son, John had intended to go talk to Minerva again. Her telling Mark that Greg's death wasn't John's fault intrigued and annoyed him as much as her apparent knowledge of his recurring nightmares. But the weeks passed and he didn't pay her a visit, partly because he was always busy, and if he were to be perfectly honest with himself, because he knew she would again ask him why he'd never told anyone that he'd seen her at Witch Falls the morning they found Greg. He didn't know the answer to that and didn't care to try to figure it out.

*Maybe she cast a spell on you.* Every so often, the thought would wing through his mind, unbidden, fueled by her knowledge of his nightmares and guilt. He did his best to quell his childish superstitions—what was he going to do, knock on her door and accuse her of witchcraft?

*No. Not in a million years.* If she *did* know about the dreams, Mark must be behind it; since he'd heard his father's night terrors, he was probably frightened and confided in her. He'd never known Mark to lie, but in this case it was likely, and he couldn't really be angry with the boy for worrying about him.

The doorknob turned and the door creaked. John swung his feet off his desk before his dispatcher's face appeared. "Damn it all, Dorothy, why won't you at least knock? What if I was changing clothes in here?"

"Then you should lock your door." The little round woman gave him the same smile she'd given him when he was eight years old and had shown up at the office to charm her out of some of her never-ending supply of caramels. "There's someone here to see you, Johnny."

"Who?"

"A very pretty young woman."

"Did you ask her to come here?" Dorothy had been trying to fix him up ever since his divorce had been finalized, years ago.

"No, Johnny," she said, barely rolling her eyes. "I've never seen her before. Her name is Sara Hawthorne and she would only say that she wants to talk to you about a case."

"Okay. I'm coming." He stood, leaned back to stretch his back, then followed her out of his office.

The young woman waiting at the tall counter was pretty, Dorothy was right about that. She had pale skin, dark eyes, and glossy dark brown hair that waved in a pageboy just above her shoulders. The tall counter unfortunately hid the rest of her from view.

"Hi. I'm Sheriff Lawson. You need to see me?"

"Uh, yes." Her voice was soft, tentative.

"Regarding?" He smiled and waited.

"Something that happened a long time ago." She suddenly sounded more sure of herself.

"How long?"

"Twelve years."

With a nod, he walked over to the end of the counter and opened the gate. "Come on in. We'll talk in my office."

"Thank you."

As she walked past him, he sensed uncertainty under the air of confidence and liked her for it, maybe because he'd felt the same way so often lately. She wore a navy business suit with a white buttondown blouse. The pleated skirt barely kissed her knees, and though she was no more than five-three, her legs looked long and slim. Noticing her low-heeled black pumps, he liked her even more; his ex-wife wouldn't have been caught dead in anything that comfortable.

As he held his office door for her, he looked back at Dorothy and saw her reaching into her bag of caramels, watching him with an ear-to-ear grin. He gave her a warning glance.

"Hold your calls?" she asked, as she popped a caramel into her mouth.

"If something important comes up, buzz me."

Dorothy nodded, then turned her attention to an office supply catalog. Lord, how that woman liked to buy cheap pens and paperclips.

John saw that the young woman was standing by his desk. "Have a seat, Ms. ah, I'm sorry—" he said, closing the door behind him.

"Hawthorne."

John rounded the desk and sat down. "Do you live in Moonfall? I don't recall seeing you around here." *If I had, I'd sure as hell remember.*

"I'm a resident as of today. I've been hired to teach history at St. Grue—St. Gertrude's."

He grinned. "Were you going to say 'St. Gruesome's'?"

She blushed and nodded. "It's rude, I'm sorry."

"Not at all. We all call it that more often than not. You must have grown up here to know about the nickname."

"I was an orphan and lived at St. Gertrude's for several years. I ran away when I was sixteen."

"What in the world possessed you to come back?" he blurted.

She tipped her head, eyeing him. Her hair caressed her jaw. Then she laughed, covering her mouth with her fingers. "I take it you're familiar with St. Gertrude's?"

He studied her a moment, then said lightly, "Everyone who grew up here knows the stories about St. Gruesome's. It's infamous."

She smiled uncertainly. "Stories? What kind?"

John suddenly realized he was treading on thin ice. "Oh, you know, kid stuff. The gargoyles come to life at night and steal children, that sort of thing." He wasn't about to mention any stories about the nubile young virgins. "The headless monk was a favorite." He paused. "What's the inside story? Is there a headless monk lurking around the chapel?"

"Some of the girls used to claim they saw him. Even one of the nuns, Sister Elizabeth. She painted a picture of him. It's so horrible that it used to give me nightmares."

"Is she the one responsible for all those gruesome portraits?"

Sara smiled. "Yes. You've seen them?"

"A few of them."

"When? Years ago?"

"No, just recently." He hesitated, then decided that she surely knew about the suicide. "There was a death last month. A teacher."

"Lenore Tynan," Sara told him, the smile gone from her face. "I'm her replacement." She paused. "If I'd known that was the reason for the opening, I'm not sure I'd have taken it. They even put me in her room." Her mouth twisted in a wry smile. "The caretaker told me about all the blood on the walls, and how they had to get me a new mattress. St. Gruesome's hasn't changed a bit, and the name is very appropriate."

Her eyes glistened, and for a brief instant, John thought she was going to cry. Instead, she sat up straighter and tilted her chin up, defying the threatened tears. "The place gives me the creeps."

"If it helps, she didn't die in the room."

Sara Hawthorne stared at him in amazement. "She didn't?"

"No. The caretaker you mentioned—was that an older gentleman named Boullan?"

"Yes, why?"

He wanted to tell her to be cautious around the man, but he had no basis for such a warning. "I just wondered. He seemed to be something of a storyteller," he added carefully.

"You're saying he let me think Tynan died in my room just to frighten me?"

"It's possible." Another careful answer.

"Just where *did* she die?"

He suddenly wished he hadn't brought it up, but he owed her an answer. "She was found in the pond at the bottom of Witch Falls. Do you know the place?"

"I think so. It's in the park on Apple Hill Road?"

"That's right."

"But if she cut her wrists in her room, how could she possibly end up at Witch Falls? That's at least a mile."

"As best as we can tell, she threw herself over the cliff. She may have known that water would keep the blood flowing, but was afraid of being discovered if she used the water in the common lavatory. Hence the falls. Or, she may simply have decided to drown herself when the bleeding proved insufficient. There's no way to be certain."

A long moment passed before Sara spoke. "Maybe she decided she didn't want to die at St. Gertrude's." She shivered. "I wouldn't want to."

"That's a possibility. People intent on suicide don't want to be saved."

"But I still don't get it." Sara pushed a stray lock of hair from her cheek. "What about the blood? How could she have traveled so far if she'd already lost so much?"

"The nuns had the room partially cleaned by the time I

arrived, but I can assure you that there was nowhere near as much blood as Mr. Boullan probably led you to believe.''

''How much was there?'' She sat forward, her eyes narrowing.

He was slightly taken aback by the abruptness of her question. He didn't really know the answer, but the nuns had claimed there hadn't been any large puddles on the floor. ''A little goes a long way.''

''How much?'' she demanded.

''Probably a pint or less.'' He didn't want to go into details with her. ''That's enough to, ah, make for an impressive crime scene.''

''Crime scene. That means you think it was murder?''

''No, I didn't mean to imply that. It was a poor choice of words.''

''Then why did you use them?'' Her eyes drilled into his.

John's emotions had been mixed, but irritation was coming quickly to the fore. ''Because I'm a cop, and that's what we say. Look, Ms. Hawthorne, we investigated thoroughly and found absolutely no reason to believe foul play was involved.'' He sat forward, causing her to move back slightly—very slightly. ''I thought you were here about an old case.''

''I am, but I think there's a connection.''

''A connection?'' He was having a hard time hiding his anger now. ''Between Lenore Tynan and an old case?''

She nodded. ''I'm surprised you didn't check your files. You'd know.''

''There is virtually nothing in our files on St. Gertrude's, Ms. Hawthorne. Despite the stories about gargoyles and headless ghosts, it's a very quiet place.''

''Do you really *believe* that?'' Sara Hawthorne's knuckles were white as she gripped the edge of the desk. ''Tell me how you explain the similarities between Lenore Tynan's and Jennifer Blaine's deaths?''

''Who's Jennifer Blaine?'' he asked quickly.

''Were you the sheriff in 1984?''

Slightly insulted—did he look that old?—John shook his head. ''I was a deputy. A rookie, in fact. And I'm not going to answer any more questions until you answer mine. Who's Jennifer Blaine?"

Sara twined her fingers together—probably, he thought, to hide the trembling in her hands. "She was my roommate. She slit her wrists in our room in 1984. It was declared a suicide, but it wasn't. She was murdered."

"How do you know?"

"She wouldn't have done such a thing," Sara said passionately. "She was getting out, going to get a job and go to college, and I was going to join her. But the sheriff said it was suicide."

"In 1984, Christopher Scarzo was sheriff, but I'd remember something like that, even if I had nothing to do with the case. We just don't get that much excitement around here." He paused. "Did Sheriff Scarzo interview you?"

"No. Mother Lucy didn't allow anyone to interview the students. She asked us the questions herself and gave the answers to him."

"That's absurd," John told her. "Did you find Miss Blaine's body?"

"Yes."

"Then there's not a chance in the world that your Mother Lucy could prevent the sheriff from questioning you, and that's what he would have done. You don't remember at least having someone in a uniform in the room when Lucy questioned you?"

She shook her head slowly. "No. Absolutely not. Some of my memories are a little fuzzy, but I'm sure about this because I wanted to tell the sheriff Jenny'd been murdered, but I couldn't. They wouldn't let me."

*Fuzzy memories. She's a fruit loop.* Even as John thought it, he realized that *his* memories were pretty fuzzy, too. "It doesn't add up. You were probably in shock. Maybe you just don't *remember* talking to him."

"I'd remember," she said, fire in her blue eyes. "Would you at least look it up? Or ask this Scarzo person about it?"

"Chris retired years ago. Moved to Wyoming," he added, as he rose and crossed to the files. "But we can take a look. That should clear things up for you." He opened a drawer and began going through manila folders. As he searched, he heard

Sara's chair scrape and her heels clicking across the room. She came to stand at the side of the open drawer and tried to peer inside. It gratified him that she was too short to see well; she was really starting to get on his nerves.

Finally, he closed the drawer and turned to her. "I'm sorry, but there's nothing here about Jennifer Blaine or St. Gertrude's."

"You didn't look inside the folders. The report has probably been misfiled." Her voice was edged with panic.

"That's possible. Look, Ms. Hawthorne, I've got virtually no backup until Monday, so it may take until then to check thoroughly. Is there a number where I can reach you?"

"You don't believe me, do you?" she spat. "You don't even want to think that you might have to get off your butt, that your little Mayberry life might be disrupted."

He glared at her and opened his mouth to tell her off, but he saw the tears welling, saw the fear, and realized she was holding on by a bare thread. Her brashness was thin armor. Memories of the fear and nausea he felt just entering the nuns' property last month flooded him. And then, dimmer memories of the nightmares that continued to plague him, of chanting, and eyes, and the moon . . .

He suppressed a shiver as his anger melted away. "I believe you, Ms. Hawthorne," he said slowly. "And a death would have been reported, whether it was an accident, a murder, or a suicide." He gazed calmly at her. "Why would you think I don't believe you?"

She let air out of her lungs noisily. "Look, I'm sorry. I've had a bad day." A tear got loose and she wiped it away roughly.

"Do you have a number where I can call you?" he repeated.

"Yes. I mean no. Don't call me at the school. I'll call you, or come to see you. Sheriff, this information is very important to me. I really need to see the report on Jenny Blaine."

"I'll do my best to find it."

"I don't know how easy it will be for me to get away after the weekend. I'll be working full time then, and I think my schedule is heavy. Do you think you might find the report by Sunday?"

He felt more kindly toward her and smiled. "I can put the night dispatcher to work when he arrives." He moved back to the desk and wrote down "Jennifer Blaine, 1984," then looked up at Sara, who was again beside the desk, watching him. "Call me Sunday." He paused. "Or are you expected to be in church all day?"

She smiled wryly. "Sheriff Lawson, I'm no nun, and the sisters aren't sticklers about churchgoing. Even the girls go to chapel only if they want to. When I was a student there, being asked to chapel was a privilege. Like a religious country club, or something."

"That's weird."

She smiled. "It is, isn't it? Maybe it's because the chapel is so small. I doubt anything has changed."

"You were in a home run by a bunch of nuns and they didn't make you pray?"

"Oh, we prayed, all right. It was all in Latin, so I never understood what I was praying about, but I had calluses on my knees. We all did. Latin class meant an hour of reciting a day. On our knees. It was hellacious."

"You must speak pretty fluent Latin, then. Or read it, or whatever you do with a dead language."

"Not at all. What little I understood, I've forgotten. What they taught was so archaic that even the English was nearly indecipherable." She extended her hand, cheeks flushing. "I'm sorry for my behavior, Sheriff Lawson. I had no right to insult you."

"Apology accepted." He shook her hand.

"I'm sorry for being such a bother, too."

"It's no bother. Frankly, I'm becoming very curious about this missing file myself."

"Then your suspicions are aroused?" she asked hopefully.

He wished she'd quit trying to pin him down. "No, just an interest. That I don't remember this case bothers me, and that it appears to be missing from the files bothers me even more." He didn't add that he still thought Sara Hawthorne might be, to put it kindly, a little imbalanced. "Once I read the report, we can talk about why you believe your friend's death was a homicide."

"And if you don't find it?" The sharp edge came back into her voice.

"Then we'll talk about that," he said, wondering if there were any Excedrin tablets left in his desk drawer.

"I guess that's the best I can hope for. Thank you." With that, Sara Hawthorne stepped briskly to the door, put her hand on the knob.

"Ms. Hawthorne?"

She turned, skirt flaring around her knees. "Yes?"

"Why did you come back here?"

"What?"

"If you hated it so much, why did you come back to St. Gertrude's to teach?"

She looked him in the eye. "To find out who killed Jenny Blaine, and to see him brought to justice."

"That's what I thought." Crossing his arms, he gave her his most authoritative look. "Don't go getting yourself into trouble. If you have suspicions, bring them to me."

"You think I can't handle myself?" she asked, holding his gaze.

"Not at all. But I'm afraid you might not be able to handle those nuns." He smiled, knowing she was the type that would rush headlong into something if she was told not to. "I'm not sure I and all my deputies could handle them, as a matter of fact."

She returned his smile. "Thanks. I'll be careful."

She left the room, and a moment later, he saw her get into a small white Sentra and drive away. She was going to be trouble, he thought. She already was, he amended, as he reopened the drawer for 1984 and grabbed an armload of files. His other deputy would arrive in about five minutes, freeing him to go home, relax, and see his son. He sat down at the desk and phoned home, but Mark wasn't there yet. Probably he was at Corey Addams's or Pete Parker's; either way, it was only four, and he wasn't concerned. He left a message saying he'd be home at six, bearing pizza. Then he sat down and started leafing through the files, looking for the missing report.

# Nineteen

"'Bye, Mark," Kelly called, as she and Minerva stood on the threshold of the cottage and watched the boy trotting up the trail toward Apple Hill Road. Mark raised his hand and yelled without slowing down, then disappeared into the thick forest.

"You need to go back before they miss you at the home," Minerva told her as they went back inside and sat down, Kelly in an easy chair, Minerva in her rocker by the stone fireplace.

"I know." She glanced at the grandfather clock in the corner of the cozy little room. It was just past four, and she had to be back by five-thirty. "I can stay a little while longer."

For the last hour or so, Minerva had told Kelly and Mark stories about Moonfall's early days. She described Jeremiah Moonfall and his family in such detail that it seemed like the old woman had known them firsthand.

Though Kelly had heard the stories before, she never tired of them. Maybe it was the stories, but it was probably because Minerva always made her feel like she was worth talking to, and that was something that didn't happen very often.

Today, the old woman told some new stories, these about the town's second most influential settler, Reverend Tobias Lawson. Kelly hadn't dared ask many questions, but Mark's last name was Lawson, and she knew from his questions that Tobias must be his ancestor. He'd gotten really excited when Minerva had said that Tobias's son had married Jeremiah Moonfall's daughter and had asked if that meant he had Moonfall blood in his veins. Minerva had laughed and said yes. When Mark left, he said he couldn't wait to tell his dad. Minerva had laughed at that as well, then told him to tell his father to stop by and visit with her soon.

Kelly and Minerva now sat in comfortable silence for long

minutes, as they always did when she visited. Only the soft creaking of the old lady's rocking chair broke the silence.

Kelly had first met Minerva by accident, about a month after she'd arrived at St. Gertrude's. It had been a quiet Sunday morning, the first time she'd ever dared to sneak off the grounds.

She had crossed the creek and had immediately felt lighter, safer, in a way she couldn't comprehend. She could only think of it as a weight being lifted from her shoulders. She had followed the sounds of water to the Falls and stood on the bridge spanning them and looked down on the bubbling white water and the pool beyond that remained clear despite the ripples from the Falls. Kelly knew nothing of the town, nothing of anything except dark, depressing St. Gertrude's, but she was now so happy, so tranquil, that as she watched the water and listened to its powerful roar, she could only think that she had found an enchanted place, a forest out of a Disney cartoon where birds sang and a princess slept, awaiting the kiss of her prince.

Time stopped for her until she sensed that someone stood next to her. She jerked her head to the left, scared that one of the nuns had followed her, but instead she saw a tall, elderly woman in a dark blue dress and a white knitted shawl calmly standing beside her, watching the water. Kelly took a step away.

"I won't hurt you, child." Her blue eyes were sharp and clear, but kind, and her high-cheekboned face seemed regal despite her wrinkles. She looked about a million years old. "My name is Minerva Payne. What's yours?"

She swallowed. "Kelly Reed."

"You are from that place." Minerva nodded toward St. Gertrude's.

"Yes." Kelly hesitated. "You won't tell, will you? I'll get in trouble."

The old lady's smile broke her face into a thousand pieces. "No, of course not. I'd do nothing to help those . . . *women.*" She practically spat the last word.

"You don't like the nuns?" Kelly asked hopefully.

"And they don't like me." Minerva cocked her head, studying Kelly. "You mean they haven't warned you about me? About this place?"

"I haven't been here long," Kelly said uncertainly. "We're not supposed to leave the grounds, and the nuns talk about 'evil influences' and stuff, like if we wander off, we might get kidnapped. Some of the little kids say that there's an old witch who bakes you into pies, like in 'Hansel and Gretel'." She looked up into Minerva's face, studied it thoughtfully. "But that's ridiculous, isn't it?"

"This is Witch Falls," she said, gesturing at the water below them. "And we're in Witch Forest. I live here." She chuckled. "You look like a smart girl. Can you guess who the 'old witch' is?"

"You?" Kelly had guessed the moment she'd spoken, but thought it was too impolite to say so. "That's hard to believe."

"Bosh, child. You know as well as I do that it's an easy thing. You don't need to watch what you say around me. Don't I look like a witch?"

Embarrassed, Kelly shrugged. "Well, you don't have any warts."

Minerva laughed heartily. "None that you can see, at least. You mentioned 'Hansel and Gretel.' Have you been to my shop?"

"I haven't been anywhere except St. Gertrude's and here."

"I own a bakery called The Gingerbread House. I live in Witch Forest and I'm as old as God ... or at least, Lucy Bartholomew. Have you met her?"

"The Mother Superior? She's as old as you?"

Minerva nodded. "She has ways of hiding her age."

"I hate her. She really *is* a witch. A mean old witch."

"Who told you witches are mean, Kelly?"

She shrugged. "They're always mean, like in 'Hansel and Gretel,' and 'Snow White.' Everybody knows that." Suddenly she felt foolish. "But there's no such thing as witches. Even if Mother Lucy seems like one."

"There *are* witches, Kelly, good and bad and in between. But Lucy and her sisters are something else."

"They're a bunch of monsters," Kelly supplied.

Minerva Payne nodded, smiling. "You'll get no argument from me."

"Do you know Mother Lucy? Have you been to St. Gruesome's?" She said the nickname with relish, her fear gone. Anyone who didn't like Lucy couldn't be all bad.

"Yes, I know her, but don't worry, dear, she's no friend to me. And I haven't been to St. Gruesome's in years. Not physically, at least," Minerva added, with a wink. "Now, would you like to come to my cottage in the woods and have a fresh cherry tart? I promise not to bake you into a pie afterward."

Kelly nodded and accompanied Minerva to her house, which turned out to be a wood and stone cottage that might have been designed by elves. The fireplace was huge, and cemented in among the smooth, rounded creekbed stones were pieces of driftwood and rocks coated with natural quartz, amethyst, and moonstone, among other gems. The floor was golden oak, polished within an inch of its life, and the braided rugs were bright and clean. There were shining copper pots and pans in the kitchen, a wood-burning stove, and another small fireplace, this one with a spit and an honest-to-God black iron kettle. The open shelves were filled with Mason jars of fruits and vegetables from the garden, along with jars of herbs and oils, many of which Kelly couldn't identify. Candles and hurricane lanterns filled each room; there was no gas or electricity here, though there was running water. The walls were decorated with all sorts of brooms, made by Minerva herself, and ornamented with dried flowers and herbs.

That first time, before she left, Kelly told Minerva that she wished she could live in the cottage with her forever. The old lady smiled sadly and told her that she could at least visit whenever she wanted. Kelly accepted that without question, and came to see Minerva whenever she could, but always on Sundays, when the nuns disappeared into the chapel with their favorite students, like her roommate, Marcia, and her stuck-up friends.

"Minerva?" she asked, breaking the silence.

"Yes, dear?"

"Why did you bring that boy here?" Though she had liked Mark Lawson, she was a little jealous, and ashamed of it.

"I thought you might like to meet him."

The jealousy fled instantly. "Really?"

"Yes. That, and more. He is in danger and needs help from me and from you."

"From *me?* What kind of danger?"

"Yes, from you. He needs your friendship. As to the danger, we'll come to that at the right time. It's just important for now that you be his friend."

Minerva's habit of being mysterious drove Kelly nuts. "He must have lots of friends."

"In his way, he is like you, Kelly. Yes, he has friends, but he's different, like you. His friends are afraid of me, just like the rest of the children in town. The bold ones dare one another to come into my store, but most stay away, just as they stay away from St. Gertrude's. Mark is different. He's not afraid, and he's interested in unusual things."

"Like what?"

Minerva smiled. "The things you see here. Herbs, oils, the things one does with them."

"What *do* you do with them?"

"I've told you before, I cook with some and heal with others. I'm an herbalist, I've told you all about herbal medicine."

Kelly leaned forward. "But what else do you do with them?"

"That's all."

"I know it isn't."

"You're too smart for your own good, Kelly. It's too dangerous for you to have that knowledge right now. When the time is right—"

"You've told Mark, haven't you?"

"Just a little. It's not dangerous for him to know these things."

"Then why is it for me?"

"Because of the nuns. It's dangerous for you to be here. If Mother Lucy found out you were visiting me, I shudder to think of your punishment. It would be far worse than if they found you in town. But if she thought you knew . . ."

"Knew what?"

"You are right to hate Lucy and her sisters, and you are right about the forest on St. Gertrude's property being different, being scary. It's a cursed place."

"How can a church be cursed?"

"There are many kinds of churches. Listen, child, and remember. The old god becomes the new devil. The god of the wood, Pan, had many names, and those we call pagans worshiped him as the embodiment of nature. The nature god was usually depicted with horns and hooves. Does he sound familiar?"

"The devil, right?"

"That's right. To the people who worshiped the old gods, nature was most important. The god of nature was believed to control the crops, the weather, birth, and death. When the Christians came along, they had to force the pagans to worship *their* god instead. So they built their churches on the pagan's places of worship, but the pagans still had a laugh or two. They sculpted their own gods into the ornamentation of the churches. The Green Man—Pan, Cernunos, Robin of the Wood, or Loki— whatever you wish to call him—is a prominent figure on older churches, and while the pagans pretended to worship the new god, they secretly worshiped the old. He had leaves for hair and vines growing from his mouth, but they left off the horns and hooves, since that was what the Christians recognized and vilified. That is how the witches—the pagans who were wise in the ways of herbs and healing—came to be considered servants of the Christian devil. They had nothing to do with Christianity, though. Witches never worshiped Satan *or* the Christian god. They were victims of fanatics. Satanists are Christians who decided to rebel against their own god."

Kelly shivered. "Are the gargoyles on St. Gruesome's old gods, too?"

"No, dear, not at all. Those are guardians, demons thought to keep evil away, though they are really evil personified."

"That doesn't make sense."

"Religion rarely does." Minerva smiled. "You're going to ask if there are green men on St. Gruesome's, aren't you?"

"Yes. I've never seen any, but I hate to look at those gargoyles. It always seems like they're looking back."

"There are no green men on St. Gruesome's. The land once belonged to Pan and his ilk, under the names the local Indians gave to the nature spirits, but it is defiled now. It is cursed."

"By God?"

"That depends on what you believe God is."

Kelly hesitated. "I don't know. I kind of like that thing John Lennon said about everybody being God. It's like the good thing that's in people, and it's all the same."

"You have a pagan soul, but that's why you're here. You are searching."

"What do you believe?" she asked, more confused than ever.

"Like you, I think God inhabits all things, but I don't necessarily think God is always good. To the Christians, God and the Devil are opposites, and they are always at war, good versus evil. I'm not so sure that they aren't one and the same. The worshipers of old thought that the gods had three faces and that the face could change according to whim or need. Good, evil, and indifferent, if you will."

Kelly nodded thoughtfully. "That makes sense. I mean, all those paintings old Sister Lizard does of the martyred saints. How could a loving god do things like that to people? It seems like a real ego-trip, even if you are God, to make people suffer just to prove how faithful they are."

"It does, doesn't it?"

"How can St. Gertrude's be cursed, though? I mean, Catholic nuns are supposed to be good."

"Do they seem good to you?"

"No. They're horrible."

"There's nothing wrong with most Christians, Kelly. Christianity is no different from any other religion; its adherents try to follow the same Golden Rule that has always been important to humanity. The credo to do unto others as you wish them to do unto you is sacred and central to every positive belief system, be it pagan, Buddhist, Christian, or any other. It is one of the few true rules of this universe. When you take away all the dogma, we all have the same god. You just have to watch out for the fanatics. And there are fanatics on both sides of every religion. Just as there were good witches, there were evil ones. They chose to be. It is the same with Christians and the rest of them. Whether or not good and evil are separate or opposite ends of the same thing, ultimately, does not matter. We make the demons and the gods fit the image we desire."

"But how can Catholic nuns be evil?"

"What makes you think they're Catholic?"

"Nuns are always Catholic, aren't they?"

"Not necessarily, and don't even think of talking about that with anyone but me."

"What are they, then?"

"Enough for today. I've talked more than I should, and you need to get back before you're missed." Minerva stood and walked to an oak hutch in the small dining area. Opening a drawer, she took something out and came over to Kelly. "I have something for you." She opened her hand to show her a thin leather thong with a small cloth bag on the end. "Inside, are some of those herbs you're so curious about. I want you to wear this amulet all the time. It will help protect you."

"They won't let us wear jewelry."

"Keep it in your pocket."

"Okay." Kelly accepted the amulet and slipped it in her skirt pocket. "How does it work?"

Minerva smiled. "It's a repellent."

"Nun repellent?" Kelly snickered.

"Let's just say it repels evil. Keep it hidden. It will be dangerous for you if the nuns find it." She walked Kelly to the door. "Be quick. It's starting to get dark early, and you can't be in that forest after dark."

Around them, daylight still shone through the trees. Kelly felt safe and calm. "Why? Will the gargoyles get me?"

"If not the stone ones, then the ones dressed in black. Now hurry, and be careful."

Minerva spoke lightly, but the concern on her face gave Kelly another chill. "Are you a witch, Minerva?"

"I'm wise in the old ways."

"I'll be back soon," Kelly said, and headed into the woods.

# Twenty

Sara stomped on the brakes, narrowly missing the red-haired girl as she darted across the road leading to St. Gertrude's garage.

The girl stood still, staring at Sara in surprise just long enough for her to jump out of the car. Then she turned to run away.

"Wait!" she called, searching her memory for the girl's name, finding it. "Kelly, wait!"

The girl whirled, her face a sullen mask of guilt as Sara approached her. "You gave me quite a scare."

"Sorry," Kelly mumbled.

"Are you all right?"

She nodded, staring at the ground. "Are you going to tell on me?"

Sara recognized the fear in the girl's voice, remembered the fear she had felt herself, and made a decision instantly. "No, but on one condition."

Kelly slowly lifted her head. "What?"

"Tell me what you were doing."

"I took a walk, but I'll get in trouble if the nuns find out."

"Just a walk? That's all?"

"We're not supposed to do anything without permission, and Mother Lucy doesn't like me, so I'd really get it."

Sara didn't think that was the whole story, but she wanted to win the girl's trust, partly because she would be a good source of information, but mainly because Kelly Reed obviously needed a friend.

"Okay," Sara said. "Maybe we can talk later."

Kelly nodded, then scooted away, disappearing into the

bushes by the eastern door of the school building, then coming out carrying books, walking sedately toward the dormitory.

Sara drove on to the garage and removed the purchases she'd made after visiting Sheriff Lawson. At the Moonfall Market she'd bought a bag of groceries—bread, cans of deviled ham and chicken, corn chips, a couple of sixpacks of Pepsi, instant coffee, a bag of M&M's, and a few apples and oranges to offset all the junk food. At a five-and-dime she'd also purchased an electric kettle, plastic cutlery, paper plates, a plastic tumbler, and a ceramic coffee mug. And, most important, a rubber wedge to push under her door.

Glancing at her watch, she saw it was nearly five-thirty, and balancing the three bags, she rushed toward the dormitory. By the time she made it up the third flight of stairs, she was panting and her leg muscles were on fire. She pushed open the door to her room, vowing to start exercising again—she hadn't realized how out of shape she'd gotten in the last year or so.

Quickly she stashed the Pepsi in the refrigerator and left everything else on the table. Then, with only the briefest glance in the tiny mirror above the chest of drawers, she raced from the dorm and over to the west end of the school building, where the cafeteria was. She would rather have eaten alone, but she was afraid she would make a bad impression if she didn't show up for dinner on her very first night at St. Gertrude's.

The heavy doors were shut and she consulted her watch again: she was five minutes late. She nearly turned around, remembering how the nuns were angered by tardiness, then reminded herself she was a teacher now, not a student. Swallowing, she pushed open one door and peered inside. The students, a sea of navy and white seated at long tables, were reciting a prayer in Latin, the same one she remembered from her youth. When they were done, she slipped inside and walked over to the table where the nuns, a dozen or so, were seated.

"Miss Hawthorne," said Mother Lucy in her clipped, hard voice, "we wondered if you were going to join us. There's a chair for you, over between Sister Bibiana and our gym instructor, Miss Roth. We took the liberty of preparing a tray for you."

"Thank you. I—I'm sorry I'm late," Sara stammered, seating herself and blushing furiously as all the nuns stared at her.

Only Sister Bibiana smiled. "I remember you, Sara," she said. "You were an excellent student. We're so happy to have you back with us."

"I'm happy to be here." She looked at her tray, remembering that the food was surprisingly good. Her plate held a slice of pot roast with golden onions, carrots, and mashed potatoes, real right down to the lumps. A bread plate held a hot roll, and there was a small dish with a square of lime gelatin with cottage cheese and pineapple. A glass of milk rounded out the meal. Suddenly, she was ravenous.

The cafeteria was quiet, except for the rattle of cutlery and the soft murmur of voices, and Sara tried to eat slowly, emulating the nuns. Beside her, Esther Roth, the quarterback of a gym teacher, with brutish features and square shoulders on a squat, powerful body, ate steadily, staring at her food as she shoveled it in. The rest of the teachers, all nuns, ate silently and sedately, and when they were all finished, Mother Lucy stood up and clapped her hands twice. "Girls," she called, "Your attention, please. I'd like to introduce Miss Hawthorne. She will be replacing Miss Tynan as your upper-grade history teacher, beginning Monday. Say hello to Miss Hawthorne, girls."

"Hello, Miss Hawthorne," came a polite chorus.

"Miss Hawthorne," said Lucy, "why don't you stand up and say a few words?"

Surprised and resentful at being asked to speak without warning, Sara rose, nearly knocking over her chair in the process. She looked across the room at the sea of upturned faces and tried to smile. "I'm looking forward to getting to know each and every one of you, and if you ever have questions about lessons or anything else, please feel free to come to me. I hope we'll have lots of fun in class." *That wasn't so bad.*

"School," intoned Mother Lucy, giving Sara the eye, "is not a place of fun. It's a place to learn. I expect you girls to remember that."

"I only meant," Sara began, trying to sound utterly calm despite her anger, "that lessons don't have to be dry and bor-

ing." She looked around the room, saw Kelly Reed at the end
of a table in the rear, and smiled in her direction. "History is
especially dry if all you do is memorize names and dates. In
my class, you'll learn some interesting things about the people
behind the names, and I hope you'll find learning an enjoyable
experience."

Sara reseated herself and the girls remained silent, their eyes
now on the Mother Superior. Lucy nodded almost imperceptibly
and there was a smattering of applause.

"We trust you'll enjoy your stay at St. Gertrude's," Lucy
told her. "Now, I'd like the other instructors to introduce themselves. Doubtless you know many of them already."

"I'm Sister Regina," said an ageless woman with heavy-
lidded eyes. Her features were nearly as severe as Lucy's, but
where the Mother Superior had a long, equine face, Regina's
was heart-shaped and rather reptilian. "I teach health and biol-
ogy, and I'm also the school nurse. I'll be seeing you through
your tests tomorrow."

*Oh, God, the physical.* Sara cringed inwardly, but gave her
a smile. "I remember you from my days as a student. It's nice
to see you again." *Let this be over with!*

They went around the table. Sister Matilda greeted her
warmly, followed by Sisters Agatha, Martha, Flora, Valerie,
Abby, and Margaret. Sister Elizabeth pursed her lips, then
offered to paint her her own saint for her room, and Sara
suppressed a chill as she thanked her: the last thing she wanted
was one of those bloody horrors staring at her every time she
was alone.

"I'm Sister Mary Oswald," said the last nun. Sara remembered her; she was so blond and pale that she was nearly an
albino, and her manner was as cold as her complexion. "Sister
Bibiana and I prepared your room."

"Thank you."

"And I'm Esther Roth," said the quarterback beside her.
"Maybe we can have a drink together, you and I being the
only lay teachers here." Her voice was rough and friendly,
maybe it was her mannish haircut or the way she looked Sara

up and down that made her decide the last thing she wanted to do was be alone with the gym teacher.

She nodded. "Were you here in '84? I think I remember you."

Esther nodded. "Sure. I was a little slimmer back then, and used to dye my hair red. It was long then."

Sara studied the woman, remembering now. She'd been less mannish back then, but had still had a reputation among the girls for oversupervising their showers. *Be nice. All students think all gym teachers are gay.* But looking at Esther now, at the short hair bleached to a nearly punkish platinum, she still thought it and felt momentarily guilty. Then she reminded herself that she had quite a few gay friends of both genders back home, and none of them made her feel this way; she knew they would no more try to seduce her or "turn" her than she would them. None of them was stereotypical, not like Esther Roth, who was not so subtly running her tongue over her lips and watching her. "Perhaps we can get together after I'm more settled," she told her.

"Sure, just knock on my door. My room's next to yours."

*Oh, joy.* "I'll do that. Thanks."

Mother Lucy stood and clapped her hands again. "Clear your tables, girls. Who's assigned to the teachers' table? Raise your hands."

Two girls did. One was a plump underclassman with horn-rimmed glasses; the other was Kelly Reed. It had been like that when Sara had gone to school. The least favored girls always got the extra clean-up duty.

"Come forward and get busy, ladies."

As Sara watched, the two took their own trays to the kitchen area, followed by the rest, who filed out of the cafeteria. "Where are they going?" she asked Sister Bibi.

"Those who aren't on kitchen duty will go to their rooms, to study or read until lights out. When you're on dorm duty, you'll find out that there's quite a bit of horseplay, though."

"That seems reasonable," Sara said, as a pale hand reached for her tray. She looked up at Kelly, gave her a subtle wink. The girl answered with the tiniest smile.

When the girls were gone and the table cleared, Lucy spoke. "The sisters and I are going to the chapel for evening services, Miss Hawthorne, as is customary. The evening is yours to do as you please. I'm sure you're tired from your journey."

"Yes. Very." Sara had taken three days to travel from the Bay Area, giving herself a small vacation, traveling down the slow, winding Pacific Coast Highway. She'd spent one night in the seaport village of Red Cay on the Central Coast, and another in Santa Barbara, before arriving late this morning, so she shouldn't have been so exhausted. But there was no doubt about it; she felt like sleeping for a week.

"Get plenty of rest," said Sister Regina, the nurse, "so you'll be refreshed for your tests tomorrow. I'll see you at one o'clock in the medical area, downstairs."

Sara nodded, her stomach twisting. She didn't like tests, be they medical or psychological or any other kind, and she didn't look forward to tomorrow. *It'll all be over soon.* She rose, along with the nuns and Esther, and was very relieved when Esther went with the sisters toward the chapel instead of accompanying her back to the dorm.

Sara entered at the far end of the dormitory and walked along the first floor, where the older girls had their rooms. Most of the doors were open and girls were socializing, moving back and forth, giggling and gossiping. When they saw Sara, most of them smiled and exhibited a politeness that she had never seen in public school. A few looked annoyed and quickly shut their doors.

She continued down the hall just past the central staircase, and stopped at the second door . . . her old room, where she'd found Jenny Blaine, her roommate and best friend, dead in a pool of her own blood. Unlike Lenore Tynan's wrists, Jenny's had been slit the long way and blood had flowed freely, spurting over the walls and furnishings. Sara shivered involuntarily, then knocked on the door, trying to ignore the portrait hanging beside it, one of some saint whose heart was being torn from her body by flying demons.

The door opened slightly and there was Kelly Reed. "Miss Hawthorne?" she asked nervously.

"Hi, ah, I didn't know this was your room, Kelly. I hope I'm not disturbing you."

"I was just studying, it's okay." Her eyes asked all the questions.

"This used to be my room, when I was a student here. I just wanted to see it again."

"Really?" she asked, her voice betraying interest. "Your room?"

Sara nodded.

"Come in." Kelly pulled the door wide, then shut it behind Sara.

The room was a bland off-white, with two metal twin beds, one on either side of the room. At the foot of each bed were small closets and on the wall with the entry a chest of drawers on either side. By the heads of the beds were small desks, each with a straight chair and a small lamp. Everything was bland and white, from the bedspreads to the desks.

"It's just like I remember," Sara said. *Except for all the blood.*

"Boring."

Sara laughed. "My thought exactly. Where's your roommate?"

"Marcia's probably hanging out in Buffy's room. Good riddance," she added.

"You don't get along?"

Kelly shook her head. "I can't stand her and her friends."

"Is Marcia the one with the long blond hair? And Buffy's is short and curly?"

Kelly's eyes widened. "You know them already?"

"I met them. And I saw them picking on you."

The girl blushed and looked at her hands. "Was Mother Lucy here when you were a student?"

"Yes."

"Do you like her?"

Of course she didn't, but Sara didn't think she should say so, at least, not outright. "She's tough."

"But do you *like* her?" She sounded disgusted with Sara's feint.

"Kelly, I'm a teacher here. What do you want me to say? I did hear what she said to you, as well as what Marcia said."

"They hate me," Kelly spat. "They all hate me."

"Why?"

"Marcia stole my locket." In a flood of words, she told her story.

"And Mother Lucy believed her?"

Kelly nodded.

"Why?"

The girl shrugged. "Because Marcia's one of her favorites. Little Miss Bitch can do no wrong." She stole a sideways glance at Sara to see the effect of the name-calling. Sara was careful not to react.

"There are always girls like that, Kelly. They picked on me, too. Do you want me to talk to Mother Lucy for you?"

"*No!*" Kelly practically screamed the word. "Please don't," she added quietly. "It'll only make trouble for me. They'll put me back in solitary."

"Don't worry, I won't say anything. What was solitary like?" She'd heard it threatened in her schooldays, but the girls it happened to wouldn't talk about it.

"I thought I'd like it," Kelly said, "you know, because Marcia couldn't bug me. But it was awful. Worse than awful. It was scary."

"Tell me about it."

"I'm not supposed to. The nuns make you take an oath that the devil will take you if you tell."

Disgust welled up in Sara. Kelly Reed was obviously frightened, and probably had good reason. "No one has a right to abuse you."

"Nobody touched me."

"Abuse comes in many forms. If they abused you, I can do something about it. Frankly, nothing would give me more pleasure."

Kelly looked up. "You don't like them, do you? The nuns, I mean."

"I never said that," she replied, with a slight smile. "What did they do to you?"

"I—I can't." Tears glistened in her eyes. "It was just so dark—"

"Hey, Ghost Girl!"

Sara turned to see Marcia Crowley, with two of her court giggling behind her, standing in the doorway. Marcia's hand stayed glued to the knob as she stared in surprise at Sara. Then a huge smile lit up her face and she walked forward, standing directly in front of Kelly. "Miss Hawthorne! How nice of you to visit!"

She was annoyed with Marcia, but decided not to say anything, since the girl would just take it out on Kelly later. "This used to be my room, Marcia. I just wondered if anything had changed."

"Has it?" the girl chirped, as her entourage smiled from the doorway.

"Not a bit. Now, if you'll excuse me, I'll leave you to your studies."

As she left the room, she clearly heard Marcia Crowley start in on Kelly in a teasing, sing-song voice. "Trying to be teacher's pet? Good fucking luck, Ghost Girl."

Resolving to find out about the nickname as soon as she could, Sara made her way upstairs to unpack and settle in, wishing to God she could stop thinking about the torments Kelly Reed suffered at the hands of Marcia and her friends. There had to be something she could do. *But what?*

# Twenty-One

Midnight, a dark, moonless shroud of a midnight that closed in around Minerva Payne, starving her lungs, making the hair in her long white braid feel tight, chilling her soul with its blackness. Here in the forest, in her cottage, she rarely felt this way, but the time was approaching, and as much as she wished to ignore it, her body told her it was so.

Tonight, she felt the aches and pains of age as she rarely did: her fingers were stiff with arthritis, though she sat close to the fire, her heart cold in her bosom. Despite the fire, the cottage would not warm as it usually did. Beyond the firelight, the air was cold and filled with portents of things to come.

She felt old and tired tonight and wondered if Lucy ever felt the same. She doubted it. Lucy had the energy of her nuns to draw on, and whenever it waned, she renewed the blood, revived the energy. It was so much easier to follow the darkness than the light; the rewards, at least on this plane, were immediately gratifying. Energizing.

Minerva rose from her rocker, for once wishing she owned a cane to lean on. *You can lean on nothing but yourself, old woman, you know that.* Steadfastly she walked into the kitchen and retrieved a blue five-pound bag of Morton's salt, then crossed to the front door and lifted the old-fashioned wooden bar latch. Her hands trembled, not with pain, which she could control, but with terror born of knowledge. *You can control that, too, so stop feeling sorry for yourself.*

Straightening her shoulders, she opened the door, letting in the night, which was thick and still and cool, though not so cold as the interior of the cottage. No crickets sang, no rodents scuttled through the brush; the night was waiting, and so was she.

Suddenly, from above, a horrible cry rent the silence and something even blacker than the night flapped heavy wings as it crossed over the cottage.

"Get away," Minerva said softly, forcefully, as she opened the edge of the salt bag. "Get away, stay away, you'll not have me tonight." So saying, she poured a line of salt across the threshold, then stepped carefully over it to walk around the cabin, encircling it completely in salt. As she walked she spoke in the old language, her tongue rolling over r's, her voice lilting and youthful, as it had been the day she'd reported the woman's body in the pond.

As she spoke the words, the aches disappeared from her hands and the stiffness from her legs, and by the time she poured the last of the salt, connecting it to the beginning at the threshold, she was moving quickly, her energy returning. She stepped over the salt, into the doorway, then turned and looked out at the night. She heard the horrible cry again, but it was distant now, repelled by the salt, as were the other negative forces. As she closed the door, the crickets, the last of the season, began their song at last, and inside the air was toasty warm.

*You've only put a bandage on a broken bone.* She threw away the empty salt bag, then retrieved a large leatherbound volume from a bookcase near the dining table. Returning to her rocker, she opened it and began studying her own words from long ago. *A bandage on a broken bone, that's all. You have to do it right this time. You have to win this battle, or the war will be lost.*

# Twenty-Two

Sara's dreams were filled with gargoyles, all of them with Mother Lucy's menacing features, all of them screeching and coming after her, razor-sharp talons extended and dripping with blood.

Suddenly, Jenny Blaine's face appeared, pale and bloodless. "Get out of here, Sara. Get out before they kill you, too!"

Sara awoke, a scream caught behind her teeth. For a moment, she didn't know where she was, only that she was in utter darkness, shivering though the sheets were soaked with sweat.

*I'm at St. Gruesome's.* The realization didn't help, but made her more fearful instead. "Jenny." She whispered the word, half expecting to see her, or the ghostly woman Basil-Bob Boullan claimed had frightened her predecessor. *Maybe they're one and the same.*

Breathing hard, she frantically felt for the cheap little bedside lamp, found the switch, and turned it. Dim yellow light filled her room. Her heart and respiration began to slow, and shakily she pushed the covers back and climbed from the bed. *What a nightmare!* It seemed silly, now. Sort of.

Thirsty, she realized that all she had to drink was Pepsi. *Damn!* She'd been in such a hurry to go to bed that she hadn't bothered to fill the water pitcher she'd found on a shelf in the closet. *So, do I drink soda, go thirsty, or walk down the hall to the lavatory and fill the pitcher?*

Her bladder put its two cents in, making her decision for her. She pulled on her robe and tied it, then grabbed the pitcher, went to the door, and kneeled and removed the rubber wedge.

She opened the door a crack, cautiously peering left, then right, down the hall, making sure it was empty, then stepped out, closing the door softly behind her.

The floor was freezing cold; she'd have to buy slippers next time she went to town. She decided not to bother with going back inside for shoes—the chilliness of the air in the hall had redoubled her bladder's demands.

Only a few of the fly-specked bulbs were on at this hour, and in between were patches of darkness which effectively telescoped the corridor. It was unnerving, but Sara continued on, refusing to look at the gruesome portraits on the wall, refusing to give in to her nervousness, her desire to run instead of walk.

She breathed a sigh of relief as she pushed open the door to the lavatory. She balanced the pitcher on the edge of a yellowed porcelain sink, then went into one of the dozen toilet stalls. Somewhere behind her, in the shower room, she could hear faucets dripping, slowly and steadily.

The shattering of glass made her scream. "Hello?" she called. "Is someone there?"

There was no reply. *The pitcher fell, that's all.* She took a deep breath, held it, exhaled, did it again, then stood, her legs rubbery as she flushed, then opened the stall door. "Hello?" she called again.

The white pitcher lay in shards on the floor. *No wonder it fell.* It had been stupid of her to leave it in such a precarious position. "Damn," she muttered, as she took a handful of paper towels from the dispenser and started cleaning up. "Damn it."

A shower turned on. Sara, brushing the last shards of glass into a towel, raised her head. *Who could be in here?* Another shower came on, and another. *Do nuns shower at two in the morning?* That was ridiculous, but someone was in the shower room, and she—or they—hadn't answered when she'd called out. The thrum of water against tiles increased as more showers were turned on.

Sara dropped the towel full of glass in the trashcan, then tiptoed across the floor toward the shower room. A sting on the bottom of her foot made her look down and she realized she'd tracked blood across the floor. She paused to examine her foot, found a small oozing wound below the toes. There was no glass in it. *The hell with it.* She flattened herself against the white tiled wall and edged along until she came to the open entryway. She peeked around the corner, and at first saw nothing but steam.

After a moment, she made out the shower heads, two dozen of them, most spewing hot water, judging by the steamy heat on her face and in her lungs. There was no movement, there were no people, just the water, pounding and pounding. She jumped as a shower head near her suddenly came to life. Not believing her eyes, she watched as the hot water handle turned by itself. "No," she whispered.

*"Sara . . . Sara . . . Sara . . ."*

The words echoed in her ears. They came from the middle of the showers, but still she couldn't see anyone. Steamy mist, like fog, pulled apart and then wafted together again, over and over. *"Sara . . . Sara . . . Sara . . ."*

Something began slowly to glide toward her, a wavery oblong of steam that took form as it neared. *"Sara . . . Sara . . ."*

She couldn't move but watched raptly as a woman took form within the steam. *"Sara . . ."* It glided toward her, and now Sara could see the eyes, dark indentations, the suggestion of a nose and mouth. *"Sara . . ."* Long hair waved around the face.

"Jenny," she whispered, no longer afraid. "Jenny, is it really you?"

The foggy specter peered at her with sorrowful eyes, then raised her arms, turning them to show the inner wrists. In the sea of white, the long red gashes, from wrist to elbow, stood out vividly. Sara's stomach clenched, and then she saw the specter's face transform from Jenny Blaine's gentle features into a monstrosity from her nightmares. At the same moment, the showers turned off and the phantom began to laugh, a horrible cackle, a screeching, gleeful, hysterical laughter that grew louder as the specter drifted away with the dissipating steam.

Suddenly, Sara's paralysis ended and she raced from the lavatory, ghostly laughter following her all the way down the hall to her door. She yanked it open and slammed it shut behind her, the cackle echoing in her ears. Frantically she shoved the rubber wedge under the door, then took one of the straight chairs from the dinette set and wedged it under the knob.

She couldn't think, couldn't even begin to comprehend what had happened. Emotions drained, feeling completely numb, she lay down on the bed, stared at the ceiling, and waited for dawn.

# Twenty-Three

"Hi, Dad!"

"Doesn't anyone ever knock anymore?" John smiled to show his son it was nothing personal. "Corey, Pete, how're you doing?" he asked, nodding at Mark's friends, who hovered in his office doorway. "You boys come to turn yourselves in?"

Corey Addams, a slight, blond thirteen-year-old, looked a little worried, but Pete Parker, of sturdier stock, grinned devilishly. "We ain't squealin', copper." The kid's Brooklyn accent stank.

"Then why are you here?" John pushed away the stack of manila folders he'd been going through since noon in a fruitless effort to find references to Jennifer Blaine's death, then folded his hands on his desk. "You look like you want something."

Mark nodded. "Caspar wants to hire us to help set up for the Halloween Haunt. Can I do it, Dad?"

The Haunt had lost its attraction for John in 1972, but his son loved it as much as he had before the accident, and he wasn't about to deny the boy his fun. Particularly, he thought, if that meant he might spend a little less time hanging around

Minerva Payne's bakery. "As long as you get your homework done on time."

"No problem, Dad. Thanks." He paused. "Can I sleep over at Corey's tonight? His mom and dad said it was okay, and Pete already asked and he gets to go."

John hesitated. Every time Mark wanted to stay at the Addamses', the old memories resurfaced, especially of how he and Corey's father, Winky, and the others had sneaked out of the house after assuring their parents they wouldn't. He'd let Mark stay at the Addamses' occasionally, but as now, he always tried subtly to change the plans, even though he knew it was a ridiculous thing to do. "Why don't you boys spend the night at our place?" he asked. "You can call out for a couple pizzas and rent some movies. My treat."

Mark glanced at his friends, who both looked amenable, but when he turned back to John, he said, "Dad, Mrs. Addams is making pot roast. I don't want to miss that!"

"Pepperoni, Mark," murmured Pete, who, like Corey, was blessed with a career mother and yearned for pizza the way Mark desired home cooking. "Olives, mozzarella."

"All the pepperoni you want, guys."

"Yeah," said Corey Addams.

"No, Dad," Mark said, almost apologetically. "We always stay over at our house or Pete's. I really want to go. Besides," he added in a sly tone, "Corey's parents are going to think I don't like them if I don't go sometime."

*Win some, lose some.* Knowing he was wrong, John made himself smile and nod at his son. "Go ahead. But don't forget your toothbrush," he added, with a trace of satisfaction. "So what are you guys going to do?"

"Caspar's gonna let us design part of the Haunted Barn," Mark said.

"We're gonna plan it all out tonight," Pete said, "and tomorrow we're gonna show it to my grandfather for approval."

Caspar was Pete's great-grandfather, but John supposed that was too much of a mouthful, and who was he to quibble? Both he and Mark called his grandfather by his first name. "Well, it sounds like you're going to be busy," John said, happier now that he knew they probably wouldn't have time to get into any mischief. "Have fun, you guys. And Corey, say hi to your dad for me, okay?"

"Sure."

The boys left the office, Corey Addams pausing to pull the door closed behind him. Corey was a lot like Winky, but he reminded John even more of Paul Pricket, the friend he missed most of all. He would never forget looking up, clinging to Greg's body, and seeing Paul above him, hearing the words, "Take my hand." He felt a pang. You couldn't put a price on a friend like that, and he suddenly wished he could see him again. After his family had moved down to Redlands in 1973, he'd heard from him once or twice, and they still exchanged Christmas cards, which of late included no more than one "Hope you're well" line. He knew Paul had gone to seminary in Claremont and was now a Catholic priest in a small parish; or at least, he was as of last Christmas. *You're seriously considering contacting him, aren't you?*

John shook his head. Maybe it was all the exposure to the nuns, maybe it was the suicide of Lenore Tynan, or the visit of the pretty young teacher alleging another suicide. Or maybe it was barely a month before Halloween, and like it or not, he always thought about the others, especially Paul, this time of year. *And you've never even admitted that to yourself until now, have you?*

He rose and put the files away, then grabbed another batch, these from 1985, and sat back down. He hadn't been able to get Sara Hawthorne off his mind, even though he thought she might be a nut. He at least wanted to find the report on her friend's death, and prove to her it was a suicide. *And to myself.*

Doubt was eating away at him, and picking up the phone, he punched in Frank Cutter's number. He should have thought of the doctor hours ago.

He was on hold ten minutes before Frank came on the line. He spent a few minutes telling him about the visit from Sara Hawthorne and the story of her roommate then waited another ten while the doctor searched his files.

"Not a trace of anyone named Jennifer Blaine here, John. You say she was a suicide?"

"Yes, though it's been alleged foul play might have been involved."

"If it happened in this county, I'd have a record of it, John. So would you."

"Maybe your file is misplaced?" John tried.

"Mine and yours both? I don't think so." Cutter cleared his throat. "Unless this was covered up by the nuns, which is unlikely, since *they* came to *us* about the Tynan woman, I'd say your schoolteacher is imagining things." There was a pause. "Of course, you might want to check with Dashwood. Maybe he didn't bother to report it."

"You mean, he covered it up?"

"Yes, that's what I mean. I'm not going to tell you your business, John, but don't get a bug up your ass and go out there and accuse the man of anything. Just say you can't find a record of the death and ask to see his copy. Don't put him on the defensive."

John suppressed a groan. Sometimes he got sick of working around the same people who worked with his father; they tended to treat him like a child. Cutter was even worse, since he was a good friend of his grandfather's too. He suppressed a childish urge to protest Cutter's assumption that he didn't know how to do his job. "I'll keep it in mind, Frank. Thanks."

He hung up and stared at the folders for a long moment before returning them to the cabinet. Before he could think twice about it, he shrugged on his leather jacket, grabbed his hat, and left for St. Gruesome's.

# Twenty-Four

"You guys are such chickens!" Mark Lawson swung off his bike outside Apple Heaven. "Minerva Payne's pies are a hell of a lot better than the nuns', and she'd let us have a price break, too!"

Corey Addams twined a chain through his front bicycle tire as Pete Parker counted his money. Neither answered.

"What d'you think, guys?" Mark chided. "That Minerva's gonna shove apples in your mouths and stick you in her oven?"

Pete took the bait. "Nah, we're just afraid she's gonna want to give us blowjobs, like she does you."

Mark talked as rough as his friends, but the remark about Minerva offended him. He tried to hide it, knowing Pete would redouble his insults if he thought he was getting to him. "You're chicken, Parker—admit it."

"I want a mincemeat pie, and everybody knows the nuns make the best in the world." Pete shoved his money back in his pocket. "I got three bucks." He looked at Corey. "You want mincemeat, too, right?"

"Yeah, sure. I have two dollars and thirty-one cents."

"What about you, Lawson?"

"I'm not gonna chip in for mincemeat. Yuck!"

"Who's chicken now?" Pete asked. "You never even tried it."

"Hell, no, and I'm not gonna," Mark said firmly.

"Why not?" Corey asked, threading the chain through Pete's and Mark's tires as well.

" 'Cause my dad calls it moose turd pie, and he knows what he's talking about."

"Do you believe everything your daddy says?" Pete asked.

Corey snickered. "Turds! I love it. It's not made of turds, Mark! I'll bet your father never even tried any, either."

"Sure he has." Mark didn't really know whether he had or not; he only knew his dad had been right about anchovies, buttermilk, and especially the true nature of sweetbreads. That was good enough for him. "You guys get yourselves a pie. I'm gonna get a pumpkin tart."

"We need two dollars more for a pie, so you have to chip in," Pete said.

"No way. That's all I have. You guys get mincemeat tarts. They're plenty big."

"Are not," Pete protested. You don't hardly get any. They're a waste of money."

Mark looked at Corey. "Your mom'll have dessert anyway, right?"

"Yeah, but it's probably apple cobbler or something."

Pete and Corey looked at each other and rolled their eyes.

"I like apples," Mark admitted, locking his bike to Corey's.

"Yeah," Corey said, "but you wouldn't if you lived in an orchard and had 'em every day."

"Damn straight."

"Okay, look." Mark dug his two dollars out and handed them to Corey. "Buy your moose turd pie, but I get your apple cobblers."

"Cool," Pete said. "It's a deal."

They walked up the wide wooden steps to Apple Heaven. The building was low and long, painted barn red with white trim. Mark pushed open the door and the fragrance of apples assaulted his nose.

The place was empty of tourists, and evidently nuns, this late September afternoon, and Mark took the opportunity to wander up and down the shop. At one end of the bakery was a seating area for tourists who needed a piece of pie on the spot. The rest of the place was lined with boxes of apples, apple cookbooks, fancy potholders, mugs, salt-and-pepper shakers made of fake mason jars, and an array of apple-head dolls. Mark thought they were the ugliest things he'd ever seen, especially the ones dressed like little nuns. Above the displays were reproductions of apple and pear company posters from earlier in the century.

One area was reserved for the bakery counter, its glass case filled with pies and tarts. Behind the unmanned counter were advertisements for Apple Heaven's wares, including "Our World Famous Heavenly Mincemeat Pies."

"You know what's really in mincemeat, guys?" he asked softly as he rejoined his friends at the counter.

Pete, his hand hovering over the old-fashioned service bell, paused. "You already told us," he sneered.

"Moose turds," Corey giggled.

"No," Mark whispered. "I mean what's *really* in it!"

"Apples and raisins and beef," Pete said. "And spices."

"What kind of beef?" Mark raised his eyebrows knowingly.

"Roast, what else?" Pete said. "You're not gonna talk us out of this, Lawson. We got your money, and we made a deal."

"I know, I know." Mark was enjoying himself, because he really did know what was in mince meat, at least the old-fashioned kind. His great-granddad, Gus, had a really old cook-book, and he'd looked it up one afternoon when he was bored. "It's got guts in it."

"Does not." That was Corey.

"Does so. It's made out of deer meat or beef, but most of the meat is guts. Hearts, livers, shit like that."

"I don't care what's in it, I like it." He tapped the bell.

"Really? Guts?" Corey asked with concern.

"Maybe even intestines," Mark said, sensing a crack in the mincemeat faction. "They just wash the shit out of 'em and—"

"I didn't quite catch that," said an angry-looking nun who had appeared in the doorway behind the counter so suddenly that Mark knew she'd heard him talking. "What did you say?"

"Ah, what's in the mincemeat pie?" he stammered.

"It's a secret recipe," the nun said. She wore a little nametag that said, "Sister Margaret." "Basically, it's made of fruit and meat."

"What kind of meat?" Corey pushed his lank blond hair from his blue eyes.

"The very best."

"Is there, like, hearts or liver or anything?" Pete asked.

"It's a secret recipe," Sister Margaret repeated, then gave them the smallest of smiles. "But you don't have to worry about things like that."

"Okay," said Pete. "One mincemeat pie, to go." He gave Mark a triumphant look.

"Very good. One moment, please." The nun disappeared into the back room, then Mark heard her say, "Cindy, box up a mincemeat pie, please."

A girlish voice said, "Yes, Sister."

"I'm telling you," Mark whispered quickly, "it's full of guts."

"Bullshit," Pete hissed back. "Nuns don't lie."

"She didn't say what kind of meat it was, dickhead."

As Pete opened his mouth to reply, the nun reappeared bearing a pink box with the words "Apple Heaven" printed on it in curlicue letters. "That will be seven twenty-five."

Pete and Corey counted out the money and laid it on the counter. The nun handed over the pie, then silently handed Pete a nickel change.

The boys turned toward the door just as it opened.

"Dad!" Mark blurted, surprised.

"Hi, Mark, boys. Whatcha got there?"

"Mincemeat pie," Pete said. "For tonight."

His dad made a face. "Mark, I didn't know you liked mincemeat."

Mark returned the face. "I told 'em what you call it, but they want to eat it anyway. I'm getting their apple cobbler."

"Are there really guts in it, Sheriff?" Corey asked, wide-eyed and worried.

Behind them, the nun manufactured a polite cough.

"I don't know, boys," John Lawson said quickly. "And I don't want to know."

"May I help you, Sheriff?" the nun asked, after another little cough.

"Yes, Sister, you sure can. Excuse me, fellas. Have fun tonight." He walked past them to the counter. "But not too much."

" 'Bye," Corey and Pete yelled as they went out the door.

"See ya, Dad," Mark called, hanging back in the open doorway, curious as to why his father was here.

"How can I help you?"

"Would you unlock the gate for me, please? I need to speak with Dr. Dashwood."

*Police stuff.* Mark closed the door softly behind him, wondering what else he'd expected. *That Dad's secretly scarfing mincemeat?* With a snort, he joined his friends at the knot of bikes they were busy unlocking.

# Twenty-Five

"Are you ready?"

Sara, shivering, clad only in a tiny white gown and a myriad of goosebumps, looked around and saw Sister Regina, the school nurse who had administered the psychological tests earlier today, enter Dr. Dashwood's examination room. She carried a tray, which she placed on a cart next to the examination table where Sara was perched, her skin sticking to the paperless leather upholstery despite the cold air of the room. The nun turned, her body hiding the tray's contents. At least today's tests kept her mind off the incident in the shower room the night before, not that she hadn't nearly convinced herself that the whole thing had been a trick of her overactive imagination.

"I'm ready," she managed, as Sister Regina shoved a thermometer in her mouth.

"Don't talk," the nun ordered, putting a stethoscope to her ears and pulling a blood pressure cuff from the wall. Efficiently she slipped it up Sara's bare arm, then began inflating it, squeezing the bulb until Sara almost cried out in pain. Abruptly she let off the pressure, removed the thermometer, then crossed to the counter area, picked up a clipboard, and began writing.

Sara saw the contents of the tray and her stomach flip-flopped. There were Latex gloves, a tube of K-Y jelly, a speculum, slides, Q-tips, tweezers, three hypodermic syringes, and several small rubber-tipped vials.

"Sister," she demanded, "what are all these things for?"

Regina turned, slowly blinking her heavy-lidded eyes. She looked more reptilian than human. She wet her pale lips, a snake in nun's clothing, then smiled thinly. "Doctor needs these things to examine you."

"He's going to do a pelvic?"

"Of course, dear. He does us all every year."

"But I brought my records. I had a complete exam by my own doctor less than three months ago."

"It's customary. Doctor likes to get to know his patients while they're healthy, so that he has a baseline to work from if you become ill." She glanced at her clipboard. "When was your last period, Miss Hawthorne?"

"I forget. What are the syringes for?"

"Tetanus, a measles booster, and flu vaccine. All customary. Have you ever been pregnant?"

"No. And I've had the measles, and everything else is up to date."

"I'll make a note of that. Doctor will decide what's best. Have you had any unusual discharges or bleeding?"

"Why are you so interested in my sex life?" She'd almost said "genitals," but stopped cold, suddenly remembering the girls' nickname for the nurse: Sister Vagina. Something flashed in her memory, disappeared before she could examine it. Had this been done to her when she was a girl? No, she didn't think so. And turning "Regina" into "Vagina" was inevitable, wasn't it? They probably still called her that.

"Do you have sexual relations?" the nun asked, blinking again.

"That's none of your business."

"Uncooperative," Regina muttered, writing something down. "Is there any history of insanity in your family?" She gave her another reptilian smile as she asked the question.

"You have my history; you know I was orphaned." She was feeling anger on top of the humiliation now.

"Of course, dear. How thoughtless of me." The nun set the clipboard on the edge of the cart, then approached her, the expression on her face softening. "Scoot to the end of the table and lie back. Doctor will be here in a moment and he expects you to be ready. If you're not," she added, her voice a falsely conspiratorial whisper, "he'll report me to Mother Lucy, and I'll be in trouble."

Sara did as the Regina requested, studying her all the while, trying to remember what she'd been like years ago. Aside from appearing no older—the nuns all seemed to have retained their earlier appearances—*you, too, can stay young forever, if you give up sunlight, sex, drugs, and rock 'n' roll*—she couldn't remember anything in particular about this one except for the snaky looks and the vulgar nickname. Some of the nuns, like Sister Bibi, had been friendlier than most, and she suspected that Sister Regina's change of attitude was just a tool; more than likely, she truly was afraid of Mother Lucy's wrath.

The footrest dropped away, leaving her legs dangling uncomfortably off the end of the table, and she stared at the ceiling, not wanting to look as the nun raised the stirrups attached to the examination table.

"Just relax, Miss Hawthorne," Regina said. "I'm going to help you put your legs up. It can be a little tricky to do yourself."

That sounded odd, but Sara, resigned to her fate, let the nun lift one leg. She felt cold curved metal against the back of her knee; it seemed unusual, but not too bad.

Sister Regina put the other leg up. "Are you comfortable, dear?"

"As comfortable as can be expected." Sara decided that the knee stirrups were less humiliating than ankle ones, but wasn't about to say so.

"All right, Miss Hawthorne, or may I call you Sara?" She didn't wait for a response. "We're almost ready for Doctor." The nun stood at the foot of the table—Sara could just see her face above her bare knees, felt herself blush when she realized what the nun could see. Regina calmly flipped up an extension on the stirrup, revealing a two-inch wide strip of belting material. She heard the crunch of Velcro as the material was wrapped around her ankle.

"Hey, what the hell—"

"Please don't swear, Sara. We've found these cloth anklets much more comfortable than the old-fashioned stirrups."

Before she could protest, Regina trapped her other ankle and she lay there, shocked and humiliated, thinking it couldn't get any worse. But it did.

"Let's just adjust these a little," the nun said. She touched something at the side of the table, and Sara heard a low whir of machinery. The stirrups moved slowly apart. "What do you think you're doing?"

Sister Regina only smiled then walked to the door. "Doctor will be right in."

As soon as the nun was out of the room, Sara tried to sit up, to reach her ankles, and free them, but it was physically impossible. "Damn. Damn, damn, damn!" She flopped back. Nothing, but nothing, was worth this. She'd resign the moment she was free, and report her treatment to the authorities.

Minutes passed. *Authorities.* Could she tell Sheriff Lawson? It was too embarrassing. She'd go to the town doctor instead. Surely, that would be at least a little less humiliating.

There was a rap on the door. "Miss Hawthorne?"

She recognized the voice, deep, very masculine, and vaguely British. *Dr. Dashwood!* How could she have forgotten who he was? All the girls had wanted him, had talked and fantasized about the man. She felt herself blushing furiously as she heard him approaching.

Blessedly, he stopped by her side and looked at her face with eyes you could get lost in and not ever care. *Except now.* He smiled, showing straight white teeth, his cheeks creasing with small, perfect dimples. "Are you comfortable?"

"Frankly, no," she said firmly.

He glanced back, saw her legs. "Oh, dear. Sister Regina got a little carried away." The machinery whirred again, and he did something to the ankle stirrups, bringing them down to a normal level.

"Why am I trapped like this? You have no right."

He shook his head. "Sister Regina is much older than she appears, and I'm afraid she's become a bit eccentric. I've spoken to Mother Lucy about letting her retire, but our Mother Superior believes Reggy has a few years left in her. We don't need these." He moved to the end of the table and she heard the rip of Velcro, then her ankles were set free, lowering her humiliation level from excruciating to merely severe.

"When would you *ever* need them?" she asked, as she started to remove her knees from the metal rests.

Dashwood's hands came down gently on the knees. "No, leave them up a moment longer and we'll get this part out of the way." He left his hands, warm and dry, on her a moment longer, then, evidently sensing she'd acquiesced, removed them. "Many of our girls are very rebellious. Runaways, drug addicts, former gang members. We have to check any new adolescent for problems, and sometimes they won't allow it without the restraints. You understand."

"That's cruel," she said, hearing the snap of gloves.

"Yes, it is, but it's vital we check for disease, pregnancy, and so forth. And some of the younger girls must be examined as well if sexual abuse is an issue." He placed one gloved hand on her abdomen and palpated gently, his eyes locked on hers.

"Surely you don't make a practice of restraining the girls."

"Very rarely, I assure you. Sometimes we give them a few grains of relaxant, but usually just a cup of herb tea and gentle conversation is enough."

Sara began to believe him. The man had a bedside manner that defied description. Trapped only in his gaze, she began to feel relaxed, even as he began the pelvic. She barely realized she was being touched, and he kept talking the entire time, never looking away from her face. He was more thorough than she had ever experienced, but it was less humiliating, too, even though she'd had a female doctor in San Francisco. He talked about the nuns, gossiping a little, then went on to tell her about the girls, warning her about some of the ones who would be special problems. By the time she felt the cold metal speculum against her, she barely flinched, hardly realizing she could no longer see his face.

"Hmmm," he said.

"What?"

"Something looks just a little odd here." He stood up and smiled at her. "It's nothing, I'm sure," he added, stripping off the gloves.

"What? There couldn't be anything wrong. I just saw my own doctor." She tensed against the metal instrument as it began to hurt. "Please, get this over with."

"Relax, Miss Hawthorne." He picked up a syringe and she saw a momentary flash of a long needle as he attached it. "We'll be done in just a moment."

"What are you doing?" she demanded, on the verge of panic.

She started to withdraw one leg, but his hand went up, firmly but gently holding it in place. "I'm just going to take a small biopsy of tissue. I can virtually assure you there's nothing to be concerned about."

"What's the needle for?" She relaxed slightly, soothed by his soul-searching gaze.

"A little Lidocaine, so you won't feel anything."

"Oh." She felt stunned, couldn't think.

"Nothing but a tiny pinch. Are you ready?"

"Just finish it, please!"

He studied her a moment longer, favoring her with a smile. Despite herself, she relaxed a little more.

He disappeared, she felt the pinch, then a few minutes later, the speculum was removed. "All done," he told her, reassurance in his eyes.

She felt warmer now, especially inside; an effect of the anesthetic, no doubt. "Can I get up now?"

"Let me do the breast exam, then you can get up."

"All right."

As he lowered her gown from her shoulders, holding her gaze, she vaguely realized her legs were still up, but she didn't really care. His hands palpating first one breast, then the other, actually felt good, like a massage. Better than a massage.

"You have an incredible bedside manner," she murmured. *What the hell is wrong with me?* She wanted to scream at him to get his hands off her, but she couldn't. She was mortified by her growing excitement. Her body was betraying her; it seemed to have a mind of its own. *How can this be happening?*

"Thank you." He kept kneading, fingers pinching her nipple now. "Very good. You're an excellent patient."

The warmth in her belly grew into heat that spread through her. She felt a violent sexual ache, could count her pulse through the steady beat in her groin. She heard herself moan. *What am I doing? What is he doing?* "Stop!" she cried.

"We're all done," he told her, one hand still resting against a breast. Her panic melted as suddenly as it had formed.

"We are?" *I can't believe I said that.* The thought was dreamy and she tried to lower her legs, but it was too much effort. She heard herself giggle, was horrified in a very detached way, as if she were watching herself from a distance. Dashwood's eyes were gorgeous.

Dimly, she heard a knock on the door, then heard the Mother Superior's voice. "Well, Doctor? How's our patient?"

"She's fine," he said. "Quite ready."

She could barely keep her eyes open, and she saw Mother Lucy, her cowl off to reveal long black hair, peering into her face. "Miss Hawthorne? Are you unwell?"

"I'm fine," she mumbled. She could barely keep her eyes open. Her ears had begun to ring and she couldn't concentrate at all. The headmistress's face went out of focus.

"I thought I might give her a trial run," she thought Dashwood said.

"No, Richard, you mustn't soil the merchandise. I'll take care of your needs personally." Was that really Mother Lucy talking? She must be imagining things, dreaming. Maybe the anesthetic Dashwood had given her had a relaxant in it. *He drugged you!* insisted a little voice, but she didn't listen, instead collapsing into an erotic dream in which she eavesdropped on two people making love.

# Twenty-Six

This return to St. Gruesome's wasn't nearly so terrible as that first visit last month, and in fact, in the several times he'd been there in August and early September, John Lawson's phobic reaction had lessened considerably.

Letting himself in the school building, he crossed quickly to the stairs leading down to Dashwood's basement offices and the infirmary and started down, relieved he hadn't run into any of the nuns.

When he reached the office door, he rapped twice, then opened it. No one was there, so he moved on to the next door, the one to the waiting room, and went inside. The nurse wasn't at her desk, but two students, both attractive blondes, one with a mane of hair, the other with shorter loose curls, sat on chairs along the wall. They looked at him and almost suppressed their giggles.

"Is Dr. Dashwood in today?" he asked.

Curly Locks nodded. "We've got appointments to see him, so I hope so." A fresh giggle escaped.

"Buffy," said the other one, "control yourself." She looked at John, gave him a smile way too knowing for a high school kid. "Dr. Dashwood will be here pretty soon." The bare tip of her tongue darted out and she wet her lips, keeping her eyes on his. "I'm Marcia Crowley, and this is Buffy Bullock. We're seniors."

"I see," John said uncomfortably, as Marcia slowly uncrossed her legs and crossed them the other way, à la Sharon Stone. He pointedly kept his eyes on a grotesque painting hanging on the wall above the students. "Is the nurse here?"

Both girls giggled, then the long-haired one said, "She'll be right back. She's helping the doctor with a patient."

John walked up to the desk and peered at the closed door behind it. His discomfort was growing by the moment.

"Are you a deputy?" one of the girls asked, behind him.

"I'm the sheriff," he replied, without turning around. At that moment, the door behind the desk creaked, then Sister Regina appeared and held the door open.

"All right," she said to someone within, then turned her head and saw John. Her eyes blinked slowly. "Sheriff, I trust you haven't been waiting long."

"Not at all," he said, as Dashwood and the headmistress came out, Sara Hawthorne between them, leaning on Dashwood's arm. She appeared pale and dazed.

"Ms. Hawthorne," he said, "are you all right?"

She looked at him, red spots on her cheeks stark against the too-white skin. Her pupils were dilated, her gaze drifting past him. "I'm fine, Sheriff Lawson," she said in a soft, vague, drowsy voice.

"Miss Hawthorne will be perfectly all right, she's just had a little too much excitement for one day," Dashwood said. "It happens sometimes. Sister Regina, please see her to her room."

"Certainly, Doctor."

"Miss Hawthorne," Dashwood said, "Stay in bed until dinnertime. Doctor's orders."

Sara nodded slowly, then Regina took her arm. The young woman placidly let herself be guided past John.

"Ms. Hawthorne?" he asked.

She hesitated, almost looking at him.

"Are you sure you're all right?" He'd been about to say something about Jennifer Blaine, then remembered that Sara hadn't wanted him to contact her at the abbey.

"Fine," she said faintly, and let Regina lead her out the door.

"I take it you know Miss Hawthorne?" Lucy demanded in her clipped tone.

"No, not really. She stopped in and asked for directions to St. Gertrude's the other day."

"That's odd," Dashwood said, "since she used to be a student here."

"Not at all, if you think about it." John countered smoothly. "We never see your students in town. I'd guess that these young ladies here," he gestured at the oversexed blondes, "would have no more idea how to get back to St. Gertrude's if they suddenly found themselves in downtown Moonfall than Ms. Hawthorne did. Isn't that right?"

The pair giggled and nodded.

Lucy gave John a hard look, then turned to Dashwood and smiled. It changed her face completely. "Doctor, I have an appointment with a student in a few minutes. I'll see you at six in the private dining room for our meeting."

"Of course."

Lucy exited the room is a flurry of black, then Dashwood turned to John. "Can I be of assistance to you, Sheriff?"

"Yes. I'm hoping you might be able to clear up something for me, Doctor. Can you spare ten minutes?"

"I think that can be arranged," Dashwood said, smiling at the two girls. "I'll be with you young ladies shortly. When Sister Regina returns, tell her that I said to prepare you for your appointments."

Another flurry of giggles. "Yes, Doctor," the blondes said simultaneously. They looked at each other and giggled harder.

"Now, Sheriff, how can I help you?"

"I'd rather talk in private, if you don't mind."

"Of course. Come with me."

Dashwood led John from the waiting room, down the hall to his private office. They settled in leather chairs, before and behind the physician's massive mahogany desk. John knew he had to be careful about what he said. "I was reviewing the recent suicide at the Falls, and I have a couple more questions."

Dashwood sat back, relaxed. "I thought Miss Tynan's case was closed."

"For all intents and purposes, but something still doesn't set right with me. Call it a hunch."

The doctor smiled and locked his disturbing eyes on John's. "I understand, and I agree that the circumstances were certainly rather unusual. How can I help you?"

"Our records at the sheriff's department weren't kept as well as they should have been until the last few years. You know how it is. Moonfall is a small, quiet town and people occasionally get a little sloppy."

"Of course."

"I found a reference to a suicide similar to Lenore Tynan's, but it's little more than a note. We're currently inputting our records into a computer system—" He chuckled, hoping it sounded convincing. "—As I said, Moonfall is rather behind the times."

"Another suicide?" Dashwood's eyebrows underscored the question. "Here? At St. Gertrude's?"

"In 1984. As I said, there was little reference to it, and I don't remember anything about it except that it happened; I was a rookie at the time and not involved in any investigation into the incident that might have been undertaken."

"I see." Dashwood sat forward now, showing interest. "Like you, I was new to my job. My father had just retired and gone home to London, and I was very new here. I'd certainly remember an incident like that." He paused. "Do you have a name? Perhaps there was an attempted suicide. I could check my records."

"Yes. Jennifer Blaine."

If Dashwood recognized the name, he didn't betray the fact. Instead, he rose and went to his file cabinets, rich mahogany ones that matched his desk. "Blaine. 'B' as in boy?"

"That's correct."

The doctor opened a drawer and began rifling through the files. "Blaine, Margaret," he read. "Blaine, Emily. Aha, here it is. Blaine, Jennifer." He brought the folder to the desk and opened it. "Jennifer Blaine was a student here from 1981 through 1985. A few allergies, a tendency toward bronchitis, slightly nearsighted. She scored high intellectually and very normally on the psychological tests we administered." He looked at another page. "The only times I ever saw her were for bronchitis, allergy shots, annual checkups, and a few stitches when she cut her arm on a broken glass. She graduated in '85. She had some scholarship money and was going to college up north. That's the last contact I had with her."

"Are you sure there was only one Jennifer Blaine?"

Dashwood nodded. "I have only one file. You said this note you found concerning her led you to believe that her alleged suicide was similar to Lenore Tynan's?"

"Yes."

"Perhaps the incident with the broken glass and the stitches turned into something it wasn't. Our students don't venture into town, though our teachers occasionally do, and maybe one said something that was misinterpreted." He smiled, turning his long-fingered hands palms-upward in helplessness. "As you are probably aware, St. Gertrude's has quite a reputation among the people in town, what with all the stories about our ghosts and gargoyles. These things are blown out of proportion sometimes."

"May I see the file?"

"Certainly." Dashwood handed it across the desk and John leafed through it, saw everything the physician had said, but no more. There was a photo of the girl. She was very pretty, with long, dark hair and a sweet smile. "May I borrow this, or get a copy from you?"

"If you wish, of course. Do you have any other questions I might help you with?"

"To your knowledge, have there been any other suicides here? Or suspicious deaths?"

Dashwood appeared to think about it. "Not in the years I've been here. I believe there have been a suicide or two and a few accidental deaths over the years, but none of them occurred during my tenure. The only reason I'm even aware of them is because of the ghost stories which probably stem from them."

"Would this be the same ghost that Lenore Tynan spoke to you about?"

"One of them, I would imagine. There are several ladies in white said to roam the main building, and there is one sometimes reported in the dormitory. But as I told you before, I believe Lenore Tynan had a potential substance abuse problem and she used the ghost story as an excuse to try to get me to prescribe tranquilizers."

"How long ago did these deaths occur?" John asked.

"The headless monk dates from St. Gertrude's days as a monastery, long before the sisters took over the abbey. Legend has it he was beheaded by his own order for being in league with the devil." Dashwood smiled and shook his head. "The good old days, yes, Sheriff?"

John nodded. "What about the female ghosts?"

"Well, there's one who's supposed to be a nun who was raped and murdered shortly after the abbey was reopened as St. Gertrude's in the later 1800s. As you might know, the place had been abandoned for many years, and legends grew during that time. As far as we know, that's when the gargoyle tales began. Between the imposing architecture of the abbey, its remoteness, and the fact that owls and other raucous night birds are indigenous to the area, it's not too surprising, I suppose."

"Seems reasonable. Can you tell me about any more recent deaths that might spawn the stories?"

"Very little. The nun is said to roam this building, as are two or three others. I believe those were all students who met early ends. One hanged herself in one of the classrooms, in the 1920s; another fell from a third-floor classroom window about ten years later."

"Murder?"

"Who knows? The only other ghost is the one Miss Tynan spoke of, the one roaming the dormitory. Its origins are unknown, but it's quite popular among the students. Frankly, Sheriff, I think it was created for fun."

"What do you mean, 'fun'?"

"Older girls love to frighten the younger ones. Longtime residents do the same to the newly arrived. Children can be quite cruel, as I'm sure you're aware."

"Yes." John started to rise. "Thank you, Doctor. I appreciate the time you've spent with me." His discomfort had grown under Dashwood's unwavering gaze, and now he glanced at his watch, eager to get away from the physician and St. Gruesome's. "If I can get that copy, I really need to head back into town."

"Of course."

"Doctor?" John asked, as he followed Dashwood into his outer office.

"Yes?" Dashwood had removed the clip from the papers on Jennifer Blaine and was feeding them into the Xerox machine.

He really wanted to ask about Sara Hawthorne, but stopped himself before the words escaped. "I appreciate your cooperation." He had a dozen more questions, but he didn't dare ask them, not until he spoke to Sara again. Though he told himself it was silly to wait, that the new teacher was probably not credible, he decided to follow his instincts and question her further first.

"You're welcome. If there's anything else I can help you with, please don't hesitate to ask." He handed John the copies.

"I'll be in touch," he replied, shaking Dashwood's extended hand. Though it was a good, firm handshake, he shivered involuntarily at the doctor's touch.

# Twenty-Seven

The rapping on her door awakened Sara slowly. She had a headache and her mouth tasted of sleep.

"Miss Hawthorne!"

"Yes?" she called, her voice raspy and thick. *What happened?* Her mind was in a fog, but the youthful voice sounded familiar. "Come in."

The door opened, and Kelly Reed slipped in, closing the door quietly behind her. Her shoulder-length red hair hid her face as she bent over her. "Are you all right?" she whispered.

Sara sat up slowly and rubbed her eyes. "I—I was having a nightmare." She tried to smile, but it turned into a wince. She rubbed her temples. "I'm glad you woke me up, Kelly."

The girl smiled at the sound of her name, then perched on the edge of the bed and pushed her hair from her eyes. "I heard Sister Regina tell Sister Bibi you passed out in the doctor's office. Are you sick?"

"My God, the exam," she said, her memory returning. Sister Regina trussing her up like a chicken, Dr. Dashwood releasing her, talking, examining. He had done a biopsy. That was all she could remember.

"What?"

"I guess I *did* pass out." She looked down at herself, saw she was dressed in her flannel nightgown, and vaguely remembered Regina helping her undress and get into bed. Kelly rose and stood back as Sara swung her legs off the bed and slowly, shakily, stood.

Kelly took her elbow when her knees started to buckle. "Maybe you should sit down."

"Maybe I should."

With Kelly's help, she crossed to the easy chair and collapsed into it. She'd had a nightmare, or maybe not; maybe it was a pleasant dream? Suddenly, she was more confused than ever.

"There are some Pepsis in the refrigerator. Why don't you get us each one?"

Kelly looked surprised. "Really?"

"Of course."

"The sisters don't let us have soda. If they find out, they'll punish me—and you."

"Well, we won't tell them, then, will we?" Sara's smile was genuine now. The girl, whom Mother Lucy had depicted as a troublemaker, was shy, awkward, and lanky, reminding Sara of a fawn. She was obviously a late bloomer and would one day, in the not-too-distant future, turn into a beautiful woman.

She watched as Kelly brought back the Pepsis. "Thanks," she said, taking the cold can and rolling it against her forehead before opening it.

"I'm not supposed to be here," Kelly said, sitting on a dinette chair and opening her can. "If they find me, I'm in big trouble." She held the can to her nose and sniffed, smiling with pleasure, before taking a tentative sip.

"Then we'll keep that a secret, too." Sara took a long pull on her can, swallowed, stifled a burp. "Mmmm."

Kelly's nose crinkled as she giggled. "Thank you for not telling on me before. You aren't like the other teachers."

"Because I'm not a nun?"

Kelly smiled. "Yeah, but I mean that you seem nice."

"Thank you for trusting me," Sara said carefully. "Is that why you're here?"

She nodded. "When you didn't show up at dinnertime, I sneaked out some food." She rose, crossed to the door, picked up a lumpy black sweater, carried it back to the table, then unwrapped it. "I couldn't bring much this way. Nothing that would spill."

"This is great." Sara smiled at Kelly. She'd brought an apple, an orange, and a banana, some slices of cheese, and several dark wheat bread rolls. Revived by the caffeine, she stood and crossed to the table, sat down on the other dinette chair.

"May I ask you a question, Kelly?" she asked, peeling the banana

"Sure."

"Were you trying to run away?"

"I think about it." Kelly looked at her hands. "I hate it here."

Sara nodded. "I understand."

"How could you?"

"I ran away, too, when I was a student here."

Kelly's eyes widened. "And you came back? On *purpose?*"

Sara nodded, her mouth full. She hadn't realized how hungry she was.

"Why?"

"Curiosity, I guess. Kelly, why do you hate this place?"

"The other girls, the nuns. I told you about the locket, and solitary." There were tears in her eyes, but a hardness, too, as she spoke.

"And you really feel that my warning the girls to leave you alone or talking to Mother Lucy would do more harm than good?"

"Please! Never tell!" She calmed herself with obvious effort. "They hate me. I know that sounds dumb, but it's true. Mother Lucy never believes me about anything. She always takes Marcia's side, and she'd love another reason to punish me."

Sara nodded, then peeled the orange and offered Kelly half. As she held the fruit out, she saw fear in the girl's eyes, then uncertainty. Finally, she reached tentatively for the orange, hesitating as if she expected Sara to snatch back the gift. *Who did this to you?* she wondered, her own emotions a mixture of anger and pity. Though she knew it was possible that the girl might be exaggerating her misery, Sara didn't think so; she'd been too unhappy herself to make such a judgment.

"Kelly?" she asked, when the girl had finished chewing a segment of orange. "I'd like to ask you about something."

"What?"

"I heard Marcia call you 'Ghost Girl.' Can you tell me why?"

Kelly flinched visibly and her fingers dug into the remaining piece of orange, squirting juice. "I—I'm sorry," she stammered, trying to wipe the table with her hand.

"It's okay," Sara said, reaching out and covering her hand

with her own. Kelly stared at it, rigid at first, then relaxing as Sara added, "If you don't want to talk about it, that's okay, too."

"I have . . . nightmares sometimes." The girl spoke haltingly. "And I wake up thinking there's a ghost in my room. I get so scared that I make noise and Marcia hears. It's happened a couple times. I know how stupid that sounds."

"Not at all," Sara said, the memory of her encounter in the showers coming back full force. She felt her hand trembling and removed it from Kelly's, embarrassed. Should she reassure the girl, or should she tell her about her own experience?

"It's dumb," Kelly said. "I'm dumb."

The comment made Sara's decision easier. "You're not dumb, Kelly. And you must keep this a secret, but I think I might have seen one last night, too."

Kelly's eyes widened. "Really?"

Sara nodded. "In the shower room. I heard someone say my name, but no one else was there, and then I saw a white figure in the steam from the water. I recognized the face. It was my roommate who died here." She decided it would be foolish to alarm Kelly with tales of water spigots turning themselves on and the ghost's face becoming demonic. "I keep telling myself it was my imagination, but—"

"Was your roommate Jenny Blaine?" Kelly interrupted, her eyes bright.

Sara nodded, a chill in her belly. "How do you know about Jenny?"

"Everybody knows she killed herself in my room, and that's who the ghost is. I looked her up in an old yearbook. Wow. You were really her roommate?"

Trembling harder, Sara nodded, unwilling to think that she was sharing more than imagination with Kelly. "Maybe we both imagined her because we both knew about her," she said lamely.

Kelly shook her head. "I didn't tell you everything. I hear her when I'm asleep. That's how I wake up. And that's when I *really* hear her, Miss Hawthorne. After I'm awake."

*Dear God.* Sara nodded slowly, knowing that if she tried to talk Kelly out of her belief, she'd not only retreat, but would know she was lying to her. "Jenny was my best friend," she said at last. "She was the best friend I ever had, and I know she'd never do anything to hurt you." She looked Kelly in the eye. "Jenny's probably just lonely. I'm sure she wouldn't want to frighten you." *Except what I saw—if I really saw it—wasn't Jenny. It was something pretending to be Jenny.* She shivered, tried to hide it.

"I guess I know that," Kelly told her. "Can I ask you something?"

"Of course."

"Why did she kill herself?"

Sara stared at Kelly, unwilling to tell her the truth.

Kelly seemed to sense her discomfort. "Did you come back here because of her? Because of how she died?"

"I wasn't there for her," Sara said, reciting the tale she'd concocted for Mother Lucy and the sisters. "I should have helped her with her problems and maybe she wouldn't have committed suici—"

"Please tell me the truth," Kelly said solemnly. Distance grew in her eyes.

"What makes you think I'm not?"

"I can tell. I can always tell. Nobody tells me the truth. You did, a little, but now you're not."

Sara gazed at the girl. Despite her youth, the look in her eyes was old and very wise. Or maybe she was just imagining it. Either way, she was losing her and knew that she didn't want that to happen. "Kelly, do you promise not to repeat anything I say to you?"

"Who would I tell?" she asked, then paused. "Yes, of course I promise. On my mother's grave." Her eyes glistened with tears as she spoke those last words.

"Kelly, I came back because Jenny Blaine was murdered. She didn't kill herself."

"Did you see it happen," she asked intently, "or do you just know?"

"I just know."

Kelly nodded. "That's what I thought."

"What do you mean?"

"I don't know, exactly, but I believe you. Who killed her?"

"I don't know." Sara sighed. "That's why I'm here, but that has to be our secret."

"Jenny Blaine died in my room," Kelly said thoughtfully. "And Miss Tynan tried to die in yours. It's kind of weird to think about, huh?"

"Yeah. Kind of weird."

# Twenty-Eight

Dressed in his most comfortable Levi's and a light blue chambray shirt, John Lawson sat at a small table nursing a beer in a dark corner of Winesap's Tavern. Mark was at the Addamses' for the night, and when John had entered his empty house, he realized that he didn't want to be there alone. The house, a modest but nice three-bedroom, the one not good enough for his ex-wife, seemed to be closing in around him, to be sucking the air from his lungs. Restless, he'd wolfed down a TV dinner, then drove his Nissan pick-up into town, half intending to drop in on Frank Cutter, but finding himself at Winesap's instead.

The jukebox was playing Garth Brooks, seemingly endlessly, and people were Friday-night noisy—drinking, playing darts, a few couples dancing nearby. From the opposite side of the dark barroom came the mildly annoying sound of a television set tuned to the fights, and every few seconds the men gathered around it roared alternately with pleasure and pain.

John wasn't interested in any of it; all he could think about was Sara Hawthorne, how ill she had looked in that brief moment he'd seen her in Dashwood's infirmary, and how it seemed more and more like she was nothing but a nut case, trying to create murders and conspiracies where none existed. That saddened him, because over the last twenty-four hours, he'd been thinking about her a good deal, about her pale skin and wings of dark hair brushing her shoulders, about her mysterious eyes with their searching gaze, and her voice, smoky-soft. He'd been attracted to her, and that was something rare. He'd stayed away from women after Barbara had left him because he'd felt betrayed. He'd never even realized she'd been carrying on with that lawyer until she had told him one night, her words grinding him into the earth with their disdain. That was the night she announced in venomous tones that she was leaving him for a better life with a better man, one capable of being more than a simpleminded town cop. It still hurt when he thought about it, still angered him if he allowed it.

He'd gone out on a few dates over the years, mostly blind dates arranged by well-meaning friends, and though he'd met a few women he'd liked, none had the spark he searched for. For some reason, the blind dates had always been Barbara clones, and whether or not it was warranted, he judged these women by their perfect hair and perfect clothing, by the expensive jewelry they wore. And, always, he backed off.

Part of the problem was that Moonfall was a family town. There were few single women to meet, and he just didn't have the heart to go barhopping in the city, or the time to join health clubs where single women roamed. The fact was, he thought, as he sipped the warming beer, he wasn't attracted to the kind of woman he'd meet in either place. He wanted a lover, yes, but more than that, he wanted a friend, one he could trust, one who would enjoy Mark's company, too.

He wanted too much and he didn't think he'd ever find a woman like that, but when Sara Hawthorne had walked into his office, he'd liked her unassuming but professional attire, liked the sincerity she exuded and the kindness he sensed, even while she was driving him to frustration with her insistence that, despite a complete lack of evidence, a murder had occurred a dozen years before. She was going to investigate it herself. *She's just another nut,* he thought regretfully. *Maybe even a dangerous one.*

"Want a fresh one?"

He looked up into the eyes of Marlene May's too-painted face. The barmaid, dressed in a skimpy red dress with white petticoats and a ruffly-edged crisscrossed bodice that squeezed and pushed up her ample cleavage until it looked more like a behind than a bosom, put her red-nailed hands on his glass and smiled at him.

"No, no, thanks. Not tonight."

"Nonsense. He'll have another," came Frank Cutter's voice. "Doctor's orders," he added, as he and Gus Lawson appeared from out the dark behind her. "Mind if we join you, John?" he asked, pulling out a chair before he could answer.

"No problem," John said, as his grandfather pulled up another chair and settled into it with a satisfied grunt. "We'll have whatever you've got on tap," Gus told Marlene. She tossed her bright platinum locks and smiled—Gus was a notoriously good tipper—then swept away John's stale beer and strutted her stuff toward the bar as the old man stared after her with unabashed appreciation. "My, my, I'll bet she's a handful." Gus winked at John. "Ever date her?"

"Not my type," John said. "Maybe *you* should ask her out."

"I just might, at that," his grandfather said, smiling as the object of his lust returned and set beers before them, careful to keep her cleavage in Gus's face. "I'll get it," he said, pulling a ten from his pocket. "Keep the change, darlin', and keep 'em coming."

"You bet, Gus." She planted a kiss on his forehead, leaving a red tattoo, then moved to the next table, an extra little wiggle in her walk.

Gus beamed after her for a long moment, then looked at John. "Didn't expect to see you here, Johnny."

"Mark's sleeping over at the Addamses'. House seemed kind of empty, you know?" John caught a glimpse of a man who looked like Richard Dashwood at the bar and wondered if it was really him. Winesap's seemed too déclassé for St. Gertrude's physician, but then again, there was little to choose from around here.

"If you got yourself a wife, you'd love him to go off on sleepovers," Gus told him with another wink.

"Let the boy alone," Cutter chided. He swallowed half his beer in one gulp. "He'll get around to it when he's ready."

Gus started to open his mouth, but Cutter wouldn't let him speak. "You find out anything about that alleged suicide?"

"Yeah. I went out to the abbey and talked to Dashwood," he said, trying in vain to spot the man at the bar again. It had been a brief, hazy view and John decided he must have been mistaken. "His records show the girl graduated and left for college up north. So there's no suicide report at all. It's missing because it didn't exist in the first place. Not a suicide, and certainly not a murder."

"But why would your Ms. Hawthorne make up something like that?"

"I think she believes it."

"Do you believe her?"

"How can I?"

"You have your doubts, that's obvious."

"When I went there today to see Dashwood, I saw her being led from the infirmary. Dashwood said she'd 'had too much excitement,' but she looked like she was in a daze to me."

"Drugged?"

John nodded. "Probably. Dashwood's nurse took her to her room. I didn't get to talk to her." He sipped his beer, enjoying the cold tang for the first time tonight. "She's supposed to come back to see me on Sunday. I'll be very interested in what she has to say." He paused. "The only thing that gives her any real credibility is the fact that Dashwood and Mother Lucy jumped all over me, wanting to know how I knew her name. I said she'd stopped at the office, asking for directions to the school. And I hope to hell that she says the same thing when they ask her."

"When," Gus said abruptly.

John raised his eyebrows. "When? What do you mean, 'when'?"

"I'm not sure what you boys are talking about," Gus said, wiping foam from his white mustache with the back of his hand. "But Johnny, you said 'when,' not 'if.' That tells me you expect this young woman to be questioned by those damnable nuns."

Surprised, John looked at his grandfather. "I hate to admit

it, but you're right. All the evidence—or lack of it—points one way, but my guts are going in the opposite direction." He quickly filled Gus in on the details about Sara Hawthorne and her story concerning the alleged murder-suicide.

"Johnny," Gus said when he'd heard it all, "are you attracted to this woman?"

John tried to hide his annoyance. "Don't you ever think about anything but sex?"

Gus stared him squarely in the eye. "Just answer the question." There wasn't a trace of amusement in his voice.

"She seems like a nice person, yes, but I don't see how that has anything to do with this—"

"It might affect your instincts."

John was all too aware of that. He took a long drink of beer.

"It'd sure as hell affect mine," Gus continued, motioning for Marlene May to fetch another round. The serious look returned to his face. "That's what's worrying you, isn't it, Johnny? Whether your instincts are working right or not."

John shrugged and finished his beer.

"Nothing to be ashamed of. Your dad talked to me about the same sort of thing. Before I retired, I had my share of confusion, just like every other preacher." A little twinkle came into his eye. "You'd be surprised at the number of confessions a minister hears, Johnny. A wife would come to me, tell me all about her husband's drinking and carousing, and the husband would come to me with the same stories about his wife. If I liked either one of them in particular, it could make it difficult to get a bearing on things."

"Did you?"

"Most of the time. You want to know how I did it?" He pulled out another ten, waving Cutter's proffered money away, then smiled at Marlene as she set down the fresh glasses. He got another lip tattoo and an eyeful as she walked away. "So," he said, after his eyes were back in place, "do you want to know?"

John resisted the urge to roll his eyes. He was starting to feel the alcohol, and that made it easier to smile at the old letch. "Sure. Tell me."

"I'd rely on my past experience, Johnny, and that's exactly what *you* should do."

It was anticlimactic, to say the least. "I realize that, Gus. That's why I'm inclined to believe Sara Hawthorne is delusional."

Gus shook his head. "You're talking about logic; I'm talking about experience."

Cutter, who'd been quietly sipping his beer and listening with a half smile on his face, cleared his throat. "You referring to the Tynan suicide, Gus?"

"No, I'm not. I'm talking about the night Greg died."

John's hand shook, splashing beer on the table's thick finish. "Cut it out, Gus, right now." He took a long pull of beer, making himself count silently to ten before speaking again, but it didn't help. "I told you I don't ever want to talk about any of that again." He stared across the tavern, refusing to make eye contact with his grandfather.

"You've got to hear about it, Johnny."

"Don't call me that, and I *don't* have to hear about it."

"John," Cutter said softly. "You were on the verge of panic the entire time we were at the abbey. Something happened to you there, and you have to remember what it was. If there's something to that young woman's story, her fate might rest on it."

Livid, John slowly turned his gaze on his grandfather. "You not only eavesdropped on us, God damn it, you told Frank." His voice low and controlled to suppress his gathering rage, he continued. "I trusted you. You eavesdropped, but at least you kept it secret all these years. What'd you do, tell Frank your story, then come looking for me to perform some sort of demented intervention?"

"He told me right after it happened, John, twenty-four years ago," Cutter said, in his best bedside voice. "Gus was very worried about you."

"Jesus Christ, Gus. Who else did you tell?"

"Only one other, Johnny—your father." There was regret in the old man's voice. "And he took it to his grave."

"His grave . . ." John bent, resting his hands on the table between the two older men. "What are you implying?"

Gus looked at his hands for a long time before turning his face toward John's. There were tears in his eyes, and for the first time John could see all of his eighty-some years in his face. "If I had kept my big mouth shut, you might still have him, Johnny."

"He was answering a prowler call in the Heights and got his head blown off," John said. "That's pretty cut-and-dried, isn't it?"

"But his killer was never caught," Cutter reminded him.

"There were no footprints, no fingerprints, no clues at all. The killer vanished," Gus said.

"And there was the matter of the call itself," Cutter added. "The people living in the house in question insisted they never phoned the station, never heard a thing before the gunshot."

John sat down slowly. "I'd forgotten."

"That's not surprising. It was a long time ago—you were just a kid, and what kid wants to think about such things?"

"The new sheriff decided that the only rational explanation was that some punk who had a grudge against your father set it up and took him out," Cutter explained.

"Yeah, I remember that now. Gus, that's when you started sleeping with that loaded shotgun by your bed."

His grandfather nodded. "I was afraid whoever got your dad would come after you, too."

"Why not you or Mom?"

"Because after I told your father about your conversations with your friends about St. Gertrude's, he went out there a number of times, asked a lot of questions. I think those damnable nuns were behind his death one way or another, just like you think they have something to do with your brother's drowning. John, if they thought you knew anything, they would have killed you, too."

"That's absurd," John said, without any conviction.

"Listen to your instincts, Johnny, before you judge."

"But they're nuns, for God's sake." He was desperate to

believe his own words. "Come on, Gus, nuns don't go around killing people."

"St. Gertrude's is a cursed place," Gus said, his eyes steady on John's, his voice taking on some of the righteous force he'd used in his sermons. "And I don't know what they are, but those nuns are no brides of Christ."

"Evil attracts evil," Frank Cutter said.

"You're a *doctor,* for Chrissake. How can you talk like that?" John shook his head. "The next thing I know, you two will be telling me that the gargoyles come to life at night and steal infants for Minerva Payne to make into soup."

"I'm a man of science," Cutter said solemnly, after he finished off his third beer. "I'd never say something like that."

"Neither would I, Johnny. This isn't a joke, and I think you know that."

"Then why didn't you two say anything before this?"

"Maybe I'm nothing but an old coward," Gus told him, "but I saw no reason to stir things up again. The way I see it, they got Greg, your dad, and the Buckman boy."

"Doug. He was a suicide." He watched silently as Marlene delivered another round. She looked at his barely touched beer, then at him, questioningly. "I've had plenty, thanks."

"I guess when you're the sheriff, you have to set an example," she pouted.

"Just leave it here, darlin'," Gus said. "When you're a retired preacher, you can drink all you want."

It amazed John how his grandfather could switch his mood instantly. All the more confused and depressed now, he wished he'd inherited the old man's gift. He'd realized that Doug's suicide had been related to that Halloween night, of course, but he always thought it was because Doug was the only one who couldn't cope with the confusion about what had happened that night. It hadn't even occurred to John that his leap off the bridge at the top of the falls—like Greg, he'd landed on sharp rocks below, crushing his skull—was anything but self-propelled. Maybe, he thought now, Doug had been forced off the bridge. Maybe his death was related to Greg's, and his father's, and even Lenore Tynan's. Maybe Sara Hawthorne was telling the truth about Jennifer Blaine. *But it's all too much. If I start believing something so absurd, pretty soon I'll start taking midnight flights on UFOs . . . or seeing gargoyles in the sky.*

"John?" Cutter asked. Across the table, Marlene finished wiping lipstick from Gus's forehead.

"Marlene," John said, snagging his jacket from the back of his chair.

"Change your mind about that beer?" she purred.

"No. When these two are done, call them a cab." He took a twenty from his wallet. "It's on me."

She smiled, tucked the bill in her cleavage, and wandered toward the bar.

"I'm going home now," he announced.

"The ramblings of old men," Gus mused, obviously drunk now. "Young men think they're foolish," he told Cutter, "but they'd be well advised to listen." He turned to John. "Sit down. Since we've traveled this far, it's time to tell you one more thing."

"Gus, if I stay for one more story, my brain's going to short-circuit. You can tell me tomorrow, when you're sober. Come by the station at noon. I'll order us a pizza. No beer."

Gus barely nodded, and no smile was forthcoming. "It's important. Mark might be in danger."

"Why?" His first thought was that because Mark was at the Addamses' house, he must be making plans to spy on the girls at St. Gruesome's and Gus knew about it.

"Every twenty-four years—" Gus began.

"Gus, please—tell me tomorrow." He sighed with relief. "Frank, do you know what he's talking about?"

"Haven't a clue."

"I'll bring the family tree," his grandfather told him. "And you'll see. You'll see."

"Sure. Goodnight, Gus, Frank."

After looking around the tavern once more and seeing no sign of Dashwood, he walked out into the dark. Shrugging on his jacket, he breathed in the night air. It was getting cold and he could smell autumn on the wind. The apples were coming in, and the leaves were turning to red and gold. Tourist season had already begun.

Woodsmoke rode by on a breeze, making him think of grinning jack-o'-lanterns, the smell of burnt pumpkin. His skin turned to gooseflesh and his whole body shook with a chill not related to the weather. Quickly he walked across the parking lot to his car and drove home.

# Twenty-Nine

"Will you boys turn that television down a little?" Winky Addams asked as he entered the family room where Mark, Corey, and Pete were sprawled out on their sleeping bags. Winky held a plate containing the last piece of mincemeat pie—donated by Mark—and he had a forkful of the disgusting glop suspended halfway between plate and mouth.

"Just five more minutes, Dad!" Corey pleaded. It's *The X-Files,* and it's almost over!"

"Okay," Addams said. "Five minutes."

The show ended, and Mark glanced at the doorway, saw that Corey's dad was still standing there, watching and finishing his pie. Mark caught his eye and grinned. "Good show, huh, Mr. Addams?"

Winky returned the smile. "Not too shabby. What's your dad think of it, being a lawman and all?"

"He doesn't like to watch spooky stuff."

Winky Addams got a faraway look on his face. "Time was, you couldn't keep him away from that sort of thing. He never missed the Haunt."

"Really?" Mark asked, surprised. "He never even goes with Gus and me." He paused. "But that's because he always works during the Haunt so that his deputies can go."

Winky Addams nodded. "That's nice of him. Say hi for me, will you, Mark? It's been a long time."

"Sure. He says hi to you, too."

"Now, turn down the volume and don't have too much fun,

guys." Saying goodnight to them, he left the room, and a moment later they heard his heavy footsteps on the stairs.

"Let's get back to work on the Haunt," Pete Parker said. He sat up and snagged the notebook they'd been using before *The X-Files* had begun.

The other two boys sat up on their sleeping bags. "Mark," said Corey.

"Huh?"

"I know why your dad won't go to the Haunt."

"I already said why."

Corey shook his blond head. "That's not the real reason. My dad told me, but he said not to tell."

"Then why are you?" Pete asked, tapping his pen impatiently against the spiral-bound notebook. "Let's get to work."

"Wait a minute," Mark said. "What'dya mean, Corey?"

Corey Addams leaned in conspiratorially. "Did you know my dad and your dad were best friends?"

"Nah—you're kidding." Mark paused. "Really?"

"Yeah. That's how come my dad knows why he's scared of Halloween."

Mark bristled. "My dad's not afraid of anything. Shit, he's the sheriff, and that makes him the bravest man in Moonfall."

"He's afraid of Halloween," Corey repeated earnestly.

"Take it back," Mark said softly. He'd known Corey since kindergarten, and the boy wasn't the type who teased. He was quiet and he didn't like fighting. "Or tell me what you mean," he added stiffly.

"My dad said that he and your dad and some other guys all went to the Haunt together, and after that, they came here for a sleepover. Right here in this room," he added in a meaningful whisper.

"So?" Mark asked, trying to hide his interest.

"They were sneaking out to go camping by Witch Falls and your dad's little brother showed up."

"Greg. I know all about him. He drowned." Mark hesitated as understanding dawned. "You mean that's the night he drowned? *Halloween?*"

"Yeah."

"I wonder why he didn't tell me that." Mark rubbed his chin. "I mean, he told me how bad he still feels about it and all, but he never said when it happened. I just figured it was summer, 'cause why would you want to camp at the Falls any other time?"

"Yeah, it's too cold," said Pete, his pen no longer drumming.

"I heard something else, too," Corey whispered.

"What?"

"Swear not to tell?"

"Swear," Mark and Pete repeated.

"I overheard my dad telling my mom about a nightmare he had," Corey told them. "It really shook him up. I mean, I heard this yell that woke me up. It was my dad, and I went to see if anything was wrong, and their door was almost closed, and the light was on, and my mom was telling him everything was all right, so I just waited a minute, and my dad said he'd had this dream, you know? A nightmare. Then I was afraid they'd hear me if I moved, so I just stood there and listened."

Mark almost said his dad had nightmares a lot, but stopped himself. "So, what'd he say?"

"He said he was dreaming about the night Greg died, and that they—my dad, your dad, and those other guys—*weren't* going camping. They went to St. Gruesome's instead, and they got caught. He said all those gargoyles were flying around just like in the stories."

Pete snorted. "Your dad's afraid of gargoyles?"

"Shit, no. It was just in the dream, and he didn't even say he was afraid."

"Finish the story," Mark hissed.

"Anyway, he said all this weird shit happened, some sexy stuff, but he didn't say what—"

"Your dad's afraid of sex?"

"Shut up, Pete," Mark said without taking his eyes off Corey.

"He said he dreamed that those nuns killed them."

"Killed who? Greg?"

"No. Killed my dad and your dad and the other guys, but they all came back to life except Greg. He stayed dead. The gargoyles ate him."

"Cripes," Mark said, disappointed. He didn't know what he'd expected to hear, but that wasn't it.

"What about the sex stuff?" Pete asked. "What'd he say about that?"

"Nothing much, just something about the nuns dancing around naked."

"Gross! Naked nuns!" Pete cried in a stage whisper.

"No naked schoolgirls?" Mark asked, his mood lightening rapidly.

"Not that he mentioned," Corey replied solemnly.

"Like he'd tell your mom about that!" Pete snickered.

Corey smiled at last. "Yeah, I guess. But I don't think he woulda yelled like that if there'd been girls in it."

"Old naked nuns'd be enough to make me scream," Mark said, trying not to giggle.

"How 'bout *young* naked nuns?" Pete asked, then clamped his hand over his mouth as a laughing fit took him.

"You guys know anybody who's ever been there?" Pete asked finally.

"My dad," Mark said proudly. "Because of that dead teacher in the pond,"

"Did she really commit suicide?" Corey asked.

"And was she really naked?" Pete chimed in.

"Yeah, I guess she did. And no, Parker, she wasn't naked."

"Would'jer dad have told you if she was?" Pete prodded.

Mark shrugged and let a stupid grin slide across his face. "You so hard up for sex that dead women turn you on?"

"Yeah," Pete said sarcastically. "I like 'em all bloated and rotten, same as Corey!"

It was hard to get Corey laughing, but once you did, he was like the Energizer Bunny—he just kept going and going and going. Now, he wrapped his arms around himself, falling on his side, shaking with barely contained giggles. "Cut it out," he managed, "or my dad'll hear."

"Worms," Mark said. "I like my women wormy."

"With lots of maggots and centipedes," Pete tossed in.

Laughter erupted and the descriptions of the perfect woman

descended below Beavis and Butthead levels until Corey's dad's voice echoed down the stairwell. "Lights out, boys."

"I told you guys to shut up," Corey sputtered, wiping tears from his eyes. He got up and flicked off the overhead light switch, then turned off the TV, leaving them in the dim yellow glow of a lamp on the end table. "They can't see this from upstairs," he whispered, "but we gotta keep quiet or they'll come down."

They sat quietly and worked on the Haunted Barn plans for a while. They were doing a mad doctor's lab and they came up with some great stuff involving severed heads that talked and jars full of fingers and ears and eyeballs. Just past midnight, they put the notebook down, doused the light, and crawled into their sleeping bags.

"So, you wanna tell ghost stories?" Pete whispered.

"Not the headless monk one," Corey said. "That's boring."

"And the gargoyle stuff is stupid," Mark added.

"What about the other ghosts at St. Gruesome's?" Pete asked.

"You mean that 'lady in white' crap?" Corey said. "That's bogus."

"Huh-uh. Caspar says she's real."

"How's he know?"

"He said that about a million years ago he was hiking around and he saw her. He thought she was real, and she ran away when he called after her. Later, he talked to your girlfriend, Lawson, and she said it was one of the ghosts from the school."

"I don't have a girlfriend," Mark said, somewhat regretfully.

"Yeah you do." Pete said in a goading voice. "You're doing the old witch, aren't ya?"

"Hell, no. She's like, older than God, but she knows all this great stuff. If you guys weren't such a pair of wusses, you could hear Minerva's stories, too."

"Min-nerr-va," Pete taunted. "He calls the old witch Min-nerr-va!"

"Yeah, well, she knows all about those nuns."

"What'd she say?" Corey asked.

"That they're evil."

"What else?"

Mark hadn't actually asked her much about the nuns or the abbey. He was mostly interested in the things she knew about herbs and roots. Mark, who loved his chemistry set above all else, thought of the old woman as a kind of chemist, but if he told Pete and Corey that, he'd never hear the end of it. He could just hear them: *Mark picked flowers with the old witch!*

*That's all I need!* "Why don't you come with me to see her and ask her about the nuns yourselves?"

"Yeah, like I wanna go hang around an *old lady*," Pete sneered.

"She gives me all kinds of great stuff. Tarts and pastries and stuff," Mark said. "For free."

"Yeah?" Pete asked, his voice slurring a little with oncoming sleep.

Mark knew he had redeemed himself. If he was visiting Minerva because she was a soft touch, that made it okay. He decided to stick with that.

"We gotta get up early to see Caspar," Pete murmured. I'm going to sleep now."

Mark lay in the dark a long time after he heard Pete and Corey's soft, regular breathing. Outside, a night bird screeched. The sound was chilling and he couldn't help but think of the old gargoyle stories. Steadfastly he turned his thoughts to his father, wondering if he was sound asleep or if he was having more nightmares.

Another screech resonated to the north, and Mark suddenly wished he were at home in his own bed, there in case his father needed him.

# Thirty

John had stayed home only briefly after leaving Winesap's Tavern, just long enough to undress, shower, and go to bed. Then he lay there wide awake, thinking about Gus's revelation about his father's death. After an hour, he'd dressed and gone down to the sheriff's office.

When he walked in, the night dispatcher, Bobby Hasse, looked up in surprise. "What are you doing here this time of night, John?" he asked, taking off his wire-rimmed glasses and wiping them with a Kleenex.

"Just wanted to look something up. Where's Thurman?"

"On rounds. He'll be back soon." Bobby put his glasses back on. Although he was over thirty, he had a baby-faced look that attracted women like cats to catnip. "Do you want me to call him for you?" His hand moved toward the radio.

"No. Just wondering." He knew his night man spent time in his office when he wasn't patrolling—he was an aspiring writer, and the quiet Moonfall nights gave him plenty of time to work at John's old IBM Selectric. Jeff was his best cop, and he had John's blessing; in fact, if he was in there writing, that would have given John an excuse to go home instead of read about his father's death. He was slightly disappointed because he dreaded looking at the file. "Quiet night?"

"One DUI. He's in the cell for the night. CHP will pick him up in the morning."

"It wasn't my grandfather, was it?"

Bobby smiled. "No. Some sonofabitch redneck from San Bernardino. Good thing Jeff spotted him, too. He had a rifle and hunting gear and a dead doe in his trunk."

John shook his head. There was no hunting allowed in tiny Moonfall County, but the drunk could easily have taken the deer in the San Bernardino Mountains, a hop, skip, and jump to the north. There would be no way to tell.

"He didn't have a hunting license," Hasse added, as he turned a page of the computer magazine he was reading.

"Good. Did Jeff write him up on that, too?"

Bobby Hasse smiled. "Sure as hell did."

"Good." He glanced at the computer by Bobby. Winged toasters flew lazily against a black background. The night dispatcher was the only reason they even had one—he loved and understood them and had nagged about being behind the times until the department bought one. John noticed a stack of files beside it. "What year are you up to?"

"Just input 1947," Hasse said. "I'll do '48 after lunch." He nodded at a paper sack on the other side of the desk.

"Have fun. I'll be in my office."

In his office, John saw a sheet of paper in the typewriter and a half-inch stack beside it. A little guiltily, he glanced at the top page, saw something about an alien invasion. Knowing Jeff, the aliens were extraterrestrial, not illegal, and it made him smile and wonder if he might lose Thurman to fame someday.

He went to the files and searched through 1973 until he found and extracted the report on Henry Lawson's death. At his desk, he read through it and found Gus had told him the entire story. There wasn't much, and there certainly was no tie to St. Gertrude's. The circumstantial evidence—that Henry had visited the abbey—wasn't even mentioned. He put the file back and looked through the '72 file on Greg's death, found nothing, then looked through everything between, hoping to find something on St. Gertrude's. It was in vain: if his father had been investigating the girls' home, he had left no notes about it.

John put his feet up on the desk, leaned back, and closed his eyes. *Rely on your past experience.* That's what Gus had said. Both he and Frank Cutter had seemed to be encouraging John's suspicions about St. Gertrude's. Gus, in particular, liked entertainment and wasn't above exaggerating to get a rise out of people, but John doubted that the old man would embroider on his own son's death. He, like Sara Hawthorne, might have convinced himself that his suspicions were correct—but what if both he and the young teacher were right?

John sighed, wondering why Gus had mentioned the family tree. *It's probably nothing.* Though his grandfather wasn't showing any signs of senility, he'd always been given to vagaries and this was probably one of them. Still, John thought, as he felt sleep coming on, the old man's words had held a disturbing ring of truth.

# Thirty-One

Midnight, and Minerva Payne sat by the warm wood stove in her kitchen, drinking a cup of tea. Nothing mysterious and herbal, just good old English Breakfast.

She'd gone to bed just after ten o'clock, slept soundly for two hours, then awakened with a start at the screeching of a nightflyer. Most people thought they were owls or hawks, but she knew better, and the raucous cries froze her blood as the thing flew in circles above her house for long minutes before flying off toward town.

*A portent.* Minerva had tied her warm robe around her waist and pulled on her slippers before going to the kitchen and stoking up the fire. *Time is running out.*

*But I'm tired, so tired.* In the old days, she'd had more enthusiasm and even her repeated failures to stop many of the deaths hadn't dampened her spirits. *You can't give up now; lives depend on it.* For the first time in many years she had two possible adepts: the orphan Kelly Reed, and Mark Lawson. All the Lawsons were, of course, capable of learning her arts, but until Mark, they'd lacked the desire. At one time, she thought Gus Lawson might come to her, but he was ultimately too involved in his own religion to be open to her beliefs and practices.

Kelly Reed was especially powerful; she routinely saw the ghosts and she had a great intuitive gift, but she was also very weak and unsure of herself. She was a rebel, too, and her constant rule-breaking at St. Gertrude's had kept her in trouble. When Minerva tried to talk to her about it, she hadn't gotten very far. Emotionally, Kelly was a typical adolescent—she thought she knew everything, and she wouldn't let Minerva or anyone else prevent her from doing what she wanted, whether it was making faces at the nuns behind their backs or sacrificing herself for some imagined cause. To make matters worse, she had an aura of darkness surrounding her that did not bode well for her continued well-being.

Mark, at least, hadn't entered the rebellious phase yet, but he was brave to the point of foolishness. *All children believe they're immortal.* She had seen in his eyes that he was driven by curiosity—like a cat, he was fearless if he wanted to find out about something. His fascination with the rumors about Minerva had first brought him into her shop, and she had quickly realized that a way to hook the boy was to dangle information under his nose. Mark was interested in formulas, from the one she used to make toffee, to the ingredients that went into making a poultice for a toothache. It didn't matter much to Mark what it was, though he had a predilection for the medicinals; he just had to *know.* It was his driving force.

She rose, bones creaking, and went to the shelves where her herbs and oils were stored. Selecting several, she took them to the table, then lit a squat beeswax candle and recited a short protection spell aimed at Mark Lawson and his father. As an afterthought, she recited one for herself. Then, taking a pinch each of rosemary and monkshood, she began slowly to crumble the fragrant herbs above the candle flame.

"John Lawson," she whispered, "hear me now, and hear me well. I am in your dreams, John. I *am* your dreams." The candle sputtered, then glowed more brightly. "You must come to me, John, you must come with open mind and open heart, or your only son is doomed."

The nightflyer was back, and she did her best to ignore its horrible cry. "See me, John, know me. Come to me before it is too late."

They're angry, she thought as the creature screeched again. She heard scrabbling on her roof and another cry echoed down her chimney. *I should have spread the salt again.* The evil at St. Gertrude's had grown in strength in the last few years, as it always did when the twenty-fourth year drew near, and it was even stronger, now that Halloween approached. It was the reason the salt she'd spread earlier was already losing its potency.

There was scratching on her roof as a second nightflyer

landed. A screech echoed down through her house, chilling her blood, giving her warning. Minerva, a solitary practitioner, had never been able to defeat Lucy and her demonic sisters, and as another screech filled the room, she questioned her powers more than ever before. *No! That's what Lucy wants. Believe in yourself, Minerva! You can do it. You* must *do it!*

She took a deep breath and began reciting her spell again. "Hear me, John Lawson. See me in your dreams and I will show you what you must know."

# Thirty-Two

Gus Lawson and Frank Cutter stayed at Winesap's getting, as they liked to say, shit-faced, until eleven-thirty in the evening, when pretty Marlene had suggested they'd had enough. Probably, thought Gus, that was because he'd tried to pat her ruffled bottom. She hadn't liked that.

It had taken half an hour for Moonfall's sole cab to show up at the tavern, and he and Frank had enjoyed the wait; although they often shared a beer or two, they hadn't had a buzz on like this for years. Gus was sitting alone in the back of the cab after Cutter was dropped at his modern house in the Heights, an area where all the streets curved and the houses had central air and heat and swimming pools.

Frank Cutter's house was nicer than Gus's, but it didn't have a spot of character, except for the den, which was full of mounted fish, photos of his deceased wife, Flora, and their children and grandchildren, books, and a Meerschaum pipe collection that Gus secretly coveted.

After John left, he and Frank had lightened up. Gus knew he'd upset his grandson, but wasn't really sorry: the youngster had spent his whole life mired in guilt about his brother, never suspecting that Gus himself felt the same way about Henry, John's father, Gus's son. Maybe he shouldn't have told John— he wouldn't have, if he hadn't been drinking—but now he was glad it had come out. Maybe the knowledge would help John finally come to grips with Greg's death.

And maybe he'd made things a little more dramatic than he should have, but deep in his heart, Gus really *did* feel that the women at St. Gertrude's had something to do with Henry's death and that the place was cursed. It was something an old Baptist shouldn't admit, and again, he wouldn't have if he hadn't been drinking. *Well, what's done is done.*

As the taxi turned onto his street, he realized that what was really bothering him was that he was a little worried about what John might do about it, especially after he showed him the family tree. *If I show it to him.* Probably it was all coincidence, he told himself, as the beer fog began to clear from his brain; but maybe, just maybe, he'd put his grandson in danger, just like he had his son. "You've got a big mouth, Gus Lawson."

"What'd you say?" the cabby asked.

"That's the place, there, two houses up," Gus said, pulling out the twenty Marlene had pressed on him right after he'd tried to pat her behind. He'd have to send some flowers tomorrow, otherwise she might never flirt with him again.

Taking his change, he walked carefully up the octagonal paving stones toward the house, fishing in his pants pocket for his keys. He thought he'd left the porch light on, but the place was dark, and if it hadn't been for the brief glint of headlights as the cab turned around, he'd have had to try key after key in the lock. "Thanks for the favor, Lord," he muttered, as he walked up the steps and across the wide front porch, the key ready.

As if in reply, one of those horrible night birds screeched above, flying close enough for him to hear the heavy beat of its wings.

Gus turned and gazed at the sky. He'd never seen the bird, but it was probably some sort of hawk, out looking for a stray poodle or something. *French cuisine.* He heard the cry again, farther away. Sometimes years went by without his hearing one of the damned things, but in other years, like this one, they were a frequent sound, especially this time of year. These were the birds that the gargoyle stories must have been based on;

when he and Caspar Parker were kids, they used to tell each other the stories about the gargoyles and the old witch in the woods—there'd been one then, as well. Minerva, he assumed, was the daughter of that reclusive old woman, and he knew she was the object of the same stories about the baby-stealing gargoyles. How birds of prey and missing dogs and chickens, not to mention the occasional torn and mutilated goat in the petting zoo, had transformed into gargoyles and stolen babies and a witch, he had no idea.

He heard one more cry, closer again, but didn't bother to look, instead quickly unlocking the front door, because you didn't buy beer, you rented it.

He stepped into the darkened house and pulled the door shut then flipped on a light, sniffing. There was an odd, mildewed odor in the room. *Now what?* Maybe Frank's newer house didn't have character, but it wasn't the pain this old relic was. *Probably the kitchen sink's backed up again.* Crinkling his nose, he walked through the darkened living room and up the short hall to the bathroom, where he turned on the light and relieved himself. As he turned on the faucet to wash his hands, he shivered, hearing the bird screech again; it sounded as if it were right outside the window. He turned off the tap and turned, trying to see through the privacy glass. He jumped as the cry repeated.

And then it stopped. *Stupid old man, acting like a scared kid.* He shook his head at his own foolishness.

Back in the living room, he flipped on the lights and the television but didn't sit down to catch the last of Leno because the mildew smell was still strong. He went into the kitchen and the stench was worse there. *Guess I was right about the clogged drain.*

He turned on the cold tap full blast and watched as the water swirled quickly down the drain. "Hmm." Next he walked into the laundry room just off the kitchen and lifted the washer lid, but there were no wet clothes festering within. Back in the kitchen, he checked the trashcan, but it was almost empty. He couldn't think of anything else to check; he'd left several windows open and whatever it was must have wafted in on the breeze. It was either dissipating now, or he was used to it, so he zapped a cup of instant coffee in the microwave and carried it into the living room and settled in his easy chair in front of his huge television.

Conan O'Brien was just sitting down at his desk. Though he'd never admit it to anyone, the upstart talk-show host and his coy sidekick amused the heck out of him and he was glad it was on: at eighty-four, he didn't require much sleep anymore.

He turned the sound up and settled back, sipping at his steaming coffee as Polly the NBC Peacock began trashing the other networks. It was Gus's favorite bit, and a moment later he was laughing aloud.

Suddenly, in syrupy slow motion, he heard a dull explosion and watched the hot coffee spill in his lap as something thunked into the back of his head. It didn't hurt, but the coffee did, and for a millisecond, that intrigued him. He felt his head jerk roughly and looked up to see the television screen just as a big chunk of something red and white hit the glass and stick. His vision flickered as red spots sprayed the screen and the chunk of white—*my head, that's a piece of my head!*—began to slip down the screen.

And then, there was nothing. Nothing at all.

# Thirty-Three

*"Let me in! Let me in!"*

*John could hear the old woman calling to him through the heavy closed door. She sounded worried, but still he was too afraid of her to let her in.*

*"Let me in! Let me in!"*

*"Not by the hair of my chinny-chin-chin!" he yelled, in a voice that trembled as much as his hands.*

*"You're no child anymore, John Lawson, don't talk like one!" Minerva Payne called back sternly. "You have to let me in!"*

*"No. Go away!"*

"You can't hide from your fears anymore. Your own child is in danger. Let me in!"

"What did you do to him?" he called, approaching the door.

"Nothing, you fool. But he'll die if you don't find enough ʌrage to let me in! I'm here to help you save him. Open the door!"

His hand clasped the doorknob. It was black iron and icy cold to the touch, frosted with cold. Startled, he jerked away, staring at it, at the heavy metal around it. Light shone through the old-fashioned keyhole just below the knob, blinding at first, then dimming, turning pink, then crimson, then turning to dark blood oozing through the lock, drizzling down the metal onto the heavy wood and down onto the floor, where more blood seeped in over the threshold.

"Open the door, John. It's the only way."

He was standing in a puddle of blood. "Oh, God," he whispered, as the cold of the doorknob seeped into his flesh, into his bones.

"It's the only way. You must let me in. You must listen to what I have to tell you. You have to save your son."

He looked at the blood that was seeping coldly into the soles of his shoes. She's never hurt me, he thought, and Mark likes her. There's nothing to be afraid of . . . except the blood . . . the blood.

It oozed up to his ankles now and it was going to fill his dark little house. Frantically he glanced around. No windows, no other doors, just this one that led to blood. And the old witch.

He swallowed his fear and tried to turn the knob. It wouldn't budge; it was frozen in place. "I can't do it!" he called.

"Yes, you can. Try harder."

He twisted with all his might, but it did no good. "Help me!" he called. "It won't turn."

"I can't help you until you open the door, John. You have to do that. Believe you can. Know you can, and you will!"

Blood oozed halfway up his shins as he grabbed the knob in both hands and put all his weight into turning it. The blood *was around his knees and rising fast. He'd drown in it if he couldn't open the door.*

*He got a fresh grip. "Whose blood is this?" he grunted, as he bore down on the knob.*

*"It's Lawson blood," Minerva called. "It's Moonfall blood."*

*The doorknob groaned and gave a fraction of an inch. The blood was up to his hips, his waist. He felt it like cold sludge, chilling his gut—climbing slowly, irrevocably, toward his heart—and he knew that it would drown his very soul. He yelled with effort and the doorknob turned another fraction of an inch. "Minerva?" he cried. "Minerva? Where are you?"*

"John?"

He came awake with a start, his legs jerking off the desk, pushing him back in the precariously tilted chair. He leapt to his feet as the wooden chair toppled behind him, and, breathing hard, came out of a crouch and looked up into Jeff Thurman's shocked face, then down at his own feet and legs. There was no blood, but he could still feel the chill.

"John? You all right?"

"Yeah. I had a whopper of a nightmare."

"I guess so."

John followed his deputy's gaze to his chair. It lay in a tumble of wood slats on the floor. "Well, it wasn't too comfortable, anyway," he said, aware that Thurman was staring at him again. He took a deep breath, willed his voice and hands to stop shaking. The clock on the wall said five-thirty . . . almost dawn. "How about helping me carry this out to the trash, Jeff? I'll go down to the city and buy a new one after the stores open."

"Sure. What were you doing here, anyway?" Thurman asked as he picked up the base and John gathered the slats.

"Couldn't sleep, so I thought I'd do a little work." He forced a smile. "Guess the sandman visited after all. I just wish he hadn't."

# Thirty-Three

Saturday had been lost to Sara. She spent the day resting in her room, sleeping, reading, and picking at the light meals the nuns brought her. There were no more ghostly visitations and her dreams were pleasant. At one point, Dr. Dashwood stopped by. For one brief moment, the sight of him made her anxious, but the panic quickly passed, especially when he gave her the news that the biopsy was negative and apologized for putting her through the procedure. After that, he listened to her heart and lungs and shined a penlight in her eyes, then declared that she would be fine before she knew it. The only "medicine" he'd brought were two chocolate truffles. When he gave them to her, his hand lingered on hers for a few seconds and his touch brought unexpected tingles of excitement.

By evening she felt rested and nearly went down for dinner, then decided against it, realizing that she should enjoy her last certain hours of peace and quiet. Also, until she went back to see if Sheriff Lawson had discovered anything about Jenny Blaine's death, she wanted to talk to the sisters as little as possible, just in case she slipped and unknowingly said something she shouldn't.

Today, Sunday morning, she awoke feeling completely herself, perhaps even a little better than usual. She'd overslept—her watch said it was nearly nine A.M.—but in the dark, windowless room, she'd at first thought it was early morning.

Taking a shower was an unnerving experience. No one else was in the lavatory, which ordinarily would have pleased her, but as she stood in a stall, shampooing her hair, she couldn't help wondering whether she'd really seen the ghost, or just imagined it in the steamy mist. If it had been a ghost, which she doubted now, it couldn't have been Jenny, not with the way its face had changed from a suggestion of her friend's into something horrible and demonic. Worried, she had hurried through her shower, but nothing had happened, nothing at all.

By the time she toweled herself dry, her confidence had grown. Vaguely she remembered how she'd gotten dizzy and lost consciousness during Dashwood's exam. Until then, she'd suspected she'd been drugged, but after the uneventful shower, she began to think that the doctor had been right when he later told her she'd simply had an anxiety attack brought on by all the stress of her arrival. And since he didn't have a clue as to just how much stress she was truly under, it seemed all the more plausible.

She had wrapped herself in her thick blue terrycloth robe and hurried back to her room, where she dressed casually in black jeans, a red turtleneck, and a houndstooth blazer. After slipping into her black penny loafers, she dried and brushed her hair and applied a trace of lipstick, then slung her purse over her shoulder and headed downstairs.

The dorm was relatively quiet, with only occasional voices of the students wafting softly from some of the open doors; no music was allowed in the rooms, nor were televisions, and then, as now, that made it seem like the sisters of St. Gertrude's wanted to keep their charges ignorant of the world outside the abbey.

The only adult she spied was Sister Bibiana, who was keeping tabs on the girls in their rooms. There were many, she realized, passing the open doors: evidently as few attended chapel services today as in her time. The nun glanced up as Sara opened one of the entry doors, so she waved and smiled and stepped outside before Bibi could stop her and ask where she was going.

Happily, she saw no one as she walked along the back of the school building toward the main entrance of the garage, but she could faintly hear eerie feminine voices singing some sort of mass inside the chapel. She peered toward the old stone building, her eyes drawn to the gargoyles perched like vultures on the corners and gables of the building. There was even one crouched atop the cross above the doors. She didn't remember ever noticing the oddly placed creature before, but then, she hadn't looked very often. On the occasions when she had studied them, they seemed to have multiplied. *Maybe there are more of them.* She was sure she'd have noticed the one on the cross.

*Or maybe you're just losing your mind.* She made herself look at the cross-sitting gargoyle again and for an instant thought she saw the stone head move, just a fraction of an inch. *Maybe you need more rest. You're seeing things again . . .*

Shaking off her fear, she turned briskly away from the chapel and walked across the perfect green lawn to the huge garage. She took her keys from her purse as she walked into the wide doorway of the old wooden building and headed for her car, parked in a stall halfway down.

Walking along the center of the old stable, she saw an aging but lustrous black Cadillac, a wood-sided station wagon, circa 1970, a Geo only a few years old, a black BMW, an ancient pickup truck, and a fairly new one. The stalls on the other side contained lawnmowers, both hand and riding, a small tractor, and a plethora of other gardening tools, fertilizers, and chemicals. She came to the stall where she'd parked the Sentra and stopped. It was still there, but there were several sacks of manure on the hood, plus a spade, two rakes, and a broom leaning against it and a Rototiller blocking it. "What the . . . ? Damn!"

She approached the sacks of manure and saw that one was leaking brown crumbs from a rip in the plastic. "Damn." She couldn't possibly move them herself and remain presentable. "Is anyone here?" she called, her voice echoing down the long dark building. "Anyone?"

No one replied, and she quickly walked to the far end of the garage, where light seeped in around a man-sized door. It opened and she walked outside. To the north was the school building, to the northeast, the kitchen and dormitory. Beyond the wide expanse of lawn in all other directions was the forest, dark and looming, held back by a manicured privet hedge. To her relief, a few hundred feet away, a handful of gardeners were manicuring the hedge with pruning shears.

Sara rapidly traversed the lawn. "Hello," she called as she approached the green-clad men. Several turned to eye her suspiciously, but one stared at her, then lay his shears down and walked forward to meet her, a smile growing on his round, cherubic face. "Sara?" he asked hesitantly, amazement in his eyes.

"Carlos!" she cried. How could she have forgotten Carlos Montoya, senior gardener, and one of her few friends? Memories flooded her as they hugged. She used to volunteer to do yardwork just so she'd have an excuse to talk to him. *What did we talk about?*

"How are you?" she asked, as they stepped apart and looked one another up and down. He was older and a little heavier, and there was a sadness in his eyes despite his smile.

"I'm fine, Sara. But what are you doing here?"

"You don't sound happy to see me," she responded, remembering now how he'd taught her to prune bushes and roses, how he'd told her stories of growing up in a farming family in Mexico. She'd loved those stories, the warmth and love they carried, and she had loved Carlos's calm assurances that she would have her own family some day. Had that been all? No. She smiled, remembering how he joked about the nuns with her. She'd loved that most of all.

"Of course I'm happy to see you, Sara." He removed a baseball cap and wiped sweat from his brow. His black hair was peppered with gray now. "But what are you doing here?"

"I'm a teacher. Starting tomorrow."

"But why *here?*"

"I applied."

His brow furrowed. "But why here?"

"Because of Jenny."

He studied her a long time. "Jenny. Jenny Blaine?"

She nodded.

"We can't talk here," he said, glancing toward the main buildings.

"In the garage?" she asked. "Someone piled fertilizer on my car and I need help moving it."

"On your car?" he asked. He scratched his head, then replaced the cap. "Go back inside. I'll be there in a minute."

He trotted toward the other gardeners and Sara returned to the garage, leaving the door ajar to let the sunlight in. In a moment Carlos joined her.

"Where's the car?"

"This way." She led him to the stall and he stared at it, rubbing his chin. "My boys all swore they didn't do this," he said, as he hefted a manure bag as if it weighed nothing. He repeated the process as Sara moved the long-handled tools.

"I was thinking," Sara began. "Maybe Basil-Bob did this?"

Carlos pushed the Rototiller out of the way before replying with a shrug. He glanced down the garage toward the big, open doors, then picked up the rake and hoe. "Just a minute," he said, then carried the implements with him, looking back and forth into all the stalls until he reached the big doors. There, he disappeared into the first stall, then reappeared without the gardening tools. He peered around just as carefully as he returned and joined Sara by her car. He leaned against the wooden half-wall beside her. "Be careful what you say, Sara. And where you say it."

"You mean what I said about Basil-Bob?"

"About many things. You shouldn't be here. It's not a good place."

"But you've worked here all these years. If it's so bad, why? There are other jobs."

"None that will pay as well all year long." He paused, then added darkly, "And the sisters did me a favor a long time ago."

She sensed he didn't want to elaborate. "But *why* should I leave?"

A rafter creaked and Carlos glanced around nervously. "You just should. It's not healthy, especially if you're thinking of digging up the past."

"Carlos," she began, "I went to see the sheriff, and he couldn't find a record of Jenny Blaine's death. I need a witness. Do you think you could go with me and tell the sheriff it happened? That she died? I need to give him some proof."

"I . . ." Montoya stared at her, his dark eyes tortured. "I can't, Sara, and you have to forget about it."

"Why? You know something happened to Jenny."

"She killed herself."

"No, she didn't. She was murdered."

"Who was murdered?" Basil-Bob Boullan appeared out of the shadows so suddenly that Sara jumped. Even in the shadows, she could see that Carlos Montoya's face had drained to chalky whiteness. Basil-Bob turned his grin on the gardener. "Who was murdered?"

"No—nobody," he stammered. "Miss Hawthorne was just asking about some of our ghost stories." He turned pleading eyes on Sara.

"That's right," she said, forcing herself to smile at the leering old man. "I love a good ghost story, don't you?"

"More than you might imagine," Basil-Bob replied smoothly.

"I've got to get back outside. Several of my men are new and I have to supervise them closely," Carlos announced.

"Thank you for clearing the things off the car for me."

"You're welcome." Carlos stepped forward, opened the Sentra's door for her, and waited while she got in. He stared at her until she realized he wanted her to start the car: he didn't want to leave her alone with Boullan, and gratefully she turned the key in the ignition. Carlos stepped back and she pulled forward a few feet.

"Where are you going?" Basil-Bob asked.

"Into town," she replied calmly. "To buy an alarm clock."

She pulled forward and headed slowly out of the garage, relieved when she saw a rectangle of light far behind her as Carlos opened the small door to return to his work. She didn't like to think of him alone with Boullan, either.

As she followed the dirt road behind the chapel and graveyard, she caught a flash of blue and white clothing and a glimpse of red hair disappearing into the woods beyond. Kelly Reed was on the loose again. *Good for you, kid. Just don't get caught . . .*

# Thirty-Four

John Lawson's new desk chair was an ergonomic work of art. Hidden in the black upholstered cushions were adjustable back supports and inflatable air bladders called "posterior regulators." There were levers and knobs to adjust everything from the armrest and seat height to the amount of bounce when one sat down and stood up. Best of all, John thought, as he plunked himself down after a long, long morning, this chair didn't threaten to tip over when he tilted it back to put his feet up.

He did just that. He'd come on duty at five in the morning and now it was going on eleven, and he was tired and hungry. He'd spent the first hour patrolling the town, which was something he liked to do at least once a day: he tried to see every detail from changing sale signs in the store windows to newspapers piling up in driveways. It gave him a sense of control and, more important, made him feel like he was earning his keep.

He'd cruised down Gus's street while it was still dark, only mildly concerned that his grandfather hadn't shown up for pizza the day before. That was nothing new, though; Gus was nothing if not mercurial.

Since the lights weren't on yet, John had decided to phone him later in the day, after church hours, since Gus, like as not, would attend. He kept his religion to himself, just as he had even when he ministered to others, but he was popular with the widows and they were popular with him.

Still, John had hesitated, idling the cruiser briefly in front of his grandfather's home before moving on, telling himself that Gus wouldn't take kindly to being disturbed at this hour of the morning, and that he'd exact his revenge by unmercifully accusing him of being a mother hen. The last time John had checked up on him, about three years ago, when he hadn't heard from him for over a week, he'd had to endure the old man's teasing for the next six months. Gus had never been one to necessarily show up where he said he would—except to deliver sermons before he retired—and he never apologized. He always said life was too short to stick to plans, and as annoying as his impetuousness was, John grudgingly admired it, the same way he admired Gus's gift for turning emotions on and off.

Though he'd never admit it, his granddad had probably stayed in, nursing a hangover, on Saturday, and he wasn't likely to show his face today, either, since the widows would be vying for his attention with roast chickens and beef stew. Come to think of it, John admired his way with women, too.

He stretched, enjoying the way the new chair moved with him. For a hundred dollars more, he could have had one with a built-in vibrator. He'd sat in it at the clerk's behest, but the vibrations against his back and buttocks were disconcerting and gave him nothing but an urge to urinate. Vibrating chairs, he had discovered, fell into the same category as computers, faxes and E-mail—he didn't trust *any* of them.

After returning to the office from his rounds, he had spent some time with Bobby at the dispatch desk, watching him input files and learning how to access them. He knew his phobic reactions were silly: it was easy, logical work, but it still made him anxious. What if the machine lost the information? Winter storms knocked out electricity all the time, and no matter how many times Bobby had told him about the battery backups, he absolutely insisted that none of the old police reports would be deep-sixed, and that every new one would be printed out immediately, so that nothing would be lost.

*Like the file on Jennifer Blaine?* He sat up, troubled by the thought. He'd already searched through the files again. He'd found nothing on Blaine, but he'd ended up reading over Doug Buckman's suicide report, reliving that awful moment when his father had come to him with the news of his friend's death.

Until this morning, he'd rarely allowed himself to think about Doug, but now he had to accept that Doug had never lost the conviction that they had gone to St. Gruesome's the night Greg had drowned. In truth, Buckman's insistence grew as the other boys' disbelief increased.

Although he was a big, outgoing jock on the surface, Doug

had had another side, a darker one that, in retrospect, might have been something born of a mystical, or at least philosophical, streak hidden under the bluff friendliness and broad shoulders.

*Or are you just finding reasons to turn Doug's suicide into another unsolved murder? Like Gus wants you to?* His grandfather's love of drama was one thing he'd inherited, but only in a passive way. John loved conspiracy theories and emotion-charged movies and secretly enjoyed gossip as much as anyone else who clandestinely read the *Weekly World News* headlines at the checkout counter. Because he was aware of this attraction, he tried to be especially skeptical, particularly of his own impressions, and let Gus do all the reveling in possibilities for the both of them.

He wondered now if Gus's inebriated confessions, especially about John's father's death, had combined with his own visits to the abbey and the appearance of Sara Hawthorne, both at his office and on Dashwood's arm in the infirmary, to stir up all those carefully imprisoned paranoias he harbored about St. Gertrude's and Greg's death.

With a sigh, he sat up and reached for the phone, deciding to call Gus and get the old man off his mind before going out to forage for lunch. He wanted something he could bring back to the office because, to be perfectly honest, he wanted to be around when—if—Sara Hawthorne returned. As his fingers closed around the handset, the intercom buzzed.

He punched the button, glad that Bobby Hasse was on duty, not Dorothy, who'd be in his face by now. "Yeah, Bobby?"

"There's a Miss Hawthorne here to see you, Sheriff. She says you're expecting her?"

"Yes," he said, unconsciously running his hand over his hair. "Send her in."

# Thirty-Five

"I didn't know it was so big," Pete Parker said in an awe-struck voice.

"Me, either." Corey Addams pressed his face against the bars of St. Gruesome's front gate. "Whatcha think, Lawson?" he asked, without turning around.

Mark stood a few feet back from the gate, staring past his friends, past the gargoyles leering from the gateposts and the vast swath of lawn, at the Gothic gray fortresses beyond. He could even make out the gargoyles crouched on the buildings, much larger than the ones on the gateposts. There were more of them than were needed to serve as waterspouts; many were obviously only decorative. Off to the right, he could even see one on top of the chapel.

"Wow!" he said finally.

"The gate's not locked," Pete said, his hand working the latch up and down.

"And there's nobody around," Corey added thoughtfully.

"So?" Mark asked. "You think they're not going to see us if we go in? There are windows everywhere." As if to underscore his words, from somewhere behind the buildings a lawn mower roared to life. "Just because we can't see them doesn't mean they can't see us."

Mark knew he should have seen this coming; Pete's sole purpose in life was to go where he wasn't supposed to, to do that which was forbidden. Mark got the creeps just looking at the abbey, and from the little his dad had said about his recent visits to the place, it wasn't worth risking getting grounded over.

The boys had gotten together at seven A.M. at the Parker Ranch and had worked on the Haunted Barn until Caspar, along with Pete's parents, had gone off to church at ten. They'd be gone until about two in the afternoon, since they always went out to eat after services. Usually, Pete had to go, too, but the boys had been careful to look very busy when Pete's mom had come out to the barn to take him away, and she'd relented to his pleading that they had to keep working if they were to have their portion of the barn ready for Halloween.

Yesterday, after the sleepover at Pete's, they'd talked more about how Caspar had seen the lady in white around the orchard, back near the edges of Witch Forest. One thing had led to another and today, as soon as the adults left, they'd set off on foot across the orchard, but had found nothing interesting, so they'd ventured into Witch Forest, pausing to take a quick peek at Minerva's house from behind the trees. Fortunately, neither Pete or Corey had the guts to pull any tricks on Minerva; instead, Pete announced that they should go to Witch Falls to see if there were any bloodstains on the rocks.

It was a beautiful day, with a cold nip of winter lurking behind the warmth of the few rays of sunlight that found their way between the tree limbs. They'd crossed the stream by Minerva's and kept walking, then hiked farther west than they should have to hit the Falls. Instead, they found themselves at the other fork, the one separating Witch Forest from St. Gruesome's land.

From somewhere to the southeast, came the roar of the Falls, but the ominous dark forest across the stream captivated them. They had looked at each other, then back at the forbidding woods, and at each other again.

They could see that the trees were thicker on the other side and there were only a few dapples of light on the forest floor. Moss grew more thickly on the tree trunks than in Witch Forest, and ferns had sprouted everywhere. Mark could see some odd gray ones whose fronds resembled cobwebs more than leaves, and he wanted to examine them, maybe even take a sample to Minerva, so when Pete suggested they ford the stream, Mark had readily agreed.

The abbey's woods not only looked different from Witch Forest, they felt different, too. In silent agreement, the boys moved quickly, Mark pausing only to snag a piece of fern and stuff it in his pocket. In the brief seconds that took, Corey and Pete got ahead of him and he had to run to catch up.

Although they didn't talk about it, Mark knew that the other two were hurrying for the same reason he was: he felt as if unseen eyes were watching him, as if the trees were leaning down to leer at him. This forest seemed alive in a very different way from the pleasant wood on the other side of the stream; this one felt like a living, breathing entity, a dark thing unto itself, with its own awareness. It seemed as if at any moment they would run into the lady in white—and she wouldn't be nice. Several times, they heard raucous screeches from airborne birds, but none of them had made any jokes about gargoyles. It didn't seem so funny on the dark side of the creek.

When they had finally seen daylight up ahead, Mark had been relieved, but when they'd stepped between some over-grown hedges onto a narrow gravel road and into the sunshine, he'd realized that St. Gruesome's buildings were the reason for the clearing. His stomach knotted. To his left, he'd caught his first glimpse of the chapel, feminine voices singing eerily within, and when Pete pointed right, indicating that he wanted them to follow the hedges and the wall that replaced it twenty yards south, he'd nodded yes.

And now here they were, at the gates. But why? To go in, as Pete suddenly wanted to do? Mark hadn't expected that, even from Pete. Corey, who pretty much did whatever the majority wanted, was looking pretty distressed as Pete kept wheedling and Mark finally just kept shaking his head no.

Finally, he looked at the sky, saw the autumn sun was no longer directly south of them now. "Look, Pete" he said, pointing. "It's gotta be at least one o'clock. Won't your parents have a cow if we aren't there when they get home?"

Pete studied the angle of the sun. "Yeah, I guess we'd better go." He cast a look at the forest, then peered down the lane that led to Apple Hill Road.

"We'd better go back the same way we came," Mark said. He nodded toward the lane. "It'd take forever to get home that way."

"You really think so?" Corey asked.

"Yeah, we came as the crow flies, so we'd better go back that way."

"More like as the gargoyles fly," Pete said wryly. "Okay, let's do it."

They walked back toward the chapel, then sprinted across the road just as the doors to the church opened amid a cacophony of bells. Pete dived into the brush, Corey on his heels. Mark hesitated only an instant, but it was long enough for a black-robed nun to step out of the chapel and see him.

"You, boy, come here," she called sternly.

"Move it, Lawson!" Pete yelled. "Getcher ass in here!"

Mark looked at the nun as she yelled at him again, then he jumped through the hedge, hearing cloth rip as his windbreaker caught on a branch. "Shit," he whispered, trying to get free, but the way it clung, the damn bush must've had claws.

"Young man!" The nun's voice was close now.

"Leave it, or we'll all be in deep shit!" Pete yelled over his shoulder as he sprinted into the woods. Corey looked like a deer caught in headlights, statue-still, his eyes darting between Mark and Pete.

Mark started pulling out of the blue jacket just as the nun arrived. As he yanked his arms from the sleeves, her face appeared, pinched and angry. "Boy," she said, in a voice crackling with cold, "Stop right there."

All Mark thought in the brief instant before he was free was that the nun had too many teeth. Even though she was small, she looked like she could chew him up and spit him out, then whittle his bones down to use as toothpicks.

"Let's go!" he cried, yanking Pete along with him. He could feel the nun's eyes boring into his back as they ran into the forest.

"Stop a minute," Corey breathed, after they were deep in the woods.

They'd gone farther than any habit-wearing nun could go, so Mark pulled up short. He turned to face Corey, who was bent over, breathing heavily. "You okay?" He was winded himself and his voice hitched over the words.

Corey straightened slowly. "Yeah. Jesus, did you see that nun? She looked like the Wicked Witch of the West."

"Yeah, Corey. I looked at her, and she looked at me. And

she's got my jacket. *Cripes.*" He dug in his pants pockets frantically. "My wallet was in the jacket. She'll call my dad. I'm sunk."

Corey was staring at him, his mouth not quite shut.

"Don't worry," Mark told him. "I'm not gonna rat on you."

"She heard Pete yell, so she knows there's more than one of us." Corey sat down on a rock.

Mark nodded, resigned to his fate. In the distance, the Falls roared. He looked around at the trees, feeling them close in on him, feeling those hidden eyes again. He turned his gaze to the forest floor in time to see a dim ray of sunlight angling across his Nikes suddenly wink out. Abruptly, wingbeats broke the silence, then a horrible screeching nearly burst his eardrums. The hawk or owl, or whatever it was, was gone in a heartbeat, its next cry sounding somewhere to the south.

"What the hell was that?" Corey asked, trying to joke, despite the tremble in his voice.

Mark forced a grin. "It's probably that old nun flying around looking for us."

"On her broomstick," Corey said nervously. "I'll bet Pete'll be sorry he's by himself when he hears that thing."

"Yeah." The thought was satisfying. From somewhere in the distance another cry sounded, but this time it seemed almost human, dissolving his satisfaction.

He was about to tell Corey their rest period was over when he heard a twig crack. Goosebumps pimpled his arms and neck as he looked at his friend and saw that he'd heard it, too.

He rose slowly as another bit of underbrush crunched. Footsteps. Mark could hear them clearly now. Quickly he stepped behind a large pine, then motioned Corey to get down behind the rock. Either Pete was getting ready to scare them, or the nun had followed them, after all.

The footsteps came closer, light and swift, the sound of someone walking very quickly. Cautiously he peered around the tree.

"Kelly!" he cried, recognizing the red-haired girl.

She about jumped out of her skin as Mark stepped out from

behind the tree and Corey stood up. "Mark! What are you doing here?"

"What are *you* doing here?" he countered.

"I was at Minerva's."

"We went to St. Gruesome's and this wicked-looking nun saw me," he told her. As he described the woman, Kelly's eyes widened.

"That wasn't just *any* nun," she told him. "That was Mother Lucy. She's awful. Does she know who you are?"

"His ID was in his jacket," Corey said, his voice doing an adolescent hitch.

"You're dead meat," Kelly said sympathetically. "Your father will beat you, for sure."

Mark stared at her. "No, he won't. He'll ground me forever, though." He wondered if Kelly's father used to hit her. Maybe the nuns did. He wanted to ask but didn't have the nerve, especially in front of Corey. "Hey," he said instead. "You didn't see another guy around here, did you? He took off ahead of us."

Kelly smiled knowingly. "You mean, he turned yellow and left you behind?"

Mark shrugged, but Corey nodded.

"No, I didn't see anybody. Sorry."

Wingbeats again filled the silence between them, and then came another screech, which was answered by one farther away. Kelly folded her arms around herself and looked up at the treetops. "I hate those things."

"I wonder what they are. Have you ever asked Minerva?"

She shook her head no, smiling awkwardly. "I'm afraid of what she might tell me."

"Yeah, I know what you mean." Mark tried to smile, too, and found out how hard it was.

"Well, I'd better get back." She took a few steps, then turned. "What's your jacket look like?"

"It's blue. Why?"

"And your wallet?"

"Black, the Velcro kind. Why?" he asked again.

"If I find it, I'll take it to Minerva's. Okay?"

"Don't get in trouble for me."

"I won't. 'Bye!" With that, she disappeared into the woods.

"Who was she?" Corey asked.

"One of the orphans. She's friends with Minerva."

"Is she your girlfriend?"

"Heck, no. I only met her once before. Let's go."

They began walking, too tired to run. Mark saw Corey repeatedly glance around as they made their way through the woods, which seemed to be growing darker despite the fact that it was only mid-afternoon.

Though he tried not to, Mark kept looking around, too. The oppressiveness of the place bore down on him, making his arms and legs feel heavy despite the adrenaline that continued to course through his system and the goosebumps prickling up the hairs on the back of his neck.

At last, they plodded through the cold water of the stream separating the dark woods from Witch Forest. Eager to leave St. Gruesome's property, they hadn't even discussed finding a narrow place to jump, or at least, one with a fallen log to walk or boulders to hop. The soggy shoes and pants were worth it because the moment Mark set foot on dry ground, everything seemed lighter, safer. One of the unseen hawks screeched in the distance, but even that didn't seem so ominous now.

"She likes you," Corey said, only the barest trace of nervousness left in his voice.

"Huh?"

"That girl with the red hair, she likes you."

"Come off it." Mark tried to shake some of the cold stream water from his shoes, but his feet still felt like they were squishing in slush.

"No, really, she does. She wouldn't try to get your wallet back for you if she didn't, would she?"

Mark shrugged. "She hates the nuns so much, I think she'd do anything to bug 'em." He looked around, then cupped his hands around his mouth. "Pete! Pete!" After a long pause, he turned toward St. Gruesome's forest and repeated the calls. No answer came. He turned east, then south, Corey adding his voice, but still there was no reply.

"Do you think something happened to him?"

Mark looked at his friend, saw real concern in his eyes. He felt it, too, but told himself he was overreacting. Pete Parker, of all the guys he knew, was probably the most capable of taking care of himself. "He's okay, Corey. He's probably watching us right now, *hoping* we'll worry about him." As he spoke, he realized he was angry with Parker for running off and leaving them on their own. "That really was a chickenshit stunt he pulled."

"Yeah, I know." Corey gave him a genuine grin. "Maybe we can get back at him at the Haunt."

"Yeah, we'll scare the piss out of him. Hey, you want to go see the waterfalls?"

Mark considered. "Heck, why not? Pete's the one who had to be home by two. He'll be there waiting and then he'll have to worry about us." Besides, he knew, it might be his last taste of freedom for a long while, once his dad found out he'd been caught by a nun while sneaking around the abbey.

They turned to follow the distant rumble of the Falls.

# Thirty-Six

"Nothing? There's *absolutely* nothing?"

John studied Sara Hawthorne's pale, earnest face and wished he could give her something, some tidbit of information, wished he could find some bit of proof that would let him put more faith in her story. "I'm sorry," he said simply. "I even had the county coroner check his records. He didn't find anything, either."

"Then you must think I'm out of my mind."

Her straight-on gaze had him trapped. "No, Ms. Hawthorne. But without some kind of proof, well, I trust you understand my position,"

"I . . . I know someone who could back up what I'm telling you," Sara told him in a slightly strangled voice.

"Who?"

"A groundskeeper. He was my friend when I was a student. He knew about Jenny. And he still works there. I spoke to him this morning."

"Are you talking about Basil Boullan?" John asked, surprised.

She shook her head bitterly. "Heavens, no. In fact, I think Boullan's one of the reasons my friend doesn't want to come forward." She paused. "He seemed to be afraid of him. He warned me to watch what I say and to be careful about who I talk to." She paused. "In fact, he told me I should pack up and leave."

"Your friend might be right," John agreed, though he didn't really want to. "Maybe you *should* leave."

"I'm not leaving." Sara tilted her chin up defiantly. "And, forgive me, Sheriff, but if you don't believe me, then why do you agree with him?"

"I didn't say I don't believe you. I said there's no record. No proof."

"Can't you demand to see Dr. Dashwood's records?"

"I saw them. Remember?"

She looked puzzled. "Remember *what?* What are you talking about?"

"I arrived just as Dashwood was helping you out of his infirmary," he said, slightly alarmed. "You looked very ill, but we exchanged hellos." She stared at him, and he added, "How are you feeling now? You're a little pale."

"I'm fine." She hesitated. "And of course I remember."

She was a terrible liar. "The doctor said you'd had too much excitement and he'd given you something for your nerves. Was that true?"

She blushed and looked down at her hands. "During his exam I got a little dizzy."

"Exam?"

She still couldn't look at him. "Yes. You know, a, ah, pre-employment physical."

"But did he give you something? A tranquilizer?" He knew she was covering something up.

"I—I don't remember." As she spoke, she finally met his

gaze, her cheeks still red. "He . . . he brought me chocolate truffles later." She blushed harder. "I mean, if he told you he gave me a tranquilizer, then I'm sure he did. That is, I really was exhausted. I even thought I saw . . . my eyes were playing tricks on me before I saw the doctor, and I was very anxious about being back there."

"What did you think you saw?"

"Nothing. It's stupid. It was just my imagination playing tricks on me." She drew herself up in the chair, her effort at self-control obvious. "But Jenny Blaine's death *wasn't* my imagination."

She looked ready to bolt, so he let it drop. "I get the impression that you trust Dr. Dashwood." The remark about the truffles was eating at him, but he didn't even want to admit it to himself.

"Yes. I suppose I trust him. I mean, he's nice."

"Nice?"

She lifted one eyebrow. "You don't like him, do you?"

"Well, I can see that he possesses a certain charm," he said carefully.

"Are you implying that I was swayed by his looks?"

"Is it possible?"

For a moment, he thought she was going to get angry, but when she spoke, her voice was soft. "I hate to admit it, but you might be right."

She spoke so matter-of-factly that he could only stare at her in astonishment.

"All the sisters start batting their eyelashes when he's around, and the girls, well, they're even worse. Her nose crinkled in amusement. "Why should I be immune to his charms?"

He suddenly wanted to believe Sara Hawthorne more than anything else in the world. He'd been attracted to her from the first moment they'd met, but now her unexpected frankness reeled him in.

"Sheriff?" she asked. "Did I say something wrong?"

*You said something right.* He shook his head and smiled at her. "Your honesty is refreshing."

She shrugged, a slight blush returning to her heart-shaped face. "Thanks . . . I think."

"Ms. Hawthorne," he said, before he could stop himself. "It's nearly one o'clock, and I'm starving. Can I take you to lunch? We'll continue our conversation, of course."

"Yes," she said solemnly. "That would be fine, Sheriff. But please, call me Sara."

"John," he told her, rising. He opened the door for her and was, to be as honest as Sara, a little disappointed that Bobby Hasse's shift had ended. It would have been nice for Bobby to see him with a woman for a change, instead of the other way around. Instead, there was Dorothy, reading *Fate Magazine* at the desk.

"I'll be out for about an hour, Dorothy."

She looked him and Sara up and down, a knowing smirk on her plump little face. "Are you two going to lunch?"

He almost didn't answer because the last thing he needed was Dorothy prying into his personal life, trying to create romances for him, giving him advice, watching his every move for clues about his emotional life. Then he decided to take Sara's lead and be frank. Maybe that would diffuse her interest. "Yes, we're going to lunch," he said, escorting the teacher to the door. "Is there a problem?" he added, pushing it open.

"No." His honesty had flustered Dorothy. "Have a nice time," she called, as the door closed behind them.

"What was that all about?" Sara asked, sliding into the passenger seat of the patrol car.

"Dorothy's been trying to fix me up for eight years." He swallowed hard. "Ever since my divorce." He turned the key in the ignition and the engine hummed to life. "There's a nice little café a few blocks away. All they make are burgers and fries, but there are about twenty different kinds, and they're all good."

"Sounds wonderful." She paused, locking her seat belt. "I don't mean to pry . . ."

"Pry away," he told her.

"Your divorce. You sound very bitter. Was it that bad?"

"The worst." He glanced at her. "Except that I have sole custody of my son. Have you been through one, too?"

"Not a divorce, but I was in a long-term relationship in

college that turned, well, weird. When I tried to break things off, Eric started phoning and sending me letters, threatening to commit suicide if I didn't go back to him.''

''How'd you handle it?''

''Well, first I developed an ulcer, but then I got angry. I called a suicide hotline and gave them his number, but that just made him worse. And that made my ulcer worse, which made me angrier at him.''

''Why did that make you angry?''

''Could you stand the idea that someone else had so much control over you that it affected your health?''

He shook his head. ''It took me years to get rid of the rage I felt toward Barbara for all the lying and cheating she did. For leaving me and Mark. Then I realized Barbara was all I thought about. I was practically possessed by her. I suddenly 'came to' one day while I was daydreaming about putting my hands around her neck and strangling her.'' He glanced at Sara. ''Strangling her! Can you imagine?''

''Yes, actually, I can. How did you turn off your anger?''

''I realized that she was still controlling my life. She was winning and I decided I wouldn't let that happen. I didn't want her to have the last laugh. So I exorcised her.''

''How?''

He smiled slightly. ''By chopping enough wood for several winters. With every stroke I envisioned the hate pouring out of me. I kept it up until it was all gone.''

''I thought you were going to say that you pictured her neck under the ax.''

He was taken aback for a moment. ''Well, maybe a little of that, too.'' He paused for a stop sign. ''You're the most straightforward person I've ever met.''

''Is that a compliment?'' she asked, a trace of uncertainty in her voice.

''Absolutely,'' he replied firmly.

''Thanks. Did it work? Chopping wood?''

''Except for the occasional bout of self-pity, it's worked great. And how did you exorcise your boyfriend?''

''The next time he called and threatened to kill himself, I

told him that if that's what he wanted to do, he should go ahead and do it. He sputtered, and I hung up."

"What happened?"

"Two weeks of hell. He didn't show up at school and I didn't hear from him. Every day I was sure I'd find out he'd committed suicide and left a letter blaming me for it. Then he returned to school, on the arm of the campus slut, and, well, before long, I was back eating all the catsup and pickles I wanted." She paused. "But I didn't have as much invested in Eric as you did in your ex."

"Maybe not, but I'm still impressed." He pulled into the small parking lot at Pippin's Café and parked. Assuming the story Sara had just told him was true, she had a lot of backbone and that somehow lent credibility to her tale about Jennifer Blaine. "It sounds to me like you're not especially easy to manipulate," he added, as they got out of the car.

"Thank you for thinking so." She smiled up at him as he held the café door open. "This place smells like heaven on earth."

His favorite booth was free, the one by the corner window that gave the best view of the town, so he led her there and handed her a menu. "Like I said, the food's great."

She consulted the menu, then put it aside. "Sheriff—"

"John," he reminded her.

"John." She tried to smile, but faltered. "The sisters are masters of manipulation."

"What do you mean?"

"I mean I think I've been manipulated." She picked up her napkin and twisted it back and forth. "I shouldn't even admit this to you, since I know my story's not very credible to begin with, but I'd prefer complete honesty."

"I'd prefer it, too." The waitress chose that moment to take their orders and he waited until she bustled away to speak again. "Please, continue. The nuns manipulated you in some way?"

"I think so." Her voice trembled slightly. "That's the problem: I can't be sure. There are huge hunks of my memory missing. I saw a therapist when I couldn't remember my schooldays, and she helped me get past the blocks as much as she could."

"Blocks?"

Sara nodded. "She said that my memory had been tampered with; that either I blocked out certain things myself, or that someone did it to me. She said it was probably the latter."

"How could she tell?"

"I let her hypnotize me." She gave him a small, twisted smile. "It wasn't easy to do. I *really* don't like to be manipulated."

"A fellow control freak."

She nodded. "Frankly, I have a hard time with the idea of hypnosis. Did you know that suggestions can be planted by the hypnotist accidentally?"

"I've heard that. Did you trust your therapist?"

"Yes," she said after a long pause. "Yes, I did. She wasn't the sort that was out to prove that everyone was an abused child. I don't think she had any hidden agendas."

"What was it that you remembered? Was it Jenny's death?"

"Yes and no. I already knew Jenny had died. I found her body. But, except for my nightmares, I had no reason to think she'd been murdered, even though I never believed she had committed suicide." She silenced while the waitress set their burger platters before them. Picking up a fry, she nibbled it thoughtfully. "Have you ever had dreams that seem to be trying to tell you something?"

*Have I ever.* "Yes," he said uneasily. "I think that's normal. Your subconscious is trying to tell you something, or you're working out frustrations. That's what dreams are for, aren't they?" He bit into his bacon-cheeseburger.

"Maybe. What about nightmares?"

"Have I had them?"

"Yes."

"Of course." He felt guilty about being so flippant with her, since he was fairly certain that what she was trying to tell him would hit very close to home, but he couldn't help it. He'd denied that there was any problem for so long that it was second nature now. "But nightmares are still just dreams." He took another bite and the food sank in his belly. He thought of Mark suddenly, uneasily. But he was safely at the Parkers'.

"Usually they're just dreams." She pointed a French fry at him. "But have you ever lost something or forgotten something and remembered it in a dream?"

"Car keys," he admitted. "But misplacing a set of keys isn't exactly the same thing as forgetting a major incident in your life."

"Maybe you're more willing to accept that you found your keys through a dream than something less tangible. Or less pleasant."

"Well, when I forget to call my grandfather for a week or so, I begin dreaming about him. A guilt-induced dream, to remind me." He chewed slowly, then swallowed, the food feeling like a hard lump in his throat. He wanted badly to admit to Sara that he knew exactly what she was talking about, that he, too, had missing time and nightmares that tried to fill it. But he couldn't—not and maintain any shred of authority. She was staring hard at him, not bothering to eat. "But I think I understand what you mean," he added uncomfortably. He was having a hard time concentrating; his son was on his mind now, as much as the topic of conversation. *You just want to avoid the subject.*

"I think you do," she said solemnly.

The silence between them lay heavily for a long moment, then Sara sipped her Coke and smiled. "So, tell me all about your son."

# Thirty-Seven

Now that they were safely in Witch Forest, Mark and Corey felt no need to hurry. In fact, they had begun purposely to dawdle so that Pete would be stuck explaining to his parents and Caspar why his friends had left him alone to work on the Haunt. He deserved to suffer that much, at least. Mark doubted anyone would find out that Pete was with them at St. Grue-

some's—he had no intention of ratting on either of his friends—
and maybe, just maybe, Kelly would be able to retrieve his
jacket and wallet and save his butt, too.

"We're almost there," Corey said, as they approached the
boundaries of the small park. "You want to go to the Mezzanine
or the bridge?"

"The Mezzanine," Mark told him, almost yelling to be heard
over the Falls. Corey nodded and the pair walked another hundred feet, coming to a steep fifty-foot incline.

The ground was soft and covered with pine needles, so Mark
took the lead, turning parallel to the slope and digging the sides
of his feet into the earth with each step. Behind him, Corey
did the same.

Mark, chilled without his jacket, relished the first splashes
of bright sunlight that hit his face as the trees thinned at the
bottom of the hill. The meadow lay just beyond the last stand
of trees, and as he approached it, a chill ran down his back.

"Why'dja stop?" Corey asked, bumping into him from
behind.

"I was just thinking about my dad's little brother." The thing
was, he hadn't been back to the Falls since Minerva had told
him about his uncle's death, and suddenly he was both excited
and scared about being here.

"Yeah, that's creepy—"

A raucous screech exploded so close that Mark clapped his
hands over his ears. He glanced at his friend and saw him
standing paralyzed, his face drained of blood. Mark put his
finger to his lips, indicating silence, when Corey opened his
mouth to speak.

The cry hadn't come from above, but from somewhere ahead
of them. Mark tried to peer between the trees, but they were
still too far from the clearing to see more than a few patches
of dry yellow grass. Looking down, he saw that the pine needles
were thinner.

He gave Corey another quiet sign, then crooked his finger,
gesturing for the other boy to follow him. Mark took one silent
step, then another. On the third, a twig snapped under his
sneaker and they stood still a long moment. Nothing happened.

Ten more steps brought them close to the meadow's edge. Mark stopped behind the thick trunk of a sycamore, Corey breathing down his neck. He was about to peek around the tree when another screech tore the air, shrill and ragged and horrible, far louder than the crash of the waterfall. Mark put his hands against the tree trunk to stop their trembling and nearly jumped out of his skin when Corey tapped his shoulder. "What?" he whispered, the sound utterly lost in the thunder of the Falls. "What?" he said again, this time bending toward Corey's ear.

"What is it?" Corey hissed back.

"I don't know." He swallowed hard. "But I think it's in the meadow. I'm gonna look."

To his surprise, Corey nodded. "Me, too."

Slowly, slowly, Mark, with Corey behind him, edged around the broad sycamore. He realized he was squinching his eyes shut and told himself to stop. *One. Two. Three.* He opened them just as a breeze came up, carrying a gentle spray of water droplets with it. Instead of refreshing, it shocked him.

At first he saw only the edge of the meadow, the dry fall grass, the tree stumps and boulders, and peripherally, the white water falling. Then he let his gaze crawl across the meadow until it stopped on the back of a huge black bird. Its lowered head moved back and forth, jerked slightly.

It was feeding, and briefly he looked away.

*Nightflyers* . . . that's what Minerva called them. She claimed she didn't know what they were, just some sort of hawk. But she also said they were evil and not to be spoken of, and Mark believed that meant she knew exactly what they were. Maybe not exactly, he amended; maybe she didn't know they flew in daylight as well.

He forced himself to look again. He could see the top of the head now and then as the creature ripped flesh from its prey. Suddenly he glimpsed a flash of black, then a dirty white sneaker, as the hawk yanked and tugged.

Corey screamed.

Instantly, Mark jumped back, but the other boy was blocking his way and he landed on his ass, knocking Corey down behind him. He scrambled to his feet, but before he could do anything else, the creature's head swiveled toward them.

Briefly, he saw the glint of predatory eyes set forward like an owl's, but with a deep reddish glow. He caught his breath at the sight of a piece of stringy red flesh held delicately in a long, hooked beak. It tilted its thick neck back and swallowed the meat, then glared at Mark. He could feel its eyes boring into his, knowing him, making sure it would recognize him.

The head swiveled again and the creature spread its wings, shiny charcoal. The feathers looked more like scales this far away, and there was a batlike arch to the wings.

Its screech was deafening, the flap of its wings loud and leathery. Barely off the ground, the thing turned gracefully and flew toward them. Without thinking, Mark turned and threw himself across Corey, flattening him.

In slow motion, he felt the wind of the wings, heard the cry, and felt white-hot pain on the back of his neck.

Then it was over.

"Mark! Is it gone?" Corey's voice was muffled against the pine needles and golden sycamore leaves.

"God," Mark rolled off Corey, put his hand to the back of his neck. "Ouch, shit." There was a half-inch crater missing at the nape of his neck. He brought his hand down and felt himself go numb at the amount of blood covering it, dripping from his fingertips. "You got a kerchief or something?" he asked, clamping his hand back over the wound.

Corey felt in his pockets, shook his head no, then pulled his jacket off, yanked his yellow t-shirt over his head and tossed it to Mark. "Will that help?" he asked, slipping the jacket back on.

"Yeah." Mark folded the soft shirt and clamped it over his neck. He looked at Corey, saw tears streaming down the boy's face, and perversely was glad, because it made him feel a trace of courage, and he needed that very badly right now. *Very* badly. He glanced at the meadow, at the blue material visible in the long grass. He forced a grin. "Think I should put a tourniquet around my neck?"

Corey gave him a sick smile, then his eyes moved to the meadow. "It's Pete, isn't it?"

Mark followed his gaze. "Probably." Suddenly, the nun having his ID seemed almost funny. "I guess we'd better go look."

"Yeah," Corey said, but he didn't move.

His emotions were gone, numb, dead, and Mark was grateful as he walked slowly into the clearing. With each step he saw more, the blood-spattered jeans, the dirty shoes, finally the glistening wet black jacket and bright red shirt. Only it wasn't red; it was really blue, and the long cord wasn't a piece of clothing, it was intestine, shiny in the sunlight. He forced himself to take the final steps, and then he saw the face. Pete's face. *But you knew that already, didn't you? So why are you doing this?* He couldn't stop staring at the open mouth, at the hollow black eye sockets.

"Mark."

He barely heard the voice, didn't respond.

"Mark Lawson."

Minerva's voice. Minerva's hands on his shoulders, turning him away from the body, turning him against her, holding him to her breast for a long minute, until he finally felt the hot tears running down his face, realized that his arms were around her and it was *her* hand holding the sodden t-shirt to his neck now. "Come away, now," she said softly, and began leading him out of the meadow.

"Corey?" he asked, as they walked into the woods toward her house.

"I sent him for your father and the doctor."

Mark stopped in his tracks. "My father?" he asked, barely comprehending. "The doctor? But Pete, he's . . ."

"Yes, I know, Mark. The doctor's for you. I wasn't sure how badly you were hurt . . . everything will be all right, Mark, but we have to take care of the bite."

"Bite?" he repeated, then looked up into the old woman's eyes. "I saw it, Minerva. I saw the nightflyer."

"And it saw you," she said, and hurried him toward her cottage.

# Thirty-Eight

Kelly Reed had successfully returned to St. Gertrude's after leaving Mark and his friend in the woods, but the screeching of the nightflyers had frightened her so much that she went straight to her room instead of checking to see if she could get into Mother Lucy's office to retrieve Mark's jacket and wallet. After twenty minutes of rest, she felt better, and taking her notebook and math book, she entered the main building.

As she expected, the halls were nearly empty—almost everyone would still be in the cafeteria at this hour. Quietly, she slipped into the library and settled in an alcove, then opened her book and stared at the meaningless numbers as she built up her nerve. After a moment, she glanced at the ornate old wall clock and saw that very soon, the girls and, more important, the nuns, would be roaming the campus in far greater numbers. She had to act *now*.

Her chair rattled as she stood and the nun in charge of the library, Sister Jerome, glanced up, a scowl on her face. Kelly smiled apologetically across the deserted room, then walked to the water fountain near the door and took a drink. As she straightened, she saw that the nun was still watching her. Swallowing her fear, she walked up to her desk and whispered, "I have to go back to my room for another book. May I leave my notebook here for a minute?"

The sister nodded curtly. Kelly, smiling politely, backed away and went out the door. The corridor was quiet as she turned the corner and approached Lucy's office door. She knocked and was relieved that there was no answer. Trying the knob, she found it unlocked, so she entered, walked through the waiting room, and rapped smartly on the door to Mother Lucy's private office. She hadn't even let herself think about what she'd say if the headmistress actually answered—she was better at instant improvisation than rehearsed speeches—but she still felt butterflies swarming in her stomach as she waited. She could feel the eyes of the tortured saints in the paintings watching her.

No one bade her enter. Gently she tried the knob and found it locked, as she'd expected. Taking her student ID card out of her pocket, she slipped it under the lock and worked it and the knob for a few seconds. It clicked open.

Sneaking away to see Minerva was one thing, but breaking into the headmistress's inner sanctum was another altogether, and as she stood there staring at the portraits, at the massive desk, smelling the chill, paper-dry air redolent of Lucy's stale cinnamon scent, the butterflies turned to nausea. *Get this over with!*

Her entire body trembled as she approached the desk. The portrait of St. Lucille seemed to watch her every move. She glanced at it, thinking that Mark's wallet might be in the desk, but the coat certainly wouldn't be. She was determined to get both items.

Turning, she saw an almost invisible closet between two tall oak file cabinets. Quickly she put her hand on the brass inset in the door and pushed. The door slid smoothly into the wall.

For a moment, she forgot her fear as she stared at the closet's contents. Front and center, there was a long black cloak, several habits, a black umbrella, and two pairs of—*quelle surprise*—black shoes. What shocked her was that one pair had six-inch stiletto heels. Kelly stared at them an instant longer, fascinated, tempted to try them on. Instead, she reminded herself of her mission and rifled through the clothes, checked the dark corners of the floor. Then, on tiptoe, she checked the top shelf and hit pay dirt: one sleeve of Mark's blue jacket was hanging out of a hatbox.

She lifted the round box down, surprised at its weight. Turning, she placed it on the edge of the desk, then gingerly lifted the lid. She pulled out the jacket and found the wallet still in the pocket. Smiling to herself over the thought of presenting Mark Lawson his belongings, she was about to replace the lid when she noticed the items below.

The box was half-filled with inexpensive beads and charm bracelets, rings, ribbons and barrettes, years' and years' worth of confiscated property. And in the middle of it all, right on top, her locket. With trembling fingers, she lifted it out and opened it, saw that the photo of her mother still rested inside. Snapping it shut, she opened the clasp and put it around her neck, slipping it beneath her shirt so no one would see it.

Kelly put the lid back on the box and replaced it in the closet, slid the door shut. Looking at Mark's windbreaker, she wished she'd brought a book bag to hide it in while she took it back to her room. Probably, she reassured herself, no one would notice it since the blue material was almost as dark as her uniform. She began folding it up.

"Well, well, well. What have we here?"

Kelly whirled to see Mother Lucy, arms crossed, beady eyes glaring, standing in the doorway. Her cheeks were flushed and she sounded slightly breathless.

"I . . . I . . ." She silenced. There was no way she could talk herself out of this one.

The Mother Superior whisked past her, snagging the jacket as she moved to her desk chair. She sat down and examined the coat, drew the wallet out, and opened it.

Kelly stood watching, stunned and afraid. Suddenly, it occurred to her that she might be able to run away. Minerva would help her, if she could make it to her cottage.

While Lucy was scrutinizing the ID card, Kelly bolted into the waiting room, running blindly for the door. She slammed into a body, felt strong hands dig into her shoulders. She looked up into the leering face of Basil-Bob Boullan.

"You going somewhere, missy?"

Without thinking, she brought her knee up into his groin.

Grunting in pain, he loosened his grasp, and as he doubled over, she tried to push past him to get to the door, but he threw himself against it and glared at her, eyes watering from her attack. "You're going to have to do better than that," he growled.

"Bring her back in here, Basil," Lucy's ice-cold voice ordered from the inner office.

"Yes, ma'am." Boullan rose to his full height, his face red and furious as he took Kelly's wrist and twisted her arm behind her. He marched her into Lucy's office, pulling her arm up until she thought her elbow would pop its socket. But Kelly managed to remain silent, eyes dry, determined that she wouldn't give either of them the satisfaction of seeing her fear and pain.

"Put her in the chair," the nun commanded.

Roughly, Boullan did her bidding, then stood behind Kelly, his fingers now pinching her shoulders.

"That will be all, Basil," Lucy said stiffly. "Please go into the waiting room and allow no one to disturb us."

"Yes, ma'am."

After he left, Lucy studied her, making Kelly feel like an amoeba under a microscope. "Why?" the nun asked.

"Why what?" Kelly snipped back.

"Why were you stealing this jacket?"

"It's not yours," Kelly said sullenly.

"Do you know this boy, this Mark Lawson?"

Kelly didn't answer.

"I assume you've lost your virginity to him. He came here to have sexual intercourse with you."

"No!"

"We'll see about that. I have no reason to believe you." She paused, her pinched face as harsh as her voice. "How did you meet this boy?"

"I don't know him."

"You're lying." The nun's voice was glacial now. "Where did you meet him?"

Kelly decided that the only thing she could do was refuse to answer, so she remained silent as Lucy asked question after question.

Finally, the nun twined her fingers together on the desk. Her knuckles were white, in spite of her calm exterior. "You will be punished, of course."

"Of course."

"Impertinence will only make things worse for you."

"So?" Kelly kept her eyes on the nun, trying not to flinch or look away.

"A week in solitary, for lying. If you decide to tell me about your relations with this Lawson boy by tomorrow, I'll shorten it to four days."

Kelly felt sick. A week in that horrible dark room would drive her insane, but she wasn't about to admit it.

"For stealing, after your confinement ends, you will be responsible for cleaning all the lavatories every day for the month of October. No one will help you. I'll personally inspect your work and each infraction, every hair in a sink or fingerprint on a light switch, will extend your sentence another day. Is that understood?"

Kelly nodded curtly.

"Basil," Lucy called.

The door opened almost instantly, and the creepy caretaker came in. "Yes, ma'am?"

"Take this girl to Dr. Dashwood. Tell him I want to know if she's lost her virginity and that I'll expect his report before the dinner hour. When he's finished with her, put her in the solitary room. Bread and water only."

The smarmy grin on Boullan's face made Kelly feel sicker. She had to get away somehow.

"Get up, Miss Reed, and go with Mr. Boullan," Lucy ordered. "Don't try anything, or solitary will be extended another week."

Silently, she rose and walked to the door, Basil-Bob's hand clutching her shoulder.

"Open the door," he ordered, after they'd crossed the waiting room.

She did, instantly coming face to face with Marcia Crowley and her snotty friends.

Marcia stared at her. "Get in trouble again, Ghost Girl?" she taunted. The others giggled, and behind her Basil-Bob chuckled, too.

His hand loosened for just an instant and Kelly saw her chance. She bolted for the front doors, ignoring Basil-Bob's outraged cries behind her.

She made the doors and slammed out of them, running down the stairs, slipping at the bottom, and going down on one knee. She could hear Boullan's running steps behind her, but she was instantly back on her feet, running across the lawn, running for the forest, knowing that with a little luck, she could lose him there.

# Thirty-Nine

"How did you get down there? It's so steep," Mark asked, trying not to cringe. He sat in a chair, his head lowered, as Minerva Payne stood over him, cleaning the wound on his neck not with herbs and poultices, but with plain old hydrogen peroxide. She daubed up the excess before it could drip, and it hurt like crazy.

"I have my ways," she said. "No, don't turn your head."

"What ways?" he persisted, determined to keep thinking about things other than Pete Parker's bloody, eyeless face.

"Magic."

"Really?"

"Don't turn your head. And no, not really. You know better than that, don't you?" She chuckled softly. "Do you think I hopped on my broom and flew down?"

"No, of course not."

"I came down the same way we came up. Do you remember?"

He tried to think, but the peroxide felt like those little scrubbing bubbles on the bathroom cleaner ad were eating his flesh, and he couldn't get the image out of his head. Between that and all the other images stumbling through his brain, he couldn't remember how he'd even ended up in Minerva's house. "I don't remember," he said at last.

"We walked to the end of the meadow and came up where it's not so steep. There, I think this is clean enough, and it's stopped bleeding. It looks worse than it is. I'm just going to tape some gauze over it."

"Thanks," he said. He raised his head when Minerva finished taping. "I don't need the doctor now."

"You should have a tetanus shot, Mark, and I think maybe

Dr. Cutter will want to sew it up. He might want you to take some antibiotics.''

Mark had no use for shots or pills, and he'd thought Minerva didn't, either. He turned to stare at her. ''But you're a healer. I thought you didn't believe in doctors. Or antibiotics.''

''Of course I believe in antibiotics.'' She smiled gently. ''The healers knew about them long before modern medical science came along. I could pack your wound with myrrh or maybe penicillin mold from bread. Would you like that better than taking Dr. Cutter's pills?''

''Better than a shot,'' he replied.

Minerva crossed to the stone fireplace and stoked the embers of a dying fire, then added some kindling and a small log from a brass basket on the hearth. The fire came back to life, and satisfied, she seated herself in her rocking chair.

''Not me,'' she said. ''I'll take the shot. Modern science may have its drawbacks, but it's also made some improvements on the natural medicinals. There are times, and this is one of them, when Dr. Cutter's methods are preferable to mine.''

''I doubt it,'' Mark grunted.

''Believe me, child, if I sewed that wound up, you'd be screaming. With Frank Cutter, you won't feel a thing.''

Mark shrugged. ''Yeah, I guess. But it's a big hole. How can he sew it up?''

''It feels bigger than it is,'' Minerva said bluntly, ''and there's plenty of skin to pull together.''

They sat quietly a few moments, then Mark broke the silence. ''How did you find us?''

''You might say that you called me to you.''

''Huh?''

''I sensed you. I've told you, Mark, you have the same gift in your blood. Your terror was difficult to ignore.''

''I don't get it.''

''Haven't you ever known the phone was about to ring? Or that maybe something was going to happen before it did?''

''Yeah, the phone, a lot. One day when I decided to play hookey, some kids got killed at school. And I knew about the last earthquake about half an hour before it happened, but nobody believed me.''

''*I* believe you. You and your father both have the ability, I've told you that. I possess the same talent, so I knew something was wrong. I decided to close the Gingerbread House early and come back to the house because I thought you might be here.''

''I was in the forest.''

She nodded. ''Yes. When I came closer, I realized that. Plus, I heard the nightflyer.''

''It's a dayflyer, too,'' he said sourly.

''Yes, I suppose it is, but very rarely. Only when the time has come.''

''I never know what you're talking about.''

Another gentle smile. ''It's a bad year for nightflyers.''

''When was the last bad year?''

''Nineteen seventy-two.'' She stared at him.

Suddenly, realization dawned. ''When my uncle was killed?''

Solemnly, she nodded. ''The cycle is twenty-four years. You'll have children the next time it happens like this, the next time they fly in daylight.''

''What are they?''

''A kind of night hawk.''

''Bullshit.''

Minerva's eyes opened wide a moment, then she laughed. ''Bullshit, indeed.''

Mark studied her, more surprised at her use of the word than his own. ''I saw its face.''

''I know.''

''Did you see it, too?''

''Over the years, I've glimpsed them occasionally, but never quite so well as you.''

''Did you see it today?''

''Briefly, as it took off.''

''It had a beak.''

''Some do, some don't.''

''Is it a bird?''

''It has wings—it must be, don't you think?''

"Bats have wings . . . and *rabies,*" he added, suddenly worried.

She nodded. "They do. But it's no bat."

"Gargoyles fly, too," he said, watching her closely.

"So they do," she agreed, her expression never changing. "So they do."

"Do you know what they say in town?"

Minerva smiled bitterly. "I think so, but tell me."

"That the gargoyles steal babies and bring them to you to bake into pies."

"Yes, I knew about that." She snorted softly. "An old enemy began that particular rumor."

"Who?"

"The headmistress at St. Gertrude's."

Mark's eyes widened now. "Mother Lucy?"

Minerva looked at him sharply. "How do you know her name?"

"Kelly told me." Suddenly, the entire story of his day began spilling out of him, and with every sentence he felt better.

# Forty

Sara didn't know what to make of John Lawson as she drove back down the tree-shrouded lane toward St. Gertrude's. Personally she liked him, and she knew the feeling was mutual; he'd asked her to go to dinner with him and wasn't put off when she couldn't set a date because she didn't know her schedule. He gave her his home phone number and suggested she call him when she could.

She thought he was shy, pleasant, and sincere, and when he talked about his son, his pride and love were obvious. Professionally, though, something was going on with the man that kept him from making any commitments regarding an investigation into Jenny Blaine's death. Maybe it was just caution—she could certainly understand his position—but she had a feeling there was more to it than that. There was a haunted quality to his questions and comments, and he had been agitated by their discussion of dreams and memories. And even though he didn't say anything, she thought he had something more on his mind as well.

She reached the abbey and slowed, taking the rutted left fork toward the garage, wondering how she should proceed with her investigation. Tomorrow, she'd begin teaching, and that would cut into her time, but it might be helpful as well. She hoped to make friends with some of the nuns—a hard task, to be sure, but she thought she might be able to get the loquacious Sister Bibi to talk about the old days.

"Damn!" Sara slammed on the brakes as a girl in blue darted out from between the bushes, right into her path. The car jerked to a halt as the girl fell before it. Thank God, there was no fateful *thunk*.

Sara jumped from the car. "Are you all right?"

"Yeah." The girl scrambled to her feet, pushed her red hair from her face. "Miss Hawthorne!"

"Kelly! What's going on?" She took in the skinned knees, the tearstained face.

"You've got to help me." Tears ran down her cheeks, making tracks in the dust. "They're going to put me in solitary. Mother Lucy has Mark Lawson's jacket and I tried to get it for him and she caught me."

"Mark Lawson? The sheriff's son?"

Kelly nodded, then looked over her shoulder, toward the bushes. "I have to get to Minerva's. Please say you didn't see me. *Please!* Minerva will let me stay with her. Just don't tell!"

"Who's Minerva?"

Suddenly Basil-Bob Boullan crashed through the bushes. "There you are, you little brat!"

"Ask Mark!" Kelly cried, as she started running for the woods—but she was too late. Boullan took a running leap and tackled her.

"Hey!" yelled Sara. "That's no way to treat a child!"

Boullan rose, holding Kelly's arm twisted behind her. "Take it up with the Mother Superior," he said, smirking at her. "She'll set you straight."

"Miss Hawthorne!" Kelly cried as Boullan propelled her toward the bushes.

"Don't worry, Kelly," she called after the girl. As she and Boullan disappeared through the hedges, Sara climbed back into the car. "I'll do something," she said softly. "I promise."

# Forty-One

*Poor Mark.* John Lawson hadn't been able to get his mind off his son during lunch with Sara Hawthorne, or after, back at the station, and now he knew why. Corey Addams, frantic and hysterical, had raced into the office less than twenty minutes after John had returned, and it had taken all his patience to calm the boy enough to get a garbled story out of him. Corey had insisted that Pete Parker had been killed by a giant bird which had also taken a bite out of Mark, who had been taken away by the old witch.

After he'd called Cutter and the paramedics, he set off for the Falls, Deputy Griffin trailing in his own cruiser with the doctor. John hadn't known what to expect concerning his son, so he sent Griffin and Cutter to the Mezzanine, where Corey said the Parker boy's body was located, then led the ambulance crew as far down the dirt road to Minerva Payne's as possible. They had come the last eighth of a mile on foot, the two paramedics towing along a stretcher while John, too anxious to wait for them, trotted ahead.

When he arrived at the cottage, Mark himself opened the door. He was pale and had a bandage on the back of his neck, but he threw his arms around his father and clung to him so tightly that John knew he'd be fine. The paramedics arrived a moment later and inspected the wound, confirming what John already knew. He questioned Mark briefly and gently, then sent him along with the med techs to Frank Cutter's office to await the doctor's return.

Now he sat opposite Minerva Payne, sipping hot tea as if nothing unusual had happened . . . but it had. Wyn Griffin had let him know by cell phone that Pete Parker was very, very dead, evidently the victim of an animal attack. Frank Cutter had already left the scene to take care of Mark before the other boy's body arrived for examination.

"More tea?" Minerva asked, as he set his cup down on the gleaming oak dining table.

"Yes, please." He was cold despite the cozy warmth of the cottage. He watched as the old woman poured tea from a delicate porcelain pot, her hands steadier than his own.

She poured more for herself, then replaced the teapot on a woven trivet. "You have a fine son," she said gently. "He's special, you know."

John shook his head. "I'm surprised at his behavior, though. Sneaking around the abbey, then going to the Falls." He paused, studying Minerva. Despite himself, he liked her and understood why his son thought so highly of her. "He said you told him about my brother, and that you warned him to stay away from the Falls. I thought you'd made a huge impression on him."

"Perhaps, for a little while, but children believe they're immortal," Minerva told him. "And of course, no boy can resist an adventure, not even one like Mark. If it helps, I don't think he wanted to go to St. Gertrude's, but the other boys would have called him a coward if he'd refused. I'm sure you understand that."

"I understand it all too well."

"Don't be too hard on him, Sheriff."

"He's suffered enough," John replied, and meant it. "Finding a body, especially that of someone you're close to, well, no one should have to go through such an ordeal. I'm just glad . . ." Embarrassed, he let his words trail off.

"You're glad it wasn't your son who was killed," Minerva finished.

"The Parkers will be devastated," John said, more to himself than to Minerva. He felt selfish, first, for being relieved that it was Pete who'd been killed, not Mark, and second, for dreading the house call he would have to make later today. He cleared his throat. "How did you happen to be at the scene, Ms. Payne?"

"Minerva," she corrected. "I closed my shop early. I heard the nightflyers screeching—"

"Nightflyers?"

"The creatures that killed Pete Parker."

"You've lived in this forest most of your life. Have you ever seen them? Are they some kind of hawk?"

"I've seen them only from a distance. And I don't know what they are. Night hawks, or some other bird, or creatures of myth and superstition, I wish I knew. They don't come from this forest, though, Sheriff. Look to the woods on the other side of the west fork of Moonfall Creek for their home."

"You mean they live on St. Gertrude's land?"

Minerva nodded. "So far as I know." She gave him a small, sly smile. "The nuns probably keep them as pets, don't you think?"

"I wouldn't be surprised." He inhaled the rich, clean aroma of the tea and took a sip. "You heard the birds, and that worried you enough to close your shop on a Sunday?" That was odd behavior for any shopkeeper.

"Not by itself, but I couldn't get your son off my mind. The two seemed connected. So I followed my instincts."

Since he'd been worrying about Mark for no apparent reason, he couldn't argue about intuition. "Connected? How could they be connected?"

"I don't know. I only feel these things, just as you do. As your son does."

"What are you saying?"

"You're an excellent sheriff, like your father before you, and that's because you are *aware.*"

"Aware of what?"

"Most people have only a little intuition and rarely pay it any attention." She chuckled. "Those who have it a little stronger call it either good luck or bad luck, depending on how they use it. But you, like Mark, and your father and grandfather, and his father before him, have inherited it to a very high degree."

"I don't think so."

"Can you deny you were worrying about Mark before you knew anything had happened to him?"

He had no answer. "Did you know my father?" he asked instead.

"Not as well as I'd have liked. Like you, he was afraid of me. Afraid of what I represent."

"What the—what are you talking about?"

"You've been afraid of me since the moment you saw me watching you from the bridge the day your brother died." She hesitated. "If I had forced your father to listen to me, we might have stopped it then. Now it's happening again."

"What's happening?" *She's senile* . . .

"The cycle." She cocked one eyebrow. "And I know what you're thinking."

"Telepathy, huh?" he asked, disappointed that this woman, who seemed so fascinating, was probably losing her mind.

"No, John, not telepathy. Logic."

He looked up, surprised at his name and her crisp answer.

"You think I've lost my marbles, don't you?"

He started to shake his head.

"Don't you?"

Her bright eyes trapped him and wouldn't let him go. "Well . . ."

"It's all right, I don't blame you. That's why I'm not going to explain about the cycle. I want you to look at it in black and white. Do you have a copy of your family tree?"

"What?" he asked, surprised that she would bring this up on the heels of Gus's similar statement.

"Surely you have a copy of your family tree. One that goes back to Tobias, the first Lawson to settle here."

"My grandfather does. He mentioned it the other night, said he wanted me to take a look at it for some obscure reason."

"Gus doesn't believe, but he *knows*. Look at it, John," she said urgently. "And look at it soon. Then come back and see me. It's important to your son's safety. And your own."

"What are you saying?"

"You'll see it in the blood if you look hard enough . . . if you open your mind to the possibility that coincidences aren't always flukes, but are vectors waiting to happen. Or be prevented. It all depends on how well you listen to your inner voice. How many possibilities you allow yourself to consider. Never forget that history repeats itself."

"Minerva," he said, again at a loss for an answer. "Why are you so interested in my son?"

"You'll see that in your tree as well. If you look for it. If you can accept it. And it will explain why you shouldn't feel guilty about your brother, either. It was a vector that no one could stop. I tried to tell you about Gregory in your dreams the other night, but you wouldn't let me in. Listen to me. You can stop it this time, John. *You can stop it.*"

"You were the one who found Lenore Tynan, aren't you?" He didn't know why he said it, but he felt it was true.

"Yes, but I'm admitting that only to convince you to listen to your intuition."

"Why did you claim it wasn't you?"

"There are enough rumors about me as it is. That those nightflyers bring me babies, that I cast spells. That I'm a witch."

"Are you?" Another unplanned question, but he forged ahead. "A witch, I mean?"

"If that's what you choose to call me. I prefer the term 'healer.'" She smiled softly. " 'Witch' has such negative connotations. These days, people think it means a satanist, but it doesn't. To be a satanist, you first have to be a Christian."

"You're an athiest?"

She laughed. "Not at all. There's a bit of God in all of us, in every creature and every tree. An athiest believes there is no god as strongly as a Christian believes God requires one to be Christian."

"Gus is Christian, but he doesn't believe that."

She nodded. "Gus is a wise man. Gus is Christian for the same reason that other open-minded people are—it's the religion of this land. What do you believe, John?"

"I've never had much use for church." He felt himself blush. "I think God is a personal thing. I guess I feel closest to God, or whatever it is, when I'm out fly fishing. That probably sounds ludicrous, but—"

"Not at all. You commune with God through nature, as I do. It's not surprising. Who taught you fly fishing?"

"Gus." He paused, then felt himself smile. "He says it's good for the soul."

"You see? It's all in the interpretation."

"Do you cast spells?" he asked, uncomfortable talking about his beliefs, or lack of them, with the old woman.

"And dance by the light of the moon, or fly on my broom?" She shook her head. "No flying, but my husband and I used to dance in the moonlight." A coy smile let him see the young woman she once was. "Waltzes. Strauss, not Liszt, I assure you."

"Your husband? I didn't know you were ever married."

"He died a very, very long time ago."

"I'm sorry."

"Yes, but he had a good life. We had good children."

"Where are your children now?"

"All gone."

"I—I'm sorry. I didn't mean to pry." He could feel the heat in his face. "I have no business asking you questions like that."

"It's perfectly all right. My children are gone now, but some of their children are still alive."

"Do they ever visit?" Ever since his childhood, he'd thought of Minerva as the old witch in the woods, without husband or children, and though it was childish of him, the knowledge that he'd been wrong, that everyone he knew had been wrong about her, fascinated him.

"Sometimes they visit. Not often."

"Did one of them call in about Lenore Tynan for you?"

"No," she said, disappointment on her face.

"Who, then?"

Minerva closed her eyes and sat up straight, and John wondered if she was having some sort of seizure. Then she spoke in the voice of a young woman. "I don't fly my broom, young man, but I do have a few little tricks."

She opened her eyes and smiled. John realized that his mouth was open. He snapped it shut then, in spite of himself, smiled. "That was amazing."

"Thank you."

"How did you do it?"

"Magic." Her smile broadened.

The grandfather clock began chiming six o'clock and John looked up in surprise. It felt like only a half hour had passed since Mark had left with the paramedics, but he'd been talking with Minerva Payne for nearly four times that. He rose and walked to the door. Minerva joined him.

"Will you check your family tree?"

"You and Gus both think it's important," he said lightly. "So I guess I'd better."

"Gus is a smart man. Give him my best when you see him." She paused." There's something . . . I don't know what, but talk to him soon."

"I will. And thanks for seeing to Mark." Uneasily, he realized it was growing dark. "I'll be in touch."

"Just stay on the path and you'll be fine," Minerva said, as she put her hand in the pocket of her long skirt. "There's nothing to trip on." She brought out a thin leather cord with a small brown cloth ball attached to it. "Take this."

Dubiously, he held out his hand. It looked something like a native medicine bag. "For Mark?"

"For you," she said. "Mark already wears one."

"Wears one? What is it?" He sniffed it, smelled a heady mixture of herbs.

"It's a protective amulet," she said lightly. "Humor an old lady, Sheriff, and keep it with you. It will help keep the darkness from your path."

He nodded, smiling tightly, and put the charm in his breast pocket. "Okay. Thanks." He started down the path, dreading backing the cruiser out of the forest in the dark almost as much as he dreaded delivering the bad news to the Parker clan.

# Forty-Two

Sara had gone straight to the Mother Superior's office after she'd parked her car with its nose slightly out of the stall to remind the gardeners—or Basil-Bob Boullan, more likely—not to block it with manure and tools again.

Mother Lucy received her cordially enough, but she was intractable on the subject of Kelly Reed. The nun explained that Kelly had broken into her office and been caught stealing. She was, claimed Lucy, truculent, her only regret that she'd been caught in the act. On top of that, the girl had attacked Basil-Bob, when he'd attempted to escort her to the punishment room, and run away. "Do you expect me to congratulate her instead of punish her, Miss Hawthorne?" Lucy had asked archly.

"No, no, of course not. But isn't a week in solitary confinement abusive?"

"No, of course it isn't. Were you never put in solitary during your time here as a student?"

"No."

"Well, then, you were unusually well behaved. The solitary room is at least as comfortable as your own room. She'll be brought three good meals a day and all her study material. She is simply being kept away from her friends."

"I'd like to see her."

"She's allowed no visitors."

"But I'm one of her teachers. Surely I'll be allowed to speak to her about her lessons."

"No. You'll give your lessons to Sister Regina, and she will deliver them to the girl."

"But—"

"No buts, Miss Hawthorne. You're far too sympathetic toward Kelly, and I'm afraid your visit would be pleasurable to her. This week, she is to reflect on her misdeeds. Sister Regina will not be sympathetic. She will be efficient and cool with the girl, and that's what she needs right now."

"What if something happens to her?"

"Illness?" Lucy gave her one of those thin-lipped smiles that threatened to crack her horsy face. "Sister Regina is a nurse, and the punishment room is right next to the infirmary. If she calls out, she'll be heard."

"At night?"

"Yes. Dr. Dashwood's quarters are nearby." Lucy opened her desk drawer and pulled out a gold chain with a heart-shaped locket and a thin dark leather thong with a small cloth bag attached. She pushed the latter across the desk, then swept the locket back into the drawer. "Do you have any idea where this came from, Miss Hawthorne?"

Sara picked up the thong. The little round bag was redolent of the forest, a refreshing change from Lucy's mildewed cinnamon odor. "I have no idea where it came from," she said, passing it back. "What made you think I would?"

"It's been reported to me that Kelly has taken a liking to you. I thought perhaps she told you where she got it."

Sara remembered Kelly's urging her to talk to someone named Minerva. She suspected there was a tie there, but she shook her head. "She's told me nothing."

"Even Friday night, when she visited you in your room?"

"You know about that?" Sara blurted in surprise.

Lucy smiled condescendingly. "We know everything, Miss Hawthorne."

*Not everything.* Sara held her hands together in her lap to keep them from trembling. "It looks like some sort of charm, doesn't it?" she asked, her eyes on the thong. "Kelly *did* say she was afraid of ghosts. Perhaps she made it to protect herself from them. Sort of like a rabbit's foot." Hopefully, that would defuse things.

"Then it's even worse, Miss Hawthorne."

"Why?"

"She's resorting to pagan superstition."

"Maybe if you gave her a set of rosary beads she'd be less fearful."

"She hasn't earned them."

''Then let her keep her good luck charm. It's merely a type of security blanket.'' *Like your beads.*

''I'll tell you this once, and only once. Don't presume to tell me how to handle my students.''

''I didn't mean to—''

''Of course you didn't.'' Lucy rose and walked over to the closet, slid it open. As she moved, Sara heard the click of the nun's rosary, caught a brief glimpse of the beads at her waist, the cross dangling from them. It looked odd, but before she could figure out what was unusual about it, it slipped between the folds of black cloth again.

Lucy took something from the closet and brought it back to the desk. Reseating herself, she unfolded the blue material, revealing a lightweight windbreaker. She slipped her hand in a pocket and brought out a wallet, took a card from it and handed it to Sara. ''Do you know this boy?''

It was a student identification card for Moonfall High School. Even without the name—Mark Lawson—under the photo, she would have known his identity. He was obviously the sheriff's son, from his chestnut hair to the firm set of his jaw. ''I've never seen him before,'' she said with complete honesty as she handed the card back to Lucy. ''Why?''

''This is what Kelly was stealing,'' she said, indicating the jacket and wallet. ''Evidently she's been having trysts with the boy.''

''Kelly?'' Sara couldn't suppress a chuckle. ''She's a late bloomer, and I seriously doubt she's to that stage yet. I'm sure that if she does know him, it's an innocent relationship.''

''Don't be naive, Miss Hawthorne. Fortunately, we've nipped this in the bud. Dr. Dashwood says she's intact.''

''Intact?''

''She still has her virginity.''

''You mean you subjected her to an examination?''

''Of course.'' Mother Lucy actually appeared surprised. ''That's standard procedure in these cases.''

''Where do you think they were meeting?'' Sara asked abruptly. She couldn't bear to think about what Kelly must have gone through at this woman's behest.

"Why, in the bushes south of the chapel. Or perhaps the cemetery, behind the monuments. Why?"

*At least she doesn't know Kelly's been in the woods.* "I just couldn't think of any place around here where there'd be much privacy."

"I see." Lucy stood again, this time coming around the desk and walking to the door, which she opened. "Good luck tomorrow," she said as Sara rose. "If you have any questions, feel free to come to me with them."

"Thanks." Sara crossed the threshold.

"Miss Hawthorne?"

"Yes?" she asked, turning to face the nun.

Another smile like cracked china. "Don't worry about Kelly Reed. She'll be fine."

Sara nodded, then turned and walked away, very worried about the girl.

# Forty-Three

*I tried to tell you about Gregory in your dreams the other night, but you wouldn't let me in.*

John sat in the easy chair in front of the dark television set in the living room, unable to get Minerva Payne's words out of his head. He was glad he'd been too concerned about Mark to confess to her his dream about being trapped in the room filling with blood while the old lady commanded him to unlock the door. Talk about Freudian—that dream had been about as obvious as it could get.

Minerva had been right about enough things that he couldn't help but give her ramblings some credence. Yes, he'd been virtually obsessed with thoughts of Mark before he'd known anything had happened to him, and since his conversation with Minerva he'd thought of half a dozen other incidents that he'd "known" were coming over the years. Gus's car crash, when he was a kid, for one. He'd known his mother was leaving about a month before she died—but he'd assumed she was going on a trip to visit her sister back East. And three years ago, he'd gotten up at four in the morning and driven over to Winesap's because he'd felt compelled to—and consequently stopped a burglary in progress. Maybe he'd even known about his brother's impending death. The feelings had always been there, so natural that he'd never even given them a second thought. They weren't reliable, though: he hadn't foreseen his father's death, nor Doug Buckman's, hadn't known about dozens and dozens of traffic accidents, thefts, bar brawls, or missing children. Or Barbara's unfaithfulness. He smiled bitterly, thinking that even so, perhaps there was something to what Minerva had said . . .

He'd certainly seen the same ability in Mark—sometimes the boy answered questions before he could ask them, and once, two years ago, the boy had uncharacteristically played sick on a day his class was taking a field trip to the Redlands Museum. He claimed a bellyache and John knew he was faking but had a feeling he should let it go. Later that day, the bus had collided with a semi-truck just outside Yucaipa. Five kids had died, several had been laid up for months, and only a few had escaped without at least a few cuts and bruises. Minerva had claimed Gus had the ability as well, and John thought that was probably true.

Thinking of Gus made him realize that he still hadn't heard from his grandfather. He reached for the phone, knowing that he should be the one to tell him about today's incident. Gus and Caspar Parker were old cronies, and he would want to be with the Parkers now. For Gus, being a preacher, making the sympathy calls, providing a shoulder for crying, was second nature. For John, it was pure hell.

"Dad?" Mark asked quietly from the doorway. "Can we talk a minute?"

John replaced the phone receiver. "Of course we can. How's your neck?"

"It's okay," Mark said, as he plunked himself down on the couch opposite John. He was dressed in clean gray sweats and his hair was still damp from the shower. He'd spent at least an hour washing off the horrors of the day, the stain of death. John had done it more than once himself.

Since they'd come home, Mark had kept to himself, sullen in his grief, and John had stayed out of his way, knowing the boy would come to him when he was ready. He looked at his son now, saw his red-rimmed eyes, knew he'd been crying, and made no comment, afraid that if he said the wrong thing, the boy would bolt.

"I've never seen one before," Mark said after five silent minutes had passed. "A dead person, I mean."

"It's a hard thing to see."

"Yeah." Mark snorted, trying to hide a hitch in his voice. "You can say that again." A minute passed, then two. "You know what?"

"What?"

"You know when they found that dead teacher in the pond?"

"Yes."

"I wanted to see it. The body. I can't believe it, but I was jealous that you got to see her. Gross, huh?"

"No. It's natural. I felt the same way before my little brother drowned. After that I never wanted to see another, probably because I could never shake the feeling that it was supposed to be me that died, not him."

"Yeah." Mark intently studied his hands. "I feel like that about Pete."

"But we're both wrong."

Mark looked up, interested.

"It's called 'survivor guilt.' That's what people usually feel when they're spared and someone they love isn't. It's completely normal." He paused. "But that doesn't help a whole lot, does it?"

"Maybe a little. Dad, how do you stand it?"

"What do you mean?"

"Seeing bodies."

"Honestly, son, I don't know. I was so affected by Greg's death that it was nearly crippling." He paused. "Maybe I had to have a job where I encountered death sometimes. My dad and Doug, one of my friends, died not too long after Greg, and

I couldn't handle it. I kept dreaming about bodies. My brother's especially."

"Did you see your dad's body? Or your friend's?"

"No. And maybe that just made my phobia worse. My father's casket was closed, but I couldn't even go to the funeral. I knew he'd been shot in the head and I just kept imagining how he must look. I tried to go to Doug's services—all my classmates went—but I couldn't make myself step into the church.

"I didn't see another body until I found one stuffed in a car trunk during my first year as a deputy. That brought the phobia back full force. That corpse was the worst." He smiled sardonically. "In more ways than one."

"What did you do when you found it? Did you faint, or what?"

"My pride overcame the phobia. People were watching me. Even before I got the trunk open, I could smell what was inside—it was summer—and I was nearly paralyzed. I couldn't stand thinking about what I was going to see. But I had to do it: I was a newly sworn-in deputy sheriff, determined to protect and serve, and all that stuff. I couldn't let anyone see my weakness. So I just did it. I turned off my thoughts and jimmied the lid."

John exhaled with a rattle, reliving the moment. "When I opened that trunk, well ... let's just say, I managed not to throw up until I was alone." He smiled. "In my squad car." He smiled. "That was pretty awful in itself. I spent hours cleaning the upholstery, my shoes, the rug. But after that, the phobic part—the paralysis, the dizziness—was gone because I'd stared my fear in the face. It was bad, really bad, but nowhere near as bad as I imagined."

He hesitated, watching Mark. "Imagination's always the worst," he continued. "Do you remember when you were little and you were sure there were dismembered hands crawling around under your bed?"

Mark blushed. "Dad—"

"For me, at that age," John continued in a rush, "it was this guy who was darker than the dark in my room. Before I went to sleep, I'd imagine he was standing over my bed holding a knife, and I'd just squeeze my eyes shut and hide under the covers. It didn't go away until I was about ten."

"Wow," Mark said, his embarrassment gone. "That's a really long time. I guess you were a pretty lame kid."

"Watch it, buster," he said lightly, happy to see a little of Mark's normal personality. "Anyway, the boogeyman didn't go away until I faced him. I took a flashlight into my room and every time I'd think he was there, instead of hiding I'd turn on the light and look. After a few weeks, he never came back again. I'd taken control of the situation."

"I did that, too. With a flashlight, you know? I'd check under the bed for crawling hands."

"I know."

"You do?"

"I 'accidentally' left the flashlight by your bed, so you'd figure it out faster than I did." He grinned crookedly.

"Really?"

"Yeah. So no more teasing your old man, okay?"

"Okay."

"Mark, you were a smart little kid—brave, too. What were you, seven?"

"Six," Mark told him, a healthy trace of pride in his voice. He went back to staring at his hands. "And that worked for you with bodies, too, huh? Making yourself look at them?"

"Basically, yes. It's never easy, though." John rubbed his chin, wondering if he was telling his son anything remotely useful. "What happened to you today was devastating. Make yourself go to Pete's funeral. That's all you need to do— just face the funeral. You're already doing the other important thing—the thing I wouldn't do. You're talking about it."

"You didn't? Never?"

"Mark, this is the very first time. My dad tried to get me to talk, but I refused. I just let it fester." He studied his son, realizing that the discussion was doing him at least as much good as it was Mark. "I still dream about my brother's death."

"Is that what your nightmares are about?"

"A lot of them. And a lot are about St. Gertrude's, too."

Mark looked defensive.

"I think I went there right before Greg died. I'm not sure."

"How could you forget something like that, Dad?"

He shrugged. "I don't know, but your friend Minerva seems to think it would be a good thing for me to try to remember. Now I think so, too. Not for her rather mysterious reasons, mind you, but because it's a fear I haven't faced."

"Corey says his dad and you and some other guys went camping that night. By the Falls."

"I think that's all we're supposed to remember."

"What d'you mean?"

"I'm not sure what I mean. It's just a feeling, you know?" Mark smiled a little. "Yeah, I know."

"So, what'd you think of St. Gruesome's?"

"It's creepy. I didn't even want to go. It was Pete's idea . . ." His expression changed and he looked away.

"I figured that much."

"The woods aren't the same, either."

"What do you mean?"

Well, after we crossed the west fork of the stream and left Witch Forest, it was, I dunno—remember the forest in *The Hobbit* where it was really dark and even the trees were watching you?"

John nodded.

"It was kinda like that."

"Minerva told me that she thinks those birds live in that forest. If she's right, it's not a good place to be."

"Don't worry, Dad, I'm not going back there. Can I ask you a question?"

"Sure."

"I asked Minerva about the nightflyers, you know? And she'd hardly say anything. Why, do you think?"

"Well, those hawks, or whatever they are, have never been documented. The nuns don't allow anyone on their property— as you know," he added with a half-smile. "And no ornithologists have ever taken the reports seriously. What happened today is, as far as I know, the first proof that they actually exist. Even Minerva admitted she'd never seen one up close, not even today, and I think that gives us a clue about how she feels about them. She's superstitious and I got the impression she's something of a pantheist.''

''What the heck is that?''

''Someone who worships nature or nature gods.''

Mark nodded. ''She says there are spirits in every tree and rock, in the streams, and even in the earth. I don't buy all that, though.''

''But *she* does. And these nightflyers are part of her religion because they're a part of nature that's unexplained. For her, they're not some kind of unknown bird, but the equivalent of Christian demons.''

''It looked like a demon, that's for sure.''

''Are you sure it was a bird, not some kind of bat?''

''It had a beak. A long one, curved. Dr. Cutter thought maybe I was just saying that to get out of rabies shots, but I wasn't. Heck, I would've asked for them if I'd thought it was a bat.''

''Was the beak curved like a hawk's?''

''In a way, but bigger. I wasn't really all that close to it. All I know is that it was all black and the feathers were so shiny that they looked kinda like scales. It had big eyes like an owl's and they glowed red.''

''Glowed red?'' John asked. ''You're sure?''

Mark nodded. ''I know it sounds goofy.''

''No,'' John said slowly. Then he realized what Mark meant. ''You mean they reflected red, like when light hits a cat's eyes just right?''

Mark brightened. ''That's gotta be it, yeah.'' He pushed his damp hair from his forehead.

''Mark, how long were you and Corey separated from Pete?'' John knew the basics, but Corey had been so hysterical that his story was completely nonsensical and Frank Cutter had given the boy a sedative and sent him home to bed. Mark, until now, had only given one-syllable answers.

''He took off only a minute or so ahead of us, but we never saw him again. I think he was running really, really fast. A little while later, we heard a couple nightflyers screeching. I think one flew right over us. Then we met up with this girl

Kelly from St. Gertrude's. She's Minerva's friend. She said she was going to try to get my jacket and wallet back, and we talked to her for a couple minutes. Then we kept going. After we crossed back into Witch Forest, we didn't hurry anymore. We were kinda p.o.'d at Pete for ditching us, so we decided to make him worry a little. That's how we ended up in the park."

"At the Falls."

"Yeah, well, you know."

"I know."

"You didn't expect Pete to be there?"

Mark shook his head. "He had to be home before his parents got back from church. He really wanted to go there, though. Maybe he thought he had time." He hesitated. "Or maybe the nightflyer chased him there."

The doorbell rang and John jumped. "That might be Gus."

"I'll get it." Mark got up and opened the front door.

"Hi, you must be Mark."

Hearing Sara Hawthorne's voice, John got to his feet and joined his son. "Hi, come on in."

Mark opened the door and stood back, casting a questioning look at John, who quickly made introductions. Sara sat down on the couch, John in his chair. Mark started to leave.

"Please, stay," Sara called.

A look of surprise crossed his face, but he came back and perched on the arm of the sofa.

"I'm sorry to just show up like this," Sara began. "I was going to phone, but I couldn't find one that wasn't locked away at the school. I went to your office and your dispatcher said I should see you in person."

Obviously, John thought, Dorothy was working late. *Any chance to matchmake.* "What can I do for you?"

"Do you know someone named Minerva?"

"Why?" Mark blurted, before John could answer. There was a protective look on his face.

"Yes, we do," John added. "She owns the Gingerbread House, down the road from Apple Heaven."

"A student, Kelly Reed, was caught taking something from the headmistress's office," Sara explained.

"My jacket," Mark said quickly. "She got caught?"

"Yes. Mother Lucy questioned me about you. She thinks you and Kelly are, um, going steady."

"Heck, no!" Mark stood up, his anger obvious. "I hardly know her. I told her what happened and she offered to help out. That's all. Why do you want to know about Minerva?"

"Mark," Sara said quietly, "I like Kelly. I want to help her. She's been put in solitary confinement and I can't talk to her for at least a week. She asked me to tell someone named Minerva what happened. I just want to find out who she is so that I can do what Kelly asked."

Mark looked dubious.

"She lives in Witch Forest, but you can find her at her shop in the daytime," John said. Mark glared daggers at him.

Sara nodded. "Kelly goes into the woods to visit her," she said, looking at Mark.

"You know about that? Are you the new teacher she talked about?"

"I must be." Sara smiled warmly. "I'm the only new one."

Mark looked at John. "She's okay, Dad. Kelly said so."

"I probably won't be able to visit Minerva until five or six tomorrow," Sara said. "Can you give me directions to her house?"

John did. "You'll need to walk the last part—the road narrows into a footpath," he finished.

"What about the other way?" she asked. "The way Kelly goes, through the forest?"

Mark paled as John spoke. "Don't go through the woods, and tell Kelly not to, either." He briefly told her what had happened to Pete Parker.

"That's horrible."

He nodded. "Have you ever heard anything about the birds? According to Minerva, they nest on St. Gertrude's land."

She shook her head. "I think I've heard them. They have an awful call, but I don't know what they are."

"The nuns haven't said anything about them?"

"The nuns don't say much of anything," she said wryly. "I

can ask around, though. Maybe the groundskeeper can tell me something."

Her words set off unexplainable alarm bells in John's mind. "No, let me do the questioning."

"I'm more likely to get answers than you are," she said, irritated.

"I know, but I just don't think it's a good idea."

"Those nuns are mean," Mark said.

Sara half smiled. "Well, they're certainly not very friendly."

"I don't want you to say anything to them." John sat forward. "I wouldn't want anyone to think you're involved in this. It might be dangerous for you."

"That's absurd," she said, her voice betraying a hint of uncertainty.

"I know. It seems absurd to me, too, but I have to follow my instincts." He looked over at Mark, saw the boy's approving expression. "Don't you have some homework to finish?"

"A little." Mark said goodnight to them and headed out of the room.

"I think you're being overly cautious," Sara said.

"Maybe. But if your friend really was murdered, someone at St. Gertrude's may be involved in something, and if they think you're talking to me, things could get sticky."

"Do I detect a change in your attitude about Jenny's death?"

He shifted uncomfortably in his chair. "I don't know. Maybe. The thing is, where those nuns are concerned, people always seem to have faulty memories. Myself included."

She raised her eyebrows. "You?"

"There was—or wasn't—an incident concerning the abbey. It dates back to my childhood. I don't want to say anything more until I talk to some old friends. I'm just saying you should be very careful." He didn't know for sure whether his warning was born of any real instinct or of paranoia stemming from the conversation he'd had with Minerva. "Would you like some coffee?"

She glanced at her watch. "I would, but it's getting late. Hopefully, no one knows I'm gone."

"You had to sneak out? That place is sounding more and more like a prison."

She rose. "It's always felt like one to me. I hate it there." She smiled as she moved to the door. "But I didn't exactly sneak. I just didn't tell anyone I was going out."

"Be careful," he said, stepping outside with her. The night was cold and clear. "Keep your doors locked, okay?"

"Okay." She smiled. "Goodnight."

"Goodnight, Sara." He watched her until she was safely in her car, then went inside to see to his son.

# Forty-Four

Kelly had survived the intimate humiliations heaped on her by Dr. Dashwood and had kept quiet when he'd confiscated her locket and the amulet, but now, sitting on the cot in the dimly lit room, she wanted to cry.

*But I won't. I won't give them the satisfaction . . .*

The ten-by-ten room had one door, which was locked, and no windows. A cot with one thin moth-eaten blanket, a table with a shadeless lamp and a twenty-five-watt bulb, and a stool to sit on completed the furnishings. That was all she had, except for her schoolbooks. She should be grateful, she told herself, for the light: last time, the bulb had burned out.

Two slices of stale bread and a single cup of water had been her dinner. She'd be a skeleton by the time they let her out, she thought, her stomach rumbling.

She sat up straight, hearing footsteps clicking along the hallway beyond. They came to a stop outside her door and a key clicked into the lock. The door creaked open and Sister Regina, the snaky-looking nurse who'd held her down while Dashwood examined her, stepped inside, bright light from the corridor haloing around her.

"Turn off your lamp and unscrew the bulb," she ordered. "It's time for bed."

"I can't have the light?" Kelly asked, trying to control her sudden panic.

"Of course not. For the next two weeks, no lights at night."

"*Two* weeks?"

"You added a week to your punishment when you attempted to run away. Now, do as you're told."

Kelly swallowed her pride. "Please let me keep the light. It's so dark in here!"

"If you don't do as you're told immediately, I'll have to get the Mother Superior." Regina's mouth vee'd into a reptilian smile. "Disturbing her will probably cost you a third week. Is that what you want?"

Sullenly, Kelly flipped off the light and unscrewed the bulb. It was hot in her hand and she gritted her teeth as she extended it to the nun. Regina caught up a fold of her black habit to protect her fingers and took the bulb. As the material moved, Kelly saw her rosary glint in the light from the hall.

The cross hung upside down. She couldn't stop staring at it. Regina glanced down, then back at Kelly. "Go to bed," she ordered, as she turned and left the room, slamming the door firmly behind her. The lock clicked, then the old bitch's footsteps receded.

Kelly forced herself not to panic in the utter darkness and slowly moved back toward the bed. She raked her shin against the metal frame and tears filled her eyes. "No!" she said. "You're *not* going to let them make you cry." Gingerly she sat on the cot, then lay down, fully dressed. Closing her eyes against the dark, she warded off her fears with thoughts of being at Minerva's house, curled up by the fire.

# Forty-Five

As she drove back up the narrow road to St. Gertrude's, Sara began to regret visiting John Lawson. She was glad they had talked, but now, driving through the heavy forest all alone in the dark with God knew what flying around or lurking among the trees, she wondered why she couldn't have waited until daylight. *You're too impatient for your own good.*

If the woods weren't forbidding enough already, a fog had rolled in while she was in town. The heaviest of it lay low to the ground, but there were white patches floating everywhere, ghosts reflected in her headlights. Now, as she neared the abbey, it grew so thick that she couldn't see more than ten feet in front of her; even the low-beams were too much.

She turned off everything but the amber parking lights and slowed to a crawl. The front gates suddenly loomed in front of her and she turned the wheel hard left, barely keeping the car on the road. "Christ," she whispered, and put her foot on the brake. The fog was slowly shifting and she decided she wasn't going anywhere until it cleared.

After five minutes spent drumming her fingers on the steering wheel, she turned off the engine and lights and cracked the window, then sat back to wait it out.

Fog swirled and crept all around the car, and she heard faint singing. Evening services, she realized. The eerie tones continued, some kind of Gregorian chant going on and on and on while fog sifted and eddied. She tried not to think about the steam in the showers that had done the same thing until it formed—*seemed to form*—a phantom.

Twenty endless minutes passed before the fog began to thin. Up ahead, she could see muted light coming from the chapel. "It's about time," she muttered, starting the car, again using only the parking lights, this time to avoid drawing attention to herself. Once she was behind the chapel, she doubted anyone would notice her, but while taking the curve, her headlights might flash in its windows. She wasn't afraid of being seen, she reminded herself; she just didn't want to talk to anyone.

The road came within fifty feet of the building before curving behind it. As she approached the turn, she glanced at the chapel, looked up at the steeple. The gargoyle was gone. She braked, took a second look. Or was it? Mist swirled, obscuring her view, thinned, thickened. "You're imagining things," she said, as she accelerated.

She passed the back of the chapel and cemetery without

looking at anything but the road. She drove on slowly to the garage, aware that she was trembling, telling herself it was nothing, just a reaction to John and Mark's story, the fog, and the dark.

"Damn it." The big double doors to the garage were closed. She put the Sentra in park and jumped out, relieved to see there was no lock on the huge old stable. Shivering, she shot the bolt and slowly pulled one of the heavy doors open far enough to get the car inside.

Back in the car, she turned on the headlights and angled the car into the building, parking in an empty stall near the door because the dark within was so thick that she couldn't bear the idea of walking all the way from the center of the garage. She locked the car, then raced out of the building and closed the door, breathing a sigh of relief as she pushed the bolt home.

The fog had receded, leaving nothing but a thin mist. In the hazy moonlight, she could see the darkened school building in front of her and the faintly lit chapel to the right. She squinted at the steeple but couldn't make out anything through the haze at this distance. *Let it go.*

She walked quickly across the vast lawn, making a beeline for the dormitory. It wasn't much past nine o'clock, but very few lights were on. She hurried inside and up the stairs to her room, relieved that she saw no one in the halls.

Opening her door she stepped inside, then flopped against it, her legs like rubber, her hands trembling. Her mouth was dust dry. "Get a grip," she muttered, as she reached over and felt for the light switch. The white-walled room was almost too bright, but she didn't mind.

She went straight to the little refrigerator and snagged a cold soda, drank half of it in one long, wonderful swallow, then shucked off her jacket and flopped into the old easy chair. For the first time the room felt like home. Not a very good home, she thought, but a home nevertheless. She looked around, thinking that with a few pictures on the walls and a throw pillow or two, it might not be so bad. Her gaze fell on the bed and she saw something glinting on the spread.

She stood up and crossed to the bed. Her breath caught as she recognized the object: a double-edged razor blade.

Raps like gunshots shot through the room, and Sara screamed before she realized it was someone knocking on the door. She whirled, clapping her hands to her mouth; she'd forgotten to push the wedge under after she'd returned.

The door flew open and Richard Dashwood rushed in. "Are you all right?" he asked, grasping her shoulders.

She looked up at him, saw the concern in his eyes. "Yes, yes, I'm fine," she sputtered. She knew she was blushing furiously. "You startled me. Uh, would you like a Pepsi, or something?"

He studied her an instant longer then smiled gently and let his hands drop to his sides. "Yes, actually, I would."

Sara took another can out of the refrigerator and brought it to the small dining table along with her own. Her heart was still beating like a jackrabbit's, but her smile was genuine. "Have a seat. I'm sorry, do you want a glass and some ice?" She was almost as horrified at her own mindless babbling as she'd been by the razor blade, but she couldn't stop. She heard herself rambling on about how she had only paper cups, not actual glasses, and would he like some tortilla chips or ginger snaps?

Dashwood seated himself while she was talking and opened the soda. He smiled when she sputtered to a halt. "Aren't you going to sit?"

"Yes, of course." Humiliated, she pulled out the other chair. "I'm so sorry. I don't know what got into me."

"You're very nervous tonight."

She nodded. "Sorry." She glanced at the bed, at the blade, but said nothing.

"Did something happen while you were out?"

"What do you mean?" she asked, instantly alert.

"I saw you coming in." He smiled gently. "I daresay the sisters are aware of everyone's comings and goings as well. It's hard to keep a low profile around here."

"I wasn't trying to sneak around, if that's what you mean. I *am* free to come and go as I please, aren't I?"

"Of course you are," he said warmly. "And it's no one's business where you go. The sisters might disapprove of your leaving the grounds, but they know they can't stop you."

Between his mesmerizing gaze and his sincere smile, Sara's reserve began to melt away. "Why would they disapprove?" she asked.

"Because they are, what's the expression? Control freaks."

"Kind of makes me want to go to the bar and pick up sailors," she said, "just to annoy them."

"That would have the desired effect." He chuckled, then his expression grew serious. "Don't let them get to you, Sara. They're a pitiful group really, all set in their ways. They've been isolated out here so long that they can't imagine how other people live."

"They're all still here, too, aren't they?" Sara sat forward, intrigued.

"Most of them. Do you remember Sister Flora? Or Sisters Nicholas, Anna, or Marie Stanislaus? They were all quite elderly."

"Yes, I think I remember some of them. Did they leave?"

"In a manner of speaking. They died. Perhaps you noticed the new gargoyle on the steeple of the chapel?"

"Yes. I thought I was seeing things."

He shook his head. "Not at all. Sister Elizabeth has turned her talents to sculpting. She creates a new gargoyle for every nun that passes on. That one was for Sister Flora, who was Lucy's assistant and personal favorite. She died six months ago. She was given the place of honor."

Sara felt reassured by the laughter in his eyes. "I did think there are more gargoyles than when I left here as a girl." She made a face. "Somehow, I'd expect her to create gargoyles instead of statues of the Virgin."

"Morbid memorials." Dashwood returned her smile, then reached in his pocket. "I almost forgot. I brought you something." He brought out something wrapped in white tissue paper and set it on the table. "I hope they haven't melted."

Opening the crackling paper, Sara saw two chocolate truffles. "Are you trying to fatten me up?"

"Chocolate has known therapeutic effects."

"Yes, it does." Sara picked one up and pushed the other toward the doctor. "But one is enough. You have the other."

"Save it for later." He pushed it back.

She bit into the chocolate, savored the fudge interior. "These are delicious. Where do you buy them?"

"I filch them from Apple Heaven. Sister Margaret has a gift for candymaking."

"I like your honesty." For the first time she felt truly at ease with the man. "Chocolate cures all sorts of problems, doesn't it?"

He nodded. "If I might be permitted to ask, why were you so anxious earlier?"

"Driving through the fog. Parking in that dark garage." She hesitated, then made a decision. "And someone's been in my room."

His eyebrows raised. "Are you certain?"

"Whoever it was left a razor blade on the bed."

"That's horrible," he said. "But I'm not particularly surprised."

"You're not?" She reached for the second truffle.

"No. It's cruel but typical in a school like this. As you undoubtedly know, your predecessor cut her wrists."

"Yes." She stared at Dashwood's handsome face. The man had remarkable eyes. "And?"

"And children—girls, in particular—can be very cruel. It's a form of hazing. Or an initiation. I think your best course of action is to show absolutely no sign of weakness. Be firm and fair, and show the girls you mean business. They'll respect you for it and the pranks will stop." He paused. "I think I can even tell you who's responsible."

"If you blame Kelly Reed, you're out on your ear, truffles or no truffles."

"Not at all." He shook his head. "Poor Kelly. There's one in every group."

"One what?"

"Outcast. Pariah. It's worse than usual for Kelly, because Mother Lucy has taken a dislike to her, and as Mother Lucy goes, so go the sisters." His eyes were dark and sad. "I wish I could do more for her."

"Why doesn't Lucy like her?" All the tension had left her now and she covered a yawn.

Dashwood shrugged. "She says the girl is a pathological liar. Kelly does tell tales, but she's not pathological. However, there's no convincing our Mother Superior of that."

"It seems so cruel to lock her up. Can't you talk Lucy into a milder form of punishment?"

"I've tried. When that woman makes up her mind, there's no changing it. If it helps, though, I can assure you that Kelly wants for nothing."

"Good. I'm glad." Sara couldn't stop looking at Dashwood's eyes. They had tiny gold flecks that made them sparkle. *He's talking about Kelly's welfare, and you're thinking like a schoolgirl!* She forced herself to sit up straight in her chair, tried to fight her exhaustion. "Do you think you could sneak me in to visit her?" She heard several of her words slur.

He turned his palms upward, a helpless motion. "It would be extremely difficult. Sister Regina is Lucy's new lapdog, you know. And I know for a fact that the confinement room is bugged."

"Bugged? That's awful." She yawned.

"Not too awful. It's as much for the safety of the student being punished as anything."

Sara nodded. "I see."

"You're exhausted," he said, gazing into her eyes. "And you have a big day tomorrow."

"First day of school," she murmured.

"I'll take my leave now," Dashwood said, as he stood up. "Thanks for the soda."

Sara stood up and the room spun. She grabbed the back of the chair to steady herself, then, embarrassed, attempted a short laugh. "Was there any liquor in those truffles?"

"There might be." Dashwood came around the table and put his arm around her waist. "But not enough to affect you. You just need a good night's rest."

Everything lurched dizzily around her as he guided her to

her bed. He bent and pulled back the covers, then helped her lie down. "I feel ridiculous," she said, as he took her shoes off and set them on the floor by the bed.

"Don't." He undid the belt on her pants and snaked it from the loops, then laid it on the night table. "I'm a doctor, remember?" He pulled the covers up over her, then sat on the edge of the bed. "Is there anything else you need, Sara?"

God, those eyes. "No." She felt herself drifting away.

He bent over her, lightly brushed his lips against her forehead. "Sweet dreams," he whispered. "Sweet, sweet dreams."

# Forty-Six

No matter how many times John asked him not to, Gus turned his telephone ringer off every night at nine o'clock. He said it was because he'd been at the beck and call of his parishoners for so many years that now, in retirement, he was damned if he was going to give up a single moment of his nighttime privacy.

It was eleven P.M. John hadn't expected him to pick up, but he'd hoped that his grandfather had finally hooked up the answering machine he and Mark had given him for his birthday last June. No such luck. *Stubborn old coot.* Well, he thought, I'll catch up with him tomorrow.

He'd spent the time since Sara had left with Mark. His son had spoken at length, exorcising every horrible detail, and hopefully, some of his emotional trauma. Then, trying to assuage the boy's obvious guilt over Pete Parker's death, John ended up telling him what he remembered of the night and morning surrounding Greg's death.

Mark had benefited from their confessions; he'd finally fallen peacefully asleep. John had covered him up and returned to the living room. He hadn't benefited; recounting the story aloud after all these years, thinking about Greg's death in such detail, had left him both drained and agitated. It didn't make sense, not the way he remembered it, and he could no longer deny that whatever was missing from his memory was important. Absently he pressed his fingers to his breast pocket, where Minerva Payne's good luck charm rested. *Silly old woman.* Or was she? He wasn't so sure anymore.

He started to reach for the phone again. After all these years, he suddenly wanted to talk to Winky and Beano and Paul. He needed to know what they thought of the events of Halloween, 1972. The clock struck eleven-thirty and he withdrew his hand. Most people in Moonfall were early-to-bed types. On top of that, it would be best to sleep on things before talking to anyone. And before he did anything else, he decided, he'd talk with Gus and find out what all the excitement about their family tree was about.

In the dark, far away, came one of those hellish screeches. Shivering, John rose and checked the locks on the doors and windows, then went to bed. He didn't expect to sleep, but he wanted to be within shouting distance of Mark, should the boy suffer nightmares or wake up to the sound of the thing that had killed his friend.

# Forty-Seven

*Sara, Sara, wake up!*

"Jenny?" Eyes closed, Sara thought she was speaking, but wasn't sure. It might only be a dream.

*Open your eyes, Sara. I have something to show you.*

She tried to force her way up through layer upon layer of sleep. It was like swimming in maple syrup, making her feel as if she were drowning in it and couldn't come up for air. "Jenny," she gasped. "I'm coming, Jenny."

*Hurry!*

Cold fingers caressed her cheek and suddenly, she was awake—and afraid. What if it was the fraud calling to her, the specter that had pretended to be Jenny in the showers?

The caress again. *It's all right, Sara. It's me. Don't be afraid.* Jenny's voice.

Slowly, trembling hard, she opened her eyes.

Jenny stood before her, pale, but seemingly solid. Her long dark hair flowed down over her shoulders, just as Sara remembered. She wore a long white gown. She smiled. *Hello, Sara.*

Sara sat up, rubbed her eyes. "Jenny, is it really you? I mean . . ."

*It's me. And I have to show you something. Get up. Please hurry!*

Sara realized that Jenny's mouth wasn't moving, but inexplicably, her fear had lessened. "What?" she asked, as she stood. "What do you have to show me?" She reached out to touch Jenny, who looked so real, but her fingertips disappeared into her arm. Startled, she jumped back. The fingers were icy cold.

*I'm sorry. I wish I could hug you.*

Sara edged around the bed, then turned to go to her closet. She could barely think; she wasn't even positive she was awake.

*You're already dressed. Put on your shoes.*

She looked down, startled to see it was true. Dr. Dashwood had come to visit, she remembered, and she'd been very tired. He must have put her to bed.

The ghost was standing by the door when she looked up again. She slipped on her penny loafers. "Okay," she said, shrugging on her jacket.

*Open the door.*

Hesitantly, she did as Jenny had asked. Without allowing herself to consider the possible consequences, she followed the ghost to the far end of the building and down the staircase. The spirit didn't walk, but seemed to glide along the floor, and Sara was glad its feet were hidden beneath the gown. If Jenny was floating above ground, she didn't want to know about it; her nerves couldn't take any more.

Ground fog covered the lawn and the barest hint of a pink dawn tinted the eastern sky beyond the forest. The spirit moved across the lawn, leaving no footprints, and Sara followed, trying to keep pace, her feet slipping and sliding on the dew-moistened grass.

Even in the gloom, the spirit was easy to see: it seemed to have its own inner light as it glided between the hedges and across the road to the forest. Sara's clothing and hair caught in the bushes as she pushed her way through. "Jenny, slow down."

The ghost stopped at the forest edge. *Hurry!*

"Where are we going?" Sara panted.

*We must hurry. Follow me!* The spirit turned and moved into the woods.

"Wait!" Sara cried, still on the road at the edge of the woods. Wingbeats sounded, echoing in the fog, and something passed overhead, seeming to cast a shadow even in the dim morning light. "Wait!" she cried again, but her voice was lost in the screech of the huge bird. Frightened, she lunged into the forest after Jenny.

She ran, never quite catching up with the ghost as it glided among the trees, and sometimes right through them. It was too dark here to see anything except looming tree trunks and the phantom's white figure, a candle in the gloom. She tripped over roots and her feet caught in rodent holes. Falling repeatedly, she ripped her trousers and skinned her knees and bruised the palms of her hands. From overhead, above the trees, came the sound of wings, and sometimes the bird's raucous call.

*Hurry!*

She heard the voice in her head as loudly as if Jenny were next to her instead of fifty feet ahead. Rushing on, she saw pinkish light between the thinning trees, heard the rumble of crashing water. A moment later, she came into a vast clearing, a vaguely circular meadow. At the far end, rising above the pasture, were waterfalls. Jenny hovered near them.

With sudden dread, she realized that this was where they had found Lenore Tynan. Glancing skyward, she saw pinkish-gray light, and no sign of the bird that had dogged her run through the forest. Relieved, she trotted across the meadow to the edge of the Falls. "Why are we here?" she asked, trying to catch her breath.

*I want to tell you how it happened.* In the dawning light, Jenny's figure had become translucent, her skin the color of fog.

"But you didn't die here."

*Many have. Many more will.*

Jenny's form seemed misty now, reminding Sara of the phantom in the shower. Her eyes were nothing more than black holes, the shape of her face barely recognizable.

*You were supposed to die that night, not me.*

"What?" Sara stepped back. "What are you talking about?"

*Look in your pocket.*

Sara slipped her hand in the jacket pocket. Her finger touched cold metal. "Ow!" She pulled her hand out, stared in shock at the razor blade imbedded in her fingertip. She shook the hand and the blade flew out onto the damp yellow weeds. Droplets of blood spattered her shoes.

The phantom moved forward before Sara could react. Its face was swirling mist, its eyes huge and fathomless. *Pick it up.*

Sara couldn't scream. All she could do was stare into those dark pits, mesmerized, and bend down. Her hand seemed to be guided as she picked up the blade without looking at it. She rose, so afraid that she was beyond feeling anything but numbness. Vaguely, she felt hot blood dripping from her finger onto her palm. "You're not Jenny."

Phantom laughter resounded in her ears, then the voice came, no longer Jenny's, but something deep and hollow and chill. *It was your time to go, Sara Hawthorne, not mine. You were a coward and you let me die in your stead.*

"It wasn't her time or mine," Sara said. Fear threatened her again, and she did her best to remain calm. "Who are you? What are you?"

*You were the chosen one, the virgin, but you ran away and left your friend to die for you. You're a coward, and now you must pay.*

Dawn approached quickly now, and Sara could see streaks of pink and blue through the ghostly figure. What was it talking about? "I never ran away."

"You did." Again came the horrible shrieking laughter and the phantom seemed to grow taller, looming over her, its huge black eyes locked on her own, imprisoning her in their depths.

*Even now, on the day of your death, you don't remember, do you, you little bitch?*

Sara tried to think, tried to remember what happened before she found Jenny. But how could she recall something that even her therapist couldn't draw to the surface through hypnosis?

*Remove your coat.*

Feeling the blade cut into her palm, she blindly removed her jacket, let it fall, then watched in amazement as her sweater sleeve pushed itself up to her elbow.

*Put the blade to your wrist.*

The command overwhelmed her and she began to raise the blade. *What are you doing?* "No!" she screamed, stopping the movement with huge effort.

*Do it.*

"No!" But even as she cried the word, the phantom swarmed over her and again, she felt as if she were drowning in cold, thick soup. "No!" She watched in horror as the hand holding the blade rose of its own accord. Her other arm was yanked out straight by invisible hands, and she brought the blade toward her wrist. "No!" The word sounded muted, garbled, and blood from the cuts on her fingers and hand dripped onto her outstretched inner forearm, spattering her pale skin.

Her hand trembled as she fought, but the blade came inexorably toward her arm. The tip of the metal pressed against the flesh over the large blue vein close to the surface of her wrist. She felt a sting and saw a single pearl of blood ooze out. "No! I won't do it!" she screamed, but she couldn't fight the force of the specter.

*I will squeeze the life from your body and hurl you into the water.*

The blade dug deeper, then she felt a tugging on her hand and knew the phantom was going to make her pull the blade up through her flesh to the elbow.

"Be gone, spirit!"

The powerful voice roared above the thunder of the Falls, and at that same moment, a single ray of sunlight hit her, shining through the phantom. Sara squinted against the brilliance. The force abated slightly, the urge to pull the blade was gone, but she couldn't remove it from her flesh.

*Do it now!* The phantom's voice ripped through her ears, shrill and awful. *Do it, bitch!*

"Be gone, spirit!" cried the new voice.

Sara heard a spate of words she didn't understand, and then the coldness slowly left her and she saw the phantom before her, an amorphous glowing mass, thin in the sunlight. The eyes, bottomless coal pits, held her in their grip, but now her will returned. "No! I won't do it!" she screamed. She flung the blade away, over the cliff.

*You will die, old woman!* The specter turned toward the Falls, and Sara turned, too, saw a tall, dark figure, its arms raised, standing on the bridge over the top of the Falls.

"The sunlight takes you! Be gone!" cried the woman.

*You will die soon, old woman.* The phantom laughter rippled through Sara's mind, and the ghostly figure turned its gaze on Sara. *And you will die in pain greater than you can imagine!* The laughter surrounded her, then faded until it was nothing but an echo.

Sara picked up her coat, found a handkerchief in the breast pocket, and wrapped it around her hand. Then she looked up at the bridge, but the woman was gone.

"Let me see."

A hand touched her shoulder and Sara whirled, raising a fist. The old woman caught it in her hand. "It's all right now," she said.

Sara knew it was the voice that had stopped the phantom, but now it was softer, kinder. The woman, clad in a dress of such a dark green that it was nearly black, smiled at her. She was tall and thin, as old as time, and her dark blue eyes were kind . . . and familiar.

"I know you," Sara said, as the woman unwrapped the handkerchief and examined the cuts.

"These aren't bad, Sara. You were lucky."

"I know you," she said again. Images flashed through her mind. A cottage in the woods, warm and comfortable, with a big stone fireplace where you could warm your hands. "I know you."

"And I know you, Sara. It's been a long time." The woman took her elbow and guided her across the meadow, then up an incline to a footpath. They crossed the bridge and turned onto a well-worn trail into the woods.

"I know this place," Sara murmured, aware that shock was muting her feelings and impressions. "I know you."

"Of course you do. We spent many hours together years ago."

At that moment, the cottage came into view between the trees, and suddenly, she knew. "You're Minerva."

The old lady smiled. "Yes, Sara. I was afraid you'd forgotten about me." She took her elbow again and urged her toward the cottage. "Come. We don't have much time."

Sara let the old woman guide her to the house, waited while she opened the door. She was embarrassed because she knew the woman's name only because of Kelly, but inside the house, it was exactly what she expected, down to the crocheted throw on the sofa and the needlepoint pillows. "I've been here."

"Yes, of course you have. Come to the sink."

She led her into the old-fashioned kitchen, past gleaming copper pans and cast-iron pots. Bunches of drying herbs hung in front of the windows, and jars and vials of mysterious potions were interspersed with Crisco and vinegar and flour on the shelves.

Sara watched in silence as Minerva washed her hand and applied Band-Aids to the cuts. "There, now. We just have time for a cup of tea, then you must get back to St. Gertrude's." She took cups and saucers from a cupboard and carried them to the table, nodding at Sara to follow.

She sat down and watched as Minerva turned up the low flame under a kettle, then took a small carton of half-and-half from the century-old icebox and brought it to the table, set it beside a delicate china sugar bowl. "We haven't much time," she said briskly as she placed tea bags in the cups. "So these will have to do." She brought the kettle over and poured steamy water into the cups, before sitting down. "Why have you returned to St. Gertrude's?"

Briefly, Sara told her. The old woman nodded. "I understand."

"There are huge gaps in my memory. I know I know you. I know I've been here." Sara paused. "You're Kelly Reed's friend."

Minerva nodded. "That's how I knew you were back. She spoke very highly of you."

Quickly, Sara told her about Kelly's plight.

The old woman shook her head sadly. "She's in grave danger. Do you know if she has her amulet?"

"They took it away from her."

Minerva rose and went to a tin on the counter. She brought out two amulets like the one Sara had seen in Lucy's office. "Wear one yourself, and get this to Kelly somehow."

"What is it?"

"Nun repellent." Minerva smiled. "Ghost repellent. It will help with your willpower if you encounter the thing that had you today."

"How?"

"I don't question, I only know it works."

Sara put the charm around her neck, placed the other one in her pocket. "I don't know how, but I'll see that she gets it."

"I know."

"Minerva, what was that thing? I thought it was Jenny. That's the second time it's fooled me."

"There's nothing of Jenny at the abbey. There's only evil." She sat forward. "I don't know exactly what it is. A Christian might call it a demon. I think it's a revenant of some sort."

"A what?"

"You've forgotten many things.

Sara looked at her hands. "Yes. I've spent years trying to remember."

"I know. A revenant is a ghost. A ghost is nothing but an unintelligent ball of power. It's a shell. When someone takes control of it and directs it, using its energy for his own purposes, then it becomes a revenant. The revenant you encountered is

very powerful, as you know. And I must caution you, whoever
is directing it is also very powerful."

"The nuns?"

"Probably. As long as you're there, you must be very cautious. Trust no one. They still want to kill you."

"But why?"

"You were the sacrificial lamb that got away."

"The ghost said Jenny died instead of me." She hesitated.
"I don't remember what happened before she died."

"You came here. Do you remember how many girls disappeared from the abbey while you were there?"

Sara shook her head. "They disappeared all the time."

"I didn't tell you this then because you were too young
and sensitive, but those nuns use virgins as sacrifices for their
orchards."

"That's nuts."

Minerva looked amused. "Not nuts, apples. Most of these
girls are undocumented; it's easy for the nuns to kill them and
claim they're runaways, or have been adopted. Trust me, Sara.
I'm telling you the truth."

"Why don't the police do anything?"

"The nuns have certain abilities to cloak themselves, to make
sure the town doesn't think about them too much. They give
much to their dark god to keep it that way, and if someone
ever did catch on, there would be no proof. It would be a story
like the one about the gargoyles collecting babies for my stew
pot."

Sara nodded slowly. "What god do they worship?"

"Why, Satan, of course. Look at their rosaries. If you could
examine the cross on the chapel, you would find that the portion
set into the building is much shorter than the top. It's inverted.
Their 'bibles' are in Latin. If you knew what the translation
was, you'd be very surprised."

"But why do they dress like nuns if they're the opposite?"
Sara was having trouble swallowing all this.

"As I told the sheriff, you must first be Christian to turn to
its opposite pole. It's the same with everything. I'm a healer
who follows the right-hand path." She chuckled. "At least, for

the most part. That puts me on the same side as a sincere Christian. We try to give what we can. A sorcerer of the left-hand path and a Satanist both believe in self-gratification above all else. They take. It's very simple. And often tempting." The grandfather clock chimed six. "You must go."

Sara rose. She had many questions but restricted herself to just one more. "You talked to the sheriff about this?"

"You know him?"

"Yes. I met Mark last night, too."

"Good. You like John, don't you?"

"I—"

"It's in your eyes." Minerva took her hands briefly. "It's good that you do, because he's slow to listen to me. And he must, or he'll lose his son. Try to influence him." She walked her to the door. "Make sure no one knows where you've been, and please, return soon. We have much to talk about."

"I will," Sara said. She was having trouble comprehending it all. "What's the quickest way back?"

"Through the forest." Minerva hesitated, then took her shawl from a coat rack by the door. "I'll go with you."

"You don't have to—"

"Yes, it's for the best." She pulled the door closed and locked it. "The woods won't be safe for a while. When you come back, drive. Then, stay on the path to my house. Make sure Kelly understands this as well."

Sara had been afraid that Minerva Payne would slow her down, but she could barely keep up with her. When they crossed onto St. Gertrude's land, the old lady moved even more quickly, speaking only once.

"Can you feel them?"

Sara glanced around the dark woods. "Feel who?"

"*Them.* The dark forces, the nightflyers, the elementals. They're watching us. It's easy to get lost here. They can confuse you without much effort."

Sara did feel something, there was no denying it, and when they came to the road by the abbey, she was relieved. She turned to Minerva. "There's still time. I can get my car and drive you home."

"Thank you, child, but no; the forest can't hurt me." She smiled. "It wouldn't dare."

Sara nodded.

"Get the amulet to Kelly as soon as you can. It should buy her some time—and some safety, if the demons visit her."

"Time?"

"She's sure to be their next virginal sacrifice on Halloween night." Minerva eyed her. "And you, my dear, are in as much peril as she, and as Mark. We must stop them or many more lives will be lost."

"What—"

"Go. We'll talk later." Minerva smiled gently, then turned and disappeared into the forest.

# Forty-Eight

When John arrived at the station at eight A.M., he found Winky Addams waiting for him in his office.

"Wink," he said, as the other man rose to shake his hand. "How's Corey?"

"Not so good. He's at home. The doc's still got him under sedation."

"I'm sorry to hear that. He wasn't hurt, was he?"

"Not physically. How's your boy? Corey said he was bitten by the same thing that got Pete Parker."

"He's all right. Insisted on going to school." John sat down at his desk.

"Really?"

"That's how he deals with things. He just sort of plunges ahead and tries not to think about them." John, secretly proud of his son, didn't mention the long talk they'd had last night. He sat forward, studying his old friend. Winky's blond hair had thinned and his waistline had broadened a little over the years, but his face still bore the same boyishly benign look. "What can I do for you?"

"I want to know what killed the Parker boy."

"So do I." John paused. "Some kind of bird of prey, as near as I can guess at this point."

"What are you planning to do?" Addams's left eyelid twitched as he spoke.

"I haven't decided yet."

"You going to go looking for the thing?"

John nodded slowly. "I thought I'd go out to St. Gertrude's and ask around first. I'm told that these hawks, or whatever they are, probably inhabit their land. Maybe the nuns know where the nest is." He paused, then mused, "Remember when we were kids? We thought they were gargoyles."

The eye twitched harder. "From what Corey said, maybe we were right."

"What did he say?"

"That its eyes glowed like a cat's and the beak was long, black, and hooked." Winky paused. "The eyes were on the front of the face, predator-style. Think we have some sort of overgrown mutant owls around here?"

"It's possible. I always thought it was a species of hawk, but I guess an owl's more likely, though the description of the beak doesn't really fit."

Winky nodded. "Couldn't be a bat?"

"No. Frank Cutter said the bite on Mark's neck was definitely from some sort of bird." He paused. "Say, Winky, you still hunt?"

"Occasionally."

"You want to help me track the thing down, once I have a better idea where to look?"

"We'd have to do our hunting on St. Gruesome's land?"

He nodded. "Looks that way."

"I hate that place. Maybe you should take one of your deputies, instead."

John looked up quickly. "Why do you hate it?"

"I don't know." Winky rubbed his chin. "I just do."

*There's no time like the present.* John steeled himself. "Wink, what do you remember about the night my brother died?"

"What do you mean?" he asked, his expression pained.

"Did we go to St. Gruesome's that night?"

"Oh, Christ, John, not *that* again."

John forced a chuckle. "Hey, I haven't brought it up for over two decades."

"Seems like yesterday." Winky had a faraway look in his eyes.

"Yeah, it does. And with all that's been happening, well, let's just say it's been on my mind a lot lately. Gus told me that he overheard all of us arguing about whether we'd gone there or not."

"When was that?"

"Not long after it happened. He seems to think we went."

"No, we didn't." Winky didn't sound too sure.

"He also thinks Doug Buckman's death was related. Remember how he insisted we *did* go out there?"

"Yeah, vaguely, but Doug was always goofing. Your grandad's imagining things."

"Maybe. Maybe he is." He decided not to bring up his father's involvement. "Listen, Winky, do you think Corey will be up to it if I drop by later today to ask him some questions?"

"Call first. Hopefully he'll be okay by then." Winky stood up. "John?"

"Yeah?"

"You ever have nightmares?"

"All the time."

Winky's eye twitched again. "Yeah—me, too. See you later."

John watched his old friend lumber out the door, then picked up the phone and put in a call to Gus. There was no answer.

# Forty-Nine

"Jan, you're such a bitch," Marcia Crowley sneered, flipping her golden hair away from her face. "*I* deserved first place and *you* know it."

"Girls," warned Sara. "Take your seats. The bell rang five minutes ago." It was the last class before lunch, and obviously, it was going to be the worst one yet. Marcia Crowley and her entire clique was present—and all, evidently, were in the throes of PMS.

"Marcia, Marcia, *Marcia!*" the girl with long blond hair screeched, paying absolutely no attention to Sara, "It's always Marcia, Marcia, Marcia!" She stomped her foot. "My essay was better than yours. *Everybody* knows it."

"Then why didn't *you* get the ribbon?" Marybeth Tingler taunted.

"Because Marcia is Sister Abby's favorite." Jan scowled. "What'd you do, Marcia, lick her—"

"Girls!" Sara thundered, with a clap of her hands. "Take your seats!"

Grudgingly, turning their glowers on Sara, they obeyed.

The day had not gone well so far. By the time she'd cleaned up and changed her clothes, Sara had barely made it to her first class on time. The only good thing was that she hadn't run into anyone in the halls or in the lavatory.

The first class had been made up of sullen, silent ninth-graders and a smattering of apple polishers who were, if anything, even more annoying than the silent ones. Next came the eleventh graders, a mix of sullen, shy, and smart-alecky ones in equal proportions. This class, the seniors, would be the worst of the day.

She looked out at the sea of faces as Richard Dashwood's comment came back to her—that Marcia and her friends were probably responsible for the razor blade on her bed. But she wondered now, because of the phantom's appearance, if that was true. The whole incident had turned into something horrifying, something she didn't understand and didn't dare think about if she wanted to make it through the day. "All right, girls, I'm Ms. Hawthorne, and we'll be studying American history this semester. Open your books to page 156."

"What about roll call?" Buffy Bullock asked coyly. The girls surrounding her giggled.

"Thank you, Buffy," Sara said with as much dignity as she could muster. She took roll call, then began the lesson, one eye on the clock.

Finally the hour ended. After dismissing the class, she waited at her desk for them to file out. She'd missed breakfast and was going to skip lunch as well, hoping that she could somehow get the amulet to Kelly during the hour. It wasn't so much that she believed the charm had power as it was a strong need of her own to let the girl know she hadn't forgotten about her. Suddenly she had an idea.

"Miss Hawthorne?"

She looked up to see Marcia Crowley standing before her desk. Her friends were arrayed behind her like back-up singers.

"What is it, Marcia?"

"We didn't see you at services yesterday." The girl was positively purring.

"No, Marcia, I was busy."

"Weren't you invited?" Buffy asked with an air of superiority.

"I'm not a member of your faith," Sara said cautiously.

The girls exchanged knowing glances, then Blaire Fugate spoke. "You're the only teacher who's an outsider, then."

"Just like Miss Tynan," Marybeth said, falsely solemn.

Sara rose and walked to the door, her flesh crawling with goosebumps. "I'll see you all tomorrow," she said in what she hoped was a calm tone. The girls filed out, their "Goodbye, Miss Hawthorne"'s all in Eddie Haskell tones.

Sara closed the door after them, returned to her desk and started putting together Kelly's schoolwork. She could pass the charm to the girl in the papers if she could find something thick enough to put it in.

Taking the amulet from her pocket, she examined it. "Damn." There was no way she could do it without a book. She turned in her chair and examined the bookshelf behind her, finally chose a biography of Thomas Jefferson. It was old and thick—perfect. She put the amulet in the middle and closed the book, pressing hard to try to squash it, but it was no use. "Damn." In one of the desk drawers, she found an Exacto knife. Supressing a cringe at the sight of the sharp blade, she took it out.

She flipped the pages until she was in the last quarter of the book, surprised at what she was about to do. She'd never defaced a book in her life, but now she began carefully cutting an inch-wide circle through the pages, glancing up nervously every time she heard footsteps in the corridor. Finally it was done, and she wound the thong around the amulet and placed it in the hole. Then she glued the center edges of the cut leaves together, and the intact top and bottom pages over the hole to secure it.

Examining her work, she was pleased: unless the nuns looked very carefully, they'd never notice what she'd done. If they did find the charm, she was in trouble, but the way things stood now, she was willing to take the chance.

Sara added a report on Thomas Jefferson to the assignment sheet, then gathered everything together and took it downstairs and entered the infirmary.

The waiting room was deserted. "Sister Regina?" she called. "Sister?"

The door to the back offices opened a moment later and Richard Dashwood stepped out. He smiled when he saw her. "Sara, I trust you're feeling well?"

"Doctor. I—I was looking for Sister Regina. To give her Kelly's assignments."

"Please call me Richard when we're alone, won't you? Regina is at lunch right now," he said, taking the book and papers from her. "I'll see that she gets them."

"I don't want to bother you with this. I can come back later." She put her hands out to take the items back, but he only smiled.

"Nonsense. Have you had lunch yet?"

"No."

"Join me, then. I won't take no for an answer," he added, his eyes warm and inviting. "Come along."

He led her out of the infirmary and around the corner to an oak door. She was amused to see that in a place purportedly lockless, he, like Mother Lucy, had a lock and used it.

"Forgive the mess," he said, ushering her inside. "Bachelor quarters, you know."

The only thing that remotely resembled a mess was a stack of papers on an open rolltop desk. The rest of the living room was elegantly furnished in dark antique furniture, and there wasn't a speck of dust visible anywhere.

She followed him past a hall door, catching sight of a bathroom and bedroom beyond. Dashwood, at least, was not relegated to spartan quarters.

They walked through a small dining area and into a surprisingly large kitchen with modern appliances. The doctor set the book and papers on the counter, then opened a gleaming black refrigerator and looked inside. "What would you say to rare roast beef with cucumber and horseradish on black bread?"

Her stomach rumbled before she could reply, and he laughed. "I'll take that as a yes." He began placing the items on the counter. "There are knives in the drawer and plates in the cupboard above."

"I'm sorry," she said, mortified as her stomach continued to speak. "I didn't have breakfast this morning." She handed him a knife, then took down red china plates and placed them on the counter.

"First day jitters? No appetite?"

"No, I just miscalculated," she said quickly. "I went jogging when I got up and didn't allow enough time to eat."

He worked quickly, slicing the beef paper-thin and piling it on the thick bread. "Would you care for a glass of wine?"

"I would, but no. It make me sleepy."

He smiled as he carried the plates to the small kitchen table. "I believe you, after seeing the effect the truffles seemed to have on you. Sit down. I have sparkling water, apple juice, or iced tea."

"Tea, please."

"Coming right up."

Sara enjoyed the meal and the company. Richard entertained her with stories about the nuns, students' exploits, and nearly everything else. The only subject he avoided was himself.

"Would you like a piece of pie and some coffee?" he asked at last.

"I couldn't eat another bite, but I'd love some coffee."

Quickly, he started the coffeemaker, then turned to her. "It's mincemeat," he said.

"What?"

He laughed. "Mincemeat pie, the sisters' specialty. What did you think I meant?"

It was her turn to laugh. "I didn't know what you meant. Thanks, but no thanks. Another time." She almost told him she detested mincemeat, but decided that would be rude.

He cut himself a piece and brought it to the table, then went back for the coffee. He poured for them, then forked a small bite of pie into his mouth. "Mmm. There's really nothing else like it in the world. Would you like to taste it?"

"Honestly, Richard, I just can't. I'm almost too full for the coffee."

"May I ask you a question?"

"Of course."

"I noticed your finger is bandaged and there are some cuts on your palm. What happened?"

"I fell when I was out jogging. It's nothing, but you know how it is when there's a cut on your finger—you seem to hit it on everything. So I put a Band-Aid on it." She forced a smile and asked lightly, "Any more questions? I have to get back— my next class is in ten minutes."

"Just one." He finished the pie. "Did you sleep well last night?"

*If only you knew.* She smiled sweetly. "Like a baby." She thought she saw a look of surprise, quickly hidden, but it might have been her imagination.

Dashwood retrieved Kelly's schoolwork from the counter and accompanied Sara out the door, locking it behind him. They walked together as far as the infirmary, then Sara continued on upstairs to face the rest of her first day of school. She only hoped that the amulet would make it safely to Kelly, for the girl's sake and her own.

# Fifty

John walked into Franklin's Pharmacy, an antibiotic prescription for Mark clutched in his hand. The store looked the same as it had when he was a kid, with a rainbow of antique apothecary jars in the windows, a counter full of penny candy, and an old-fashioned soda fountain.

Beano himself was behind the pharmacy counter at the rear of the shop. His dark hair was cut short, and he was as round as ever; his white coat had popped a button. When he looked up and saw John, he nodded hello as if they were nothing more than fleeting acquaintances. Beano had retreated more than any of them after Greg's death, and completely broke relations after Doug Buckman's death.

John put the prescription down on the counter and pushed it across to Franklin. He read it, then nodded. "This will only take a minute." He turned and began working. "Heard about the Parker boy," he said over his shoulder.

"News travels fast."

"Heard your boy got a chunk taken out of him."

"Just a nip. He's fine. Frank just prescribed the drugs as a precaution."

Beano nodded, but said nothing until he brought the container of pills back to the counter. "So, was it one of those damned hawks? Been hearing them a lot lately."

"From the description the boys gave, it's probably an owl." He paused. "You've been hearing them, too, huh?"

"Yeah." Beano scratched his chin thoughtfully. "I don't remember them being this noisy since we were kids."

"Around the time of Greg's death we heard them a lot, remember?"

Beano eyed him. "Yeah. I remember."

"What else do you remember?" John asked lightly.

"What do you mean?" Beano's tone was suspicious.

John told him Gus's eavesdropping story. "What do you think, Beano? Did we go there?"

"Hell, no, we didn't go there. Thinking that way is what made Doug crazy enough to kill himself."

"Well, then, you and Gus almost agree on something."

Beano glowered at him from beneath his dark brows. "Doug and I were like this," he said, crossing his fingers tightly. "Until Greg died, just like this. Then he just kept going on about all that St. Gertrude shit, and I couldn't stand being around him." He leaned forward on his elbows. "Doug told me he saw one of those things, but I think he was full of shit."

"Why do you think that?"

"Remember my big brother, Brian?"

"Sure."

"He claimed the same thing, and you know how full of shit he was."

"When?"

"He claimed it was the year he left for college '71, I guess. He said it to scare me."

"How come you never told us?"

"Because it was a load of bullshit. I wanted to go to St. Gertrude's to check out the girls, and if you guys knew about the birdies, you wouldn't have gone."

"But Beano, I remember you saying he said we shouldn't go."

"Yeah, well, I guess I was a kid back then, so I believed him a little." He grunted, his face reddening. "I didn't tell you about the bird because it sounded too stupid. Guess we missed our chance to see some pussy. If Brian wasn't dead already, I'd like to give him a piece of my mind. Christ, you know what that son-of-a-bitch said?"

"What's that, Beano?"

"He said it wasn't a bird."

"What was it?"

"Claimed it was a gargoyle. I can't believe he scared me with that bullshit now. He just wanted to keep all the pussy-lookin' for himself."

"A gargoyle?" John asked, interested.

"Yep. Doug said the same thing. Those must be godawful ugly owls, that's all I can figure."

"They must be."

Beano put the pills in a bag, clearly done with the conversation. "Tell your grandad his pills are ready. I called him a couple times, but he didn't answer."

"I'll take them to him. I'm going by his place right now to check on him. Haven't heard from him for a few days."

"He's probably off fishing somewhere."

"Probably." John paid for the pills and left for Gus's house.

# Fifty-One

Last night, Kelly had been too nervous to sleep, and now she fought the almost overwhelming urge to take a nap. She had no intention of giving in to the desire because she wanted to be so exhausted by the time Sister Regina came to take away her lightbulb that she wouldn't care it was gone.

Nothing had happened during the night, but the utter darkness had seemed filled with evil, and Kelly had trembled beneath the thin blanket, awaiting the sound of the crying ghost. It never came, and now she almost wished it had: it wouldn't have been as bad as the waiting.

Her stomach rumbled and she was very thirsty; lunch had been a cup of water and a stale bran muffin. She tried not to think about her hunger as she sat down at the table and began examining the schoolwork Sister Regina had delivered a few minutes earlier.

There was a copy of *The Scarlet Letter* to read with her English assignment, some pages of Latin, and way too much algebra. Then she found what she was looking for: Miss Hawthorne's history assignment. She read the sheet and noticed that the report on Thomas Jefferson had been hurriedly written at the bottom in a different color ink.

Hoping to find a personal note hidden in the book, she flipped through it and found the last part stuck together. She could tell that something was hidden in it. Casually she stretched, looking around at the camera she knew was hidden behind a portrait of a naked female saint being eaten alive by rats. She knew it was a stationary mount, and after making sure it wouldn't be able to see what she had on the desk if she was careful, she turned casually back to the desk.

She looked through the rest of the assignments, then sighed aloud—she figured they could hear her if they could see her— and picked up a pencil. She opened the Jefferson book and pretended to read, all the while using her fingernail to poke a hole in the pulpy paper. After a moment, she exposed the hole and saw the amulet. Elated because Miss Hawthorne had obviously visited Minerva. she curled her fingers around the necklace, drew it out and dropped it in her pocket. She'd put it around her neck when she couldn't be seen, after the light was taken away from her.

# Fifty-Two

John pulled up in front of Gus's house feeling slightly embarrassed. The old man would tease him mercilessly for worrying about him, but there was no hiding it from him, no saying he was just in the neighborhood. Gus would *know*—he always did.

He climbed out of the cruiser and checked the mailbox by the driveway, mildly alarmed to find an electric bill, a couple letters, one perfumed, and some ads inside. Gus's mail was delivered in the morning and the old man was usually prompt about retrieving it: he loved those perfumed notes from his lady penpals. *Don't jump to conclusions. He probably* did *go fishing today.*

He took the mail, then started up the path, pausing to snag a rolled-up sales flyer, then climbed the porch steps and knocked on the door. "Gus? Gus? You home?"

The drapes were drawn, but that wasn't unusual. Gus didn't like to answer his door, and if Jehovah's Witnesses had been prowling around, he became militant about it. He could hear the television playing inside as he knocked again, but that didn't mean much, either; Gus usually left it on whether he was in or out. After knocking and calling out once more, he went back down the steps and around the house to the small garage. It was padlocked shut, but he cupped his hands and peered inside. Gus's Oldsmobile was parked within.

John's stomach twisted, then he reminded himself that, like as not, Gus had gone fishing or shopping or whatever, with a friend who had done the driving.

Still, as he walked back to the front door and pulled his keys from his pocket, he couldn't shake his nervousness. He found the right key, then pulled open the screen door and tried knocking one last time. No answer. *You should have called him Saturday when he didn't show up for lunch.*

The lock turned and John pushed open the door. Cool, fetid air wafted out. "Dear God," he choked, recognizing the smell. "Oh, dear God."

He took his gun from its holster, then forced himself to step inside the darkened house. "Gus?" The smell of blood and death choked him as his eyes went to the only bright spot in the living room—the television set. *General Hospital* was on, but parts of the screen were obscured by dark spatters and drips, and gobbets of something thicker. On the floor in front of the set he could make out a lumpy puddle of dried gore.

Lifeless fingers were just visible on the arm of the easy chair facing the television, and he dreaded what was to come. It was almost a relief as he made his way along the wall of the living room and into the hallway beyond to check the rest of the house for intruders before he faced the chair.

There was no sign that anyone had been in any other rooms, and finally, he was satisfied that he was alone. He walked slowly back into the living room, his legs rubbery, his heart jittering as he forced himself to go straight to the easy chair.

The top of Gus's head was gone, the jagged edges of his skull jutting up like a broken eggshell. Flies crawled sluggishly on what remained inside.

"God," he moaned and raced to the bathroom, barely making

it to the toilet before his lunch came up. That hadn't happened since the body in the trunk when he was a rookie. He rinsed out his mouth and pulled himself together then returned to the living room, trying not to think of the corpse in the chair as his grandfather, but as a homicide under investigation.

Obviously, a shotgun had done the damage. Probably a cut-off, definitely from behind at close range. The body would have been thrown forward—there were stains on the rug confirming that. But the killer had put the body in an upright position, one hand resting on the armrest, the other in its lap, loosely holding the TV remote. Whoever did this had a perverse sense of humor.

He walked out onto the front porch and took deep lungfuls of fresh air, then called in the crime on his cell phone.

# PART FOUR

## OCTOBER, 1996

# Fifty-Three

The day of Gus's funeral dawned foggy and cold, and as the casket was lowered into the grave, John rested his hand on Mark's shoulder. The little cemetery, which had served Moonfall since pioneer days, was filled with friends and neighbors, and in a way, that only made him feel worse. He had let Gus and the whole town down because he and his deputies hadn't been able to turn up a thing. Not a footprint, fingerprint, or suspect—not a damned thing.

Mark nudged him, and he realized everyone was waiting for him to act. He stepped forward and scooped up a handful of dirt, then sprinkled it in the grave. "Ashes to ashes," he said and choked on the words.

The next moments were confusing as everyone came up to offer his sympathy. He shook hands and nodded and said "thank you" more times than he could count, and even found some trace of amusement in the sheer number of grieving older women, many of them from out of town, who threw red roses into the grave. Gus had always brought his dates a red rose, and now he was smothered in them.

"John, I'm real sorry about Gus." Caspar Parker shook his hand solemnly. "You let me know if there's anything I can do."

John looked at the old man, Gus's best friend, Pete Parker's great-grandfather, the mainstay of Moonfall. There was true kindness in the eyes of this man and it surprised him since he hadn't gotten to the bottom of his great-grandson's death. "Thanks. Is the Haunt still on?"

"Pete would want it that way," Caspar said, loosening his tie. "But now, with Gus's death, the violence of it—I don't know."

"Please, go ahead with your plans. Gus wouldn't want it any other way."

Caspar nodded, then looked down at Mark. "You still want to help?"

"Can I, Dad?"

"Of course you can." Mark was part of the reason he wanted the Haunt to run as scheduled: it would give the boy something to concentrate on.

Caspar stood beside the grave a long moment, hat in hand, then walked slowly toward the cemetery gate.

"How are you two holding up?" Frank Cutter asked as he stepped forward.

John turned toward him and realized that the cemetery was nearly deserted. Only Minerva Payne lingered, twenty feet away, at the grave of Jeremiah Moonfall. "We'll survive, Frank."

"Terrible thing," Cutter said.

"Yeah."

"A few of us are going to have a little wake at Winesap's tonight, raise a few glasses in Gus's honor. It's what he would want. Care to join us?"

"Uh, no," John said, glancing at Mark.

"Dad? Corey asked if I could spend the night," Mark said. "I said I didn't think I could, but I'd like to, if you want to go out."

"Well, sure, I guess."

"It'll do you both good to get out," Cutter said.

John nodded, his eyes on Minerva Payne, who was walking purposefully toward them. "Minerva, thank you for coming."

"You're welcome," she said, then turned to Mark. "I hope you'll come visit me sometime soon."

"I will."

"I have to do some heavy cleaning at the Gingerbread House next week. Would you be interested in working for me after school?"

"Yeah. Can I, Dad?"

He nodded, realizing Minerva's intentions—keeping the boy occupied—matched his. "Just so your homework gets done." As he spoke, the old lady shot him a subtle wink, and for the first time since Gus's death, he actually suspected that life might go on.

"Sheriff," she said, drawing an envelope from a pocket in her dark dress. "This is for you. No, no, don't open it now. But come see me next week, after you've perused it."

He nodded. "I'll do that."

Gentle rain began to fall, not much more than a mist, and Minerva pulled her shawl closer around her.

"Can I give you a lift?" Frank Cutter asked.

"Yes, that would be very kind of you." She stepped forward and kissed Mark lightly on the forehead, then rested her hand briefly on John's. "Take care," she told them. "Be careful." With that, she turned and took Cutter's arm, and they walked slowly away, leaving John and Mark alone.

"Why can't you find the killer, Dad?" the boy asked softly.

The question tore him apart. "Mark, I won't stop looking until I do find him. I promise."

Mark didn't reply. He was staring at the grave, silent tears that had been held back throughout the services, now coursing down his cheeks. John felt his own tears spill, and didn't bother to wipe them away.

"It must've been horrible finding him like you did," his son murmured at last.

"Yes. But no worse than you went through when you found Pete."

Mark looked up at him. "Thanks, Dad."

"For what?"

"For—I don't know. For everything. For not punishing me when Pete died. For being nice to Minerva. For not dying."

The tears came harder, mingling with the rain, and John put his arm around Mark's shoulders, drew him close, suddenly wondering how he'd survive if something ever happened to the boy.

# Fifty-Four

"Here's to Gus." Frank Cutter said, raising his straight shot of Wild Turkey.

"To Gus," said John and Caspar Parker in unison.

They drank, then Caspar poured another round and raised his glass again. "To Pete, a hell of a little guy."

"To Pete."

They drank again, then Caspar poured more liquor into their glasses. John hoped there would be no more toasts: he just didn't have the stomach for it. And it felt strange to be sitting in Winesap's without Gus. *Be honest; it's depressing as hell.*

"Anyone else coming?" he asked.

"I asked Winky Addams and Beano Franklin, but it doesn't look like they're going to show," Cutter said.

"Joe didn't want to leave Helen home alone," Caspar said. They were Pete's parents. "Johnny, I wanted to talk to you about Pete a little bit."

"I'm sorry, Caspar, but I don't have anything new yet."

"No, no, son, I know that. And you've had more on your mind. Trying to find a human killer takes precedence over an animal attack." Caspar downed his third shot and poured himself another. "I want to tell you something about Pete's death." He cleared his throat, then looked John in the eye. "He's not the first."

John sat up in surprise. "He's not?"

"No. Way back in 1898, my uncle was killed by one of those murdering bastards. My dad saw it, but he told everybody it was a bear. We had a lot of griz around here back then."

"Why'd he say it was a bear, Caspar?" John asked.

"Simple. He knew everybody'd think he was nuts if he told 'em what he really saw. He only told me on his deathbed, and I never told anyone else until now. Not even Gus." He downed another shot. "I didn't want to be thought of as a space cadet, either, and I wouldn't have spoken up if Mark and Corey hadn't seen it, since I wasn't too sure about it." He sat forward. "I've seen a lot of strange things around here. Saw one of those white ladies in the orchard not once, but three different times over the years. Saw some other things I'm not sure I believe, either. There was a house up on the hill where the Heights is now, when I was a boy. Just a little cabin. A woman and her daughter lived there. Pretty little things, both of 'em. But one night, stones commenced to rain on the house. Everybody saw it. They appeared out of the sky—*pop*—like that." He snapped his fingers. "Went on for a couple months. Big ones, little ones, river stones, lava rock. No one could ever explain it. Not even Minerva."

"She must've been just a girl then," Cutter said. He was on his fourth shot.

"Well, maybe she was and maybe she wasn't." Caspar poured a double. "She claims her ma and her ma before her and so on have always lived in the cottage, since about the time Jeremiah Moonfall came to town. But no one never saw a youngster around there. Just the old woman."

"What're you saying, Caspar?" the doctor asked. "That Minerva's been living there for a couple hundred years?"

"Nah, that's too crazy, even for the likes of me. I'm just saying there's something strange about Minerva, too." With liquor-glazed eyes, he stared at John. "Your boy likes her, doesn't he? Pete said he did."

John nodded. "He likes her a lot. But Caspar, tell me what your father said—"

"It's okay, Johnny, if young Mark likes her. She's a witchy old woman, but she's not evil. She's got nothing to do with those gargoyles, that's just rumor."

"What killed your uncle?" John asked, as Caspar paused to pour another whiskey.

"Just told you, Johnny. A gargoyle got him."

"A gargoyle?" John stifled a chuckle.

"That's what I said. They roost at St. Gertrude's."

John and Cutter exchanged glances.

"I know what you're thinking," Caspar said to both of them. "But it took a lot of good whiskey for me to get up the nerve to tell you, and you're gonna listen. My daddy described something a lot like what your son and Corey talked about, only this one was a little different. It had a long tail whippin' around behind it, and it had little fuzzy ears like a bear's. What do you think's been screeching in the forest all these years? Hawks don't sound like that; neither do owls. We had a few bird nuts come through here looking to find themselves a new species, but they never did. Never will. They couldn't find eggs, nor nests, and you know why?" With a satisfied look, he glanced back and forth between the two men.

"Why?" Cutter asked.

"Because they turn to stone in the daylight."

"Yeah," John said. "I hear that's what gargoyles do."

"Oh, they don't have to," Caspar said, his volume rising with every word. "That's just their way, most of the time. That way, nobody can catch 'em. All those stories about 'em carrying off babies are based in fact, you know. My daddy told me they got a few, back when people weren't quite so careful."

"Sheriff Lawson, allow me to extend my condolences."

John jerked his head around and found Richard Dashwood staring sympathetically down at him. What was worse was that Sara Hawthorne was with him. He stood up, glad he hadn't been drinking. "Dr. Dashwood, Ms. Hawthorne. This is a surprise."

"I heard about your grandfather," Sara said softly. "I'm so sorry."

"Thanks."

"Who're you?" Caspar asked Dashwood. "I've seen you before."

"I don't think so. Perhaps you met my father." Dashwood extended his hand, but Caspar was too drunk to bother with such amenities. "I'm Richard Dashwood, St. Gertrude's physician. This is Miss Hawthorne, one of our teachers."

Caspar paid no attention to Sara, but kept his eyes on Dashwood. "I know you."

"Perhaps you've seen me at your Halloween Haunt. I attended last year."

"That must be it," John said, sensing trouble brewing. He smiled at Sara. "Out for a night on the town?"

She looked uncomfortable. "Just one drink. I've been so busy I haven't been able to get away."

"At least you've made a friend," John said.

"Something's wrong with my car, so Richard offered to drive me."

John didn't like the way she looked at the physician, but he knew he had no right to say so. *You're jealous, you idiot.*

"Care to join us?" Cutter asked.

"No, thank you. We have a table."

He nodded at a dark alcove less then ten feet away. Plenty close, John realized, to have eavesdropped on Caspar's loud comments about the gargoyles. "Thanks for stopping by," he said, and turned his back on the pair.

# Fifty-Five

*I shouldn't be here. What am I doing?* Sara Hawthorne waited while Richard made a show of pulling her chair out for her after they left John's table.

"Another glass of chardonnay, Sara? It's an excellent vintage. I'm frankly surprised to find something of this caliber in an establishment like this." His nose wrinkled in distaste. "Unlike the tavern," he added, topping off her glass without waiting for a reply, "this has an excellent bouquet."

*And an interesting afterbirth.* Sara wondered how he'd react if she'd joked aloud. Not well, she thought, her eyes drifting to the back of John Lawson's head. She hadn't realized he had such broad shoulders until now.

*The man's in mourning. Stop lusting after him.* She smiled at Richard, and thought that maybe she was losing her mind. Kelly had had been locked up for a week, and she hadn't tried to send her any more encouragement, not even a scrap of paper with a note saying "Hi." She hadn't gone back to Minerva's, either. Instead, she'd spent all her free time in Richard's company. The man was a gourmet cook, and she'd gained several pounds in the last week, judging by the way her clothes fit.

She didn't know what the physician's attraction was, but it had put her in some sort of self-indulgent haze. Every time she was with him—for breakfast, lunch, and dinner every day since their first lunch—she came away not caring about anything else. Tonight, she knew, they would probably make love for the first time.

"To pleasure," Richard said, raising his glass.

She smiled mechanically and clinked glasses, then sipped the wine. Was she in love? Was that why she was behaving so out of character? She'd thought so, but now she wondered if she was just rationalizing her behavior. The moment she'd looked into John Lawson's eyes, she'd found herself, at least for a brief instant. *He's the one you want to make love to, not Richard.*

"Sara? What are you thinking?"

"Nothing," she said, avoiding his eyes. If she looked into them, she would be captivated. It always happened that way.

He started talking about wine, and her thoughts drifted, though she was careful to nod at the right moments. She hadn't had another bad dream—or other experience—since the episode in the woods. Instead, she'd had very pleasant dreams, almost too pleasant. They were so intensely erotic that she awakened repeatedly in the throes of orgasm, positive that a phantom lover had just left her bed. It was almost enough to make her believe in incubi.

*What's wrong with me?* As Richard yammered on, she watched John's back, saw the slump of his shoulders, the tilt of his head. He was sad and he wasn't drinking. The old man at his table was making up for that, still holding forth, but in tones too soft to hear anymore. Earlier, before Richard insisted they say hello, she'd been eavesdropping with fascination, even though she could tell the old fellow was completely plastered. Richard, on the other hand, had grown more and more irritated. She was sure that was why he wanted to talk to them: to shut the old man up.

At that moment, John stood up and took his coat off the back of his chair. He was leaving. She had to talk to him.

"Excuse me a moment, Richard," she said softly. "I need to visit the powder room."

"Of course."

"No, don't get up. I'll be right back."

John was just going out the door. She left the table and glanced back. Richard wasn't watching. Quickly, she made her way across the common room, and out the door into the chilly night.

"John," she called across the lot.

He turned, squinting against the tavern's lights. "Sara?"

"Wait!" She ran to him. "I need to talk to you."

"Go ahead." His tone was cool.

"Not now. I don't want Richard to get suspicious."

"Look, I don't want to be part of whatever mating dance it is you're conducting."

Her first reaction was anger, but she quelled it, remembering his stories about his wife's affair, realizing trusting women was probably difficult for him. "It's not what you think. I—I don't know how to explain."

"It's pretty clear." He hesitated. "Look, I have no right to speak to you this way. I certainly have no claim on you. I've just had a hard day. A hard week."

She touched his arm and he didn't draw away. "I know. I'm sorry. Look, I don't know what's going on. That's what I need to talk to you about."

"Sara," he said, pulling back, "I'm in no shape to hear about your love life."

"I have no love life."

"Are you really that naive? Dashwood's laid claim on you. If you don't have a love life now, I guarantee you will before the night is over."

"No," she said, thinking more clearly than she had in a week. "When I get back to the abbey, I'm going to have the headache of the century."

"Don't—"

"If I have a love life, you'll be part of it. Believe me, I have no interest in that man. He's an egomaniac."

"Then why are you with him?"

"I—I don't know. Like I said, it's part of the reason I need to talk to you. And it has nothing to do with sex. It has to do with things that are going on at the abbey. Things I don't understand. Please, believe me."

He studied her a long moment, then slowly put his hands on her shoulders. "God help me, I believe you." With that, he pulled her against him and tilted her chin up gently with his fingers.

They brushed lips tentatively, once, twice, and the fire in her belly stirred to white hot flames. She could smell his skin, a mixture of clean aftershave and his own scent, whatever it was that made him a unique person. It was intoxicating. Their lips brushed again and she drew his lower lip between her own lips, lightly touched it with her tongue, tasting him.

She heard herself moan as his tongue met hers and they began to explore one another, his hands in her hair, hers feeling the ridges of hard muscle in his back. She pressed herself against him, feeling her heat, and his.

Finally, the kiss ended, both of them panting. His eyes were bright. "Sara . . ."

She smiled up at him. "I'll come see you tomorrow afternoon."

He nodded, then she turned and walked quickly back to the tavern while she could still pull herself away.

# Fifty-Six

Letting Sara go was one of the hardest things John had ever done. As he watched her walk away, he wanted to stop her, to take her home with him, not only to make love to her, but to keep her safe. She was in danger, he knew that as well as he knew his own name.

It was a powerful feeling, the kind that Minerva Payne had rightly accused him of having. Instinct, intuition, precognition: whatever it was, he knew it was true.

He drove home. Trying to keep his mind off Sara—he

couldn't do anything for her until he heard her story tomorrow—he concentrated on Minerva. Until now, he'd forgotten about the envelope she'd given him at the cemetery and he was suddenly very curious about its contents.

As always, the house seemed empty with Mark gone, so he turned on the TV to fill the void, then went to the closet and retrieved the envelope from his suit. He returned to the living room. *The X-Files* was just starting. It was Mark's favorite, and John knew he and Corey were probably glued to the Addamses' set. Normally he avoided the show, as he avoided anything with a touch of the weird, but he found himself watching it, engrossed. During each commercial, he examined the envelope but didn't open it; now that it was in his hands, he wasn't so sure he wanted to know what was inside. Whatever it was, it would no doubt complicate his life even more. *But it might have some bearing on Mark's safety . . .*

The ending credits rolled and grimly, slowly, John opened the envelope. First he drew out a note written on a piece of stationery in an elegant, precise hand. ''Please study the enclosed history and then return it to me. It is more important than you realize. Sincerely, Minerva Payne.'' He set the note aside and unfolded a sheet of typing paper. It was a hastily written copy of the Lawson family tree.

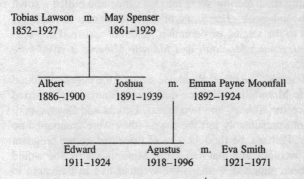

```
Tobias Lawson   m.   May Spenser
1852–1927            1861–1929
        |
   _____|_____
   |           |
Albert      Joshua      m.   Emma Payne Moonfall
1886–1900   1891–1939        1892–1924
                |
      _____|_____
      |              |
   Edward        Agustus     m.   Eva Smith
   1911–1924     1918–1996        1921–1971
                    |
```

| Howard | Henry | m. | Chloe Raines |
|--------|-------|-----|--------------|
| 1934–1948 | 1938–1973 | | 1939–1975 |

| Gregory | John | m. | Barbara Tyler |
|---------|------|-----|---------------|
| 1962–1972 | 1959– | | 1963– |

Mark
1983–

He had never looked at the family tree before; it just wasn't something that had interested him. But now he found it fascinating. For a moment, he wondered how Minerva had come to have a copy, then he saw that Tobias's son Joshua had married a woman named Emma Payne Moonfall. By the birthdate, she had to be Jeremiah Moonfall's daughter. That surprised him, but it was Emma Moonfall's middle name, Payne, that intrigued him. Was there actually a tie to Minerva, as well? He wondered if Minerva came from some offshoot of the clan. Was that why the old woman kept insisting he and Mark and Gus had the same "gift" for intuition as she?

Taking the paper, he went into his office and pulled a small paperbound book, *The Story of Moonfall,* from a shelf. He turned to the section on Jeremiah Moonfall and read one sentence: *Jeremiah Moonfall and his wife Minerva arrived here in 1875.*

"Minerva?" he asked aloud. He scanned the pages and found that the Moonfalls had three daughters; Emma, who married his ancestor, Tobias, and two others, Leticia and Desma, both of whom presumably left the town—they were mentioned no further. Perhaps, he thought, one of them had gotten pregnant out of wedlock and that had led to Minerva's line. She would have been shunned. Perhaps she went to live in the cabin in the woods where Minerva now lived. The townsfolk wouldn't have wanted to have anything to do with an unwed mother, and the witch stories might have been started at that time.

Whether he was right or not, he didn't know, but it did make sense.

He returned to his chair in the living room and perused the chart again. The blood tie couldn't be the only thing Minerva had wanted him to see, could it? If so, then she was reading importance into it that just wasn't there. Study it, she had said.

And then there was Gus. That night at the tavern, he had talked about cycles, something to do with a passage of years. Gazing at the chart, he saw that the Lawsons seemed to produce only male children, which was probably nothing but coincidence. Tobias Lawson and his wife had had two sons, Joshua and Albert. Albert had died in 1900 at the age of fourteen, while Joshua had grown up and married Emma Moonfall. Together, they'd produced his grandfather, Agustus, and another son, Edward, who'd died in 1924, aged thirteen. Gus, in turn, had had two sons, John's father, Henry, and Howard, who'd died in 1948, aged fourteen. Then came John and his own brother Greg, who'd died in 1972, at the age of ten. And now there was only Mark, who would be fourteen on October twenty-first.

There was no pattern to the deaths of the surviving brothers—all died at well-advanced ages except for his own father.

But there was a definite pattern to the early deaths. All were between the ages of ten and fourteen, and they had died in 1900, 1924, 1948, and 1972. All the deaths were twenty-four years apart—and that was what Gus had said: there was a twenty-four-year cycle.

Minerva had told him it was important to his son's safety that he talk to her after reading the family tree. *It's 1996. Mark is the right age.*

*It's nonsense . . . isn't it?* He stared at the chart, trying to convince himself it was all a huge coincidence. But if this had been an impersonal case he was investigating, he knew he wouldn't deny the link. Not in a million years.

But why had no one said anything before this? Why hadn't anyone noticed the pattern? *Twenty-four years is a long time. And Gus knew about it.* His grandfather had seen it happen twice; why hadn't he spoken up sooner? Maybe because he didn't really believe it. Lord knew John himself was skeptical.

He glanced at the clock. It was far too late to visit Minerva tonight. He sat back and tried to remember how his father's brother had died, but he realized that he had no knowledge of any of the youthful deaths except Greg's, and what he knew of that was terribly sketchy, even though he must have been present. He needed to know the dates the others had died. He had a feeling, though, that he already did: the same day of the year as Greg. He also wanted to know the ways they'd met their deaths.

Gus would have stored the information somewhere in his house, but it would be easier emotionally to check the county records on Monday. For that matter, he could possibly get the dates at the cemetery on his way to Minerva's tomorrow.

He folded the sheet and replaced it in the envelope, then sat back and tried to concentrate on the television's mindless babbling. It was a losing battle.

He turned his thoughts to the kiss he and Sara had shared, and finally he fell asleep, lulled by remembered pleasures that soon fled under nightmare visions of Gus, Pete Parker, Greg, and finally, his own son, all begging him for help he was incapable of providing.

# Fifty-Seven

"Thank you for a pleasant evening, Richard." Sara stepped out of the doctor's black BMW before he could come around to open the door for her. She pulled her coat close around her, nervous in the dark garage. Although Richard had been chivalrous since she'd returned to the tavern after seeing John Lawson, she was uneasy, unable to stop wondering if he might have seen them together, even though he gave no indication that he had.

The garage was unbearably dark and she gladly let Dashwood take her arm and guide her outside.

"Would you like to come to my apartment for a nightcap?" he asked after they navigated the damp lawn and were safely on the stone walkway.

"I would, but I'm getting a headache," she said, cringing at the sound of the hoariest old excuse in the book coming from her mouth.

"I can give you something for it."

"No, thanks, it's just from the wine. It'll go away when I go to bed. To sleep," she corrected lamely.

"I have something that will get rid of it much faster." As he spoke, he gently put his finger under her chin and tilted it up to make her look at him. At his eyes.

Sure enough, once she gazed into them, she was tempted to change her answer. "I'm sorry," she said with effort. "Not tonight."

He kissed her gently on the lips, and while it wasn't unpleasant, she felt none of the magic, none of the passion that she had experienced with John. There was, she decided, no comparison.

"Are you certain?" he asked.

"Another time," she said, forcing a smile and setting her gaze at a point just above his eyes. She knew she would have acquiesced if it hadn't been for the fresh memory of John Lawson's kiss.

He smiled, unoffended. "Then at least allow me to see you to your building."

"I'd like that."

They strolled to the dormitory, then Dashwood stopped in the shadows. "I'll watch until you're safely inside. I don't want to sully your reputation among the girls."

She nodded. "Richard, this probably isn't the right time, but I wonder if you might do me a favor."

"Anything, as long as you promise to see me again."

"Of course."

"What is it, then?"

"Kelly Reed."

"She's fine."

"I know, but she's been locked up for a week already, and

I can't stop worrying about her. Do you think you might be able to convince Mother Lucy to stay her sentence?"

"She's very strict about such things."

Sara smiled. "But she dotes on you." "Dotes" wasn't the right word, she thought—"lusts after" was closer. "She'll *listen* to you."

"I don't know," he said slowly.

"You sound as if you're afraid of her." That, she thought, should kick in the testosterone.

"How little you know," the doctor said gently. "If you're wise, you'll be afraid of her, too."

She hadn't expected the answer. "Why?"

He hesitated a long moment, then bent and kissed her on the lips. "I'll see what I can do."

"Thank you. Once she's out of solitary, I'll be able to concentrate on other things."

"Like me?"

She smiled coyly, and after the barest of nods, turned and walked swiftly to the door, smiling to herself. She'd behaved as badly as Marcia Crowley and her crowd. Normally, that kind of manipulative female behavior repelled her, but not this time. She smiled to herself. *Desperate times, desperate measures.* She'd finally won a round and probably secured Kelly's freedom.

# Fifty-Eight

John sat on the little overstuffed sofa across from the old lady in the rocker, a cup and saucer in his hands. Anxious to get his questions answered, he'd tried to refuse the tea, but she had insisted on the amenities and he'd found he didn't really want to resist her. "Minerva, you said you still have some relatives who come to see you now and then."

"Yes," she replied, her face unreadable.

"Would that be Mark and me?"

The mask evaporated into a broad smile. "You've done your homework."

"You're named for Jeremiah Moonfall's wife. It wasn't too difficult to figure out."

She chuckled softly. "Named for Jeremiah's wife. I've never thought about it that way before."

"May I ask you a personal question?"

"Of course." She smiled. "I might even answer."

"Was your grandmother one of Emma Moonfall Lawson's unmarried sisters?"

She rocked for a moment, then looked him in the eye. "No."

"Then one of them must have been your mother."

"No. Neither girl bore children. My mother's identity isn't important. What is is whether you understand why I'm concerned about Mark."

He nodded. He had briefly stopped by the cemetery on his way to the cottage and now knew that all the young Lawsons had died on October thirty-first. "Every twenty-four years an adolescent Lawson child dies. This is the twenty-fourth year, and my son is the only candidate."

"Exactly. I've tried to break the cycle, but I've been unsuccessful."

"You mean you tried when Greg died?"

"Yes, among others."

"Minerva," he said, sitting forward. "I don't understand any of this." He raised his hands helplessly. "I'm willing to listen, I *want* to listen, but you're speaking in riddles. I think like a cop. I need plain answers."

"Then you shall have them. More tea?" she asked, a twinkle in her eye.

He didn't take the bait. "No, thanks. Are you telling me that Greg's death wasn't an accident?"

"Nor were any of the others."

"Then you're alleging that the same murderer has been active for nearly a century."

"Longer, and plural. But to understand, you must listen to my story. Will you?" She fixed him with bird-bright eyes.

He settled back, resigned. "Yes, I'll listen."

"In 1876, shortly after the arrival of Jeremiah and Minerva Moonfall, a son, Gerald, was born to them. He died on Halloween, two weeks after his birth."

"Why isn't he in the cemetery, or mentioned in any histories of the area?"

"Except for the nuns who had recently moved into the old abbey, Minerva and Jeremiah were virtually the only people on the mountain. Even Tobias and May Lawson wouldn't arrive for nearly two years. There was no cemetery in those days, John." The old lady's eyes glistened. "And even if there had been, there was no body."

A tear ran down her wrinkled cheek. "Gerald was carried off by a nightflyer." She dabbed her eyes with a handkerchief. "Ironic, isn't it? Generations of Moonfall children tell stories about the nightflyers stealing babies to bring to me. Instead, they took one away. From Minerva Moonfall," she added quickly.

Having seen the condition of Pete Parker's body, John had no trouble believing such a thing could happen. "Yes, but I don't understand how this connects with my son."

"Blood ties and blood feuds. And friendships. The Lawsons arrived here in 1878, and they quickly became close friends with the Moonfalls. Tobias and May had two sons, Albert and Joshua. Minerva and Jeremiah went on to have three daughters, Emma, Leticia, and Desma, but no other sons. Emma was the only one who inherited Minerva's gift. Perhaps that's what helped keep her alive." She sat back, a faint smile on her face as the chair rocked gently. "Emma Moonfall and Joshua Lawson were a match from the time they were in diapers. Time passed, and hardships tested both families. Leticia drowned in the falls, and Desma disappeared into the woods one day never to be seen again. Then, in 1900, on Halloween night, Albert Lawson disappeared. His body was found four days later in St. Gertrude's woods. He was torn limb from limb. That death was attributed to a bear attack, but it was no bear that killed him. He died because it was time for the sacrifice and he was chosen because the murderers knew of the friendship between the two families."

"Who were the murderers, and why were they out to hurt the Moonfalls?"

"All in good time. You promised to listen."

John nodded, biting his tongue.

Minerva closed her eyes a long moment, then peered closely at him. "Fortunately, Joshua and Emma lived. Minerva had tried to use her powers—witchcraft, magic, whatever you wish to call them—to save all the children from harm, but there was too much evil for a solitary practitioner to control, and she knew she was lucky that her own Emma and Joshua Lawson both made it to adulthood.

"They married and officially mingled the bloodlines, bringing Edward and your grandfather, Agustus, into this world. And on Halloween night, exactly twenty-four years after Albert's death, Edward disappeared. The next day, his body was found in a ditch by Apple Hill Road—it was just a dirt track back then. It was decided he'd been run over by a horse-drawn apple cart belonging to a local drunk." She shook her head. "But it wasn't true. The drunk wasn't even in town that night. The body had other wounds that couldn't be explained. Knife wounds. But he was buried and that was that.

"A month later, a final blow was struck to Jeremiah and Minerva. Emma was found dead, a rope around her neck, in an old oak that used to stand where my vegetable garden is now. It was widely believed that she killed herself out of grief over her son's death." Anger sparked in her eyes. "But she was murdered for nothing but spite."

"How do you know all this?"

"I *know*. The deaths of the daughters were deaths-in-effigy. Minerva was the one who was supposed to die, but they could not touch her."

"Who are 'they'?"

"Patience, young man. Agustus married and produced your father, Henry, and his brother, Howard, who died Halloween, 1948, another sacrifice. Supposedly, he died in a thresher accident, although why he was operating one in the middle of the night was something the sheriff never investigated." She paused. "There are, as you may already realize, powers that fog the mind."

"What—"

"Hush. Finally, you came along. Then Greg. Probably, you were the one meant to die—you were the preferred age. Instead, Greg drowned. It was no accident, John, and you couldn't have prevented it."

"Are you saying you know what happened to him?"

"Only in so far that what happened to him was what happened to the other boys. He was a sacrifice. I don't know the details . . . but you do."

"I *do?*"

"It's in here," she tapped her forehead. "Waiting for you to find it."

"Well, do you think you could give me a clue as to who these immortal murderers are?" He couldn't keep the sarcasm out of his voice.

"The sisters of St. Gertrude's."

"The nuns?" he asked, incredulous.

"You know it in your heart,"

"You want me to believe that my brother died because of some century-old feud carried on in the name of nuns and a woman who all must be dust by now?"

"And they killed your father, for delving into things. He was a good man. He never believed his brother died by accident, and that's what made him become a sheriff. It's the same with you, isn't it?"

"I—"

"And Gus," she continued. "What I have told you, he was going to tell you. He never wanted to because he knew the knowledge would put you in jeopardy, as it did your father. He felt it was his fault your father died."

"He told me that," John said, nodding. "But even assuming this is true, how could nuns do such grisly things? Why?"

"First, no one suspects them. Second, they are brides not of Christ, but of Lucifer."

"*Satanic nuns?*" he asked.

"They used to call themselves the Order of Lilith. Named

for the night demon—the original succubus—mentioned in the bible. They've been around for centuries. They came to America before the Revolution and settled in Massachusetts, not far from the old Moonfall homestead. They didn't wear the garb of nuns then, but they were a sisterhood responsible for much of the witchcraft hysteria.

"Minerva had been aware of them, had even been persecuted by them, before she married Jeremiah. She knew what they were, and when the sisterhood left Massachusetts, Minerva convinced Jeremiah to come here and settle. It may have been a foolish decision, but she felt that it was the only one she could make—to follow them and continue to try to diffuse their evil as best she could." She shook her head sadly. "As many deaths as there have been, there might have been even more if she hadn't come."

"If I understand you correctly, these nuns have been responsible for many deaths besides the ones on Halloween." He was again wondering if she was senile or had a sick sense of humor, but he decided to play along for now.

"Of course. The twenty-four-year cycle is a high ritual sacrifice to their god. That's when they need a child's soul, a young male, preferably on the verge of manhood, yet still pure. They have procured them for centuries from here and there. It is a personal vendetta that has caused them to pick those of the Lawson-Moonfall bloodline. That and the fact that Minerva's power has been passed down to several of them, including you and Mark."

"You said they meant to kill me, not Greg?"

"Yes, but don't feel guilty. You have the gift and you've passed it on to your son. Greg did not have it. Because you did, along with your age, you were the more desirable sacrifice."

"Caspar Parker said his uncle was killed by a bear," John began, unwilling to think about Greg any longer.

"Yes—at least, that was the story. In truth, a nightflyer got him."

"So they don't just prey on Lawsons." For the moment, at least, John realized he was buying her story.

"Of course not. The sisters are subtler now than they once

were, but they prey freely, usually on those with whom they have no quarrel."

"I had a friend, Doug Buckman—"

"Yes. They said he committed suicide, but it was murder."

John nodded. "I've always suspected it. Doug was sure we went to St. Gertrude's Halloween night. The rest of us didn't quite believe it."

"Some people are almost impossible to brainwash. Doug was one of them, and he paid for it with his life."

"Brainwash?"

"Yes. Brainwashing, spell-casting, sorcery. Take your pick. Do you ever wonder why it's so easy to forget about St. Gertrude's? It's in your mind one moment and gone the next. There are twelve nuns in the coven, any number of acolytes, many recruited from the orphans, and one high priest, who is a very powerful sorcerer. He and Lucy, his priestess, are capable of things you cannot imagine."

"Dashwood is the priest," John said with satisfaction.

"Of course."

"What about Boullan?"

Minerva snorted. "You might call him the waterboy from hell. He seems formidable, but that's just a touch of madness." She paused. "He has no power, no magic, but don't get me wrong: he could be dangerous in a purely down-to-earth way. He likes to eye the girls, but I don't know if he's ever laid hands on one. I suspect he has."

"How do you even know about him?"

"Remember your dream? I tried to visit you in your sleep and came up against a door?"

He nodded slowly.

"It's a taxing procedure, but that's one way I know. The other way, you'll understand much better. I have friends."

"The girl Mark mentioned?"

"Yes. Kelly is in great danger, I fear. The same as your son. I'm virtually certain they've marked her as the other sacrifice. She has the gift, the same as Mark, and since they can't convert her, they'll kill her."

"Other sacrifice?"

"A virgin female."

He nodded slowly. This was getting too weird. "What you're telling me is useless, legally. If there's abuse going on, if a victim would step forward, I'd have just cause for a search warrant."

"No one will talk. They don't remember." She hesitated. "Kelly might—she's not very susceptible to brainwashing, but she doesn't really know anything of value."

John sat back, his feelings a mix of fascination and disgust. He decided to keep things light until he sorted out his impressions. "You said Emma Moonfall Lawson died here. Is this the original Moonfall home?"

"Yes. Your great-grandfather was born here. Minerva was the midwife."

"All the histories of the area say that the original Moonfall homestead burned down."

She eyed him. "Do you think I want some historical society coming around trying to hang brass plaques on my front door? Many, many years ago a self-appointed historian came around, asking questions. She'd connected my last name with Emma's middle name. I claimed there was no relation."

"But there is."

"Of course."

"How are we related?" he asked. "Are you from another branch of Minerva's original family?"

"You wouldn't believe me if I told you."

"Well, then, tell me this. What was Minerva Moonfall's maiden name?"

She colored slightly and years washed away from her face with a coy smile. "You already know."

"Payne?"

"Yes. It means 'pagan,' you know."

"I know now." He studied her. How much was truth, how much was senility, and how much was her sense of whimsy, he had no idea. Whatever the mix, he realized he liked her, liked the idea of being related to her. "Are you my aunt, or cousin, or . . . ?"

Minerva stared at him a long moment. "Sara Hawthorne is

a wonderful young woman," she said abruptly. "She needs you. Your protection."

"You know Sara?"

"She used to visit me when she was a student. Her friend Jenny died in her stead."

"You know about Jenny Blaine?" Finally, something he could use.

"Of course I do, and yes, she was used in a minor ceremony, then made to commit suicide."

"Sara thinks she was murdered."

"She was."

"That doesn't make sense."

"It would if you better understood Richard Dashwood's abilities to manipulate the mind." She rose and went to the couch, sat down beside him, and took his hand in both of hers. "Your friend Doug Buckman was forced to jump to his death. Jenny and many other girls were murdered, by their own hands or others'. You have no record of Jenny Blaine in your police files, do you?"

"No."

"That's the beauty of their set-up. The sisters keep to themselves, they keep their girls to themselves. Have you ever wondered about their apple orchards, John?"

"No. Should I?"

"Even in the bad years, their trees never fail. They rely on rain for irrigation, which no other orchard would do nowadays, and they have bumper crops even during the worst droughts. They advertise that their apples are organically grown, and that is true. Worms wouldn't dare touch one, no blight ever strikes, even in years when other growers lose entire orchards."

"What are you saying? That they use magic to grow apples?"

"They're organically grown, and when I say 'organically,' I mean it literally. Those apples are fed blood. Human blood and human flesh."

"Then why these sacrifices of Lawson males? Why risk taking someone from town if they have such a supply of orphans?"

"The orphans are merely fertilizer, for the most part. They

also sacrifice one at each equinox and solstice. As for the Lawson boys, they have little access to young male virgins and there's also the matter of the vendetta."

She had an answer for everything. He looked down at her wrinkled hands covering his own. They were warm. "Minerva, where do the nightflyers figure in all this?"

"They are part of it."

"You know what they are, don't you?"

She laughed, a sad sound. "What they are is even beyond my belief."

"Caspar Parker claims they're gargoyles. That they turn to stone in the daylight."

"Do you believe him?"

"He was very drunk when he said it." He laughed softly and shook his head. "I don't know what I believe. I know they exist, and that animals that have been thought to live only in myth have been discovered recently. I read about a giant sloth that was discovered in South America a few years ago. The natives in the region thought it was a powerful god and had told stories about it for centuries, but there had never been any proof of its existence before. And a species of horse that was thought to be extinct for thousands of years was recently discovered thriving in Tibet. Giant squid, sea serpents." He raised his eyebrows and shrugged slightly. "Why not gargoyles? Bats sleep in caverns during the day and come out at night. Other animals hibernate in the winter. Why not a creature that sleeps during the day in plain sight?" He smiled. "I draw the line at their turning to stone, though."

Minerva nodded. "I call them 'nightflyers' because 'gargoyles' sound even more ridiculous. I have some odd ideas about them, but they're only theories, and not worth talking about right now. But you're right, they don't turn to stone during the day because they've been flying in the daylight again, just as they have before."

"Every twenty-four years."

"Exactly. John, there's precious little time left. You have to save Mark, and you have to save yourself. And others as well. I will do everything I can to help you."

"With magic?"

"Yes, and knowledge. I will help you remember what happened when your brother died. Knowledge, as they say, is power."

"Why won't you tell me about yourself? How did you inherit this job, if that's what it is, from Minerva Moonfall?"

"It is my lot. It has always been and always will be. I'm much older than you think I am."

"You're not implying you're . . ." His words trailed off into silence.

"That I'm your great-great-grandmother? Is that what you think?"

He smiled tightly and shrugged. "You tell me."

"No. You will tell me when the time is right. For now, what I will tell you is that I am a healer, a practitioner of the right-hand path. I have developed certain abilities I was born with. I have studied and worked at it, and I am proficient. I am quite old, and it is duty, magic, and willpower that increase my lifespan." She paused. "Perhaps willpower *is* magic. It is the duty of a healer to pass on the knowledge to someone who can use it. I cannot rest until I have trained an apprentice and put aside my own power. Training takes years, and I have yet to find my student. I have one in mind, however."

"That's what you're trying to do to Mark?" he asked, anger rising.

"Yes and no," she said bluntly. "It is solely up to Mark. The boy has the gift, but I believe he will turn it toward chemistry or modern medicine. He needs more proof than I can offer. He'd make a fine doctor, you know; a rare one with the insight to see more possibilities than most. He might make great strides in medicine."

John nodded. He had exactly those thoughts about Mark's future himself. "If not Mark, then who?"

"The girl I mentioned, the orphan, Kelly. She is very raw, but the abilities are within her, and she wants to learn."

"I see—" He shivered, suddenly freezing cold.

"It's all right, John." He heard Minerva's voice, felt her hands, the only warmth on his body.

His teeth chattered. "What is it?"

"Someone's after you. Are you wearing the amulet I gave you?"

"N-no." He was growing colder, feeling like he was immersed in ice water.

"I told you to wear it." She took away one of her warm hands and plucked a charm out from under her collar, removed it and draped it over his head. "Don't take it off, and make sure Mark wears his. *Make absolutely sure.*"

Even his eyeballs felt frozen. Minerva put her other hand down to his and he grabbed it, held tight, draining the warmth from her.

"Hold on, John. It will pass." Minerva's voice was calm and firm, her grip like iron.

Slowly, he felt warmth begin to seep into his fingers, up through his hands and arms, into his chest, where the chill had been a knot constricting his heart. Minerva spoke unintelligible words, something with a Celtic sound, very foreign, yet not. Scottish, perhaps, or Welsh, he didn't know, couldn't think. Slowly his heart pumped warming blood up into his brain and down into his abdomen, legs, and feet. And as suddenly as it began, it was over. He looked at Minerva, saw her open her eyes. Her cheeks were flushed, and for a moment she looked far younger than she normally did—then, far older. "What the heck was that?"

"I told you," she said. "A spell. If you'd been wearing your amulet, it would have repelled the sorcery, and you'd have felt no more than a brief shiver."

"How?"

"You ask questions, just like your son. I don't know precisely how it works, I just know it does. Accept that, at least until we get safely through October."

As real as it had seemed, now that it was over, he couldn't believe that he'd felt anything but a herald of the flu. That was all he needed. "Tell me something."

"Yes?"

"It seems to me that if I take Mark out of town for Halloween, he'll be safe. Isn't that correct?"

"That works in theory, but you must be prepared. There are vectors coming together and you must be aware that things may not follow your plans." She cocked her head. "You wouldn't drive without wearing your seatbelt, would you?"

"Of course not."

"Then look upon the amulet as a seatbelt and alternative plans as locking your doors and looking both ways."

He laughed. "That's an odd way of putting it."

She smiled and let go of his hands. "I thought I might better convince you if I spoke in your terms."

"It does make more sense when you put it that way."

"They are already after you. They know you will interfere with their plans, and that makes you a marked man. Watch your every step, John. If you don't survive, neither will your son. Or Sara."

"We'll wear the amulets," he said, realizing he was serious. It couldn't hurt. Maybe it would help.

"Good. Digest what I've told you, then come back and let me help you remember. You cannot fight them successfully if you remain ignorant." She rose. "Someone is waiting for you."

He looked at his wristwatch. It was past one o'clock, and this time, he had been so engrossed in Minerva's stories that he hadn't even heard her grandfather clock's chimes. "Sara?"

Minerva nodded and saw him to the door.

He turned toward her. "Did Sara tell you she was coming to see me today?"

"No. But I hope she tells you everything that happened to her last week. I witnessed some of it. She's under attack, make no mistake. John, if she tells you, don't scoff. Just listen and accept it at face value."

"I will." He wanted to ask Minerva what she was talking about, but fought the urge. "How do you know she's coming to see me? I don't even know for sure."

"I can feel her. Can't you?"

"Yes," he said reluctantly. "Yes, I suppose I can."

# Fifty-Nine

"Well, Richard, do you think our meddlesome sheriff is warming up yet?" Mother Lucy sat back on Dashwood's leather sofa and put her feet up on his mahogany coffee table.

The doctor knelt in the middle of the carpet, rolling up the black pentagram cloth they had used for the spell. "Take your shoes off, Lucy. You'll scratch the finish." He lifted the cloth, folded it in half and took it to the armoire in his office. When he returned to the living room, one of Lucy's spike-heeled shoes flew at him, grazing his leg. "Bitch," he said fondly.

"Bastard." She tossed the other shoe at him and smiled. "Well, did it work?"

"It worked, but something interfered."

"The old woman."

Dashwood was amused. Lucy refused to speak of Minerva Payne by name. "I'd say so. Lawson certainly wouldn't know how to protect himself on his own."

"I hate her." Lucy removed her black cowl and tossed it on the floor. "She's a pain in the ass."

Richard sat down at the other end of the couch. "I want you to let Kelly Reed out of solitary confinement, Lucy."

She laughed, combing her fingers through her long black hair. "*You* want me to release her? You mean your precious little twist wants her released, don't you?"

"Yes, Lucy. It will help keep Sara in line if she has the girl to dote on."

"Is our little Sara giving you problems, then?" Lucy's voice oozed venom. "Would she rather fuck the sheriff than you?"

Dashwood smiled despite his annoyance. Lucy was and always would be the most jealous woman in the world. She'd ordered him to seduce Sara to keep her from causing trouble, but she hated that he spent any time with the young woman and tortured him for it.

"Yes," he said, knowing it would make Lucy happy. "She'd

rather fuck the sheriff. She followed him out of the bar last night and they kissed. I couldn't get her to come back to my apartment afterward."

"Does she know you saw them?"

"No, of course not."

"And those mesmerizing eyes of yours didn't work?"

"I couldn't even get her to swallow a truffle."

"So she didn't dream last night?"

"I doubt it."

"And now you want me to release the Reed girl to do the job you couldn't do?"

"Yes." He hated the Mother Superior for her need to humiliate him, but there were other things he loved about her. Her power, her intelligence; her greed; her lust. All those little deadly sins that made her Lucy Bartholomew.

"Come closer." Lucy stood and unbuttoned her habit, then sat back down, positioning herself so that he could see the black lace garter at the top of her stocking, and a curve of breast above the black demi-bra. He moved closer. "You say the sheriff kissed our little Sara?"

"Yes, Lucy."

"Show me what sort of kiss it was," she ordered.

He did. Kissing Lucy was always repulsive at first. The ridiculous old–fashioned concoction she used to keep herself young, with its overtones of cinnamon and dampness, permeated her skin and breath. It was, he thought, like kissing a freshly prepared and spiced mummy. But mummies didn't move, and Lucy certainly did. She could do tricks with her tongue that still astounded him, and as she worked her magic, he began to respond. Finally she pulled away and put her hand over his erection. "I'll release Kelly Reed, but first we must do something to put the fear of—" she barked a laugh, "—God into her."

"The lady in white might pay her a visit," Dashwood suggested.

"Just what I was thinking. But first," she said, squeezing him hard, "we need to renew our strength."

"Yes." He was breathing raggedly, aching with need and repulsion. The combination increased his passion.

"Call Regina and tell her to remove Kelly's lightbulb now. We'll let her sit in the dark for a while while we exercise your magic wand." She laughed throatily. "After an hour or so without light, Kelly should be quite ready to receive the white lady, don't you think?"

"Yes, Lucy. Excellent." He stood up, the erection painfully pushing against his trousers, and made the call to Sister Regina. Then he turned to Lucy. "Where?" he asked hoarsely.

"Your bed, I think. I'm in the mood for handcuffs and leather."

"Your wish is my command," he murmured, as he scooped her up and carried her to her chosen fate.

# Sixty

Sara Hawthorne sat back in her chair and gave John Lawson a twisted grin. "And that's when Minerva Payne came along and banished the ghost. I suppose you think I'm hopelessly insane."

"No," he said, after a long pause. "I have to admit that your ghost story sounds perfect for telling around a campfire on a summer night, but I do believe you."

"You do?" she asked, not hiding her surprise. "*You* believe in ghosts?"

"I don't know what I believe in anymore," he told her. Deep in his bones, he could still feel the inexplicable chill. Briefly, he told her about the experience at Minerva's. "How can I possibly judge your story when I've just been through something nearly as weird?" he asked.

"Minerva gave me this," Sara said, pulling a leather thong and small cloth amulet from beneath her dark green sweater. "She says it will protect me."

John sheepishly showed her his, then replaced it under his

shirt. "Minerva told me that you used to visit her when you were a student."

"It's funny. Even when Kelly Reed asked me to speak with her, I didn't recognize the name. I didn't remember anything, but I recognized her when I saw her by the waterfalls, and I remembered the house when she took me there."

"Do you remember her now?"

"No, not exactly. But it seems right. I know it's true. I guess there's more missing from my memory than I thought."

He nodded. "She says the nuns fog people's memories. Today, she told me that my brother died in my place. And that your roommate died in yours."

"Maybe Minerva is the villain in all this," Sara suggested hesitantly.

"I've thought about that, but it doesn't feel right. Know what I mean?"

"Yes, I do, believe it or not."

He shook his head. "I'm beginning to think we're living in the Twilight Zone."

"What are we going to do about it?"

"Get out of town?" he asked lightly.

"Are you serious?"

"Well, there's no reason for you to stay here," he began. "I have to. My position . . . and it's the culmination of something my family has been involved in this since the beginning. I have to put a stop to it. I have to see it through or I won't be able to live with myself."

"Why do you think I feel any differently?" she asked archly.

"I don't mean it that way. But if any of these things are true, you're living in a viper pit." He hesitated, trying to gauge her anger. "Speaking of vipers, tell me about Richard Dashwood. You said he drove you into town last night because you were having car trouble."

She studied him, then nodded. "I did. The car wouldn't start, but this morning, I had Carlos check under the hood. Something was just loose."

"What?"

She smiled sheepishly. "I honestly don't know. Why?"

"Do you know much about cars?"

"Squat," she admitted.

"It's always possible someone—Dashwood, for instance—loosened a wire to keep you from going out."

"I hadn't thought of that," she said. "What is it you want to know about Dashwood?"

"Is he courting you?"

"Well, he's been bringing me truffles every night. Does that count as courting?"

"In my book."

"I need a twelve-step program to get over chocolate—I can't resist the damned stuff. The thing is, last night I didn't give him a chance to give me any, and last night was the first time I didn't get unaccountably sleepy and have excruciatingly pleasant dreams."

"Huh? What does 'excruciatingly pleasant' mean?"

"Sexual dreams," she said, blushing.

"Are you sure he's not drugging you, then coming to your room and—"

"I suspect he *is* drugging me, but I know he's not coming to my room because I always wake up, um, near the climax of the dream, and I'm alone."

"No one can get in? If you're drugged—"

"The minute I come in at night, I put a rubber wedge under the door. No one can get in, and whatever is in those truffles is mild. Once I wake up I feel normal, and when I go back to sleep there aren't any more dreams."

"Can you bring me one of the chocolates? I'll have Doc Cutter analyze it. If Dashwood is drugging you, we'd have proof. That'll allow me to do some serious investigating. I can't do anything without a search warrant, but if you can get me the truffle, well, watch out, sisters. You hungry?"

"Famished. One thing first, though. I don't want you to think I'm going to turn tail and run. I won't leave."

"You shouldn't be living there."

"I know, but I have to."

"Why? Solving an old murder isn't worth risking your life."

"Maybe not, but Kelly is. She's been locked up in solitary confinement all week. They have it in for her."

"Minerva mentioned that."

"Yes. I asked Richard—Dashwood, I mean—to intercede with Mother Lucy and get her sentence lifted. I have to be there for her."

"What makes you think he'll do it?"

"I used every catty trick I've ever seen in the movies."

"You promised to sleep with him," he said sourly.

"Well, I promised to see him again, but I guess I implied more."

"You know damned well that's what you implied." Half his mouth smiled, the other half refused. "I admire your resourcefulness, but—"

"But what?" she asked, ready to be offended again.

"But after that kiss last night, I don't want to share you with anyone, especially not that psychopathic charlatan."

Slowly, so slowly, a smile spread across her face. "You're jealous?"

"You bet."

"Good." She stood up and walked around the desk, leaned against it, and looked down at him. "I'm glad."

John glanced at the door, saw it was latched but unlocked. He decided to take a chance on Dorothy's staying out for another minute and go for it. Placing his hands on her waist, he tugged her closer. She bent down and they shared their second kiss. Though it lasted only an instant, kissing Sara was as thrilling as the first time.

# Sixty-One

Kelly Reed stared at the glowing white figure that hovered in the corner. It wasn't the crying ghost she had heard in her room; this was something else, and she thought she knew what it was: an infamous Lady in White.

She was frightened, barely able to control her trembling,

but Minerva had told her about the phantoms and how she'd encountered this one more than once. Sometimes it did nothing but float along through the forest or orchards, a simple ghost, but at other times it was a revenant, fueled by a human enemy.

*Kelly,* the voice called. Since appearing a few moments before, the thing had repeated her name over and over until it echoed in her head. Kelly clutched the amulet under her shirt. It would protect her. It had to. *A revenant can hurt you only if your fear allows it. It will tell you things, try to make you do things you don't want to do. If you ever encounter one, ignore it. Eventually it will go away.* Kelly remembered Minerva's lesson as the phantom glided closer to her.

"Go away," she whispered, and turned her back on it. Trembling fiercely, she felt her way to the wooden chair and sat down facing the wall. "Go away."

*Sara Hawthorne is dead, Kelly. So is the old woman. They're dead, the life squeezed out of them. They're floating in the pond at the falls. The water is red with their blood.*

No, she told herself. *It's trying to scare me, just like Minerva said.* She even thought she knew who was doing the talking: that old bitch Lucy.

She remembered the camera and wondered if all the nuns were gathered around watching her, or at least listening, since it was dark. Or maybe Marcia and Buffy and the rest were laughing at her right now, waiting for her to crack. Anger calmed her terror and she sat stolidly at the desk, even when icy fingertips caressed her face and a frigid tongue licked her neck.

The phantom moved right through the table to stand before her. Its face was featureless except for the black eye sockets. Then it opened its mouth, wide, wider, impossibly wide, barring rows of triangular shark teeth. *No! You won't scream!* She bit her tongue, telling herself it was an illusion, *just an illusion!* and then the phantom's mouth widened even more, yawning over her, enveloping her. She heard herself screaming, as if from a distance, then everything faded to black.

# Sixty-Two

Sara had intended to return to the abbey hours ago, but after lunch John Lawson had invited her to his house for dinner and she'd impulsively accepted. After leaving the station, she had a feeling she wouldn't make it back to town if she spent the free time at St. Gertrude's. Somebody might tamper with her car again—she was sure John was right about that—or the sisters would assign her some time-consuming task. Something would happen to spoil the evening.

So she spent the hours exploring Moonfall's shops, and when she tired of that, Sawyer's Petting Zoo. It was a wonderful autumn afternoon and she relaxed and fed the sheep and goats corn from the vending machines scattered around the park. She spent the last hour before dusk sitting on a bench, watching the fluffy-tailed gray squirrels search the ground for acorns and pine nuts to hoard for the coming winter.

At five o'clock she drove to John's house and was welcomed by his son Mark, who was obviously trying to be polite but was full of questions about St. Gertrude's and the nightflyers. It was a little awkward; she didn't really know all that much, plus she didn't know how much John wanted the boy to know. She steered the conversation toward Minerva Payne, asking him questions about the vials of herbs and tinctures in the old lady's house. The boy seemed to know everything about them, or at least, their medicinal purposes. In the next twenty minutes, she heard an entire lecture on the antiseptic properties of myrrh, aspirin, and wintergreen oil, and how witches knew about digitalis and ephedrine long before doctors began using them for heart disease and asthma. His knowledge seemed inexhaustible, but it was fascinating nonetheless.

John soon showed up bearing dinner: two pizzas, one with everything, one Hawaiian-style, plus a bag of salad fixings, a bottle of dressing, a six-pack of Coke, and two pints of Ben and Jerry's New York Chocolate Chunk.

After the gourmet efforts of Richard Dashwood, John Lawson's version of dinner was refreshing. She didn't have to worry about which fork to use, the napkins were paper, not cloth, and he offered her a choice of Coke from the can or in a glass with ice, which was doubly refreshing. In contrast, Richard had an endless supply of exotic teas and juices, and his efforts to ply her with expensive wines combined with her own lack of knowledge to play hell with her self-confidence.

But it was the rich chocolate ice cream that impressed her most of all: he had listened to her when she'd confessed her addiction, and he had remembered.

The three of them talked about witches and nuns and gargoyles, nothing too serious. Then, after dessert, Mark made himself scarce, leaving Sara and John on the sofa, mellow flames crackling in the fireplace nearby. John had left the choice of music up to her, and she loaded his CD player with a mix from his eclectic collection. A little Jelly Roll Morton, Scott Joplin, and Charlie Parker for a classic jazz fix, followed by Mozart's "A Little Night Music," some early Springsteen and recent Garth Brooks. John Lawson seemed to like everything she did, and she was pleased to see no sign of the Wagnerian epics that crowned Richard's opera collection. It was all so refreshingly normal.

The music played softly while they talked, filling one another in on their lives. Finally, they reached the subject of St. Gertrude's, and John told her the details, as he remembered them, of his brother's death. She talked about Jenny Blaine and some of the runaways from her time as a student, and they both knew that the blots in their memories were more massive than they had realized. The missing pieces were similar in form and nature, and it was something that had doubtlessly been done to them. John told her about Minerva's offer to restore his memory, and she encouraged him to do so.

Finally, the talking done, they indulged in some old-fashioned necking. He could have had her in a minute, but he didn't make the move, and she was glad. There were things that had to be worked out in both their lives, and although she wouldn't have resisted his advances—she wanted him too much for that—

she knew it would be even better after they worked out their individual problems.

Now it was past midnight and Sara, braver than usual, had parked her car in the garage and walked to the dormitory. No one was around, so she tiptoed down the hall to her old room, the one Kelly now shared with Marcia Crowley. Opening the door a crack, she peered inside. Neither Kelly nor Marcia was in the room. Obviously, Richard hadn't come through—at least, not yet. She wondered briefly where Marcia was but decided she wasn't that interested.

Disappointed at Kelly's absence, she went up to her room, flipped on the light, and shoved the wedge under the door.

"Hi."

She whirled. "Kelly! You scared me half to death!"

The girl was sitting at the dining table, an open book in front of her. "Sorry."

"You must have cat's eyes," Sara said, coming to the table and setting down a small bag of groceries she'd picked up during the day.

"No." She produced Sara's flashlight from her lap. "I used this. I hope it's okay."

"Of course it is. Want an apple?" she asked, pulling a small bag of Granny Smiths from the grocery sack.

"That'd be great." Kelly took the fruit, then hesitated. "Are these from the nuns' orchard?"

Sara grinned. "Heck, no. They're from the Addams Family Orchard way down the road. They're untouched by nuns."

"Is that really what it's called?"

"Yep." Sara sat down and took an apple for herself. "You look thinner. Didn't you eat?"

"I ate everything they gave me," Kelly said, between ravenous bites. "Bread and water. I'm starving."

"Are you serious? They told me you were getting three squares a day."

"More like three *slices* a day."

"That's horrible." Sara got up and opened the refrigerator, took out a quart of milk, a package of ham, mustard, and bread, then quickly put together a sandwich for the girl. She brought it to the table, along with the whole carton of milk and a cup. "Eat. All you want."

"Thanks."

Sara studied the girl while she ate. There were dark patches under her eyes, and her cheekbones stuck out under her thin flesh. Kelly ate voraciously. When she finished the last crumb, she looked up. "Thank you."

"You could have eaten something before I got here."

"That'd be stealing."

Sara doubted she'd learned her morals from the nuns. "Do you want anything else?"

"No, thanks. I'm fine now."

"When did they let you out?"

"Sometime late today. I don't know exactly. I passed out and woke up in my dorm room."

"You fainted?"

Kelly nodded.

"From hunger?"

"I wish. I got scared. God, Miss Hawthorne, it was horrible."

"Call me Sara when we're alone."

"Really?"

"Really. What frightened you?"

"You'll think I'm nuts."

"Try me."

"A ghost." Kelly eyed her. "Nuts, huh?"

"Not unless I'm nuts, too. I've seen one twice."

"Did it have teeth?"

"Teeth?"

"Yeah. Like Jaws. I tried to ignore it. Minerva told me all about revenants, and that they go away if you don't get scared."

"Minerva told me that, too."

"Well, it kind of worked. Then it opened its mouth and I saw those teeth. It swallowed my head, and I fainted."

"I don't blame you. I would've, too." Sara studied the girl, wondering how much she should say, what would help and what might do more harm. "If a revenant is directed by a person, do you know who it might be?"

"Lucy," she said firmly. "At first I thought it was Marcia

and those guys, because they'd love to get me, but I decided they don't have the brains. It's Lucy or the nuns, for sure."

Sara nodded. "What about Dr. Dashwood?"

"I dunno. Lucy said he got me out of the second week, so I kind of doubt it."

"Don't trust him, Kelly."

She looked up in surprise. "Why?"

"I think he's been drugging me."

Kelly's eyes widened. "Really?"

"Maybe. Did he tell you why he got you out?"

"Because he felt I'd learned my lesson." She rolled her eyes.

"He got you out because I promised to go out with him if he did." Sara felt petty telling her this, but she needed to know that Dashwood wasn't a knight in shining armor.

"You did that for *me?*"

"I was worried about you." She finished her apple. "Kelly, do you ever have problems with your memory?"

"What do you mean?"

"Do you realize sometimes that pieces of time are missing, especially after you've been around Dr. Dashwood?"

She rubbed her chin thoughtfully. "Dashwood does this thing with his eyes. I think he tries to hypnotize me, but it doesn't work."

"Listen, Kelly, the sheriff says he might be able to do something if someone will come forward. Feeding you bread and water for a week is abuse."

The girl hesitated. "No. If it didn't work, the nuns would really get on me, and if it did, they'd send me away."

"You don't *want* to be here, do you?"

"No, but I've been in foster homes and stuff, and it's just as bad. I don't want to leave Minerva. Or you."

Kelly looked ready to bolt, so Sara nodded. "Okay, but if you change your mind, tell me."

"I want to live with Minerva."

"She's very, very old. I don't know if she could take care of you."

"I can help her."

"Maybe so. Kelly, Minerva asked me to tell you something.

She said that you shouldn't go through the woods to visit her. It's too dangerous right now."

"I always go that way."

"Remember the day you got in trouble trying to get Mark's jacket? One of the boys was killed by a nightflyer."

"Not Mark!"

"No. A boy named Pete Parker. Did you know him?"

Kelly shook her head. "No. Is Mark all right?"

"Yes. He was wounded slightly. The thing took a bite out of his neck, but he's fine."

"Are you sure?"

Sara smiled. "Absolutely. I just saw him."

"Were you at the sheriff's office?"

"No. I had dinner with Mark and his father."

"And he's okay?"

Young love, thought Sara. "Fine. He asked how you were, too."

The girl beamed.

"Kelly, it's really important that you not travel through the forest. A nightflyer might get you."

"But I *have* to see Minerva."

"I'll take you tomorrow, if you think you can sneak away."

"Of course I can. I'll wait for you outside the front gate. Behind the trees. What time?"

"Noon?"

"Okay." She got up. "I'd better get back before Marcia does."

"Where is she, anyway?"

"Off with the nuns. They do stuff in the chapel."

"What kind of stuff? I didn't see any lights when I drove in."

"They have ceremonies or something. They use candles, so you can't see. I snuck up to the window once. Marcia and those guys are like novices or something. They all wear these black robes, like the nuns." She paused at the door and removed the wedge. "I couldn't see much."

"Be careful," Sara told her, as Kelly slipped out the door.

She shoved the wedge securely under the door again and went to bed.

# Sixty-Three

*Sara, my darling Sara.*

*Warm lips touched her cheek, rained kisses over her face, then down her neck, across the ridges of her collarbone. She moaned softly as strong but gentle hands cupped her breasts and the lips moved lower, joining the hands to explore her flesh.*

*Who are you? she wondered.*

*You know. A tongue hardened one nipple, then the other, lighting exquisite, torturous passion deep inside her. Dream lover, she thought. You're here.*

*I am. Hands caressed her waist and hips, then moved to the inside of her thighs, gently but firmly parting them. Lips and tongue followed, trailing down her stomach, her abdomen, then lower, kissing her thighs, circling closer and closer to her core, but never touching it, driving her mad with desire. She pushed her hips toward the dream lover, strained toward his lips and teasing tongue. The fire burned unabated, and still the dream man refused her satisfaction.*

*Please, she moaned. Oh, please. Who are you?*

*You tell me. Kisses came closer, fingers parted her, but did not touch. She burned.*

*John, you're John. She opened her eyes but could not see him in the dark, could only hear his soft laughter as he manipulated her.*

*John? asked the dream lover. Or am I Richard? Or maybe someone else? This is your dream.*

*He moved up over her body as he spoke, pinning her shoulders with his massive hands. She felt his hardness against her and strained toward him. Make love to me, she pleaded. Make love to me, John.*

*I'm not John! The words blasted through her head as he*

*plunged into her. His hands dug into her breasts, squeezing and kneading, and she screamed as teeth pressed into her soft flesh, biting and pulling. The hands moved everywhere, squeezing, pinching, and the weight of his body held her down as he thrust again and again, growing larger with every move. He was tearing her apart.*

*You're killing me! Blindly she reached for his face, but where his head should have been there was only icy cold air, thick and slimy. Hollow laughter filled her head as the pounding continued, and suddenly she knew who it was—what it was— that was raping her.*

Her own screams woke her, the laughter still resounding in her ears. She opened her eyes and saw the white vaguely man-shaped mass glowing in the dark. Slapping on the bedside lamp, she sat up. "Get out of here! I don't want you! Get out!"

The phantom disintegrated into small dots of light that blinked out one by one as the laughter faded.

"Oh, God," she whispered, and jumped from the bed. Her entire body hurt. She ran to the long mirror she'd mounted on the closet door and pulled her nightgown over her head. It dropped to the floor unnoticed as she stared at her body.

"Oh, my God." There were vivid pink fingerprints every-where, quickly turning into dark bruises, and a perfect set of toothprints surrounded one nipple. Tiny drops of blood beaded on the skin. Her abdomen bore scratches and her inner thighs were mottled with bruises. A thin trickle of blood was drying on one leg.

She needed a doctor, but what could she say? That a ghost raped her? She could go to Richard, but what if it was him fueling the attack? What might he do?

*Go to John. He'll know what to do.* The thought was humiliat-ing, and she knew beyond a doubt that he'd insist she leave the abbey. She couldn't do that, not without Kelly. *Take her with you and get out!*

She threw on the clothes she'd worn today, grabbed her purse, and swiftly ran down the stairs to the first floor. The corridor lights were out, so she trailed her hands along the doors, counting them off. As her fingers found the right doorknob, she heard a rustle of skirts behind her, but before she could turn around, a damp, foul-smelling cloth was clamped over her nose and mouth, and darkness spiraled around her.

# Sixty-Four

Naked, sitting cross-legged on black satin sheets, Richard Dashwood opened his eyes and smiled at Lucy, equally naked, sitting opposite him on his bed. "That was quite a treat," he told her.

"Yes, wasn't it?" She took two brandy snifters from the bedside table and handed him one. "We outdid ourselves, didn't we, darling?"

"To us," he said.

"To us."

"You know, Lucy, I'd been paying our little Sara dream visits on my own, but it was nothing like this. This was . . . sublime." He drained his glass and set it aside as Lucy did the same.

"Supremely sublime," she agreed. "We must do it more often."

"One shouldn't let one's sex life get into a rut." He smiled and lay back, watching her watch his bobbing penis.

"Do you think we managed to mark her?" Lucy asked, crawling up between his legs.

"Yes, I believe we managed to do all sorts of things to her. Sister Regina has been instructed to chloroform her and put her in the infirmary. They should be arriving about now." He smirked. "If the poor girl's been raped, she must be examined, you know."

"I know." Lucy's nostrils flared and her pupils were dilated. "Do you want to go there now?"

"No, I want to come now. There's only so much a man can take, you know."

"I know," Lucy said. "What will it be this time, dear doctor? Handcuffs? Rubber? Leather? Feathers?"

He smiled. "Nothing so fancy, Lucy. After all, I must see to my patient. Let's just play doctor. See my thermometer?"

She nodded, eyes bright.

"I think I'll take your temperature. Open wide."

"Yes, Doctor."

# Sixty-Five

By October twenty-ninth, Moonfall was a gem of red and gold. The days were cool, the sunlight brilliant as it slanted between the trees, catching the colors of the falling leaves.

The nights were frigid, the sky so clear and bright that the Milky Way was startlingly brilliant. Houses and cabins took on a cozy look as wood smoke filled the air and pumpkins roosted on porch railings. The apple harvest was in full swing, and store shelves were lined with bright baskets laden with shining fruit, red, green, and yellow. Fresh cider, hot cider, spiced or not, apple butter, apple jelly, and apple pies were in demand, and Apple Heaven's mince pie business was booming.

Despite the festive atmosphere, John Lawson was in a funk. He'd made no progress in the deaths of Gus or Pete Parker and had been plagued by increasingly terrifying nightmares, both the usual ones about his brother and the now familiar one about the room filling with blood while Minerva Payne ordered him to open the door for her.

Mark was completely involved in the Halloween Haunt, giving John little choice but to let him stay in town on Halloween. And worst of all, Sara hadn't contacted him since their dinner more than ten days ago.

The station had been hopping. As the festivals began, so did bar fights, drunk driving, and thefts, and this year it was all worse than usual. He'd been working twelve to fourteen hours a day, and his deputies were all on overtime. In his few spare moments, he entertained all sorts of half-baked theories about Sara's lack of communication, his main one being that she had chosen Dashwood over him. Sometimes it occurred to him that she might be in danger, and that's what was on his mind at the moment.

He'd tried to avoid such thoughts, even when they were so powerful that he could barely tolerate them. He told himself it was paranoia, lack of sleep, or stress, but he knew what it was: avoidance. The dreams about Minerva and the room filling with blood stemmed from the same source. He had been avoiding everything that smacked of the bizarre, trying to pretend to himself that it was just another tourist season in Moonfall. He knew he had to stop. Now.

He turned his cruiser onto Apple Hill Road and glanced at his watch. It was just past four; there was nearly an hour of light left. First, he would visit Minerva, then go out to St. Gertrude's. He'd never gone back to ask the nuns about the nightflyers, and that would be the perfect excuse to nose around.

He pulled into the little parking lot at the Gingerbread House, saw the "Open" sign, and got out of the car, relieved because he'd expected to have to go all the way out to the cottage.

The bell jingled on the door as he went in and he was surprised to see Mark, wearing a white apron, sweeping the floor. "Hi, Dad!"

"Hi, Mark." Guilt washed over him. He'd forgotten his son was working for Minerva. He'd spent so much time avoiding the whole subject of the old woman that he'd convinced himself the boy was spending all his time working on the Haunt. "Is Minerva here?"

"Sure. She's in the kitchen. Go on back." Mark returned energetically to his chores.

"I was hoping you'd come see me," Minerva said, as she turned from a huge oven, a tray of cookies in her mitted hands. "I've been trying to contact you."

"I know. You should have used a phone."

She ignored that. "We're running out of time."

"Yeah." Everything he'd been avoiding came rushing back at him under her gaze. "Have you seen Sara Hawthorne?" he blurted, suddenly wondering how he could have let so much time pass.

Minerva set the cookies down. "No, but Kelly Reed has

come to see me. That girl's still running through the woods. At least she's not traveling at night. Still, I'm afraid she's not going to make it one of these times. The nightflyers are hungry. Have you heard them?"

Indeed he had. Several animals—goats and sheep and a pig—had been mutilated, and chickens and rabbits had disappeared. People were on the lookout for mountain lions, coyotes, even bears, but certainly not for gargoyles. The cries of the creatures in the dead of night had awakened him from his nightmares more than once. He nodded and told her about the attacks on the zoo animals.

"We're lucky that's what they're going after," Minerva said. "Come on outside with me. You can bring that garbage can along."

He picked up a half-filled kitchen trash can and carried it out behind her. She lifted the lid on a large can and he dumped the trash.

"Thank you, John," she said. "I thought it best we talk out of Mark's hearing. Come on over here."

He followed her to a low ranch-style fence at the edge of the property and they leaned against it. "You've raised a fine boy," she said. "A hard worker."

"Thanks." He stared out at the acres of Parker orchards. "I haven't been paying enough attention to him lately."

She nodded. "You have a lot to deal with right now. You're worried about Sara, aren't you?"

"Yes. And I've been avoiding it."

"Kelly says she hasn't been herself lately."

"She's ill?" He remembered the vacant, drugged look on her face that day in Dashwood's infirmary.

"She's troubled, I think. Tormented. She needs you, John, but you already know that."

"I might be the source of her torment."

"You know better than that. She loves you. You love her. Be a little more confident. You torture yourself unnecessarily. Just listen to your inner voice, and you'll know the truth."

"Minerva, how can you know she loves me? Did she tell you?"

"No. I've only seen her once since she arrived, but when I mentioned your name, I could see it in her eyes. She didn't know it yet. But she does now. You should go see her."

"I'm going as soon as I leave here."

"Good. Watch out for that damned Dashwood. I'm certain he's unhappy about you. He's after Sara for his own purposes."

"Did you divine that as well?" he asked, half-smiling.

"No. Kelly told me that Sara got her out of solitary confinement by promising to go out with him. I'd imagine he's behind that episode at my house."

That was another thing he'd conveniently forgotten. The attack of freezing cold seemed like a dream now.

"Are you wearing your amulet?"

"Yes," he said, lifting the leather string slightly. He was wearing it primarily because Mark had taken to nagging him to do so.

"I want you to go see Sara now, John, but I want you to come back and see me at my cottage *tomorrow*. We have to find out what happened to your brother before it happens to your son."

His stomach turned at the words, but he knew she was right. "I will."

"Promise on your father's and grandfather's graves."

He hesitated. "I promise."

# Sixty-Six

"So, Mother Lucy, you don't know anything about these birds?"

Lucy smiled at John, as serene as the Virgin. "No. We hear them, of course, but we never see them. They've never given us any trouble."

"I was told that they nest in St. Gertrude's forest."

"I wouldn't know. I always thought they came from Witch Forest. Wasn't that child killed by the Falls?" she asked smoothly.

"Yes," he replied, just as smoothly. "Just above where Lenore Tynan died."

"Then perhaps you should be looking around there."

"Perhaps. If you don't mind, I'd like to ask some of your staff about them."

"Of course."

"Where would I find your gardeners?"

She looked pointedly at the wall clock. "Getting ready to go home for the day, I'd imagine. Go out to the garage—the old stables across the lawn. You'll probably find some of them there. But you'd better hurry if you want to catch them."

"Thanks."

John followed her directions and found the long building. Sara had mentioned that she had a friend, a groundskeeper, who'd been at the abbey when she was a child. Later, she'd dropped the name "Carlos," and that was who he wanted to talk to. First, to ask about the nightflyers, then for the real reason: to find out where to find Sara.

The garage doors were swung wide open, and he heard men's voices speaking Spanish as he entered. He spotted them halfway down the long building and strode swiftly toward them, spotting Sara's white Sentra along the way. It gave him a little jolt to know with certainty that she was here somewhere.

"Excuse me," he said to the men, who had turned and now watched him suspiciously. Several backed into the shadows, and he realized that they were probably illegal immigrants.

He smiled. "I'm not here to arrest anyone, don't worry." They continued to eye him dubiously, but one man, square-shouldered and with a thick head of salt-and-pepper hair, stepped forward. "What can we do for you, sir?"

John stuck out his hand. "I'm John Lawson, sheriff of Moon-fall. And you are?"

"Carlos Montoya. Chief groundskeeper." He shook John's hand with a firm dry grip.

*Bingo*. "Can you spare a few minutes, Mr. Montoya?"

"Sure. My men are just getting ready to go home. Do you want to talk to them as well?"

"No, no. I realize this is an inconvenient time. I'm sure you can answer my questions, Mr. Montoya. If I have any for your men, I'll come back."

Montoya nodded, then spoke in Spanish, and watched his crew finish putting the equipment away and quickly leave. Very quickly. "They like to be out of here before dark, Sheriff. They're superstitious," he said, as the last one left the building.

"Are they afraid of the nightflyers?"

"Nightflyers?" Carlos asked.

"Yes. The birds. One killed a little boy recently."

"Yes, they fear them." Carlos peered around the garage in one direction, then the other. "They fear many things."

"Do you want to go somewhere else to talk?" Montoya's nervousness seeped into John, and he wondered if anyone was lurking in the shadows, listening.

"Let's go outside." Carlos led him out the far end of the building, away from the chapel. He shut the small door behind him. "What do you want to talk about, Sheriff?"

"Have you worked here a long time?"

"Twenty years."

"Have you ever seen one of those birds?"

"Yes. They're demons." He whispered the words, glancing around nervously.

"Do you know what they are? One of them bit my son, and the doctor is concerned about rabies," he added, thinking that might get Montoya to speak more freely.

"They are demons. They are servants of the devil, but that's all I know."

"When did you see one?"

"One night many years ago, when I was late leaving. It flew at me as I went to my car. I swear, it sounded like it was laughing at me." He paused. "I know how ridiculous that sounds. Recently, I saw one land among the gargoyles on the chapel. My men saw it, too, which is why they were so eager to leave. It wasn't even dark yet. No darker than it is now."

"Mr. Montoya, I believe you. And I want to ask you a question *you* might find ridiculous."

"Yes?"

"Have you ever noticed any of the gargoyles missing?"

"You mean . . . ?"

"Is it possible that the thing you saw flying *is* a gargoyle? That maybe a few of them aren't really made of stone?"

Montoya crossed himself, the fear in his eyes unmistakable. "They breed," he said, so softly John could barely hear him. "There are many more now than when I first came here."

"I was told that Sister Elizabeth sculpts them as memorials to sisters who have died."

"That's what they say, but I don't think so. The nuns, they look the same as they did when I first came here. They don't age. They don't die, except by accident. And when they do, more gargoyles appear."

"What kind of accidents? Have many died?"

Montoya peered around in the growing darkness. "Yes, many. New ones, usually, ones that don't fit in. They have accidents."

"You mean, they're murdered?"

"Please, speak softly, Sheriff. There are ears everywhere."

He nodded. "Can you answer the question? Were they murdered?"

"I didn't say it, you did. Many die here, many disappear."

"Besides the nuns?"

"Students run away, they say. I'm sure a few do. And my men sometimes leave without a word. They just disappear, and usually, it is out of character for them."

"What do you think happens to them?"

"I don't know. I try not to think of such things. It's dangerous. I should go now."

"Wait. There's something else."

"What?"

"Are you Sara Hawthorne's friend?"

Carlos's eyes opened wide, then slitted. "I know her. She used to be a student here."

The man tried to keep a neutral expression, but John could read his terror. "I'm concerned about her safety," he told Montoya. "She's a friend of mine. I expected to see her several days ago, but she never showed up."

"She is here. Her car is in there." He nodded toward the garage.

"Can you tell me how to find her? I have to talk to her."

"It might be trouble if they see you with her."

"Where's her room?"

"On the third floor of the dormitory building. But you can't go in. They'll stop you." He hesitated. "Do you want to see her tonight? Now?"

John nodded.

"I'll get her. I can say I need her to move her car. Go back inside the garage and wait."

"Thank you. I won't forget this."

John turned and entered the darkened building, leaving the door open. He watched Carlos Montoya trot across the lawn and wondered how the man lived with all the fear inside him.

# Sixty-Seven

Sara sat alone in her room, picking at a plate of cheese and crackers and fruit that she'd forced herself to prepare. She wasn't hungry, hadn't been since the night she'd been raped. She'd passed the time in a daze, teaching her classes, then returning to her room, not wanting to be around anybody.

She looked at the little bottle of Valium sitting on the table by a can of Pepsi. Richard had given them to her, and she knew she was abusing them, but didn't care. *That's because you're abusing them, idiot!* She reached for the bottle, then drew her hand back. She had to stop relying on them.

She remembered the rape in every detail, right down to the fact that it was ridiculous. She even remembered running from her room to get Kelly but then her memory clouded. Richard said she'd evidently fainted. One of the sisters had found her lying in the hall and taken her to the infirmary.

When she woke up, she was in one of the five beds that comprised the tiny hospital ward. Richard sat beside her, holding her hand. He told her how they'd found her and that he'd examined her and tended to her wounds. He confirmed that she'd been raped, but no real damage had been done. He had, he said, given her something to help her relax.

When he'd asked her for the identity of her attacker, she'd told him it was a ghost. She'd just said it outright, and he'd squeezed her hand and told her she was in shock. It could only be one of a few people, assuming her attacker was male: Basil-Bob Boullan, or one of the gardeners. She said it wasn't any of them. He told her there was no evidence of semen, so it might have been one or more of the girls, though he personally thought that the physical education teacher, Esther Roth, who was also her neighbor, was the most likely culprit. Roth, he told her, had an extensive collection of marital aids and a borderline personality. Lenore Tynan had complained to the Mother Superior about advances she'd made toward her. Sara hadn't argued. What was the point?

The next morning, Richard told her that Esther Roth had confessed, and that the police had taken her away. She would have no more problems. And that was the end of it, except for the bottle of Valium that had helped her keep from thinking about anything.

Every time a pill wore off, as one was doing now, she started to relive the horror, the sheer terror and humiliation. What had happened? She knew it wasn't Esther Roth who'd attacked her, and she couldn't shake the notion that it had something to do with Richard Dashwood. But what? The thing that had attacked her was the same thing that had led her to the Falls, that had frightened her in the shower. Probably the same thing that had come after Kelly. Was it a revenant, as Kelly thought? It was just all too much. Sara reached for the bottle, unscrewed the lid, and shook a pill into her hand.

Someone rapped sharply on the door. Startled, Sara's hand shook, hitting the bottle, sending the Valiums rolling everywhere. "Damn."

"Miss Hawthorne?"

She recognized Sister Bibi's voice. "Coming." She looked at the pill in her hand and let it drop with the rest, then went to the door and bent to remove the rubber wedge. Then she saw she hadn't even bothered to use it. *What the hell's wrong with me?*

She opened the door a few inches and peered out. "Yes?"

"Carlos is downstairs. He needs you to move your car. It's blocking something."

She nodded. "Tell him I'll be right down."

Closing the door, she slipped off her robe, trying not to look at the ugly bruises on her legs as she pulled on a pair of jeans and her penny loafers. She gingerly slipped on a bulky V-neck sweater that would hide her lack of a bra—her bitten breast was still inflamed and anything tight was sheer torture. She hunted for her keys, finally found them in her coat pocket, then left her room. Walking down the hall, she tried to clear her mind, tried to concentrate, and by the time she met Carlos at the entry, she felt like some of the cobwebs had been swept away.

"I'm sorry to bother you, Sara," Carlos said as they walked across the lawn. "I wouldn't if it wasn't important."

"I'm glad you bothered me, Carlos. You kept me from doing something stupid."

He glanced sideways at her but said nothing.

"Why are you here so late?" she asked as they entered the garage.

"Because of me," came a voice from the darkness.

"John!"

He stepped out of the shadows, and she fell into his arms. "John! I'm so glad to see you!"

"Sara, are you all right?"

She nodded, her head tucked into his shoulder. His arms tightened around her, and she couldn't suppress a cry as her sore breast was crushed against his chest.

He let go of her. "What's wrong?"

"Nothing," she said, trying not to cry. The emotions she'd denied all week were right on the surface, threatening to break free.

"I'm going to go home now," Carlos said.

She'd forgotten about him. "Carlos, thank you," she managed.

"My pleasure. See you later."

They heard a motorcycle start, and hum away. "Come on," John said. "Let's get out of here."

"There's no place else to talk."

"I mean, let's leave the abbey. My car's by the gate. I'll bring you back later."

She knew that if she left with him, he'd see her in brighter light. The sweater, though bulky, was low-cut and he'd spot the bruises near her neck. *But he already knows. He arrested Esther Roth.* "Okay."

"Have you eaten?"

"Not lately," she said. He put his arm around her waist and she moved away. "I don't want the girls to see us," she told him. The truth was, it hurt too much.

In the police car, he put on his seatbelt and started the engine. He glanced at her. "Better buckle up."

"Oh, sure." She tried to smile as she pulled the belt across her chest with one hand and held it away from her body with the other.

"What's wrong? Are you hurt?"

"You know."

"No, I don't. Tell me."

"Your department arrested Esther Roth."

"What? Who's Esther Roth?"

"The P.E. teacher." She stared at him. "You didn't arrest her?"

"Sara, I haven't arrested anyone from St. Gertrude's and neither have my deputies. Who told you I did?"

"Richard. The sisters. They told me."

"They lied. What was I supposed to have arrested her for?"

Tears overflowed, spilling hotly down her cheeks. "Let's go," she said, her voice shaking. "Let's get the hell out of here."

He looked at her a long moment, then nodded and started driving. She couldn't stop the silent tears, and they didn't speak again until they were safely on Apple Hill Road.

"We'll go to my house, okay?"

"I don't want Mark to see me like this." She wished she'd taken a Valium; she felt like a sniveling idiot.

"He's having dinner at the Parkers'. They won't bring him home before nine o'clock."

"Okay. Your house."

They soon pulled into his driveway and she couldn't even bring herself to open the door and get out. Intellectually, she knew the shock was coming back; she felt the chill on her body, the numbness behind the tears as John opened the door and helped her out, then escorted her into the house.

"Come on," he urged. "Sit down." He put her on the couch, then brought a box of Kleenex and set it on the coffee table.

"Thanks." She wiped her eyes, then blew her nose. "I feel so stupid. I'm acting like a baby."

"You're acting like someone who's undergone some kind of trauma."

Laughter bubbled up from under the tears. "Trauma?" She heard her voice, the incipient hysteria within it, but couldn't help herself. "Trauma? I guess you could call it that." She put her hand over her mouth to stifle the laughter.

"What did Esther Roth do to you?"

"Nothing!" She spat the word. "They said she did it. They even said she hit on Lenore Tynan. The woman's a horrible creature, but she didn't do it."

"Sara," he said, gently turning her toward him. "Tell me." She saw his expression change as he caught sight of the bruises at the edge of her sweater. "Did someone beat you up?"

"Oh, God." She couldn't hold back the hysteria any longer. "Oh, God. No, John, no one beat me up." She laughed uncontrollably.

"Sara! Get hold of yourself!"

He tried to take her hands, but she yanked them away. Everything the pills had dulled was rushing back and she was feeling emotions she should have experienced a week ago, not now, not in front of John. Hurt and anger filled her. Outrage.

"What happened, Sara? I can't help you if you don't tell me." His eyes pleaded with her.

"Tell you?" she growled, jumping to her feet. She was out

of control now, and she didn't care. "Hell, no, I'll *show* you!"
She turned away and yanked the sweater over her head, then
turned back to face him. "Here's what happened! I was *raped.*"

He was on his feet in an instant, his eyes wide, jaw open.
"Sara, my God! Who did this to you? Why didn't you come
to me?" He stared at the bite on her breast, then looked into
her eyes, searching.

"It wasn't a who, it was a *what*. A *ghost* raped me. A *ghost*.
What do you think I should do, give you a description of
something that had no face, no form? How could I report that?
It's ridiculous."

"You could have talked to me—you know that."

Her anger transformed into sadness as she looked at him. "I
couldn't talk to you. I passed out and woke up in the infirmary,
and I've been eating Valium ever since. I was about to pop
another one when Carlos called me. You don't have any, do
you?"

"No, and you don't need them. You've got me now."

She bit back tears.

"Who examined you? Dashwood?"

"Who else? Fortunately, I was unconscious, but he said there
wasn't any sign of semen, and that probably Esther Roth and
her dildos attacked me."

"You need to see a real doctor."

"The hell I do. I'm fine."

"The bite looks infected." He moved closer and put his hand
near the breast, but didn't touch it. "I can feel the heat an inch
away. Let me call Dr. Cutter. Human bites are very dangerous."

"You're not hearing me, John. This *isn't* a *human* bite. It's
a *ghost* bite."

John placed his hands on her upper arms, carefully avoiding
the bruises. "We both know about their ability to fog the mind.
They've probably made you think the rapist was a ghost so
that you couldn't identify him."

Frustration and sadness nearly overwhelmed her. "No, John.
I don't remember what made me faint—that's foggy, as you
say, like it is for you with your brother. I remember I was going
to Kelly's room—I was going to take her and leave—and then,

there's just the haze. But I remember every detail of the rape. *Every* detail."

He nodded slowly. "I believe you," he said, though she could hear the uncertainty in his voice. He made a half-assed attempt at a smile. "The bottom line is, I can't bring in the bastard who did this to you because I can't handcuff him."

His words broke the tension and she put her arms out to him, the shock and hysteria flowing away as wrenching sobs shook her entire body. He held her as if she were made of eggshells and let her soak his shirt with her tears. She had no idea how long they stood there like that, but finally the sobs lessened and with that came release.

"Thank you," she whispered. She felt drained and purified and she knew she loved him. "Thank you."

He kissed her chastely on the forehead. "You're welcome." He bent and picked up her sweater, then led her to the couch. "Would you like me to draw you a hot bath?" he asked, as he handed her the sweater.

"Yes, I'd like that very much." The thought of relaxing in a tub made her smile. She hadn't realized how much she'd missed bathing at leisure, without fear.

She heard water running, and when he returned he was carrying a plush navy robe. He handed it to her. "If you need me, just call. I'll be right here."

"Thanks." She took the robe and walked down the hall to the bathroom. The tub was modern, slightly oversized, with bubble jets frothing the water. *Heaven.* She undressed and stepped in, easing down into the water.

As the warm bubbling water massaged her sore muscles, she sighed and relaxed for the first time in a long while. She was safe here, she thought, and it was a wonderful feeling. No Lucy, no Richard, no ghosts.

But could they find her here? She touched her neck, realizing she hadn't had Minerva's charm since the attack. Had she been wearing it that night? She tried to remember, and thought perhaps she'd left it on the night table. She hadn't seen it since. *It's silly, anyway.* She shivered despite the warmth of the bath.

"John?" she called.

Instantly she heard footsteps coming up the hall. "Yes?" he called from outside the door.

"Please come in," she said, slipping down into the water to hide her nudity.

He slowly opened the door and walked in, his eyes averted. "Do you need something?"

"You. Sit down. Keep me company, please?"

He looked at her face, carefully keeping his gaze above her neck as he sat on the broad edge of the tub. "My pleasure."

"You're a knight," she told him.

"What?"

"A white knight, rescuing me from the castle, remaining chivalrous at all times. I feel so safe with you."

"I'm not sure that's a compliment."

"Oh, it is." She brought her hand out of the water and took his, kissed the back of it. "It most definitely is." Butterflies flew into her throat and she swallowed them back down. "Would you care to join me?"

He didn't answer for a long time. "Yes, I would. But we should wait until you're not so sore, don't you think?"

Sara nodded, giving him a disappointed look.

"Would you like me to wash your back instead?"

"Yes." She picked up the round sponge and the bar of soap, put the two together, and rubbed, building up a lather. "Here you are."

He look flustered, then stood up. "I didn't do the laundry," he said sheepishly. "I have to wear this shirt again tomorrow."

"Take it off." She smiled.

He grinned. "If you can, I can." A slight blush on his face, he unbuttoned the tan uniform shirt, undid the buttons at his wrists. He turned as he took it off, and she admired the broad shoulders and the muscles in his back.

"You must work out," she said, as he hung the shirt over a hook on the door.

"A little," he said, "but not like I should."

He turned toward her and she liked what she saw: a flat stomach, moderately developed pecs, and muscles in his upper arms that were impressive but decidedly not of the gaudy Stallone variety. His chest was bare except for a modest thatch of reddish-brown hair that trailed down his abdomen and disappeared beneath his belt buckle. She felt passions stirring within her and was surprised and pleased. She'd thought that after her experience last week, she'd never want sex again. She wanted it very badly but wondered if it was a reaction to all the stress she'd experienced.

He sat behind her and rubbed the sponge in lazy circles over her back, then set it aside and used his fingers on the back of her neck and spine, pressing gently but firmly against the stiff muscles, never once hitting a bruise.

Finally, his fingers pushed over the front of her shoulders. "That's wonderful," she told him.

He moved around to face her, used the sponge to soap one of her arms, then the other. Then he massaged each one in turn until all the stiffness had left her. She moved up higher in the tub so that her breasts bobbed at the surface, then she saw his expression and remembered the wound. She dropped lower in the water.

He picked up the sponge. "How about a leg?"

She lifted one, enjoyed the friction of the sponge as he soaped her feet and legs, stopping just above the knee. Then he began the slow, steady massage, spending ages on her foot before kneading her calf muscles. Again, he stopped at her knee, even when she lifted her leg farther out of the water. He moved to the other foot instead.

"You're a very frustrating man," she said.

He grinned. "You have no idea how frustrated. You're a real test for my willpower."

"Let's make love, John."

He lowered her foot into the water and moved off the tub and onto his knees. Gently he pushed her hair back from her face. Cupping one hand behind her head, he put his lips to hers. Their passion grew and his free hand slipped into the water, caressing her belly, then working up to cup her uninjured breast.

Then he stopped and pulled back. "We can't do this."

"Yes, we can." She ached for him.

"No, not yet."

"Why?"

"Because you're still in shock, and if I take advantage of you now, you're likely to hate me later, and I don't want to risk that."

"I won't hate you."

He kissed her lightly. "Well, I'll hate myself."

She nodded, knowing he was right.

"Also, you've been raped. I want to know you're all right. What if I hurt you?"

"I'm fine."

"I want to hear that from a doctor."

"Dashwood said I was fine."

"He doesn't count." Anger flashed briefly in his eyes. "I want you to go see Dr. Cutter tomorrow. I'll make an appointment for you."

"No."

"Yes. If nothing else, your breast is infected."

"But—"

"It's not a human bite, I know. But it's still infected and you need treatment. You could end up with blood poisoning, and maybe we'd never get to make love."

"Hand me the robe." She stood up and stepped out of the tub, angrily taking the robe from him and wrapping it around herself. She turned to leave, but he was blocking the door. "I have to get back to the abbey."

He didn't budge. "Are you afraid of doctors?"

"I'm not submitting to any more humiliating poking and prodding."

"You said you were unconscious when Dashwood examined you."

"I was," she spat, "or I never would have allowed it again."

"Again?"

She could feel more tears coming, breaking down the wall of anger she'd built. "He gave me a very thorough physical when I arrived. *Very* thorough."

"What do you mean? Did he—?"

"Not that I recall," she told him, staring down at her hands. "But my memory is a little foggy."

"Sara, was that the day I saw you being led out of the infirmary?" He put his hand under her chin, forcing her to look at him.

"Probably. Maybe. I don't know."

"Why did he examine you?"

"It's customary." Tears ran down her cheeks, but with effort she stopped them. "He examines the girls when they arrive, too. I thought that was strange, but he said that he has to make sure they don't have venereal disease, and that they haven't been abused. That makes sense, doesn't it?"

John shook his head. "I don't know. I mean, yeah, it does, but I can't stand the man, so I'm automatically seeing him as the abuser. I'll ask Cutter to look into it. And speaking of Cutter, is Dashwood's exam what's made you gun shy?"

"Well, it was never my idea of fun, anyway."

"Look, I'll take you. He's an old family friend. Hell, Sara, the man looks like Mel Tormé. How frightening can he be? He delivered Mark. He delivered me, for that matter."

"Okay." She tried to smile. "I'll do it for you."

"Thanks. I'll call him. His house is right by his office."

"You said tomorrow."

"Sara," he said, parting the collar of the robe to reveal the top of the injured breast. "Do you see those little red lines radiating off the bite?"

She looked down, saw them, very faint. "That's nothing. It can wait until morning."

He put his hand on her forehead. "You have a fever. It can't wait. It's the beginning of blood poisoning. Do you want to go with me now, or end up in a hospital? Or dead, if you do nothing?"

"You're blunt," she said. "I'll give you that. Go ahead. Call him. I'll get dressed."

# Sixty-Eight

"Where the hell is the little bitch?" Lucy stormed as she paced back and forth in her office. "You were supposed to be keeping an eye on her."

Dashwood watched Sister Bibi's round eyes fill with fear. "Her car's still here. I checked. Carlos asked to see her. He said he needed to have her move it out of the way and she went out with him. She hasn't come back."

"She wouldn't wander off into the forest, would she?" Dashwood suggested.

Bibi gave him a grateful look. "She had her keys. If she was going to leave, wouldn't she have taken her car?"

"Why didn't you watch to make sure she came back?" Lucy demanded. "What's the matter with you?"

"She was with Carlos. I didn't think—"

"Precisely. *You didn't think.* We have to have her for the All Hallow's Eve ceremony. If she's not back, Bibiana, you'll replace her!"

The little nun quivered. "I'll check all the rooms again." With that, she was out the door.

Lucy paused. "Where's Carlos?"

"He must be home by now," Dashwood said softly. "Would you like me to—"

"We'll deal with him tomorrow. I should have realized. Richard, I believe I know exactly where our Miss Hawthorne is. Carlos will pay dearly for this."

"Where?" Dashwood asked.

"That damned sheriff was here earlier, asking about the gargoyles. He went out to talk to the gardeners. He must have had Carlos fetch her. She's with him." She went to her desk and pulled out a phone book, consulted it, then punched in a number. She waited, drumming her fingers on the desktop, then slammed the phone down. "No answer at his house."

"I'll deal with him," Dashwood said. The thought of killing John Lawson excited him.

"What, Richard? Kill the sheriff two days before the big night? Where's your subtlety?" She paused. "On the other hand, perhaps you have a point. No one would suspect us. Very well. Take the same shotgun we used on Gus Lawson."

"With pleasure. I'll be off as soon as I fetch a sedative to take to Sara."

"Do it," Lucy said. "If the boy is there, sedate him and bring him along. They'll think he found his father dead and ran off in fear." She laughed. "Or maybe they'll think he killed him."

Dashwood left her office, her laughter shrieking in his ears.

# Sixty-Nine

"You were right," Sara told John, as she sat down beside him in Frank Cutter's office. "He's a gem."

John squeezed her hand, glad to see the calmness in Sara's eyes. Even when she'd seemingly relaxed in the bath, he'd detected a trace of hysteria in them, and being a white knight, as she'd called him, had been extraordinarily difficult in the face of her passion—and his. He'd had to keep reminding himself the passion wasn't coming from the right place, and if it hadn't been for the visual reminders of what she'd been through, he would probably have given in. "Frank's one of the good ones," he told her.

The door opened and Cutter walked in and sat down at his desk. "You said Dr. Dashwood treated the bite, Miss Hawthorne?"

"That's what he told me."

"Then I'll be looking into the state of his license tomorrow. You are very fortunate John brought you in. He was right. You were headed for blood poisoning, but the injection and the antibiotics should take care of things. I want to see you again in three days, though." He paused, pulled an amber pill bottle from his pocket. "Pharmacy's closed by now. These are on the house." He pushed them across the desk.

"Thank you, Doctor. Now, will you please tell John I'm all right?"

"She'll be all right, John." Cutter glanced from one to the other, then smiled benignly at Sara. "Do you want me to get personal with this big lug in here?"

"Yes," she replied firmly.

"All right. First, the bite on your breast. I don't understand why you believe a human isn't responsible—it was made by human teeth." He paused. "Do either of you want to explain that to me?"

Sara looked at John. "Just accept it for now," he said. "I don't understand it, either, but I believe Sara." He almost added that it might have something to do with magic, but he stopped himself. He didn't need to open that can of worms.

Cutter folded his hands on his desk. "All right, I'll accept it for now. The bruising is consistent with large hands. There is evidence of penetration by a large object, human or man-made. There's bruising, swelling, and some vaginal tearing, which is healing nicely. Don't have sexual relations for another week, and I think you'll be fine."

John felt his face redden and he couldn't meet Frank's gaze.

"I've taken blood and I'll have the tests back by the time I see you again, but so far, everything looks good. You're not pregnant, by the way."

"I told you, it wasn't a man who did this."

John nudged her with his knee. "Sara was told that it was likely that a woman assaulted her with a dildo." He nudged her again and she remained silent, thank God.

"Sounds reasonable. Now, would you two like a cup of coffee? Got a whole pot full at my house."

John glanced at his watch. It was eight-thirty. "Sara?"

"Yes, I'd like that."

"Let me call home and leave Mark a message, in case he

beats us back." Frank pushed the phone over to John and he made the call. Then he rose and joined Sara and the doctor at the door just in time to hear Cutter say, "When John was born, he was blond from head to toe. Had fine blond down all over his body, and until it fell out, the family cat seemed to think he was her kitten. She was always trying to groom him."

"Thanks a lot, Frank. Shall I tell Sara about your birthmark?" He grinned at Sara. "Rumor has it, it's a perfect profile of Elvis."

# Seventy

John Lawson wasn't home. Richard Dashwood had broken into the house after making sure it was empty, and the ease of entrance had been surprising. Most likely, Lawson arrogantly assumed nobody would dare break into the sheriff's house. He hadn't even bothered to use the deadbolt on the front door. A quick flick of a credit card was all it took.

The lights were on, the drapes closed, so Dashwood prowled through the house. The man had common tastes: light oak furnishing, distastefully modern, with a television taking center stage. The kitchen was a sterile white, the pantry full of canned soup and the refrigerator held canned ham and leftover pizza, peanut butter and jelly. The freezer was, of course, loaded with frozen dinners, which, in Dashwood's estimation, was reason enough for the man to die.

His bedroom had, of all things, a large waterbed with a bright spread patterned with geometric blues and greens. It clashed with the curtains. The boy's room was done in Early Adolescent Rubble. The bathroom was steamy, the towels damp.

Lawson's office showed little more of the man's personality. The desk held a PC clone with bouncing eyeballs on the screen. He pressed a button with a gloved finger and some obscure computer war game came up, a little square box in the middle of the screen asking if he wanted to play again. "Cretin," he muttered. Checking the drawers yielded little of interest, except a small roll of twenty-dollar bills stuck in with a package of pencils and several boxes of paper clips. He didn't touch any of it.

More interesting were the bookshelves that lined the room. The man could, at least, read. Criminology books of all kinds lined one wall, history books, another. Lawson had an interest in the Civil War, just like every other would-be intellectual these days.

Another set of shelves held an eclectic mix of nonfiction, everything from cryptology to Egyptology, and the last case held fiction, mostly paperbacks. John Lawson was the ultimate common man. He favored Nero Wolfe, Tony Hillerman, and Larry McMurtry. At least there weren't any of those tacky horror novels on his shelves. Dashwood smiled to himself. Perhaps if the sheriff had read a little Poe or King, he'd have some clue as to what he was getting into.

The phone rang. He stared at the answering machine on the desk. It was on, and on the fourth ring, it picked up and rattled off an insipid message, then beeped. John Lawson's voice came over the speaker.

"Hiya, Mark. It's about eight-thirty, and I'm at Dr. Cutter's with Sara Hawthorne. She had a little accident, but she's fine now. We're going to his house for coffee—we have some things to talk over with the doctor. We won't be too late, though. Do me a favor, son, and check and make sure the guest room's made up. Sara's going to spend the night at our house. If you need me, the doc's number is in the Rolodex on my desk. Remember to lock the doors and do your homework. 'Bye."

"Damn it." The dullard of a sheriff had already talked. If he killed Lawson now, he'd have to kill the doctor as well, and there was always the possibility he'd alerted his deputies. But as it was, Lawson didn't really have anything except a Valium-popping woman claiming she'd been raped by a ghost. He decided it would be best to let Lawson live another day or two.

Dashwood whirled, hearing a noise in the living room. "Dad?" called a boy's voice. "Dad? You here?"

He smiled to himself. At least something had gone according to plan. He pulled a small bottle of chloroform and a handkerchief from his jacket pocket, poured a little on the cloth. Taking Lawson's son would get the man's mind off Sara Hawthorne, and it would also take care of the most difficult aspect of the All Hallow's Eve preparations: procuring the boy.

He stepped behind the door and waited. It didn't take long before the boy walked up the hall and entered the office. Without looking around, he went straight to the flashing answering machine and pressed the button. As soon as Lawson's voice started prattling on, Dashwood crossed the room in three long strides and clamped the cloth over Mark's mouth. The boy struggled hard, but Dashwood kept his grip, and finally the boy went down in a heap.

Leaving him there, Dashwood went to the boy's room, found a backpack, and took jeans, shirts, socks, and underwear from his drawers, stuffing the bag with them. Then he took an extra blanket from the boy's closet and quickly fashioned a long lump under the bedspread that resembled a sleeping body.

Going to the kitchen, he looked in the cupboards, found a container of Slim-Jims and half a dozen Twinkies, and threw them in, too, then carefully shut the cupboard doors. Returning to the office, he removed the roll of twenties from the desk and shoved it into the bag.

Last, but not least, he entered the guest room and made up the bed for Sara Hawthorne. When he finished, he messed it up a little, so that it would look like the work of an adolescent boy.

Now came the hard work. He dragged the boy out of the office and hoisted him over his shoulder fireman-style, then snagged up the backpack. He walked boldly out the front door, locking it behind him. The street was quiet, and he made it to the BMW without being seen.

# Seventy-One

"No arguments, Sara," John said, as they pulled into the driveway. "You can't go back to the abbey. You're sleeping in our guest room."

"John, I have to go back. I promise, all I'll do is get Kelly to Minerva's so she's safe, hand in my resignation, and grab my stuff."

"You're stubborn," he said, as he unlocked the front door and ushered her inside. "I could put you in protective custody, you know."

"You wouldn't dare!"

"Don't tempt me." The clock chimed eleven. "Mark?" he called, then turned to Sara. "We're late. He might already be asleep. Just let me check on him, then we can resume our argument."

She smiled and sat down on the couch.

Mark's room was dark, but a stray beam of moonlight shone across the bed, revealing his son's sleeping form. John was sorry they were so late getting back—he and Sara had told the doctor enough wild tales to fuel conversations for years to come—but he was not sorry Mark was already asleep. It made everything much easier.

He left Mark's room and checked the guest room. Mark had made the bed and even turned back the covers. It was a little messy, but John was impressed; for Mark, this was exquisite work. And it meant he approved of Sara.

"You have to stay," he said, returning to the living room. "Mark's made up the guest room for you."

"I'm willing to stay the night," she said. "I just have to be there in the morning."

"About Kelly," John began.

"What?" She was suddenly alert. "I've neglected her for a week. Lord, John, I just remembered. I promised to drive her to Minerva's last Sunday, and then the . . . incident occurred and I forgot all about her. Is something wrong?"

"No, but I don't think you need to worry. The girl gets around. Minerva says she's been visiting her. I'll go over in the morning and ask Minerva to keep her until we can sort things out."

"Do you think Minerva's safe out there?"

"I know it sounds strange, but yes, I do. And I think anybody who's with her is safe." He studied her. "Where's your magic necklace?"

Sara laughed. "It disappeared that night."

"We have an extra. It's in my bedroom. I'll get it for you when we turn in."

She smiled. "You're taking this pretty seriously now, aren't you?"

"It can't hurt," he said lightly.

"If we can get Kelly out of there, then put St. Gertrude's under investigation, I'll be very satisfied, but I still wish I knew what really happened to Jenny."

"We may never know, but I'm going to do my best to find out for you. You just let me handle that part."

"I have to get my things."

"That's fine. I'll go with you."

"Okay. Then I'm going with you to Minerva's."

He opened his mouth to object, then realized they'd run out of reasons to spar. "Sure. I'd like that."

Sara lifted an eyebrow. "What happened to the he-man routine?"

Grinning, he pushed his hair away from his forehead. "Simple. You stopped talking like Wonder Woman. Want some hot milk or something?"

"Hot chocolate?" she asked.

"I think we can manage that."

Soon, they sat at the kitchen table sipping steaming mugs of chocolate made Sara's way; so strong he could barely drink it. "You really are addicted to chocolate," he mused, adding a spoon of sugar to his mug.

"We all have our vices. John, do you know if Dr. Cutter is

right about that history teacher retiring from Moonfall High at the end of the semester?"

"Frank Cutter is all-knowing."

"Do you think I'd have a chance at the post?"

"Are you kidding? With your background, you'd be in like flint." He tried to suppress a sudden yawn. The day was catching up with him.

"I'm tired, too," she said, rising. "Are you done with that?" He nodded, and she took his cup, drained the bitter chocolate, then set both mugs in the sink and filled them with water.

"John? You don't happen to have an old T-shirt or something I can wear to bed, do you?"

"How about a pajama top? Mark gives me pajamas every year in the hopes I'll start wearing them to bed." He realized what he'd said, and added, "I wear shorts."

She followed him past Mark's closed door to his bedroom. He gave her a long pale blue pajama top then guided her to the guest bathroom where he showed her hotel soaps, toothpaste, shampoo, and even a new toothbrush sealed in plastic.

# Seventy-Two

Sometime during the night, Sara awoke from a nightmare and for a moment she panicked. She didn't know where she was. Then she remembered and tried to relax.

In her dream, the ghost had come to her, and instead of black pits, it had Dashwood's eyes. The creature swarmed over her and she came awake clutching her throat, certain she was drowning in ice-cold slime, sure her lungs were filled with the stuff.

Lying there in the dark, trembling and wishing she wasn't alone, she realized she could hear something; a voice, not in her head, but somewhere outside her room. She rose and tiptoed to the door and opened it a crack.

"I can't open it!" came John's voice, tortured and loud, even behind his closed door. "Help me!" he cried hoarsely.

*He's having a nightmare, too.* She walked to his room and knocked softly on the door.

"Help me," he pleaded softly.

Opening the door, she saw him thrashing around under the covers on the tall bed.

She crossed to him. "John, wake up. You're having a bad dream." She spoke quietly, not wanting to startle him.

"It won't open," he grunted.

In the dim moonlight from the window, she made out his face, saw his contorted features. She reached out and placed her hands on his shoulders. "John! Wake up."

He sat bolt upright, eyes opening wide, breath coming in ragged pants. He stared at her, seemed not to know her, then relaxed.

"Sorry about that," he said. "Nightmares. Did I wake you up?"

"No, my own nightmare did that."

"I hate being alone at night," he said a little shakily.

"Me, too. What do you say we sleep together before we sleep together?"

He stared at her a long moment. "I'd like that."

She closed the door to his room, then climbed into his water-bed. It was warm and it sloshed as she positioned herself, turning on her side and spooning against his body. He put his arm around her waist and tucked her closer to him, not saying a word.

Soon he was asleep and she lay there listening to the soft, regular rhythm of his breathing. In his sleep he nuzzled against her neck and pressed his legs against hers so that there was no space between them. She smiled to herself as sleep finally came. For all his insistence that he had to protect her, she knew that he needed her as badly as she needed him.

# Seventy-Three

John squinted as morning sunlight streaming through the window washed across his face. More asleep than awake, he turned over and snuggled deeper under the covers—and then realized he wasn't alone. Sara lay on her back sound asleep, her dark hair feathering across the pillow, her face angelic and peaceful. God, she was beautiful.

He glanced at the alarm clock and was startled to see it was past 7:30. *Damn.* He'd meant to set it last night—he should have been up an hour ago.

Moving slowly to avoid waking Sara, he climbed out of bed, then padded out into the hall and down to Mark's room. He rapped on the door. "Mark?"

The boy didn't answer. He must have slept in, too—he would have knocked on John's door, otherwise. He opened the door and walked in. "Mark? Wake up. You're going to be late for school." He reached down to shake Mark's shoulder, but his fingers closed on nothing but soft material.

"Mark?" He pulled the covers back, saw the blanket wadded on top of the sheet. "What the hell?"

"Mark?" He called his son several times as he walked through the house. There was no sign of him, not even a note saying where he'd gone.

"What's wrong?" Sara rubbed her eyes and sat up as John reentered the bedroom and started dressing.

"Mark's gone."

"To school?" she asked.

He shook his head. "No. I don't even think he was in bed last night—he faked it." He tucked in his shirt and buckled on his gunbelt. "I'm going to make some calls," he said. "This isn't like him, not at all."

# Seventy-Four

Sara had been surprised when John had handed her the keys to his blue Nissan pick-up and asked her to drive to Minerva's to see if she knew where Mark was, but she gladly did it.

She'd driven as far as she could, then began walking the rest of the way. John had been nearly frantic to find Mark, and she finally asked him if he thought the boy had seen them in the same bed and taken off. To her relief, he didn't even hesitate before he said no.

She reached the cottage and the door opened before she could knock. Minerva's worried face peered out at her, then the door opened wider. "Come inside."

"Have you seen Mark?" Sara asked, before she even sat down.

"No, not since yesterday afternoon. He was going to the Parker place."

"Yes. Caspar Parker said he dropped him off at home around 9:15 and saw him go inside." Briefly, she explained how John had discovered the boy was missing this morning. "Minerva, do you think Mark would run away?"

"No," the old woman said firmly. "He loves his father, and even if he didn't, it's not the sort of thing he'd do. He's too conscientious for that."

"John's very worried about him."

"With good reason."

"Minerva, you don't think he's at the abbey, do you?"

"Not of his own free will, but I wouldn't be surprised if he's been taken there." She rose from her chair and put the teakettle on to boil. "I have a story to tell you. You may have heard some of it already, but you must hear it now, because lives depend on it. John, his son, and Kelly Reed—and you, for that matter—are all in great peril."

She began the story of the Moonfalls and the Lawsons, stopping briefly to brew more tea, then continued, telling Sara things she already knew, as well as facts that were new to her. Nearly an hour passed before Minerva sat back and sighed. "And that's why I fear Mark may already have met with foul play. Tell John to check the school and to take his deputies with him. Check the basement."

"Where the infirmary is?"

"Yes, and I believe there is a sub-basement as well. Sara, Mark will die tomorrow night, and so will Kelly. John must get them out of there."

"He wanted me to ask you if you would keep Kelly with you if she shows up today."

"Gladly. I should have prevented her return weeks ago."

"You couldn't know."

"Oh, but I did. I thought it best to let her go back. I thought it would strengthen her resolve to learn the magic of the right-hand path."

Sara nodded, not quite sure what the old lady was talking about.

"You said John took you to see Dr. Cutter. May I ask why?"

Sara launched into the story, beginning with her gentle dream and ending with the rape. "I'm not sure how I fainted, but I woke up in the infirmary."

"You surmised correctly that the thing that attacked you was the same phantom that nearly took your life at the Falls. It's a revenant, probably empowered by Dashwood and Lucy. I've encountered it myself, and it reeks of those two."

"Did it attack you?"

"It has tried." She paused. "Not sexually, not even when I was young. Lucy hates me too much for that. But it's come near my house a number of times and tried to scare me with monstrous appearances and threats. It's even invaded my dreams now and then. But it never lasts long. It takes a tremendous amount of energy, you know, even for those two, to make the phantom take physical form." Minerva took her hands. "Close your eyes and concentrate, Sara. I want you to think about that night. Think about walking down the hall to Kelly's room. Try to see through the fog."

Sara did as she asked. The old woman began speaking words

she didn't understand. Rough and lilting at the same time, the unknown phrases mesmerized her and her mind began to clear. "My God," she blurted. "I was drugged. Someone put a rag over my face. It smelled like chemicals."

"Chloroform, I'd imagine. That was the easy part. The sexual attack on you must have left them absolutely exhausted."

That didn't make Sara feel any better. "What about the pleasant sexual dreams that occurred before the attack?"

"There were never any marks on you before the attack?"

"No."

"I expect that was Dashwood alone, simply visiting you in your sleep. You've heard of astral projection?"

"Yes, I think so."

"It's simple. Most people can learn to do it. His mind communicated with yours, so in a way, it was a real encounter. A mental one that can't hurt you."

"It's so . . . invasive."

"Yes. It's horrible. John was right when he stopped you from spending another night there. You are probably meant to be one of their sacrifices. The dreams are a way of warming you up for what is to come."

"Warming me up? What does that mean?"

"My dear, the sisters and their high priest don't just kill their victims. They torture them sexually and then present them to their god for sexual intercourse."

"You mean, they rape you in its name?"

"That's the foreplay, Sara. They conjure their demons, who then have sexual intercourse with the victims. Then the coven kills them, if the rape hasn't already."

"Dear God." Sara could barely comprehend what Minerva said, but after the experience with the revenant, she had to believe her. "Do they attack the boys as well?"

"They attack whatever they wish, though I don't think they are as violent with the boys—the Lawsons, at least. You see, they've always wanted the Lawson bodies to be found, but they don't want to give any clue to their involvement in the deaths. That's why they always make it look like an accident or suicide. They're very cautious."

Minerva cleared her throat. "Nothing more will happen until tomorrow night, but John *must* get his son and Kelly away from there. Tell him he must stop them completely or they will kill other innocents. He needs to come to me first, though; he'll fail without my kind of help."

"Who are they?" Sara asked. "John told me about the Order of Lilith and all that, but who are they? Who is Dashwood? Are they descendants of the original group?"

Minerva didn't answer for a long time. "I didn't tell this to John, but you've seen the phantom, so you might be willing to believe me."

"I'm ready to believe anything."

She nodded. "They are not descendants. They are the originals. So am I."

Sara stared at her. "You mean you're . . . ?"

"I came here with my husband Jeremiah in 1875. John is my great-great-grandson."

"How old are you?"

"Older than you're guessing. I was born in England sometime in the late 1690s. The gift ran in my family, and though my mother did not possess it, my grandmother did. She apprenticed me when I was twelve, and by the time I was eighteen, I was proficient enough to be able to slow my aging to a crawl by normal standards. When I met Jeremiah, I let myself age normally until he died, then I slowed the process again. For all intents and purposes, I'm pushing seventy. If I had known then what I know now, I'd have slowed the process before Jeremiah died. This body doesn't have the strength it needs."

Sara shook her head. "That's amazing."

"And very hard to swallow, I know, but nevertheless, it's true. Dashwood and Lucy are older than me. Dashwood, under other names, is mentioned in histories dating back to the days of Joan of Arc, and Lucy, nearly as long. Both were active in the Church in their early days, both rejected it, and when they found one another, their evil grew a hundredfold. A few of the sisters are quite old as well. Some came here with Lucy and Dashwood."

"Can they be killed?"

"Yes. They are mortal. Like me, however, they have protective magic surrounding them, Because there are many, their magic is strong."

"How are they recruited?"

"A practitioner of magic recognizes his own kind. They find their members many ways, often recruiting them from among the students."

"Those are the girls that attend the chapel services?"

"Yes. Those who wash out are disposed of. Killed. Kelly has the gift but she won't bend to their wishes, so she will die."

"What about the nightflyers?"

"As I told John, they are quite real."

"Are they the gargoyles?"

"I believe they comprise some of the figures that ornament the buildings, but I've never seen a gargoyle take flight, so I'm not sure. They are part of the evil, though, I promise you that." The clock chimed nine times. "It's time for you to talk to John."

"Should I tell him who you really are? Who the nuns are?"

"Only when you truly think he's ready to believe you. I think it's better to wait and let him concentrate on his son. He has to understand the danger. That's the important thing."

Minerva saw her to the door. "Remember, go straight back to John."

"I will."

Sara started up the path to the truck. The day was beautiful, the sunlight compensating for the chill morning breeze. She heard a screech to the west and picked up her pace, sighing with relief when John's blue pick-up came into view. When she was only a few feet from it, a bone-chilling shriek sounded overhead. She looked up and saw a huge black creature sweeping over her, its wingspan at least six feet across. Instinctively, she ducked and ran for the truck, shoving the key into the lock and opening the door as fast as she could.

She leapt inside, slamming the door behind her. Breathing hard, she looked up through the windshield. The creature had disappeared.

# Seventy-Five

Mark Lawson awoke to darkness and a throbbing headache. He was shivering from the cold and had no idea where he was. The last thing he remembered was listening to his dad's message on the answering machine—and that was it. There was nothing. *No, not nothing.* His mind cleared and he remembered smelling chloroform. Someone had drugged him.

"Hello?" he said to the dank darkness.

There was no reply.

He realized he was sitting on damp, smooth stones and got to his feet, slightly dizzy, and leaned against the wall, also of dank, wet stone. "Hello?" he asked again.

He felt his way around the room, jumping when he heard the squeak of a rodent. *Great, just great. A rat'll bite me and I'll end up getting rabies shots, after all.*

He kept moving and finally came to a door of heavy unfinished planking that filled his hands with splinters. Gingerly he felt for a doorknob, and his fingers came to rest on a cold metal handle. He pulled with all his might, but the door wouldn't budge.

"Help!" he yelled, pounding on the door. "Let me out of here!"

He yelled and pounded until his hands and throat were raw, but no one came.

# Seventy-Six

"Quite a set of lungs on the Lawson boy," Dashwood said, as he turned off the microphone switch in his office.

Lucy's lip curled. "I'll be glad to be rid of him. And his disgusting father, too. But first we must get Sara Hawthorne back here."

"Yes. That should be fairly easy. Why don't we just have the sisters take care of that?"

"A compulsion spell?"

"Yes. That should work fine. You and I have better things to do. Preparations to make for the black mass."

Lucy nodded. "I'll have them do it during the lunch hour."

"What if Lawson comes with her?" Dashwood asked. "By now, he's discovered his son is missing. I took the backpack so that he'll think the boy ran away, and I reset the answering machine, but there's no guarantee he'll fall for it. I wish I knew who he's already talked to."

"No matter. If he shows up today, we'll be pleasant, and if he persists, Richard, we'll cloud his mind."

"Do you still want to kill him?"

Lucy rubbed her rosaries thoughtfully. "Yes, but we might want to wait a while so that no one suspects that we know he's at least spoken to Cutter about his suspicions. For now, we'll kill his son, and perhaps drive him mad with our friendly ghost. Won't that be fun, Richard, darling?"

"I can hardly wait." He smiled. "I trust Kelly Reed is well in hand?"

"The sisters and our novices are keeping an eye on her. She's attending classes as usual and doesn't suspect a thing."

"Lucy, you're an amazing woman. I don't know how you do it all. Spells, torture, administration, bondage, and discipline. I'm in awe." He took her hand. "Perhaps we should focus and combine our energy again to replenish one another, since the ceremony is so close."

"Richard," she said coyly, "you read my mind. I'll call Sister Agatha and have her gather the sisters. Then you and I can indulge ourselves." She smirked at him. "I'll meet you in your apartment in twenty minutes. Make sure you have some matches. I want to get hot."

# Seventy-Seven

They had been watching her all morning, but when the lunch hour arrived, Kelly Reed was overjoyed to see that the nuns had disappeared. Of course, Marcia Crowley and her gang of twits had their eyes on her—no doubt under the sisters' orders—but they would be easy to lose.

She went through the lunch line and sat down at the far end of a table by herself to wolf down the tasteless food: macaroni and cheese, lime Jell-O, and puke-colored canned green beans. She was hurrying because Sara Hawthorne hadn't been in class today and she wanted to find out why. Finishing her milk, she got up and turned in her tray, then walked toward the cafeteria's back door.

"Hey, Ghost Girl," Marcia called in a singsong voice. "Where do you think you're going?"

Kelly turned and glared at her. "I have to clean the third-floor bathroom. Do you want to help?"

"Gross," Buffy Bullock whined.

"We're supposed to go with her." Marcia didn't sound too enthusiastic.

"Then *you* go," Buffy sniped back.

"Yeah, Marcia, *you* go," echoed a couple of the other girls.

Her face set in an ugly sneer, Marcia stared at Kelly. "I'm going to come and check up on you in a few minutes, so you'd better be there."

"I'll clean a toilet just for you," Kelly called, as she headed for the door.

"Use your tongue," Marybeth Tingler called after her.

Kelly didn't respond. A moment later she reached the dorm and went straight to Sara's third-floor room. She knocked. "Miss Hawthorne? Sara? Are you okay?"

She waited a moment, then opened the door and walked inside. The bed was unmade and Sara's robe and nightgown were tossed across it. Her purse was on the table. Kelly thought she must be on the grounds someplace.

She left the room and hurried downstairs. If anyone saw her running around, she'd end up in solitary again, and she didn't want that. She stepped outside and flattened herself against the wall as Buffy and Marybeth passed by.

Kelly held her breath until they were out of sight, then glanced at her surroundings. The big kitchen building was nearby, and since the nuns weren't around, it would be the perfect route out to the garage to see if Sara's car was there. She knew it was more likely that Sara might be in the infirmary, but she didn't want to risk looking there—at least, not yet. It was too dangerous.

She sprinted the fifty yards to the old stone kitchen, then around to the back. She'd never been inside; this wasn't the cafeteria kitchen, but the monstrous antique one used by the nuns to bake the pies and make jams, jellies, and candies to sell at Apple Heaven.

Moving to a window, she peered inside and saw wooden tables just under the window and ovens lining the far wall. A long central counter was piled with large chunks of meat, and the grinders—huge, old-fashioned ones with hand cranks— had meat oozing out of them. *Gross.*

But no one was around. Wherever the nuns had gone, they'd left everything in a hurry. She moved to a door and tried it, breathing relief as it opened. She slipped inside, crouching low and listening, ready to bolt if anyone came along.

No one did. She crossed the huge kitchen and saw large pots simmering on the stoves on the far walls. The place stank of simmering meat, a cloying scent she had smelled on the wind before. She despised it.

Flies buzzed around the top of an open garbage can and she glanced into it as she passed. Kelly stopped in her tracks as she saw a pair of eyes staring up at her. Dead eyes in a dead face. The severed head of a man, one of the gardeners, gazed blindly up at her. She caught sight of fingertips poking out from beneath the bloody neck. Her stomach roiled, and she couldn't move, couldn't think.

The slam of a door startled Kelly out of her paralysis. She crouched and moved quickly toward the far door, which she thought would bring her out fairly close to the garage. Behind her, women's voices chattered. Someone laughed, high-pitched and witchy.

Trying to push the grisly image from her mind, she reached the door and turned the knob. It opened silently. She glanced around, saw no one, and sprinted toward the small garage door. She made it in a few seconds, and breathing hard, let herself inside.

Dim lightbulbs illuminated the long, gloomy building. At the far end, sunlight shone through the open double doors. She waited a moment, but heard nothing except a lawnmower somewhere in the distance.

Keeping to the shadows, she walked through the building until she saw Sara's car. *Okay, she's still here, for sure.* Kelly shivered, thinking of what she'd seen in the garbage can, knowing that the chunks of flesh on the counter and oozing out of the grinders probably belonged to the dead man. *God, that's the secret ingredient in their mincemeat pies—people!* Might they have done the same thing to Sara? She had to find her, and *fast.*

She continued on toward the other end of the building, knowing it was less likely someone would notice her if she went back that way. Near the end of the building, she saw Dashwood's black Beamer, noticed something bright red poking up above the seat. She peered in the window. It was a backpack, with a Hootie and the Blowfish patch on it. *Mark's!*

What was happening? Whatever it was, she knew she'd better get help fast. Cautiously, she peered out the garage doors, waited forever for a pair of nuns to walk from the chapel to the school building. Finally they disappeared inside and Kelly sprinted across the lawn, then raced past the chapel.

"Hey!" someone called. She glanced back and saw Marcia running after her. Kelly increased her speed, racing through the cemetery, and broke through the bushes, onto the road. Marcia's voice was more distant now. Kelly crossed the road and entered the woods, zigzagging through the trees until she was deep in the forest. Marcia wouldn't find her now. She probably wouldn't even follow her.

After resting a few minutes, she started walking. She'd check Minerva's cottage first, since it was closest. If the house was deserted, she'd go to the Gingerbread House, knowing Minerva would let her call the police from there. Overhead, above the trees, a nightflyer screeched. Another replied and a shadow momentarily blotted out what little sunlight filtered through the trees. *They're hunting for me.* The creatures circled, their screams hurting her ears, and she crawled under a giant conifer and waited until their calls receded into the distance before moving on.

# Seventy-Eight

Sara Hawthorne had told John that Minerva was sure Mark was at St. Gertrude's. He had thanked her, then asked her to go back to his house and wait.

She'd been irritated as hell—he was worse than Minerva. He'd promised to take her with him to the abbey, but he'd gone back on his word, saying instead that he would pick up her property and turn in the letter of resignation for her. She'd paced his living room for an hour and a half, wanting, *needing,* to do something. *Like pick up my own property and formally resign. Right in Lucy's face!*

Now she was in John's blue mini-truck again, driving up the road to St. Gertrude's. She'd finally given in to the need to go there, to pack up her things, grab Kelly, and get the hell out. John would be furious if he found out, so she pulled the Nissan around to the back of the abbey and parked in the first stall in the garage, just in case he showed up while she was here.

She stepped out of the truck and locked the door, then turned and found herself face to face with Richard Dashwood.

"Hello, Sara," he said, beaming at her. "I missed you."

# Seventy-Nine

John rubbed his throbbing temples, then reached in his desk drawer, found a couple Excedrin, and popped them in his mouth, washing them down with the dregs of a two-hour-old Coke.

His son was missing and he hadn't even managed to leave the station yet to look for him. His deputies, Scotty Carroll and Wyn Griffin, were cruising, at least, and they'd already alerted many of the merchants in town to keep an eye out. John had spent half the morning dealing with citizens of Moonfall and the other half on the phone, calling Mark's friends and their parents, but no one knew anything.

Sara had come by to tell him that Minerva was sure the nuns had taken the boy. He didn't want to believe it, and he'd been spending much of his time arguing with himself about it. Minerva Payne was old, maybe crazy, maybe senile—maybe both. She made no secret of her hatred for the sisters, and the stories she told him were patently absurd. All that, and she had no proof to back her allegations. So why, he asked himself once more, was he inclined to believe her?

*Listen to your inner voice and you'll never go wrong.* She'd told him that every time he'd seen her, and he realized now that it was his inner voice that was trying to be heard over the voice of reason and logic.

Someone rapped on the door. "Come in," he called out. "Jeff," he said, as Deputy Thurman stepped in. "Take over here for a while," John said, rising. "Whole town's a zoo today." He moved to the door.

"Must be the full moon." Thurman paused. "Sorry about your son."

"Yeah, thanks." He fought down a lump in his throat. "No reason to be sorry. He'll turn up." He rushed out of the station before Dorothy could torture him with yet more pity, climbed in his cruiser, and drove over to the Gingerbread House.

# Eighty

"Did it go according to plan?" Lucy asked, as Dashwood entered her office.

"Miss Hawthorne is resting, none too comfortably, I might add, in the old root cellar."

"Why didn't you just toss her in the vault with the boy? It's more secure."

"My dear Lucy, you're far too soft-hearted. Do you really want them to have one another for company? It would lessen their fear." He gave her his most charming smile. "They wouldn't be as much fun tomorrow evening. And the root cellar is secure enough. It doesn't have a padlock, but it does have that nice big bar latch."

Lucy pursed her lips. "You're right, Richard, on both counts. I like the way you think," she added, smiling. "She came like a moth to the flame. I'll have to compliment the sisters on their spellcasting. Now, regarding the boy. . . ."

"Yes?"

"You mentioned taking his backpack to make it appear as if he's run away."

"Indeed I did."

"Where is it?"

"In my car."

"We're likely to be entertaining the sheriff soon, Richard. Make sure you ditch it. Throw it in with the boy, or something."

Dashwood nodded. "Immediately." He started to leave, but Lucy wasn't done yet.

"We have only two flies left in our ointment, Richard. Three, if we count the old woman, but I hardly think she's worth counting." She laughed. "Our flies are the sheriff, who has no proof of anything, and Kelly Reed."

"Have they found her yet?"

"Not yet, but I expect good news soon. She can't get far in that forest without being spotted."

"I have one more problem to take care of." Dashwood dangled Sara's car keys from his fingertips, eager to be on his way. "Our runaway teacher returned in what I believe is Lawson's personal vehicle. A small blue truck."

"She *what?*" Lucy stood up, her eyes blazing. "Why didn't you tell me this before?"

"You didn't give me a chance to tell you, Lucy dear. Don't worry. I'll take it into town and leave it in a crowded parking lot, where it will be so obvious no one will pay any attention to it. I'll have Sister Regina pick me up in the station wagon."

"Don't take it into town, you fool. Too many people are likely to recognize the truck and wonder why you, not Lawson, are behind the wheel. Honestly, I expected better of you, Richard! Just drive it up the fire trail on the other side of Apple Hill Road, and be careful no one sees you when you cross the highway. Take it at least a few miles away."

"Lucy, the station wagon can't go up that road."

She smiled thinly. "Walk. You need the exercise."

"You're right, of course," he said, keeping his temper with great effort. "It wouldn't pay to get sloppy for the sake of my comfort. But, Lucy, I should be here when Lawson shows up. He'll want to talk to me."

She nodded. "Have Boullan take it, then. But be quick about it."

# Eighty-One

*Can they smell me?*

Kelly had traveled very little distance since the first time the nightflyers had passed overhead. She thought there were at least a half dozen of them, circling, screeching.

She knew they were trying to find her, and if they did, she thought she wouldn't survive. At times, when the cries sounded very far away, she sprinted as far as she could—fifty feet, one hundred, who knew?—and had so far been lucky enough to find trees to hide under or outcroppings of boulders to crouch below.

The nearly impenetrable forest of St. Gertrude's had aided her, but now she was ready to cross the stream into Witch Forest, which meant there were more places where the nightflyers would be able to see her. *Minerva.* She thought the name as hard as she could, picturing the old woman's face in her mind. *Minerva, help me.*

She continued the thought as she waited for the screeches and wingbeats to fade. After an eternity they did, and she ran the twenty feet to the stream, then pounded through it to the other side. Hearing a nightflyer approaching, she threw herself under a wide-limbed pine and waited, her thoughts still on Minerva.

# Eighty-Two

"If they have Mark at St. Gertrude's, I'm going to need a search warrant," John told Minerva Payne. "Even if they let me search the place without one, I can't have a free hand with the nuns and Dashwood looking over my shoulder. The place is a warren. They could have him right under my nose and still keep him hidden from me."

"I have no proof for you," Minerva said. "I wish I did."

"Sara mentioned the basement or a root cellar below it."

"The sub-basement. You should begin your search there." Minerva cocked her head as if she were listening to something he couldn't hear. She turned her gaze back on him. "John, you may have to go clandestinely. Not as a sheriff, but as a father." The faraway look came into her eyes again.

"I suppose I might have to, at that." The thought sent adrenaline coursing through his blood. His uniform and badge were armor that gave him a sense of authority and purpose. Without them, he would feel like he was fourteen again, sneaking around where he shouldn't. *Greg lying on a slab, an altar of black stone, candlelight flickering across his nude body . . .*

"John?" Minerva asked. "Are you all right?"

"I—I remember something. About Greg. An altar, candles, dark figures around him."

"Good. I told you weeks ago that you must remember in order to save your son. Your memories will lead you to Mark, if you let them." Minerva put her hand over his, then suddenly flinched, her nails digging into his skin.

He drew away. "What's wrong?"

"I'm sorry. I have to go." Minerva took a set of keys from her apron pocket and crossed to the front door. "You remember what I've told you, John," she said as she opened it for him. "Come to my house in an hour or two and I'll help you capture your memories."

"Minerva," he repeated, as she almost pushed him out the door. "What's going on?"

"I'm needed."

She strode away before he could open his mouth to offer her a ride. He watched, amazed at her speed as she crossed the parking lot and started down the narrow road to her cottage. She was out of sight within a minute, and he wondered how a woman that old could move so fast. Magic, he thought wryly.

He sat down in his cruiser and rubbed his forehead. Time was wasting and he didn't know what to do next. The brief flash of memory was promising, and for a moment he thought he might spend the next hour with his eyes shut and his mind open, trying to remember more, but he knew himself better than that. Sitting still wasn't one of his talents. He had to do something.

He picked up his cell phone and punched in his home number to talk to Sara. He'd rushed out of the house this morning with barely a word, certainly nothing that would reassure her. Then he'd been short with her when she'd come to the station to tell him about her conversation with Minerva. After spending the night in the same bed, he felt he should at least say hello and let her know what was going on—or, more precisely, what wasn't. Besides, he was worried about her.

He phoned the house twice, but the machine picked up both

times. Where was she? Cursing away his fear, he started the car and drove home. His truck wasn't in the driveway.

*Damn it.* He left the cruiser idling while he ran up to the house and let himself in. "Sara?" he called, knowing she wasn't there. *"Sara?"*

In thirty seconds he was back out in the cruiser. For a moment he tried to convince himself she was in town, shopping or driving around looking for Mark, even though she'd promised to wait for him here. But in his gut he knew where she was: St. Gertrude's.

He used his phone again, this time to call the unlisted number for his office. He didn't want to talk to Dorothy, and this was the only way around her.

"Sheriff's office." Deputy Thurman answered halfway through the first ring.

"Jeff, it's me. Sara Hawthorne isn't at the station, is she?"

"No, not as far as I know. I'll ask Dorothy—"

"No. Just take a look out the window and see if my pick-up is in the lot."

"Sure." He heard a clunk as the phone was laid down. Ten seconds later, Thurman returned. "It's not there, boss."

"How busy are we right now?"

"Scotty's on a domestic, and Wyn's at the high school. Principal Simmons found a pistol in a student's locker."

"Great, just great," he sighed. "What about you?"

"I'm on my way out to Parker's. Larry Finney got drunk and is exposing himself to the ladies again."

Suddenly, John missed the annoyances of normal life. Finney, a retired insurance salesman, had a love of apple wine and a problem with his pants. Ordinarily, John would pass the call off to his deputies, but right now he wished he had the luxury of taking it.

"Do you need help on something?" Thurman asked.

"No. I'm going out to St. Gertrude's to take a look around. If you get freed up, feel free to join me."

"Sure thing."

"And Jeff?"

"Yeah?"

"If I don't call in in two hours, come and get me. And bring at least one other deputy along."

"You got it. Are you expecting trouble?"

"I don't know," John told him. "But it's possible. I have a weak lead on Mark. He might be out there. I'm just going to take a look around. And Jeff, tell the others to keep an eye out for my truck and for Sara Hawthorne. If you find either one, give me a call." John clicked off the phone and grimly set off toward St. Gruesome's.

# Eighty-Three

She had heard the faraway cries of the nightflyers for several hours, and they had made it nearly impossible for Minerva Payne to concentrate on her baking. She'd burned two batches of cookies and ruined a tray of cream puffs because of the sounds, which were no less ominous because of their distance.

She'd felt great relief when John Lawson had shown up at her shop; she'd been afraid he wouldn't come. But there was no time to help him because shortly after his arrival, Minerva began feeling something else: someone—Kelly, she thought—was asking for help. It was a mental scream so loud that Minerva could barely think and only Kelly Reed was capable of sending such a strong message.

*But what if it's a trap? What if it's Lucy or Dashwood, trying to get me out of the way before tomorrow night?*

She had to take the chance. She'd kept a low profile these last few years, casting only protection spells to keep the coven away. In fact, her spells weren't so different from the ones that Lucy and Dashwood used to keep their own presence shrouded from the minds of the townsfolk. Hopefully, Lucy and the rest didn't think of her as a major threat any longer, but as a decrepit old woman far past her prime.

Two nightflyers swooped across her path just as she reached the clearing around her cottage. They were so close she could smell their decaying scent. Their wingspans were at least six feet wide, their faces ugly, shrunken monkey-like masks, and their eyes flashed red even in broad daylight.

Minerva had restrengthened her protection spells, and unless Dashwood and Lucy's magic was stronger than she had reckoned, the nightflyers wouldn't be able to come any closer to the cottage. She raised her arms and extended her fingers at them, reciting a few lines of Celtic magic. The things edged back over the trees. *"Be gone!"* Minerva cried, mentally shooting her magic from her fingerprints into the monstrosities. *"Be gone!"*

The pair gave a few more feet, and Minerva walked safely into the clearing, past her gardens, and into the house. She wondered if it really was Lucy and Dashwood, not Kelly, who had called her. Imprisoning her in her own house would keep her out of the way.

*Minerva! Help me!*

The voice resounded in her ears, closer now, but not so close as the nightflyers circling the clearing. Nearly certain it was Kelly, she knew she had to risk a trap and find her.

The screeching of the nightflyers grew more distant as Minerva took an old Remington rifle from her bedroom, made sure it was loaded, then put extra shells in her pocket. What magic couldn't manage, a weapon could. Whispering more protection spells, for herself and for Kelly, she opened the front door, peered out, then stepped outside. She shut her eyes a moment, sensing the direction she would need to take, then set off into the woods, toward St. Gertrude's.

There were more than two nightflyers, more than she'd ever heard at once. The creatures flew above the forest, their raucous cries echoing among the trees, and she paid them no mind but kept walking steadfastly toward the source of the cries for help.

*Minerva!*

She paused, shocked by the voice that boomed in her head. A screech, just as loud, sounded above, and she looked up to see one of the nightflyers perched on a high limb, wings folded, watching her with bright, bloody eyes. Minerva raised the rifle, took aim, and fired.

The blast shoved the butt of the gun painfully into her shoulder, but she paid it no attention. She'd hit the creature. It rocked on the tree limb, then screamed, a sound far worse than the screeching. Minerva thought it would burst her eardrums. The nightflyer glared down at her, started to unfurl its wings.

She raised the gun and gave it the other barrel. The creature squawked angrily and swayed on the branch as Minerva quickly reloaded. Before she could raise the gun, the creature fell. She backed away and reloaded as it hit the ground, wings flapping weakly.

"Let's have a look at you," she said, as the nightflyer stilled. Glancing upward she realized the other flyers were farther away now. Perhaps she'd scared them off. She hoped so. Keeping the rifle aimed at the black creature, she came within two feet of it and stopped.

There was no blood visible on the body, only gaping holes showing dull dark red below the feathers, or scales, she wasn't sure which.

The face was out of a nightmare, with predatory, close-set eyes under heavy brow ridges. This one had no beak but a piggish snout, and the slightly open maw revealed gleaming onyx teeth.

One eye opened, blackish-red, and glared at her. The mouth moved. Without a second thought, Minerva aimed at the head and let both barrels fly.

At first, there was only a gaping reddish hole where the face had been, then the red began turning to black. As Minerva watched, the black wounds began to lighten to gray and so did the hide—the feathers or scales, or whatever they were. There was a crackling sound and the head began to break apart in chunks, then the body. After a few moments, all that remained was broken stone. Minerva remembered to reload, but couldn't stop looking at the thing. When John Lawson had suggested that the nightflyers might really be creatures that hibernated during the day and resembled stone gargoyles, she had been pleased with his openmindedness and amused at the thought. But he was right. She bent to pick up a piece of stone, thinking that she'd enjoy seeing his face when he found out they really did turn to stone. She stopped short of picking any up. The heavens only knew what effect carrying a piece with her might have; probably none, but possibly, it could prove disastrous. Perhaps she would bring the sheriff here and show it to him.

"Minerva!"

She turned at the whisper, scanning the woods. "Kelly?" she asked softly. Somewhere overhead, the nightflyers screeched. "Kelly, where are you?"

"Here."

The girl crawled out from under an ancient pine tree, brushing needles from her hair. She ran to Minerva and put her arms around her. "You found me. Thank heaven you found me!"

"You were hard to ignore, child." Minerva held her and stroked her hair. "I'm glad you're all right."

"They've got Sara," Kelly breathed. "We have to help her."

The nightflyers were coming closer. Minerva stepped back and looked up between the trees as a shadow passed overhead. "First we have to help ourselves, Kelly." Above, there were three cries in succession, answered by two more. They were coming for their prey. Minerva saw the fear in Kelly's eyes. "Come along, we'll be safe at my house. *Hurry!*"

# Eighty-Four

"You should, of course, ask the other sisters," Mother Lucy told John, "but I haven't seen Miss Hawthorne or your son today. Have you, Dr. Dashwood?"

"No," Dashwood said, all charm and smarm. "But if I do, I'll tell them both you're looking for them."

*I just bet you will.* John stood uncomfortably in Lucy's office, trying to keep his eyes off the bloody portraits decorating the walls. Being alone with Lucy and Dashwood was definitely an unpleasant experience, and he wished Thurman were here to back him up. "I've been told that Mark might be here."

"Who told you that?" Lucy asked, forcing a smile onto her brittle face. "It must be a joke. We have no boys here, only girls. Someone was having fun at your expense."

"I can't reveal my sources," John said, "but they were quite serious."

"It's all right, Sheriff," Lucy said. "I know exactly who fed you such nonsense. That senile old creature in the woods—that Payne woman." She arched an eyebrow. "Aptly named, isn't she?"

"Do you have a problem with her?" John asked casually.

Lucy shook her head. "No, except that she's rather senile and eccentric and has gotten it into her head that St. Gertrude's is some sort of haven for devil worshipers. Nothing could be further from the truth. We're godfearing people."

*Especially if you* are *Satanists.* John smiled gently. "I'm sure you are. My son was sneaking around outside the gate the other day and he lost his jacket and wallet. That's why I think he may have come back."

"He was?" Dashwood asked, then broke into a sham grin. " 'Boys will be boys...' isn't that what they say?"

"I suppose so. Mother Lucy, he told me you chased him." John stole her gaze and kept it.

"That's absurd. Except for the photo you've been kind enough to bring, I've never seen the boy. And I doubt he's seen me, and he certainly doesn't know my name. He's imagining things, Sheriff."

"Maybe so." He almost brought up Kelly Reed, then decided not to for the girl's sake.

"You are certainly free to talk to the sisters and look around all you want," Lucy said, her sympathy as false as her smile.

"Thank you. Now, about Sara Hawthorne—"

"She didn't show up for her classes today," Lucy interrupted. "When we checked her room, we found no sign of her."

"Frankly, Sheriff," said Dashwood, "we're quite concerned. Her mental state was a little uncertain. Nerves, you know. She had convinced herself she was seeing ghosts."

"Was she?"

Lucy and Dashwood glanced at one another, then both looked back at John and laughed. "You mean you believe in our notorious ladies in white, Sheriff?" Lucy asked.

He shrugged. "Just covering the bases, Mother Lucy." There

was no point in further questioning. "Mind if I take a look around?"

"Please do. Dr. Dashwood will accompany you and answer all your questions."

"I'd prefer to be on my own," John said.

"I'm afraid the sight of a man, especially in uniform, prowling our halls might frighten the girls," Lucy said.

"Come along, Sheriff Lawson," Dashwood said, opening the door. "What's your pleasure?"

"I'd like to see Sara Hawthorne's room." He turned back to Lucy. "Ms. Hawthorne is tendering her resignation, and I promised to pick up her personal items."

"After you check her room, the doctor will see to it that one of the sisters boxes up her property and places it by your car."

"Thanks."


They went through Sara's room, the dormitory, and the garage, all without results. "What's in there?" John asked, pointing at the old stone building set back from the school building.

"The bakery." Dashwood smiled. "It's the home of the sisters' Heavenly Mincemeat Pies. Would you care to take one home with you?"

"No thanks." He was tempted to request a tour, but it was unlikely he'd find Mark or Sara hiding in a busy kitchen. "I'd like to see your root cellar and basement area."

"Root cellar?" Dashwood asked. "We don't have one. It was filled in years and years ago. Before my time. The only basement is where my infirmary is located. You're welcome to examine that, of course."

"I've seen drawings of the abbey," John said. "There was a sub-basement under the floor where the infirmary is located."

Dashwood studied him, and John thought he saw a faint trace of anxiety in the man's expression, but it fled so quickly that he couldn't be sure. "There was a seepage problem, Sheriff. I'd like to oblige you, but the sub-basement is entirely filled in with brick and stone and earth. There's no entrance anymore."

John nodded acquiesence and let Dashwood lead him through the school building and infirmary. Nothing seemed unusual, and he didn't spot any doors or stairs leading farther under the building. Back outside, he turned to the doctor. "One more thing I want to see, Doctor. The chapel." With those words, he turned to face the building and stared, realizing that the gargoyle he'd seen on the cross was missing.

"We don't ordinarily let any but those of our denomination inside its doors, but of course we'll make an exception for you, Sheriff."

"The gargoyle is gone," John said, as they walked toward the little church with its odd crucifix.

"Gargoyle?"

"The one on the cross."

Dashwood stopped moving and stared at the church. Finally, he turned to John. "I believe I heard Mr. Boullan mention something about taking it down for Sister Elizabeth to do some work on. Something wasn't quite right, evidently."

"It must weigh a thousand pounds."

Dashwood smiled. "No. Perhaps the old ones do, but the new ones Elizabeth makes are composed of some sort of plastic resin which is nearly as impervious to weather as stone."

"I see." It sounded like bunk to him, but he wasn't going to say so at this point. "Let's go inside."

"As you wish."

Dashwood unlocked the chapel doors and held one open for John. The place was dark except for the flickering of rows of votive candles and a few tapers near a covered altar. Dim light, filtered reds, blues, and greens, came in through a round, featureless stained-glass window high above the chancel.

"Would you turn on the lights?"

"I'm sorry, Sheriff. The chapel isn't wired for electricity. We prefer to keep it as it was in the old days."

John nodded absently and walked slowly up the center aisle. His stomach had knotted the minute he'd entered the building, and suddenly, he knew—absolutely *knew*—that he'd been here before. Swallowing hard, he stepped up onto the chancel and approached the altar.

He poured sweat. In his mind, he could hear chanting, feminine voices raised in eerie song. He looked at the altar. It was long and covered with a cloth. *Greg was here. There were people singing, and they wore black robes. I was here. I had to watch while they . . . while they . . .*

"Sheriff? Is something wrong?"

John realized Dashwood was standing next to him. "No," he said, trying to keep his voice from trembling. He reached out to lift the altar cloth, but Dashwood stopped him.

"It's sacred, Sheriff. That's why we keep it covered. I'm afraid I can't allow you to touch the cloth. It's sacred as well."

John couldn't stay in this place any longer, not with Dashwood there, watching him while the memories came back. "It's late," John said, striding up the aisle, hiding his panic under a gruff demeanor. "Thank you for your time, Dr. Dashwood. I'm sure we'll be speaking again soon."

"I'm sure we will."

Dashwood's words echoing in his ears, John forced himself to walk instead of run to his cruiser.

# Eighty-Five

Sara awoke in darkness, her head throbbing, her mouth tasting of earth. Slowly she lifted her head and spat dirt from her mouth. "Oh, God," she muttered. "What the hell happened?"

She shivered and pressed her hands against the dank soil, pushing herself up into a sitting position. "What happened?" Faintly, she heard a voice calling, "Let me out, let me out," over and over.

*Where am I?* There wasn't a speck of light, only darkness so thick she felt as if she were choking on it. *Dashwood. The garage.* Images flooded her. She'd come to the abbey to resign, to get her things and Kelly, too. Her mind cleared further, and suddenly she recognized the voice in the distance.

"Mark!" she screamed, as loud as she could. She pushed herself to her feet.

There was momentary silence, then, "Let me out!" louder than ever.

"Mark! It's Sara," she called. "Where are you?"

"I don't know. In the dark! *Get me out of here!*"

"Help is on the way," she yelled, wondering who else could hear her and the boy. "You don't have to yell anymore. Just wait."

Silence answered her. Slowly, she felt her way around the low-ceilinged room. The earthen floor was damp in places, muddy in others, and the stone walls were cold and slick. She finally found a set of stairs. There were only six, but at the top was a heavy wooden door with only a handle. She pulled, then pushed, and knew she couldn't open it.

She got down on her hands and knees and pushed the caked, muddy soil away from the threshold, squinting when she saw dim light coming in from beyond the door. She couldn't see anything but a small square of brick floor outside, but when she pushed her fingers between the door and the threshold, her hand came back with a small chunk of rotten wood.

*Please stay quiet, Mark.* She dug out more wood, until a faint beam of light illuminated her torn, filthy hands. It wasn't much, but at least she could explore the cellar and try to find a way out.

# Eighty-Six

Night lay heavily over Moonfall and the silence of his empty house lay equally heavy over John Lawson. He'd come home to catch a few hours of sleep before relieving Deputy Thurman around two in the morning. He'd been the only officer on duty and John knew he was exhausted.

*Mark, where are you?* He fought back anger first, then tears, as he made a grilled cheese sandwich and zapped a bowl of tomato soup in the microwave.

He took the food to the table and stared at it, unable to eat. He'd spent too long nosing around the abbey and hadn't made it to Minerva's. He'd driven past her shop in the twilight, but it was closed, and he just didn't want to make the trek into the woods to see her. Not with those nightflyers screeching all over the forest. Tomorrow morning would be time enough, he told himself. Surely, if Sara or Mark had turned up at her house, the old lady would have come to tell him or brought them out. She, at least, wasn't worried about traveling the dark path from her cottage to the road. Or at least, she didn't let on, if she was.

He left his soup congealing on the table and went into his office. Digging through his files, he found a Christmas card list from last year and read down to the address of Paul Pricket's parrish, then called information and got the number for the rectory.

The phone was answered on the third ring. "Hello, St. Florian's. Father Pricket speaking."

"Paul," John said. Though the voice was deeper, Paul Pricket still sounded like himself. "This is John Lawson, up in Moonfall. How are you?"

"John?" Paul hesitated. "I'm fine. I was just thinking about you. You've been on my mind, though I don't know why."

"Gus is dead, Paul."

"I'm sorry—"

"He was murdered, just like my father was, and I can't find the bastard who killed him."

"I'm sorry—"

"Please, Paul, just listen. Mark is missing. I think he was taken by the people at St. Gertrude's, but I'm not sure. I've been all over the place. I know it sounds ridiculous to tell you a bunch of nuns kidnapped my son."

"John," Paul said softly. "They're not Catholic. There's no record of them in our files."

"When did you check?"

"A couple days ago. I've been having nightmares. I always do around Halloween, about, you know . . ."

"Greg. You can say it, Paul. I have them, too. So does Winky Addams."

"Beano?"

"He's closed himself off from us, but I wouldn't be surprised. "Paul, do you ever wonder if we went to St. Gertrude's the night Greg died?"

"Yes," he said without hesitation. "I've prayed over it, I've meditated, I've done everything I can think of, but I can't remember." He paused. "But Beano was sure we didn't go. Remember?"

"Yes. Paul, before he died, Gus told me he overheard the five of us talking, right after Greg drowned. He said that we had gone. And I've been talking to Minerva Payne."

"Who?"

"The old witch in the woods."

"Really? Why?"

"She seems to know more than anyone. She says the sisters used to be called the Order of Lilith."

There was silence on the other end of the line. Finally Paul cleared his throat. "Lilith was a night demon, John. She's mentioned in Isaiah."

"That makes sense, considering what these women are like." He briefly told Paul about Sara's ghostly rape. "What do you make of that?"

"Well, it fits in with the Lilith stuff. Lilith was the original succubus—a spirit that uses men at night. Rapes them." He chuckled lightly. "Personally, I always thought that was nothing more than an excuse for nocturnal emissions among the celibate."

"Is there a male spirit that rapes women?"

"Yes," Paul said, serious again. "It's an incubus. But succubi and incubi are the same spirit in different forms."

"Minerva believes it's a revenant," John said, and explained.

"That makes sense, I suppose. Are you sure this really happened?"

"One hundred per cent."

"Well, if those nuns are a group of Satanists and they know what they're doing, maybe they've figured out how to do things like that. There are many powers we don't understand."

While John told him everything of the events of the past weeks, Paul listened in silence.

"It's a fantastic story, John."

"The thing is, I'm beginning to remember things. I've been in that chapel at the abbey before, Paul. I recognized it. They had Greg laid out on the altar, and there were a bunch of people in black cowled robes. I watched. *You* watched, Paul. We all did, and we couldn't do anything to stop it. Do you have any recollection of a man named Dashwood?"

"No, not offhand."

"Do you ever dream about eyes?"

"Yes, I dream I'm being sucked into them."

"Those are Dashwood's eyes. And you *were* sucked into them. We all were."

"How can you be so sure?"

"I feel it. And Minerva Payne told me. Well, she called him a sorcerer. I'd call him a man with a vast knowledge of hypnosis and hypnotics."

Another long silence. "What can I do to help, John?"

"You've already helped." He forced himself to chuckle. "I understand now what all these people see in confessing to priests." He hesitated. "Paul, can you come up tomorrow?"

"To Moonfall?"

"Yes. If what Minerva tells us is correct, the nuns' big celebration will occur then. I have to save my boy, Paul. And Sara, and a girl who's a student there who's evidently slated for sacrifice, too. I could use some backup, Paul."

"But if this Minerva has the powers you say she does—"

"I know she can do things, but I don't pretend to know or understand how far she can go. But *she* was the one who pointed out that to be a Satanist, you must first fear the Christian God. Paul, even if Minerva could spin that abbey into outer space, I think it would be a good idea to have you here with your own kind of magic."

"Essentially, you're talking about exorcism. The church probably won't allow it."

"Don't tell them. Come to see an old friend. Me."

The silence lasted so long that John began to think Paul had hung up. Then the priest spoke. "I'll be there sometime after noon tomorrow. Is that okay?"

"It's great, Paul. Thanks."

# PART FIVE
## HALLOWEEN, 1996

# Eighty-Seven

"When do you think they'll go away?" Kelly asked Minerva as they sat by the blazing fireplace. The clock had just struck midnight; it was the first minute of Halloween.

"I don't know, child. By morning, I suspect." Minerva hoped she was right. The trip back to the cottage had been harrowing only for a few moments; then the nightflyers had disappeared. Minerva had hoped the attack was over, but an hour later they'd returned, their power even greater.

She and Kelly had been outside, picking vegetables to go with the chicken frying in the kitchen, when they'd returned, swooping in over the clearing as if there were no spells protecting the property. The women had had to run into the house for cover.

No doubt Lucy and Dashwood had added their sorcery to the nightflyers'. She looked at Kelly. "We're safe here."

"But if they can break into the clearing, can't they get into the house?"

"If they could have, they already would have."

"Why are they doing this?"

Though the girl was terrified, Minerva could see that she was fighting her fear with her questions, and that, she thought, was a very good sign. "They are doing it because I killed one of them, and because they don't want me interfering with the ceremonies tomorrow night."

"And because I'm here."

Minerva nodded slowly. "Yes, because you're here."

"What can we do? We have to help Sara and Mark."

"That is for John Lawson to do, but we can help him. You can do your part by reciting the protection spells I taught you. I am going to try to help John find his memories." She rose.

"You're not leaving?" Kelly jumped to her feet.

"No. I'm just going into the kitchen. I need to be by myself for this. It's quite difficult." She walked across the threshold. "I'll be back in a little while."

# Eighty-Eight

*John, let me in.*

John, dozing in his chair, turned uneasily. He heard Minerva's voice in his mind, knew the dream was coming and that he could still make himself wake up before it took him.

He'd already remembered some of Halloween, 1972, on his own, but if Minerva was right about his being able to remember how to get into the basement at the abbey, then he couldn't just wait for his memories to kick in. He needed to let the dream come. But he was afraid.

*Remember for Mark. Let me in.*

Hearing those words, he let himself fall into the dream. He spiraled down into the locked room and saw that blood was already seeping in under the door and drizzling down the keyhole in the black iron latchplate.

*You know how, John. Open the door.*

He grasped the knob and turned it with all his might.

*That's it, don't stop! You can do anything, John, it's your dream.*

The knob began to turn, but just barely. Minerva's words echoed in his ears and he applied them with new strength. Abruptly the knob turned and he began pulling it. The door groaned as the hinges began to give, then suddenly, it flew open. A wave of blood followed, filling the room, drowning him as it flowed into his lungs. He choked.

*It's a dream, only a dream. Do what you must.*

He began to swim for the door but ran into one wall, then another. He couldn't breathe, couldn't see through the red fog. And then he found the doorway and swam out of the room.

Into utter darkness.

The blood was gone and he was sitting on a hard wooden bench. He was paralyzed, and as candles flickered to life around him, he tried to call to Minerva, but his vocal cords wouldn't work. All he could do was sit, unblinking, and stare at the black altar within the candles. He felt others sitting, unmoving, next to him and though he couldn't turn his head, he knew that Paul, Winky, Beano, and Doug surrounded him.

Figures draped in black walked into view, each carrying a black candle. They filed around the wide altar to stand in a half-circle behind it. A tall figure—Dashwood, he knew—walked up to the altar and laid out Greg's small, pale body.

Next, a girl of thirteen or fourteen walked in. Dressed in white, she was supported between two cowled figures. She let herself be guided up onto the altar and placidly laid down next to Greg. Two more black figures dragged a grown woman in. Unlike the girl, she was unconscious. As the others began a low chant, two dark figures stepped forward and helped the other two bring the woman around the altar and hoist her up so that she lay crosswise across Greg and the girl. As they positioned her, her arms, then head, then breasts came into John's view. She was made up in colors so bright that he could see them in the near darkness. Her lips and nipples were red-black, and her eyes, open and staring, like John's, were rimmed with dark blue. Her cheeks were bruised with blush.

The chanting continued, growing louder, more ominous, until the air turned frigid and thick. Behind him, he heard the doors blow open and a gust of foul wind filled the room. Something was coming, something large and horrible, and he knew what it would do to the young woman.

*The same thing will happen to Sara. And Mark will be the living altar, as Greg was. And then, like your brother, your son will die. You must find the basement.*

*I can't!* He was stuck in his own fourteen-year-old body, as paralyzed as he'd been that night. He struggled, hearing the Beast coming down the aisle, smelling it as it filled his nostrils with the pungent odor of death. No matter what he did, he couldn't make his body move, and he needed no reminder of what was to come next. He remembered in full detail, first the rape of the woman by something inhuman, something he could only think of as a devil. It tore the woman apart, and she had been awake the whole time, unmoving, paralyzed, though her eyes, leaking silent tears, conveyed all her pain and horror. He remembered how, as the Beast reached orgasm, blood had spurted from her mouth, coating her unblinking eyes, filling her nose. He had seen the life drain from her, had seen her eyes go blank. As awful as it was, it was a relief when she died.

He remembered the demon tossing her aside and tearing the white dress from the girl, the virgin. She was waking up and begun to scream as it nearly tore one of her legs from its socket in its desire to take her. Greg had awakened, too, and begun to scream with her. The demon paid him no mind and no one stepped forward as the little boy rolled off the altar and tried to crawl away.

*He saw me. He was crying for me.* The truth hit John in a jolting flash. Greg had crawled to him, had begged him to look at him, to talk to him. He'd felt Greg's tears falling on his deadened hands, and he could do nothing.

*It's a dream.* Minerva's voice ripped into the vision. *You aren't tied to the body. Leave the body there and find the prison in the basement. Find it for Mark! Find it now!*

The chanting deafened him as the demon attacked the young woman and he remembered how he'd escaped the dream's bloody room. *I can do anything. I can fly.*

Suddenly, he found himself in the air, high above the chapel, his ears filled with the cries of nightflyers. One swooped at him and he escaped, jumping down into darkness, spiraling down.

He opened his eyes and saw his living room. *Am I awake?* The Regulator chimed half past midnight, Halloween. He blinked and then Sara was standing before him, luminously nude in the darkness.

*John, I need you.*

"Sara?"

She stepped closer. *Make love to me, John. I want you.*

He stared at her, thinking he had to be dreaming, but it seemed too real. He lifted one hand and pinched the back of the other. It hurt like hell. "I'm awake," he said.

*I know.* Sara was nearly on top of him now, her lips moist, her eyes sparkling.

"Sara, my God, Sara. How did you get here?" He stood up and put his arms out to her, closed them.

They closed on icy cold air, nothing more, and then he felt her slide into him, felt his bones begin to chill, his heart to stutter. Blindly he reached under his shirt and pulled out the amulet. "Get away!"

Instantly, the coldness left him and Sara was standing before him, a sad smile on her face. *We never got to make love when I was alive. Can't we now?*

"You're not Sara. Get out of my house!"

Sara's image shifted and flowed before him, losing color, the body disappearing and the face elongating until it was an amorphous white head nearly as tall as he. The eyes were burning black pits. *This is what raped Sara.*

Laughter filled his mind, shrill and maniacal, and the mouth yawned open, revealing short, sharklike teeth. The phantom rotated until it was sideways, then suddenly it rushed him and he felt the teeth dig into his chest and back, biting into his flesh like hundreds of short, sharp knives.

*Begone, spirit!*

In the back of his mind, he heard Minerva's voice, and then he caught a glimpse of her at the edge of his vision, translucent, glowing amber in the darkness.

*Begone!*

Slowly, the pressure on his body dissipated, the sharp pain stopped, and then he stood alone in the darkened room.

Breathing hard, trembling, he turned on a lamp and looked down at himself. He couldn't comprehend what he saw. His shirt was torn and bloodstained, and he realized he was in pain. He ran down the hall to the bathroom and turned on the light, tore off his shirt, and stared at himself in the full-length mirror.

Blood seeped from a neat half-circle of razorlike cuts running from his left side to three-quarters of the way across his chest. Turning, he saw the same marks on his back. Dumbfounded, he did nothing for a long moment, then he forced himself to move, turning on the shower, stripping, and climbing in. He scrubbed himself for twenty minutes, not caring that the wounds still dripped blood.

Finally, he turned off the water and dried, keeping the towel wrapped around himself until he knew the bleeding had stopped. He let the towel drop and took a tube of Neosporin from the medicine cabinet and used the whole tube on the cuts. Bruises were already purpling around them.

He was practically running on automatic as he entered his bedroom and took a T-shirt from his drawer and slipped it on, wincing at the pain the movement caused. He pulled on fresh socks and underwear, then a new pair of dark brown Levi's, and laced his shoes up.

The clock chimed once as he left for the station. The first hour of Halloween was over. He would have a long night alone, and with a little luck, maybe he would remember on his own where the entrance to the basement was. He realized he was praying he would, and was very nearly amused, but he knew that if he let himself laugh, he wouldn't be able to stop.

# Eighty-Nine

Sara's hands hurt, but she had made progress in her efforts to open the door. The wood had been damp for years and was rotting away, and Sara had used that to her advantage, eventually pulling off a large, firm length, which she had used until there was a six-inch square of faint light entering the ragged hole at the bottom edge of the door.

At that point, she explored the room again. She found shelves above eye level lining one wall, and realized there were long metal ells holding them up. She shoved on the lowest shelf and it creaked and groaned and finally cracked.

Pulling it from the wall, she went to work on the metal shelf support, trying to pry it out of the brick wall. It had taken hours, but now she held it in her hands, one end bare, the other still with a piece of wood stuck to it.

Now, she was at the door, slowly working the metal between

the door and the jamb, pushing it upward, toward the latch. It was tedious work and all for nothing if anyone came down to check on her, but she had already cleared several more inches. With luck, she just might make it.

# Ninety

"Minerva? Are you okay?"

Minerva opened her eyes and saw that she was looking up into Kelly Reed's worried face. She gave her a small smile. "Help me up, child. This floor is too cold and hard for my old bones."

"Should you move? I mean, maybe you need an ambulance."

"Nonsense. Help me up."

Kelly did as she was told. "You fainted," she said as she led Minerva to her rocker by the fire. "You were talking. I heard you, so I didn't come in until you stopped, then I found you on the floor."

Outside, a nightflyer screeched. It sounded like laughter. "First of all, Kelly, that was a trance that got away from me. I was guiding John Lawson's dream, then it was interrupted by the revenant. John was in trouble and I had to expend a lot of energy to help him. I believe he's all right now."

"What did you do?"

"A little astral projecting." She patted the girl's hand, trying to dispel her panic. "I'll teach you how someday."

"Someday?" Kelly asked, her eyes bright. "Does that mean I can stay with you?"

"That's what it means. You're a gifted student of the occult arts, Kelly, and I'll expect you to apply yourself."

"Oh, I will. I promise." Outside, a nightflyer screeched, but the girl barely noticed. "You're really going to keep me?"

"We'll have to pull a string or two, but that won't be too hard. Now, I need some sleep. Just an hour or so will do. Keep watch and wake me around two. Then you can sleep."

"An hour's not enough—"

"Yes, it's plenty. When you have learned to be a healer, you won't need more than a few hours yourself. And when you're very old, all you'll need is an hour." Minerva stood up and went over to the couch, laid down on it. "Hand me that afghan, child."

Kelly placed the knitted forest green blanket over Minerva, then sat down in the old woman's chair. "Minerva?" she asked quietly.

"Yes?"

"Do you think I'm going to get to live long enough to get old?"

"I'll see to it. Now, let me sleep."


# Ninety-One

"What time is it, Lucy?"

"Just past six A.M."

Dashwood felt Lucy's warm but bony body stretching next to his. They'd spent the evening making plans, everything from holding Minerva Payne captive in her own house until they could retake Kelly Reed, to the type of make-up they would use on Sara Hawthorne when they prepared her for the Beast. They'd made love twice, and after that, they had expended the rest of their energy sending the revenant spirit to John Lawson's house.

Naked, he slipped out from between the black sheets just as Lucy reached for him. He didn't like to have her sleep with him and wouldn't have allowed it if he hadn't been so exhausted by their lovemaking and spellcasting. "Get up, Lucy, dear. We have much work ahead of us."

She pushed the covers back with her legs and spread herself across the wide mattress. Despite the reek of the cinnamon-mildew chemicals she bathed in, Dashwood found himself responding. The chemical bath might stink, but Lucy's body appeared young and firm. *And bony.*

He was looking forward to checking on Sara Hawthorne. To

preparing her for tonight. She was slim but possessed firm, round breasts and an ass with enough flesh on it to dig his nails into. And she didn't smell like rotting cinnamon.

"What are you thinking about, Richard?" Lucy stretched, revealing her innermost secrets.

He tried not to respond. "I was wondering if we should feed Miss Hawthorne and the boy."

"No," Lucy said. "Leave them alone until it's time to prepare her." She fixed him with her cold stare. "And Richard, Regina will take her into the infirmary, tranquilize her, and do the preparatory work and the make-up. You don't need to worry yourself about that."

*Bitch.*

He smiled, his ire diminishing under the strength of his desire. "Are you jealous, Lucy?"

"Of course not."

"I think you are."

"Then spank it out of me," she ordered, rolling over.

Sometimes, Dashwood thought as he joined her on the bed, he rather enjoyed following Lucy's orders.

# Ninety-Two

"It's *what* time?" John Lawson leapt out of his desk chair, ignoring the pain and stiffness of his chest and limbs. He stared at Dorothy.

"Just past noon."

"Good God, you let me sleep?"

"You looked pale, exhausted. I thought you needed it."

"Dorothy, my son is missing, Sara Hawthorne is missing, and it's Halloween. Don't ever let me sleep again."

"See how much you needed it? You're still cranky."

Cranky, he thought, didn't begin to describe how he felt. Enraged came closer. He counted to ten before speaking. "Dorothy, who's working right now?

"Wyn and Scotty. Jeff's due in at two."

"What are they doing?"

"Running calls." She shook her head. "There's already been a fight at Winesap's and a brawl at the Cozy-Up Inn. Two women fighting over one man. I don't think there's a man on earth worth *that.*"

John ignored her. "Why did you decide now was the time to wake me? Why didn't you wait another hour?"

His sarcasm was lost on her. Dorothy giggled and actually blushed. "Because you've got company. A priest."

"Paul's here already?"

"Paul?" she shrilled. "I thought he looked familiar. That's little Paul Pricket out there, isn't it? I used to be great friends with his mama. She must be so proud of him."

"Dorothy, give me two minutes, not a second longer, then send him in."

"Okay."

She rushed out the door, no doubt to pounce on Paul. John combed his hair, then popped two Certs in his mouth and straightened his clothing. He waited. And waited. After five minutes, he sighed and walked out of the office. Sure enough, there was Paul Pricket, wearing a priest's collar and a pained smile as he nodded at Dorothy's questions.

"Paul," John said, striding across the room.

"John!" Paul's relief was obvious as they shook hands and then hugged. "It's been a long time."

"It sure has. You look the same. Except for the collar, of course."

"A little less hair, and a little taller. You're a lot taller than I remember, and you still have all your hair. What's your secret?"

"It's in the genes, I guess."

"Oh, yes. You said Minerva Payne is—"

"Come into my office," John interrupted, glaring at Dorothy. "I don't want to be disturbed unless it's important," he said sternly, then led Paul behind closed doors.

"Wow." Pricket ran his hand through his thinning blond hair. "She hasn't changed." He sat down in the chair opposite John. "You look like hell, Lawson."

John stood up and started unbuttoning his shirt. "You want a look at hell?" He pulled his T-shirt over his head and heard Paul gasp.

"What happened?"

"If I were Catholic, Padre, I'd have to say a demon bit me."

Paul circled him, gingerly touching some of the marks. "Does it hurt?"

"Oh, yeah."

"What'd the doctor say?"

"Haven't seen him yet. This thing showed up around midnight. I came here shortly after and fell asleep, and Dorothy decided to let me go on sleeping until you showed up."

"By the looks of you, you needed it. Tell me about the demon."

John put his shirt back on, then sat down and spent the next hour and a half telling Paul everything, finishing with the dream that preceded the demonic attack. Paul showed shock, surprise, and horror as John talked, but the look of revelation on his face as John recounted the details of the events in the chapel was the most terrifying of all.

"Dear God, John. It happened, didn't it? It really happened."

John nodded. "I think so. I *know* so. I can't deny it any longer. If nothing else, the visit from that mouthful of teeth last night convinced me it's all true."

"Do you believe your demon and the one that attacked Sara are one and the same?"

"Absolutely."

Paul nodded. "So what do we do now?"

"We pay a visit to Minerva Payne."

# Ninety-Three

Sara shoved the metal rod through the jamb and met solid resistance. "Give me a break," she prayed to whatever god might be listening. She was exhausted, and had almost given up a number of times, but Mark's occasional calls for help had sustained her. Now, she pulled the rod back and replaced it, slightly below the handle on the door. It slid through this time.

Slowly, she worked it upward, met resistance again, and knew she'd found the lock. She had no hope of breaking a padlock, but if the door was secured with an old hasp, she might be able to pry it out.

She pushed upward, her tired arms trembling with the effort. Something gave, barely. Heartened, she bent her knees and got a better grip on the metal, then pushed with all her might. Slowly, the resistance lifted, inch by inch, and then the door yawned open so suddenly that she gasped.

She stepped into a large, dimly lit area and looked back at the door. It didn't even have a lock, just a wooden bar that fit into a metal rest. *Finally, my luck is changing!*

"Mark?" she called. She couldn't see far into the gloom, but she figured she must be in the long, low-ceiling basement.

"Sara?" The voice was muted, but close by.

"Keep talking, Mark. I'm on my way."

She followed his voice to a heavy door, her heart sinking when she saw the padlock securing it.

"Mark, I can't unlock the door, but I'm going to get your father. I'll be back as soon as I can."

"Okay," he called, his voice betraying disappointment.

Overhead, a door opened. *Please don't talk, Mark!* Sara fled into a shadowed corner and crouched behind some mildewed wooden crates.

Footsteps clicked down the stairs and across the floor to her prison. She heard a gasp, an oath, and then the footsteps, rapid now, approaching. From behind the crates she watched as Sister Regina knocked on Mark's door.

"Boy, are you in there?"

"Let me out," Mark called. "My dad's coming and he's going to arrest you if you don't let me out *now!*"

Sara cringed, wishing Mark hadn't said anything. Regina crossed to the stairs. Her hand on the rail, she turned.

"Sara, I know you're here, and I'll be back in a few minutes with Mother Lucy and Dr. Dashwood. Show yourself now, or you'll be severely punished."

Sara waited until the footsteps went upstairs and the door opened and closed. She knew she had to get out before Regina alerted the others, and she didn't have time to be picky. After counting to a hundred, she sprinted across the room and tiptoed up the stairs.

She found a blank wall where a door should be. Frantically she felt for a latch, and finally her fingers found one. The wall slid slowly and silently away, and she found herself in Richard Dashwood's bedroom. She could hear voices in the living room, Richard's and Lucy's and Regina's.

"The boy is still there, but Sara Hawthorne managed to get away," Regina said quickly. "She's still down there. There's no way out except through this apartment."

Sara crossed to the bed, lay down, and worked her way underneath it.

"I told you, Richard," Lucy stormed. "I told you to put her in with the boy for safekeeping, but no, you had to do it your way."

"Let's go get her," Dashwood said in a stern, angry tone.

Sara saw their feet as they entered the bedroom. Dashwood's came right up to the bed, then she heard a drawer open. He took something out, then closed it again. "Dart gun," he said to the women. "It'll put her out at two hundred feet, if necessary."

Lucy made an irritated noise, then the entrance slid open and the trio disappeared. As soon as the door shut, Sara crawled out from under the bed. She started to pick up Dashwood's phone, but realized it was too dangerous to stay here.

She left the apartment, trying to keep to the shadows. Classes would be in session right now, so her best bet was to make it to a safe phone, in case she got caught leaving the abbey.

She could hear voices in the infirmary waiting room, so she passed it by and went up to the first floor, emerging near Lucy's office. She sprinted through the empty hallway, made the office, and entered.

It was empty, thank heaven. She crossed to the inner office door and made short work of the locking knob with the metal rod she still carried. She picked up the phone.

"What are you doing in here?"

Sara whirled, saw Sister Elizabeth blocking the exit, her hands on her hips, her pale face set and hard. Her tongue flicked out and she licked her lips. "Answer me."

She was out of options. Raising the metal rod, she charged the nun, swinging at the side of her head, and, to her surprise, connecting. The sister went down, her eyes rolling back in her head.

Quickly, Sara stripped off Elizabeth's habit and cowl, pausing only an instant when she saw the nun's lingerie—red bra, panties, and garterbelt and black fishnet stockings. Opening the closet, she dragged the nun inside and closed the door, then quickly donned the habit and draped the rosary around her waist. She wiped the dirt from her face with a handful of tissues from a box on Lucy's desk after dipping them in a pitcher of water, also on the desk, then placed the cowl on her head. Again, she turned to pick up the phone, but she heard the door to the outer office open. Sara grabbed the rod and plastered herself against the wall by the door.

"What the—" came a female voice.

Sara brought the rod down on the back of the nun's head as she came through the door. It was Margaret, and she went down like a sack of potatoes.

There wasn't room for two nuns in the closet and classes were about to let out. Not sure where she was going, Sara stepped over Sister Margaret and walked boldly into the halls and out the front door.

Two nuns were on the walk, coming up from the gate, and she figured they couldn't recognize her since she wasn't sure of their identities. Mentally cursing, Sara nodded hello at them, then turned and briskly walked toward the dormitory. Passing them was too risky.

# Ninety-Four

John drove the cruiser to the end of the road leading to Minerva's. He was worried now; he'd expected to find the old lady at the Gingerbread House, but it was plain she hadn't been there today.

"Hear them?" he asked Paul, as he killed the ignition.

Paul nodded. "The gargoyles, huh?"

"Yeah. You know how to handle a rifle?"

Paul shook his head. "Haven't a clue."

John took it from its holder anyway, and showed Paul how to use it.

"Look!" Paul cried, staring out the front windshield. "Look at that!"

A nightflyer was circling in front of the car. As they watched, two more joined it. "They're not going to let us in," John murmured. "Hand me the rifle."

Paul did. John rolled down his window and took aim. Without warning, one of the nightflyers dived straight for the window. John fired, missed, and fired again, but the ugly malformed head was in the car, ripping at his arm with its short beak. Talons yanked the weapon from his hands and he watched in amazement as the creature flew off in the direction of St. Gertrude's, still clutching the rifle.

"It's intelligent," Paul said softly. Then, just as softly, "Get that window closed, *now*."

John hit the button and the window closed just in time for another nightflyer to crash against it, cracking the glass.

"Let's get out of here," Paul urged.

John barely heard him; he was staring at the dazed creature on the ground as it shook its head and flapped its wings.

"John, let's go. Another one's coming and your window won't hold."

"Right." He started the car, backed it up until he could turn around, then headed out of the forest. At least he knew why Minerva hadn't been at her shop. He hoped she was still alive.

"What next?"

John pulled out onto Apple Hill Road. "How about a reunion? We've all been tormented by the nightmares. Let's see if Winky or Beano are ready to shake theirs and give us a hand."

"All right," Paul said, then fell into silence.

John drove to the Addams Family Orchard first. Winky would be more likely to say yes, and that might help convince Beano. *Convince him of what? To relive that night twenty-four years ago?* John didn't know what he was doing, calling on his old friends. He didn't have a plan. But maybe Minerva was right about following his instincts. What he was doing *felt* right, if nothing else.

# Ninety-Five

"They won't leave," Kelly said as the afternoon shadows lengthened. "They're going to keep us here until we starve."

"No. They'll leave at dusk. They'll be at St. Gertrude's for the ceremonies." Minerva didn't mention her fear that the nuns would make another attempt to recapture Kelly. If they made it until sunset, she doubted they'd come; they would replace her with another girl. *John,* she thought, *please follow the voice within you. Follow your heart, or many will die.*

"What will we do at sunset?" Kelly asked.

"You will wait here and continue the protection spells while I go to the abbey."

"I'm going with you!"

"No, Kelly, you're not. I am going to send Sara and Mark here when I find them, and you must be here when they arrive."

"I can go. I know my way around, and—"

"No. Your powers aren't developed enough, and you're one of their targets. You *must* remain here." Minerva paused, then shook her finger at the girl. "An apprentice does as her teacher says."

"Okay," Kelly said sulkily. "I just hate waiting."

Minerva put her arm around the girl's shoulders. "I know, child, I know. I've been waiting for this night all my life."

# Ninety-Six

"You're frigging crazy, Lawson, and you, too, Pricket, for listening to him." Beano Franklin glared at them from behind his pharmacy counter. "You boys go play your Halloween games, but leave me out of it."

"Beano," Paul said. "It *happened*. You *know* it did. I can see it in your eyes."

"Oh, yeah, priesty-boy? I don't see Winky here. Couldn't you see it in *his* eyes?"

"Yes, Franklin, we saw it," John said. "He admitted it, but he has his family to consider."

"And I don't?"

"You're not married. You have no kids," John said harshly. "Your life's been on hold ever since that night."

"Blow it out your ass, Lawson, and get out of my store. You too, butt-boy."

"Come on, Paul." John led his friend outside. "We're on our own. Are you with me?"

"Of course I'm with you. I think I became a priest because of that night." He smiled thinly and wiped his wire-rimmed glasses with a tissue. "Besides, how could I resist that line you gave me about your needing my priestly magic to fight Satan?"

John smiled back, then looked up, knowing dusk wasn't far off now. "Let's get your bag of tricks ready, and try to figure out a plan of action. We're running out of time."

"Are your deputies going with us?"

"No. I can't tell them what's going on, and I won't risk their lives without their permission. This is strictly non-police business. I'm going to turn civilian for the night and stop playing by the book."

Paul gave him a real grin this time. "Let's do it."

# Ninety-Seven

"Richard, I wanted everything to be perfect tonight, but thanks to your pigheadedness, it looks like I won't get my wish."

Dashwood sat opposite her in her office. They had fruitlessly searched the basement for Sara Hawthorne. Then, when they'd returned, they'd instead found Sister Margaret sprawled on the floor of the office. She wasn't even sure who'd hit her—a nun, but not one she recognized. *Damn her weak eyes.* Dashwood was virtually certain it was Sara Hawthorne, but Lucy didn't care for virtuals. She wanted proof. And she wanted Sara in her hands.

"Lucy," Dashwood began, "we have to deal with the possibility that Sara may have escaped."

"And if she has, she may have gone to the sheriff. She'll give him the proof he needs to come in here and disrupt the festivities."

"Did you hear something?" Dashwood asked.

"What?"

"There it is again. It sounds like groaning."

The pair stood still, listening, until the sound rose again. Dashwood pointed at the closet. Lucy nodded and mouthed the words, "Open it."

He reached out and grasped the knob, then rapidly twisted it and flung the door open. "Hello, Sara—"

He silenced, staring at the scantily clad Sister Elizabeth. After a moment, he bent and helped her up.

"There's an extra habit in the closet," Lucy said tartly. "Put it on."

Elizabeth slipped the clothing over her head, smiled at Dashwood, then turned to Lucy. "I caught Sara Hawthorne in here. She attacked me."

"I gathered as much. What was she doing in here?"

"She was about to use the phone."

"Thank you, Elizabeth. You may go ready yourself for the ceremonies."

When she was gone, Dashwood turned to Lucy. "Sara obviously didn't manage to make any calls. We'd be crawling with police by now if she had."

"She's either escaping on foot and taking her time about it, or she's still here somewhere." Lucy smiled. "Maybe one of our pets got her."

"No. I would know if that were the case. I think she's still here."

"Well, we're running out of time," Lucy snapped as she checked her watch. "We'll need replacements for Hawthorne and Kelly Reed, just in case we don't retrieve them. Go through your records, Richard, and find us a suitable virgin. You *can* manage that, can't you?"

*Dried-up old bitch.* "Of course I can," he said, all sugar and spice.

"I expect the Reed girl will show up here before the appointed hour, but even if she doesn't, we must dispose of her, preferably tonight. She's trouble."

"Big trouble," Dashwood agreed. Kelly Reed had power, and one of the things she could do was resist his efforts at hypnosis. Even when he'd drugged her, she resisted. His astral projections had had no effect on her, and even when he and Lucy had banded together and sent the revenant to her, she had resisted admirably. She couldn't be allowed to live. "Who will replace Sara Hawthorne?"

"I promised that honor to Sister Bibiana, remember?"

"You're serious?"

"Yes, quite. I've put up with her dimples and giggles long enough. I'm going to bring Marybeth Tingler into the order to replace her. She's adequate, don't you think?"

"Yes."

"Now, go find us a virgin and have Regina slip Bibi a mickey. It's nearly time to begin the opening services."

# Ninety-Eight

It was after six P.M. and Sara was still at St. Gertrude's. For the last forty minutes, she'd been hiding in the dormitory's third-floor lavatory, in a stall with an Out-of-Order sign taped to it. Her legs were cramping from hunkering on the toilet seat, but there hadn't been a single second in which she could leave.

She'd ended up in the dorm after fleeing from the two nuns coming up the walk when she'd first left Lucy's office. Students were all over the place—nuns, too—and she'd taken a chance and let herself into Kelly and Marcia's room. Fortunately, Marcia wasn't there; unfortunately, there was no sign of Kelly— *no* sign. Her books were gone, her toiletries, her clothing . . . and the bed had been stripped. Something had happened. Kelly was gone, but whether she had run away, or something worse, Sara had no idea. Were they preparing her for sacrifice? Sara could only think of rescuing her and Mark, and that meant she had to get away from the abbey and find John. She had been about to leave the room when the doorknob turned and she'd heard girlish giggling outside. She'd stepped inside Kelly's tiny closet and pulled the door closed just as Marcia Crowley and Buffy Bullock came in. She'd heard bedsprings squeak as the girls flopped down on the beds.

"So, old Lucy sure was pissed at you for letting Ghost Girl get away," Buffy said.

"What are you so happy for? You have to scrub toilets for a week, too."

The pair went on sniping at Kelly, the other girls they hung out with, and the nuns. Sara listened from the dark closet as the minutes ticked by, relieved to know that Kelly's whereabouts were unknown, but more anxious than ever to alert John about Mark.

"So," said Buffy, "I heard this rumor that that bitch Hawthorne ran away, too."

"Yeah, me, too." Marcia's voice lowered. "Old Lucy thinks

she's such hot stuff, but she can't even keep her hands on those two assholes. I wonder who they're gonna get instead."

"Do they have a boy?" giggled Buffy.

"Well, I heard Sister Vagina tell Sister Lizardbeth that they got the sheriff's kid."

"What are they gonna do with him?"

"Hell, I dunno. I don't know what they wanted Ghost Girl and Hawthorne for," Marcia confided. "But I have a good idea."

"So did they really get rid of Esther Roth?" Buffy asked. "There was a sub again today."

"I know, idiot. I was there." There was momentary silence. "She and that gardener, Carlos What's-his-name, they're both gone. Lucy got rid of them."

"Why?" Buffy whispered, as Sara cringed. If something had happened to Carlos, it was her fault.

"Who knows? I asked Sister Bibi, because lots of times, she talks, you know?"

"Yeah. So what'd she say?"

"She said they baked them into pies and fed them to the tourists."

Both girls laughed, but all Sara could think of was the sickeningly sweet odors that sometimes wafted from the old kitchen.

"Maybe it's true." Buffy giggled some more.

Marcia laughed. "Yeah. What if it is? Esther Roth ought to be happy, if it is. Finally, somebody's eating *her!*"

The laughter swelled, then finally died down into a few snorts and snickers.

"Tonight's gonna be great," Buffy said at last.

Bedsprings creaked. "Did you get your robe yet?" Marcia asked.

"Yeah. Mine's black. What color's yours?"

"Black," Marcia replied. "Why?"

"Marybeth got a red one."

"She's Lucy's favorite."

"Yeah. You think Lucy's a lez, like Roth was?"

"No. She fucks Dashwood."

"Does not."

"Sure she does. You've seen them at the regular masses. They're all over each other."

"Yeah, well."

"You're jealous!"

"Am not. Let me see your robe."

More squeaking bedsprings, then a door opening. "Here it is," Marcia announced.

"Hey, bring it to my room and we'll try them on. I'll show you Marybeth's."

"Okay, but we're on hot chocolate duty in fifteen minutes. We gotta be there or Lucy'll really have a shit hemorrhage."

*Hot chocolate duty?* Sara had had no idea what that meant. All she'd known was that the girls had left and she could escape.

But it wasn't to be. She'd left the room, then ended up going up the stairs to avoid running into Marcia and Buffy and the rest of their gang. They were carrying steaming carafes—the hot chocolate, no doubt—and little Dixie cups. As Sara took the first step, she saw them open the first dorm door.

*They're drugging them.* Sara stopped at the second-floor landing, intending to walk to the other end and go back downstairs behind Marcia and the rest. But she ended up hurrying to the third floor to avoid a nun who came up the center stairwell and turned toward her.

The third floor was the worst place to be, since most of the sisters' rooms were located there, but at least the hallway was empty. She had barely started down the hall when a door began to open. Sara backed up, pushed the lavatory door open, and slipped into the broken toilet stall.

A moment later, two nuns entered, then two more. They went into the shower room, but Sara stayed put because more nuns arrived. As they entered, others finished and came out to dry themselves. Sara watched through the crack between the door and the stall, shocked to see them all nude. A large make-up bag sat on the counter in front of a wide mirror, and one by one they used it, each applying a whore's worth of blush, eyeshadow, mascara, and crimson lipstick, before rubbing red rouge into their nipples and genitals.

When they were done, they walked into the locker area and reappeared wearing cowled robes of shimmery black satin with red trim.

The lavatory emptied as a charley horse knotted Sara's leg. She bit her lip against the pain and climbed off the toilet seat, willing the muscle to loosen. Finally it did. She peered out the crack, saw no one, heard nothing except dripping showers, then let herself out of the stall and tiptoed to the locker area. She started looking through the lockers and finally found a robe. She shucked off the habit and slipped the satin gown on, pulling the cowl down to her eyes and close around her cheekbones.

The corridor was empty as Sara left the bathroom. She walked swiftly to the far end of the building and down the stairs to the first floor. Outside, she moved across the back of the school building and around the corner and ran into a cluster of robed figures. She stayed where she was, and a few seconds later, Mother Lucy's voice broke the silence. "Our priest and our missing sisters and acolytes will join us later. They are preparing our gifts to our lord and master. We shall enter the chapel now and begin our prayers. Follow me."

There were perhaps twenty women in all, and Sara fell into line with them. They began a minor-keyed chant and followed Lucy into the chapel.

It was beautiful, Sara thought, grotesque and beautiful at the same time. The entire chapel was alight with black tapers. As they all filed into the front pews, Sara saw the shining black altar, and behind it, a crimson drape. She barely suppressed a cry of surprise as she saw black gargoyles lining the sides of the church, their eyes glittering red. She almost thought they were alive, but they didn't move, and she told herself the eyes were red glass or stone and merely reflected the candlelight.

The nuns and students continued to chant as they sat down, and Lucy stepped onto the chancel and pulled a cord beside the red drapes. Sara stifled a gasp as an inverted black cross appeared. The Mother Superior then went to the altar and began singing a prayer in counterpoint to the chanting. It was beautiful, Sara thought again, in a very grotesque way.

# Ninety-Nine

"The Halloween Haunt," Paul Pricket said as John pulled the passenger side door of the priest's green Honda Civic closed. "I used to love it."

"Yeah." John hadn't wanted to use Paul's car, but he didn't want to take the cruiser to the abbey—that might have unwanted repercussions—and his own mini-truck was still missing. Plus, Paul had insisted on driving, even pointing out that the dark green vehicle would be easily hidden among the trees.

They had visited the Haunt in the hope that Mark had shown up there, on the slim chance that he had taken off on some impetuous adventure of his own. No matter what, he wouldn't miss that. But Caspar hadn't seen him, nor had Corey Addams, who was manning the boys' section of the Haunted Barn with the help of a couple kids John vaguely recognized.

With Paul's help, he had threaded through the Haunt, asking virtually every partygoer if he'd seen his son, but the answer was always no. Now, as they pulled out of Parker's Mills's parking lot, everything caught up with him. The sounds of the festivities behind them, the smell of smoke from fireplaces all over town, kids in costumes roaming the sidewalks, grinning jack-o'-lanterns on steps and porch rails, made him feel infinitely sad. He'd never celebrated the night with Mark, had always relied on Gus. Since his brother's death, John had thought he hated Halloween, but that wasn't true; he was afraid of it, and now both his grandfather and his son were gone.

"We'll find him, John," Paul said, catching his thoughts.

"I hope you're right."

"Don't lose faith, now. These people have been killing your family members—and God knows how many others—for a century. They undoubtedly killed your grandfather and your father and plan to kill your son. *They're devils.* We saw proof of that today. And if Minerva Payne says you're the one who's going to stop it, then . . ." Paul's voice trailed off.

"I'm surprised you're so willing to believe."

Paul shrugged. "It's my job. There's Apple Heaven."

"The turn-off for the abbey is right behind it."

"I remember." Paul turned and drove through the parking lot, coming to a halt before the chain closing the private road. "Now what?"

"Now I start breaking the law. Flip the trunk release." John hopped out of the car and opened the long red toolbox he'd placed there while they were at the house. He withdrew a pair of bolt-cutters, sliced the chain, and pulled it loose.

"Let's go," he said, after he'd shut the trunk and climbed back in the car. "Better douse your lights."

Paul did. "This trip is going to be a slow one. I can hardly see a thing."

"Wait'll we hit the forest," John said. He could see only Paul's profile in the greenish dash lights.

Paul glanced at him. "We used flashlights back then."

"If we hadn't, maybe they wouldn't have caught us. We can't take any chances this time."

"Okay."

They drove through the orchards by the faint light of the low harvest moon, but when the apple trees gave way to pine and juniper, Paul had to slow to a crawl. "I'm driving blind here, John."

He nodded and pulled a penlight from the pocket of his black shirt. "It'll be faster to walk the rest of the way. Stop and let me out. I'll find a place off-road to hide the car."

"If you say so."

John got out and walked a few yards, then came to a place where the car could be pulled safely among the trees. He indicated the spot and Paul pulled in.

John was dressed all in black, Paul the same, except for his clerical collar and the navy knapsack slung over his shoulder. It contained his priestly tools, vestments, a crucifix, and several flasks of holy water. John's tools, a pistol in a shoulder holster, a hunting knife, skeleton keys, and a smoke bomb that Mark had concocted. John had taken it for safekeeping, promising the boy that at the right time and place, they would set it off together. *Together.* He hoped he could keep his promise.

"Ready?" Paul asked.

"Let's do it," John said, as they stepped onto the road to St. Gertrude's.

# One Hundred

As Minerva had hoped, the nightflyers stopped circling her house after darkfall, but they left considerably later than she had expected. The helpless waiting and wondering had been nearly unbearable. Alternately, she'd spent the minutes and hours of the day anxious or angry at herself for letting the passage of years steal her strength.

She tried to hide her emotions from Kelly and had spent the time casting spells of protection on everyone who might need them.

Kelly had continued to argue about staying behind tonight, and Minerva had had to be quite stern with her before she was convinced she would be more helpful if she stayed at the cottage and kept working the protection spells. Now, as Minerva walked alone through Witch Forest, knowing it so well that she needed no light, she had no idea whether or not she was right in leaving the girl behind. She was brave, cunning, and knowledgable about the abbey, but she was also undisciplined and impetuous, and, most important, the nuns had marked her for sacrifice.

She had left the rifle behind with Kelly after making sure she could handle the weapon, taking with her only a century-old hunting knife and her amulet. To the north she could hear the thunder of the Falls, and soon she came to the stream that divided the two forests.

She stared into the onimous darkness across the water. There were no forest sounds tonight, no animals, no insects, not so much as the soft sigh of a breeze or the rustle of leaves. Minerva waded into the water, feeling its icy chill soak through her shoes. Her bones would ache in the morning.

But that chill was nothing compared to the one she felt as she stepped onto St. Gertrude's property. It was cursed land. When she had first come here, the local Indians had spoken of it only in hushed tones. It was a place to be avoided, and their name for it translated into "the forsaken land." They had told her their own legends, which dated back many centuries, and had told her as well of the monks who had built the abbey. They had been plagued with death and disaster from the time they had first broken ground, and as the years had passed, things had grown worse, the monks eventually indulging in all forms of depravity, from bestiality to cannibalism.

Minerva walked into the murky wood, reciting old Celtic spells to keep her fear at bay. She had rarely been in these woods and now had to keep her mind clear to find her way through the dark. When she was a girl, her grandmother had taught her how to travel without her eyes, using her senses of hearing, smell, and space and direction, as well as sheer instinct. She had learned to run through forests in the dark without tripping over roots or plowing into tree trunks. As she called on these skills now, they came back in full force, and she faltered only if she allowed her mind to fall into fear.

Minerva traveled on, ignoring the feeling that she was being watched, ignoring the unnatural silence. Time passed and she knew she was nearing the abbey, but she felt as if she were making almost no progress.

It was a trick of the sisters', a protection spell of their own, meant to keep away the curious on this night. Minerva redoubled her concentration and continued on, but the nuns' magic had played hell with her sense of direction, and eventually she realized she was hopelessly turned around.

Not hopelessly, she corrected. Closing her eyes, she concentrated, taking herself beyond the physical senses, into a deeper place. She meditated, pushing away the sisters' cobwebs, then finally opened her eyes and set out once more.

# One Hundred One

"Where the hell is the abbey?" John muttered. It was past nine o'clock, well past, and he and Paul should have arrived at St. Gertrude's hours ago.

"I don't know how we lost the road," Paul said.

"God damn it, we were *walking* on it," John spat. "How the hell could we lose it?"

"I'm sorry, John, I just don't know."

"No, *I'm* sorry, Paul. I didn't mean to jump all over you. Time's wasting and I'm worried. Maybe you could ask your boss for a little help or something?"

"I've *been* asking," Paul said softly. "I trust he'll send some soon."

They walked on in silence, feeling their way among the trees, trying to find the road in the dark. John's penlight had died at least an hour before, and his hope was dying now as well. He felt like a rat in a maze.

"John?"

"What?"

"Do you hear that? In the distance?"

He listened, heard the faint crash of water. "Great. Just great. We're going toward Witch Falls."

"At least we know we're heading east instead of south." Paul had always been the king of silver linings.

"Okay, then we should go . . ." John suddenly realized that he couldn't sense direction, even though the sound of the Falls gave him all the help he should have needed. On the rare momentary occasions he'd lost the sense previously, he'd felt an unaccountable but faint nausea, a trace of dizziness. Now those feelings nearly overwhelmed him. "Paul, which way is south?"

"I don't know," came Paul's voice from the darkness.

"I believe I do, gentlemen."

John drew his pistol before his brain recognized Minerva

Payne's voice. "Minerva," he said, reholstering the weapon. "What are you doing out here?"

"The same thing as you."

He heard a snap, then a match flamed in front of Minerva's face. She looked at them. "You've brought a priest, John?"

"This is Paul Pricket. He was with us that night." John spoke quickly. "I remembered what happened."

"I know. You let me in. Do you know where the entrance to the old basement is?"

"No. Not yet."

The wooden match was burning down. "Why have you brought a priest, John? No offense, young man," she added, then blew out the match before it burned her fingers.

"Because of what you said. You said that every religion has its own demons. What better to fight Christian demons than a Christian holy man?"

Minerva chuckled softly, sadly. "You have a point, John. Paul, why did you agree to come?"

"When John called me, I agreed to visit. I've been having nightmares for years, just like him. And then, when I arrived today and he told me what happened in the chapel, I knew it was true. On some level, I've known it all along. I know it was behind my decision to become a priest."

"Well, do you think you can work with an old pagan, Father Paul?"

"It would be an honor."

"Good. If you gentlemen will come with me, I believe I might be able to find the way. Stay close, now."

# One Hundred Two

The services were going well. Richard Dashwood had entered the back of the chapel to check on them several times, and the prayers, in twisted Latin, were being sung on schedule.

He and Sister Regina had been very busy since the services started. First, they had begun the preparation of Sister Bibiana to serve as the devil's bride. Although she knew a great honor was being bestowed upon her, she had protested rather violently until he had administered a dose of his paralysis drug and hypnotized her. Now she was in one of the examining rooms, being bathed and shaved, perfumed and made up by Regina.

Once that process was begun, Dashwood had administered a mild tranquilizer to Mark Lawson, to make him docile so that when he was led from the basement vault to the chapel, to serve as part of the living altar, he would be fully awake for the experience. And for his own slow, very painful death.

Dashwood had hoped to rip his heart, still beating, from his body, but Lucy insisted they use an overdose of the paralysis drug, as was usual when they had to return a body to be found. The drug, in high doses, not only paralyzed the voluntary muscles, but slowly seeped into the involuntary ones, slowing the heart and the respiration, so that the victim felt as if he was dying. It was an ancient concoction similar in nature to a modern drug that had been targeted for use on child molesters, then was withdrawn because it was considered too cruel. Dashwood's drug was superior: in small doses, it wore off without an antidote and when used to induce death, broke up in the bloodstream so quickly that it was impossible to identify. Dashwood smiled, thinking about the modern doctors, like Frank Cutter, who thought they knew everything: they had overlooked the old medicines, dismissing them as old wives' cures, and in doing so, had turned their backs on a world of knowledge.

He had also tranquilized a twelve-year-old girl, Denise Somebody-or-other. Her name didn't matter and he didn't intend to use her; perhaps Sara Hawthorne was a lost cause, but he still intended to deliver Kelly Reed to the altar. That would redeem him with Lucy.

He glanced at his Rolex. In an hour, he would have to join the services to do his duty as high priest and deflower the novice, Marybeth Tingler. It was a task he looked forward to, but first, he had other work to do.

He left his office and went to his apartments, where the black cloth with its inverted pentagram was already laid out on the carpeting.

He stripped off his robe, then sat, naked and cross-legged, in the center of the pentagram. He drew a deep breath, exhaled, and repeated the process. Controlling the revenant would be grueling work alone, but it was worth it if it would lure Kelly Reed back to the fold.

# One Hundred Three

The cottage, so warm and cozy when Minerva was there, now seemed full of shadows and ghosts. Kelly knew that was stupid, but she couldn't help it.

She couldn't concentrate on the spells, either. They seemed as idiotic as her own growing fear. For her, being left behind in the supposed safety of the house was far more frightening then accompanying Minerva to St. Gertrude's. It was almost unbearable.

"Kelly!"

She jumped, whirling as someone knocked on the door.

"Kelly! It's Mark. You have to help me. Minerva's hurt!"

She pulled back the curtain and saw Mark staring at her. "Just a minute," she called. Grabbing a coat Minerva had lent her, she raced out the door as Mark turned and began to trot away. "Mark, wait!"

"Hurry!" he called without turning around. "Follow me!"

# One Hundred Four

Hours had passed, and still the women and girls in their black hooded robes continued to chant. Sara's knees were killing her from kneeling on the hard wooden riser.

She kept her cowl pulled past her cheeks and forehead so that the nuns on either side wouldn't recognize her, and she fortunately remembered some of the chants from her Latin classes a decade ago.

The chant ended and the cowled figures rose as an ancient pipe organ wheezed to life. At first, she didn't recognize the music, but slowly it came to her: it was Mendelssohn's Wedding March, played in a minor key. Around her, the others turned to face the doors. Suddenly, they were thrown open, and the girl in red—Marybeth Tingler—began walking slowly down the aisle. Under the red cowl, her eyes shone with pleasure and her reddened lips smiled. Sara bent her neck slightly so the girl wouldn't see her face, then turned to face front as the others did, once she finished her walk.

Marybeth stood in front of the altar, Mother Lucy behind it. "Tonight, our first order of business is to initiate our novice. This year, we have chosen an outstanding student, Marybeth Tingler. After the ceremony, she shall be known forevermore as Sister Mary Elmo."

The chapel doors sounded as if they'd been blown open, but Sara couldn't turn to look, since the others didn't move; but a few seconds later, a tall, robed figure strode by—Dashwood. As he stepped up toward the altar, Marybeth Tingler stripped off her robe, revealing a pale, slim body, the tips of her small breasts painted an obscene red-black.

Lucy moved out of the way as the girl climbed onto the altar, her legs facing the inverted cross, her head tilted back over the edge of the altar. For a brief instant, Marybeth's eyes locked on Sara's, and the girl smiled. Sara tensed, but the girl looked away without any other reaction, and Sara told herself she didn't recognize her.

Dashwood walked around the altar and let his robe fall from his shoulders, revealing a thin, lightly muscled body and an enormous erection. "Mary Elmo, do you desire to become a bride of Satan?"

"I do," she answered in a husky voice.

"Do you promise to obey His laws, to do whatever He asks of you, and never to question Him?"

"I do."

"Do you agree to die whensoever He wishes, be it tonight or centuries hence, and when you die, do you agree to become one of the guardians of the order as the sister you are replacing will do tonight?''

"I do."

''Then, in Lucifer's name, I take you as His bride.''

He plunged forward, and Marybeth's eyes bulged in shock. She screamed once, then her eyes glazed with pain, then pleasure, as Dashwood continued to thrust.

Out of the corner of her eye, Sara thought she saw one of the black gargoyles move.

# One Hundred Five

Kelly had followed Mark into St. Gertrude's forest, and nearly to the abbey grounds before she lost him. He'd never slowed, and she'd run blindly after him, mindless of the tree limbs and bushes that snagged and tore her clothing, not caring about the scrapes and bruises she endured on her frequent falls.

''Mark?'' she called. ''Mark? Where are you?''

He didn't reply, and suddenly she began trembling very hard. *It wasn't Mark.* Until now, she hadn't had time to think, just to run after him, but now she realized that he had been easy to see, despite the dark. The nuns had used him to lure her here.

But she was alone. If he hadn't disappeared, she probably would have followed him straight into the church, or Lucy's office, or wherever else he wanted. But he had. She could hear chanting, and though she felt a little turned around, she followed the voices and soon saw the dark outline of the chapel and the faint flicker of candlelight behind the stained glass windows.

*Now what?* She wondered where Minerva and Mark were. Should she try to get to town and find the sheriff? Somehow, she didn't think they'd let her make it.

Minerva had told her the sisters wanted to sacrifice her, and that frightened her now, but not too much. She'd spent so much time successfully evading them over the past months that she knew they weren't omniscient. She decided to hide in the bushes near the chapel door for a few minutes and try to figure out what to do next.

# One Hundred Six

"Get up, boy."

Mark Lawson squinted into the beam of a flashlight. His limbs felt heavy, his mind muddled, and he remembered a man holding him still while a nun gave him a shot. The room had spun, and then—nothing.

"You drugged me," he tried to say, but his tongue tripped over itself, and his lips felt rubbery and thick.

"Unless you get up right now, you'll get more of the same."

Mark pushed himself up off the chill floor, his hand against a wall to steady himself. There was a single nun standing between him and the open door, and he thought he could get past her, but the minute he took a step, his knees buckled and he fell. The woman's cold hand closed on his upper arm and yanked him to his feet, then she dragged him to the door and out, following the flashlight's beam across a fathomless room to a flight of stairs. She pushed him ahead of her and forced him to crawl up the staircase.

Dizzily he looked around and saw that he was in a room that was sort of like Dr. Cutter's examination room. A girl in a white gown stared at him blearily from a chair, and he figured she'd been drugged, too. Her wrists were bound together and attached to a leg of the exam table next to the chair.

"Take off all your clothes and put this on." The nun held out a white robe like the girl's.

"Why?"

"Do it, or I'll do it for you."

"I'm not gonna undress in front of a girl."

"Yes, you are—that, or you get another shot."

"I have to go to the bathroom."

The woman pursed her lips and stared at him a long moment. "This way," she said, roughly pushing him out of the room, and about ten feet down the hall to another door. She opened it to reveal a small, neat restroom. A tiny, dark window over the toilet promised freedom. The nun pushed him inside and stepped in after him. "Do your business," she ordered.

He felt his head clearing and realized he should hide it. He looked at her, keeping his eyes unfocused, his body limp. "I can't with you watching," he slurred.

"If you have to go, you will."

"I think it's diarrhea. Please, just wait outside—*please?*"

She glared at him, and he put his arms across his belly and stumbled against the sink. At that, she made a disgusted sound and walked out. "Be quick. If you try anything, you'll be very, very sorry." She closed the door and he could hear her tapping her foot just outside.

Groaning, he carefully climbed on top of the toilet seat and saw that the window had a crank. He groaned again, then made a gross sputtering sound with his mouth as he tried the crank. It turned, and cold air hit his face.

"Hurry up."

"I am," he moaned, then made more wet sputtering noises as he shakily stepped onto the tank top and pushed his head out.

The window was in an alcove, half below ground, and he quickly slithered out, turned, and moaned and sputtered once more before climbing unsteadily out of the alcove, then crawling on his hands and knees behind a row of bushes against the building. He was still shaky and his limbs wouldn't obey as well as they should, but he was at least twenty feet away when he heard the nun shriek, "You'll pay for this, you little shit!"

He almost laughed, but caught himself. Peeking out from behind the bushes, he saw no one, so he pushed through them and half-ran, half-staggered toward the end of the building.

# One Hundred Seven

Even with Minerva leading, two more hours passed before they found the front gate of St. Gertrude's. In the distance, John heard chanting, and as he looked up at the twin gargoyles on the gateposts, memories suddenly flooded his mind. Memories of Halloween night, 1972.

First, the five of them, John, Winky, Paul, Doug and Beano, boldly walking through the gate, then skulking along the shadowy bushes toward the school building. Suddenly, a scream— *Greg's scream*—pierced the night. They halted in their tracks at the base of the steps and, shocked, glanced at one another, then, as one, turned and ran across the lawn toward the gate, toward Greg.

But the gate was blocked by a half-dozen black-cowled figures. The tallest held Greg's limp body in his arms.

John ran at the tall one, intent on tackling him and rescuing his brother, but the other figures stepped forward, blocking his way. The man had laughed in a deep, rich voice as strong hands clamped onto John's arms. The figures grabbed the other boys, too, harshly ordering them to be quiet. They spoke in feminine voices and John remembered wondering how normal women could be so powerful. Then a silver needle flashed in the moonlight, and he felt a sharp pain in his arm. His knees buckled and the world spun away.

He and the others woke in a dark, dankly cold room. They were all there, including Greg. John felt his way to his brother, following the sound of his moans. Groggy himself, he tried to revive Greg, but he wouldn't do more than groan feebly. One by one, the other boys began to talk, then move, exploring the room with their hands. He remembered hearing Doug Buckman call out in a slurry voice that he'd found a door, but that it was locked.

A few minutes later, the door was unlocked and the tall man stepped in, the revolver in his hand fanning across the boys.

Flanking him were the robed women, one holding a bright lantern that cast swinging shadows on the stone walls.

"Take the young one and prepare him for the ceremony," the man said, as two of the women stepped forward and pulled Greg from John's weak grasp. The leader locked his dark eyes on John's. "It will hurt you more, I think, if we allow you to live." He'd laughed again and disappeared from the room, his followers behind him. Again they were locked away in darkness.

Time passed slowly, but finally, three of the women, one holding the gun, returned and took Winky out of the room. They came again and again until John, the last, was finally led across a vast chamber and up a flight of stairs, into a doctor's examination room. Winky, Paul, Beano and Doug were there, sitting on straight-backed chairs, staring straight ahead as if they weren't even aware he was there.

The women restrained him and the man gave him another injection. That was when he thought he had died . . . but he hadn't. And while he struggled in vain to move, even to breathe, as he felt his heart slow down, the man stared into their eyes and told them the story of their camping trip to Witch Falls. He told them that Greg had fallen into the water and drowned.

"My God," he whispered, turning to face Minerva and Paul. "It was Dashwood."

"What?" Paul asked, without taking his eyes from the gate-post gargoyles.

"I know how to find the basement."

Minerva stared at the sky. "It's late. They may have already moved your son. John, check the basement, but be careful. And quick. Paul and I will go to the chapel and prepare for what will come at midnight. Meet us on the north side as soon as you can."

He nodded, then drew his pistol and ran toward the school building.

# One Hundred Eight

His duty as bridegroom-in-effigy long completed, Richard Dashwood had gone into a small anteroom located behind the chancel of the chapel, to prepare himself for the midnight ceremony. In the chapel, the women continued to build power through the sacred chants, power that would be channeled through him at midnight, when he called the Beast into this world.

His timing had been off in regard to Kelly Reed. When he was forced to break off the revenant contact to initiate the novice, he had known Kelly was near the abbey, but now he had neither the time nor the energy to search her out. The other girl would serve in her stead, and after the ceremonies, he would track the Reed girl down and dispose of her. He smiled to himself. He would bring her to Lucy and they would take their time killing her; that would give the Mother Superior great pleasure.

He sipped brandy from a snifter and closed his eyes, reliving the taking of the novice, then someone rapped urgently on the door. He looked around, but before he could ask who it was, the door opened and Sister Regina peered in, her face a pale mask of worry.

"What is it, Sister?"

"Doctor, it's the boy."

"Come in and shut the door." He set the snifter down and gazed at her as she stood before him. "What about the boy?"

"I—I'm afraid he's escaped," she stammered, fear growing in her eyes.

"How?"

"The window in the bathroom by your office. He said he was sick, and—"

Dashwood stood, drawing himself to his full height. "What about the girl and Bibiana?"

"They're ready. Basil-Bob is guarding them."

He nodded. "I'm very disappointed in you, Regina."

She lowered her eyes. "I'm sorry."

"You will be flogged for this."

"I know," she replied softly.

"Go quietly into the church and fetch three of the girls from the back row to help search for him. Then go back to the infirmary and guard the sacrifices yourself. Do you think you can do that without fouling things up?"

"Yes, Doctor."

"Good. Apprise Boullan of the situation. Tell him to use any means short of death to recapture the boy. We need to bring him and the others into the chapel in exactly fifteen minutes."

"What if we don't find him?"

He studied her. "Then you will answer to Mother Lucy, and she will be far more severe in her punishment than I will."

Regina fled the room and Dashwood followed, walking out into the night. Of the three sacrifices, the male was the least important. It was not a gift for the Beast, but a sacrifice that was more truly for the orchards and for Lucy's pleasure. The ceremony could continue without him, but Lucy would be enraged, and Regina wasn't the only one who would suffer her fury. She couldn't punish him, as she would anyone else, but she was a vindictive bitch, fully capable of making his life miserable.

"Damn it." He walked into the dark cemetery, his eyes darting among the moonlit gravestones, hoping to see movement. First Kelly Reed escaped, then Sara Hawthorne, and now the boy. The sisters were getting very sloppy, and he and Lucy would have to do something about it. More new blood, perhaps.

A twig cracked and he turned to see Marybeth Tingler, in her red robes, picking her way around the gravestones.

"Doctor Dashwood?"

"Yes?" He moved to join her. "What are you doing out here? You're supposed to be inside."

"I—I know, but I thought I should tell you something."

"And what would that be?"

"I think I saw her. Miss Hawthorne, I mean."

He took her shoulders. "Where?"

"In there." She nodded toward the chapel.

"When?"

"When we were . . . during my initiation. She was in the second pew from the front, on the right." She hesitated. "I'm not positive, though."

"Why did you take so long to tell me?"

"It was the first time I could get away without being noticed."

He kissed her forehead chastely, then let go of her shoulders. "Thank you, Marybeth—I mean, Sister Mary Elmo. I won't forget this." He smiled beneficently. "Go back inside now, and try not to draw attention to yourself. I'll take care of everything." He drew a small notepad from a pocket in the robe and wrote a short note to Lucy, apprising her only of Mark Lawson's disappearance. "Give this to Lucy when you can," he said, folding the paper and handing it to her.

"Yes, Doctor."

Still smiling to himself, he watched her disappear into the chapel, where the chanting was rising to monumental proportions as midnight approached. When he wrote the note about Mark, he considered alerting Lucy, but the thought of surprising her had been far more appealing. There was a chance, too, that the girl was wrong, but he doubted it; he didn't believe Sara had been able to leave the grounds, and what better place for the prey to hide than under the hunter's nose? It required courage, something he admired.

He strode across the lawn to the school building and downstairs to the infirmary, where he found a cowed-looking Sister Regina watching the two female sacrifices like the proverbial hawk. He told her the procession would begin shortly, boy or no boy, then went into his office and prepared a syringe of mild but fast-acting tranquilizer to jab Sara with when the procession began.

# One Hundred Nine

Kelly Reed hadn't moved from her hiding place in the bushes on the north side of the chapel. Once she was safely hidden, she didn't know what else to do. People had come and gone constantly, and she'd seen several robed figures prowling the grounds, perhaps looking for her. She had little doubt that Mark was here, perhaps in the chapel, and that he needed her help, but what could she do?

She rested her elbows on her knees, her brow on her hands. Hot, silent tears cascaded down her cheeks, and she gave up trying to stop them.

"Kelly."

Thinking she only imagined Minerva's whisper, she lifted her head. Minerva stood before her and Kelly flinched, thinking of the revenant. Then she realized that she could barely see her in the darkness. "You're real," she whispered.

Minerva folded herself down in the bushes next to Kelly. "This is Father Paul," she murmured.

Startled, Kelly saw the blond man who stood in the shadows. He joined them, kneeling on the ground, and for an instant, Kelly thought he had a hunchback, then realized it was a knapsack when he swung it onto the ground.

"He's a Catholic priest, Kelly, not like Dashwood."

"I was here on a night like this many years ago," he told her. "I'm here to help save Mark."

"What are *you* doing here?" Minerva asked, and Kelly quickly explained about the phantom of Mark that had led her into the woods.

Minerva nodded. "Have you seen anyone coming or going since you've been here?"

"Yes. Some of them are prowling around like they're looking for someone. Dashwood and Boullan are both out. Dashwood just went into the school building. Minerva, what's going on?"

"At midnight, they call their god into this world to feast on human flesh."

"Satan," added the priest.

"It's an evil force, whatever its name," Minerva said. "Father Paul and I are going to try to banish it before another innocent is killed."

"What should I do?" Kelly asked.

"It's not safe for you to leave, so for now, stay here with us. Sheriff Lawson will join us soon, hopefully, with Mark. I believe Sara is here, too. You've seen no sign of her?"

Kelly shook her head. Within the chapel, the voices rose to frenzied levels.

# One Hundred Ten

John had slipped into the school building and downstairs to the infirmary without being seen, but finding the exam room containing the entrance to the basement had been far more difficult.

The infirmary was not deserted; Dashwood's prune-faced nurse had been sitting in one room with the lights on and the door ajar. With her were two people—a woman and a girl—dressed in white robes. He hesitated long enough to make sure it wasn't Sara under all the make-up, then whisked past the door successfully, hoping the basement entry was not in the occupied room.

There were four more doors, all closed. The first, he knew, was to Dashwood's office. The next door yielded a restroom, and he noticed that the window over the toilet was open far enough for a man to climb through. It was something to keep in mind, he thought, as he opened the next door. It was an exam room, but the door inside led only to a linen closet.

One door left. John slipped inside quickly as voices sounded down the hall. He crossed to a door similar to the one in the previous room. Opening it, he felt a surge of relief. The closet was empty, without shelves. He stepped inside and quickly found a small latch on the back wall. He depressed it and the door opened.

After closing the outer door, he made his way down into the darkness, cursing his dead penlight. Halfway down the stairs—or so he figured—he halted and listened. "Mark?" he called. "Mark? Are you here?"

Only the echo of his own voice answered him. He called louder, but still there was no reply. The only thing he could see was the glow of his watch face when he lifted his sleeve: ten minutes until midnight. Without light, there was no way John could explore the basement, so he turned and carefully made his way back up the stairs and into the closet.

He exited the closet and crossed to the door, then paused, listening. Silence. He slipped into the hall. Light glowed from the exam room where the woman and the girl were waiting. The door leading to the front waiting area was shut, just as he'd left it. He paused, wondering if he should try to get the women out now, then the waiting room door opened and the decision was made for him. Before he could move, a half dozen robed figures came in, led by Dashwood, his cowl thrown back. The doctor saw him and started running.

John opened the door to the bathroom and ran in, leapt onto the toilet, and shimmied through the tight window, pulling free just as Dashwood entered. John crashed through the bushes and ran across the back of the building, not slowing until he reached the end.

He had to make it to the chapel, but it was impossible because the doors were wide open and robed figures were filing out. He crouched in the shadows of the bushes and checked his watch. It was only a few minutes until midnight.

The figures formed into two rows lining either side of the chapel doors. They began to chant and their voices carried eerily through the night air.

Something rustled in the bushes behind him. Turning, he aimed his gun at the sound. "Come out or I shoot," he hissed.

"Dad?"

"Mark?" He pushed between the bushes and came face to

face with his son, who was hefting a football-sized rock, the sharp point aimed right at him.

Mark's eyes opened wide and he set the rock down. "Dad!"

"*Shhh.* They'll hear us." As he spoke, he stuck the gun in his waistband and pushed the rest of the way through the bushes, not caring about the twigs scratching his hands and face. He grabbed Mark and hugged him. "Oh, God, I thought you were—"

"Dead," Mark finished, as he returned John's hug with a near stranglehold. "I almost was. They drugged me. I got away through the bathroom window."

"So did I," John said. "They'll be looking for us. Minerva's waiting by the chapel; we have to get to her."

The boy nodded, then tensed as the door at the end of the school building opened, less than eight feet away.

Dashwood and Mother Lucy came out and turned toward the door, raising their cowls. "Richard," Lucy hissed, "kill Lawson on sight. He can't disrupt the ceremony."

"Don't worry, my love," Dashwood said softly, his tone irritated. "Nothing can happen now. And I have good news for you, Lucy. Sara Hawthorne has been located."

"Really? Where?"

"See the faithful waiting for us outside the chapel?"

Lucy nodded.

"She's among them. I'll inject a tranquilizer as soon as I pass her. Then we can give her to the Beast, or keep her for ourselves, whatever you desire."

"Richard," she purred. "I'm impressed. Here they come."

John watched as the pair stepped back and two more stepped out, supporting the white-clad girl between them. They were followed by another duo, these guiding the woman in white. Finally, the third pair exited. John shivered, knowing that if things had gone their way, they would be bringing Mark to the altar.

Lucy and Dashwood started across the lawn toward the chapel, the others following at a stately pace. John knew he couldn't get to Sara before Dashwood did, but at least the doctor had said he was only giving her a tranquilizer.

# One Hundred Eleven

Minerva and Paul entered the chapel from the rear as soon as the congregation had filed out, and now Minerva saw that Paul was staring in shock at the inverted cross, the black altar, and the gargoyles lining the walls. "Come, Paul," she whispered. "Begin your rites. We don't have much time."

The priest nodded. He now wore a large crucifix around his neck—his own sort of amulet, Minerva thought—and held an open vial of holy water. Speaking softly in Latin, he began sprinkling the water. When some hit a gargoyle mounted near the chancel, it sizzled.

Minerva began her own ancient rites. The chapel was charged from the sisters' magic, and as she spoke, she felt as if she were breathing cold oil into her lungs, not oxygen. Her ears rang and hurt from the changing air pressure in the room. She approached the gargoyle that had sizzled and put her hand on its ugly muzzle. It was ice-cold, but the eyes, dull and reddish, began to glow crimson. It was stone . . . living stone.

# One Hundred Twelve

Kelly edged nearer the front of the chapel, keeping to the shadows, careful to make no sound. The nuns and chosen students stood on either side of the doors, their heads turned toward the school building. A small procession came out the door, led by Dashwood and Lucy, and slowly began walking across the lawn.

Trying not to worry about Minerva inside the building, she tried to see some of the faces, soon recognizing several of the nuns, plus Buffy Bullock and Marcia Crowley. Marybeth Tingler wore a red robe and a smile. For an instant, she saw a flash of face from under a cowl, and she jumped, thinking she recognized Sara Hawthorne. She kept her eyes on the woman, and finally, she showed her profile for a split second. *It is Sara!*

# One Hundred Thirteen

Sara shivered as she stood in the line of Satanists watching as Dashwood and Lucy approached. She strained to see the white-clad figures being brought behind them and as they neared, she nearly sighed with relief. Mark wasn't among them. He'd escaped.

Or had he? Had he made it home and alerted John? Her eyes darted as she searched for him in vain. Where was he? Where was Minerva? Maybe the nuns and Dashwood had gotten to both of them. Maybe they were all dead. *Don't think like that!*

Sara turned her gaze back to Dashwood and Lucy, and her heart skipped a beat. Lucy was walking slowly down the opposite line, pushing the cowls back to reveal the faces beneath.

Dashwood was doing the same thing on her line and was quickly approaching. Her mind raced. She had to get away, and her only choice was to run. She swallowed hard, wondering if she could make it into the woods. Her chances were small, but if she didn't run, they were nil.

Suddenly, Dashwood moved straight to her, skipping the two women before her. He grabbed her cowl and yanked it back. "Did you know, my dear Sara, that fear has an odor? I can smell it on you." He grabbed her arm with one hand and raised a hypodermic with the other.

"*No!*"

Sara heard Kelly's cry and saw the girl racing toward her. Dashwood grunted and slammed into her, the syringe flying from his hand.

"Come on!" Kelly yelled, trying to yank her out from under Dashwood, but the man shook her off and pinned Sara's wrists.

Sara heard Kelly scream, saw movement behind her, heard more shrill cries. Dashwood pulled Sara up, twisting her arm behind her, almost breaking it. Then he put a knife to her throat.

Lucy had Kelly in a similar hold, minus the knife. "It's time!" she called out. "All of you, line up and enter the chapel. *Now!*"

Sara and Kelly struggled in vain while the Satanists filed into the chapel. Last came the sacrifices, then she and Kelly were alone with Dashwood and Lucy.

"What shall we do with them?" Lucy asked.

"Bring them in. There's no time."

# One Hundred Fourteen

Minerva had hurried Paul out of sight behind the drapes framing the inverted crucifix as soon as they'd heard the screams. She knew they had Kelly and Sara.

The church bell began to chime, heralding midnight. She glanced at Paul, wondering how much good they'd done. He smiled tightly, sweat beading on his forehead despite the preternaturally chill air.

She heard the congregation returning, heard their feet, their soft chanting. The air began to thicken and electricity lifted the hairs on her arms and neck as the bell chimed on. The Beast was on its way.

# One Hundred Fifteen

John cringed at the sound of Kelly Reed's scream; his stomach clenched when he heard Sara's voice. For a moment, he saw nothing, then the robed figures moved into the chapel, and he saw Lucy holding Kelly's arm and Dashwood standing behind Sara.

It was time to strike. "Wait here, Mark."

"No way! I'm going with you. You have a gun."

He couldn't argue with that. "Stay behind me."

He drew his gun and dashed out of the bushes, running straight across the lawn toward the chapel.

"Let them go!" he ordered. Dashwood and Lucy both stared at him, Lucy's face a scowl, Dashwood's amused. He pressed the knife against Sara's neck, and John saw a crimson bead seep from her throat.

"It seems, my dear Lawson, that we're at a stalemate," the doctor said smoothly.

Suddenly, Kelly moved, and John saw her foot come down hard on Lucy's. The nun cursed and Kelly was free. She ran at Dashwood. "Let her go!"

*"Kelly, no!"* John yelled, and the girl stopped short of tackling Dashwood, paralyzed like a deer caught in headlights. Lucy lunged at her and John turned his gun on the nun. "Stop, or I'll shoot!"

"Fuck you!" Lucy screamed, as she wrapped her hands around Kelly's neck and began to squeeze.

John squeezed the trigger. Blood spurted from Lucy's head and she went down and lay still. He'd scored a direct hit.

Then something began to happen to her body. Under the black robe, it moved, the legs drawing up and disappearing beneath the cloth, followed by the arms and head.

Suddenly, a nightflyer shrieked. The black robe flapped and then was thrown aside to reveal a creature, hideously ugly from its lizardy tail to its mouthful of sharp teeth. It flapped its wings, shrieked again, then took off, flying up to the top of the chapel cross. Awestruck, John watched it, and realized that some of the gargoyles were missing from the chapel roof. Most of them, in fact.

Dashwood was laughing, though it was hard to hear above the frenzied chanting. "Where else would Lucy roost?" He laughed harder. "Good shot, Lawson, and thank you. I was tired of her tyranny. And now, if you'll excuse me, Sara and I are late for a date with the devil."

Dashwood turned, backing toward the church, using Sara as a shield. John watched helplessly, Mark and Kelly beside him.

"You two, *run*. Get outside the front gate and wait for me."

"But—" Mark said.

*"Do it.* If you have to run farther, stay on the road. Whatever you do, stay on it, all the way to Apple Hill." As he spoke the words, his heart thundered. He'd said almost the same thing to his little brother exactly twenty-four years ago.

The kids ran, and John turned his attention back to Sara. Dashwood was entering the chapel, dragging Sara along with him. John ran after him.

He stopped short on the threshold, staring in shock at the spectacle before him. It was almost identical to the dream he'd had the other night. Only the first four pews on each side were filled, and Dashwood was passing them, still holding onto Sara. He rounded the altar and John saw the white-clad figures laid out across it. Glitter-eyed gargoyles lined the edges of the chapel.

The air was thick and cold, and when Dashwood opened his mouth and began speaking something that sounded vaguely like Latin, it became thicker and so cold that it hurt John's lungs.

Dashwood, his knife still at Sara's throat, stepped back from the altar. He came to a halt before the red drapes flanking the reversed crucifix, still reciting the foreign words. The women in the pews began to chant in counterpoint to Dashwood, and above the black altar, the air began to vibrate, like heat waves over desert sand. A sound like roaring wind filled John's ears and the swirling air above the altar, above the human sacrifices, began to darken.

Dashwood's voice rose, and red sparks appeared within the swirling blackness. Suddenly, a nightflyer shrieked, and John looked toward the sound, saw first one, then another gargoyle stretch its wings. More shrieks followed.

Dashwood yelled and jumped forward, and Sara spun away from him, dropping to the floor, then getting to her knees, ready to run. Dashwood barely glanced at her, but turned and yanked the drape.

Minerva and Paul stood there. Minerva moved instantly, the

hunting knife in her hand pointed at Dashwood. Paul went straight to the altar, a bible in one hand, holy water in the other. He began chanting in recognizable Latin, and as he did, he shook the vial of water and threw it at the boiling black mass.

A sound louder than a thousand screams nearly burst John's eardrums. He ran up the aisle. Seeing him, Minerva turned from Dashwood and joined Paul at the altar, beginning her own arcane work.

The robed figures in the pews were in confusion without their leaders. Ignoring them, John ran at Dashwood, and the man surprised him by kicking the gun out of his hand. It spun across the floor and Sara grabbed it.

Dashwood punched John in the chest, knocking the air out of him. He dropped to his hands and knees, and before he could get to his feet, Dashwood struck again, delivering a kick to his ribs.

*Concentrate!* Doggedly, John got to his feet and swung at Dashwood. He missed the first time, but the second swing connected squarely with the doctor's jaw and knocked him backward.

He didn't go down, but came back swinging. John blocked a punch, then connected his fist with Dashwood's abdomen. Air wooshed out of him and Dashwood glared, his eyes fiery pits.

John kept eye contact as they feinted, but he could hear chaos behind him, could feel the chill in his lungs. Dashwood leapt at him, knocked him down. John kneed him in the stomach and they rolled off the chancel. He heard screaming from the pews as they rolled to a stop at the feet of the worshipers.

Dashwood's knee slammed into his groin, and John doubled up on the floor, vaguely aware that the doctor was on his feet. Groaning, he got up and ran after him, not stopping when Sara called his name.

Dashwood ran into an anteroom and John followed, his eyes watering and his stomach roiling from the pain in his groin. The doctor was gone, but a door to the outside hung open. John stopped on the threshold for a split second, panting, aware that the air wasn't as cold now, his ears weren't under pressure, and the nightflyers' screeches had died down. Whatever Paul and Minerva were doing was working.

He set off after Dashwood. He could barely see the man in the dark as he fled through the hedges and across the road into the forest.

Dashwood was fast, but John kept up, chasing his dark silhouette between the trees more by sound than by sight. They ran on and on, splashing across the creek, running until the roar of Witch Falls drowned out the sound of Dashwood's footsteps.

Moonlight shot through the thinning trees as they approached the Falls, and John, holding his ribs where Dashwood had kicked him, was able to spot the doctor as he moved up an incline and ran onto the old wooden bridge spanning the top of the Falls.

With a new burst of energy, John made the bridge. "Dashwood!" he yelled. "This gets settled now!"

Dashwood, halfway across the bridge, turned to look at him. "You can't win, Lawson. You're no match for me."

John stalked toward him, wishing he had his gun.

"You Lawsons are easy. Your ancestors were easy. Your father was simple. He came nosing around, and we set him up and blew his brains out. Your grandfather was even easier."

"Go to hell," John spat. He was only a yard from Dashwood now. "You're out of tricks, Doctor. Now it's just you and me, one on one. No magic, no gargoyles, nothing."

Dashwood cocked his head, studied him, then laughed. "Whatever you say."

Dashwood threw himself at him, exactly as John had hoped. He sidestepped neatly, then whirled, throwing his arm around Dashwood's neck from behind, pulling him backward, trying to strangle him.

Dashwood gasped, then kicked John's shin and broke away. John blocked the first punch, took the second on the shoulder, then hit the doctor with an uppercut to the jaw. Dashwood staggered back against the bridge's wooden handrail, and John plowed into him, his hands wrapping around the man's neck.

Suddenly, the bridge creaked and groaned, then they were falling and falling into the water. It seemed to take forever before they hit, and John, on top of Dashwood, felt the shock as the doctor crashed into the sharp rocks at the bottom of the Falls. They bounced and hit another rock, and despite the thunder of the water, John heard Dashwood's spine snap, felt the body bend unnaturally beneath him.

They'd come to a stop, teetering on a rock at the base of the Falls. John squinted through the spray and the dark, saw Dashwood's eyes were open and blank. Blood oozed from his mouth. "Go to hell," he said, and rolled himself off the body and into the deep water. He paddled slowly away from the rocks into the old swimming area, his memories of his last swim here, when he'd dragged his brother's body from the water, dominating his thoughts.

Barely aware of the icy water, he swam by memory to the steep trail that led up to the Mezzanine. He crawled slowly toward the top, his mind reeling. It was over at last, and Mark was alive, Sara, too. As he made the ridge and dragged his body onto the flat ground, he realized he was already lapsing into disbelief, already rationalizing everything that had happened the way he would on his police report.

"John?"

Sara's voice, far away. "I'm here," he called. Sara, he thought, Sara. She brought new concerns, new feelings, new problems. And he looked forward to them all.

"John?"

He looked up, saw her silhouette on the bridge. "Down here," he called. "Get off the bridge. It's broken."

She screamed, and he staggered to his feet, shouting her name. Then he heard the ungodly shriek of a nightflyer.

He looked at the Falls and saw a huge black form rise above the cliff. Batwings, a tail, red eyes. It hovered for an instant, then flew at him, and he remembered how Lucy had transformed when she died. The thing flew at him and he curled into a ball and rolled, hiding his face and stomach. He had no way to fight it.

Talons ripped into his back and teeth tore at his shoulder. *After all this, I'm going to die.* It was almost funny.

A shot rang out and he felt the wind of a bullet pass near his face. The gargoyle shrieked in his ear, then he heard another shot, and this time the creature screamed, deafening him. Its claws ripped from his flesh as it thrashed away. John rolled and got to his feet. "Sara?" he called.

"*John!*"

She was no longer on the bridge, but running across the meadow. "John, are you all right?" she asked, throwing herself into his arms.

"I'm fine," he said, trying not to flinch as the gun, still in her hand, hit his shoulder.

"You're hurt." She pulled away.

"Not much," he said. She held out the gun and he stuck it in his waistband again, knowing that putting it in its shoulder holster would hurt like hell. "How about you?"

"I'm fine," she said. "Thanks to you."

"What happened back there? In the chapel."

"I don't know, really, except that black ball of whatever-it-was started to take human form, then it turned back into a ball and began to fade. It wasn't as cold. Did you notice?"

"I did. Minerva and Paul?"

"John, I followed you out of there, but they seemed to have things under control."

He put his arm around her waist and they stepped back so that the moonlight hit the fallen nightflyer. Its chest had been blown out, and it was hard to see in the dim light, but the blood appeared to have turned black and solidified. The open eyes were no longer red. John toed the body and was surprised to meet solid resistance. He bent and touched it: it was cold and felt like stone.

Taking the gun from his waistband, he backed up, Sara with him. At a safe distance, he aimed and fired, then they approached and saw rock shards where the head had been.

Sara took his hand and squeezed. "So I guess we should go back and shoot all the gargoyles at St. Gruesome's."

"That's probably a good idea."

"Let's go. I left Mark and Kelly waiting at the gate." He

hesitated, then faced her and took her other hand. "Sara," he said before he lost his nerve, "I love you."

"I love you," she said softly, turning her face up toward his.

They brushed their lips together. It was barely a kiss, but it was wonderful just the same.

# EPILOGUE

# HALLOWEEN, 1997

"Here he comes," Mark said as a spotlight blinked on deep in the Parker orchard.

"Who's coming?" Sara asked.

"The Headless Horseman," the boy replied, turning to watch the orchard.

Sara jumped as a horse's frenzied whinny shrieked through the loudspeakers, and John put his arm around her, pulling her close as hoofbeats sounded. "It's just like it was when I was a kid," he told her as the Horseman began his journey toward the crowd gathered outside the cider mill.

She glanced up at him. "Beats the hell out of last Halloween, doesn't it?"

John smiled. "Sure does."

St. Gertrude's was empty now, except perhaps, for a few ghosts. The nuns had vanished by the time he and Sara had returned from Witch Falls, leaving behind a cluster of furious and indignant followers. Paul Pricket had insisted that the girls—both the cultists and the vast majority, who had slept through the night unaware of the events thanks to the tranquilizers in the hot chocolate—should be taken in by Catholic orphanages. They had, he explained, already been under the influence of the Church's "enemies" and needed to experience the "other side." John had agreed and by the middle of the following day, buses had taken all the girls away to start their new lives.

To put it mildly, John had ignored the letter of the law in the matter, but he had never regretted his decision. Though he wasn't pleased by the way the Church had covered things up, he knew it was best for the girls, so as sheriff of Moonfall County, he'd done a little sweeping under the rug himself.

He had also been cavalier about legalities in the case of Kelly Reed. She had lived with Minerva for a year now, going to school at Moonfall High—she was in one of Sara's history classes and working at the Gingerbread House. She'd transformed from ugly duckling to swan over the last few months, and Minerva, whatever her age really was, seemed younger and more invigorated under Kelly's influence.

A year ago, John felt he was a prisoner set free, and tonight, watching the horse and its headless rider gallop closer, he felt exactly the same way. His entire adult life had been plagued by fear and guilt until last year, when his memories had returned.

The afternoon of All Soul's Day, he, along with Paul Pricket, Frank Cutter and Caspar Parker, had returned to the deserted abbey and blasted every last gargoyle to Kingdom Come. Most merely shattered, but a few were nightflyers, and their blood-curdling screeches rent the air before their bodies crumbled.

Now, the Horseman, on his mount, rode to the center of the clearing. The horse reared and whinnied, just as it had twenty-five years ago, and with fond sadness, he remembered his brother's excitement.

Mark, eight inches taller than last year, his voice cracking into adulthood, glanced back at him and grinned. "Cool, huh?" He smiled at Sara. "Next year, we'll bring the squirt. That'll be great."

Sara nodded, unconsciously touching her expanding stomach, her eyes on the Horseman as he charged away into the night. John squeezed her closer as a chill breeze ruffled their hair. "Tired?" he asked, wondering if he'd ever told Mark he'd called his own younger brother "squirt." He decided not to ask.

"Not tired," Sara murmured. "Just thinking. Next Hallow-een, we'll have another son." She smiled up at him. "And he'll be safe. And Mark will be safe. And you." Standing on tiptoe, she kissed him.

"Yeah." John barely heard Caspar's traditional goodnight, liberally laced with warnings about hitchhiking spirits. Last year he'd lost Gus, but he would be the last. Sara was right; Mark and the unborn baby she carried would be free of the curse. "Let's go home," he said, resolving never to take his new life for granted.

The trio walked out to the parking lot, and John opened the pick-up's door for Sara, who awkwardly slid in. Mark squeezed in beside her and John went to the driver's door, but didn't open it. He stared up at the moon, smelled burnt pumpkin and woodsmoke and smiled to himself, enjoying the night, musing over the fact that he needed to trade in his pick-up for something roomier. A minivan, maybe.

A shadow passed in front of the moon, and in the distance, something shrieked. Only a hawk, he told himself as he opened the door and slid in. *Only a hawk.*

## ABOUT THE AUTHOR

Tamara Thorne lives with her family in California. She is the author of nine horror novels published by Pinnacle Books. Her next novel will be published in August 2004. Tamara loves hearing from readers and you may write to her c/o Pinnacle Books. Please include a self-addressed stamped envelope if you wish a response. Or you can visit her website at www.tamarathorne.com

# BOOK YOUR PLACE ON OUR WEBSITE AND MAKE THE READING CONNECTION!

We've created a customized website just for our very special readers, where you can get the inside scoop on everything that's going on with Zebra, Pinnacle and Kensington books.

When you come online, you'll have the exciting opportunity to:

- View covers of upcoming books
- Read sample chapters
- Learn about our future publishing schedule (listed by publication month *and author*)
- Find out when your favorite authors will be visiting a city near you
- Search for and order backlist books from our online catalog
- Check out author bios and background information
- Send e-mail to your favorite authors
- Meet the Kensington staff online
- Join us in weekly chats with authors, readers and other guests
- Get writing guidelines
- AND MUCH MORE!

**Visit our website at**
**http://www.kensingtonbooks.com**